ACCLAIM FOR
JEFF ABBOTT'S THRILLERS

BLAME

"I could not tear myself away from Jeff Abbott's mesmerizing, gripping, and claustrophobic novel. *Blame* is the perfect blend of complex characters, plot twists galore, and great psychological suspense. Don't miss it."

—Harlan Coben

"Abbott does a stellar job.... This story is in the hands of a true thriller master. And the payoff is glorious."

—Associated Press

"Abbott's perfectly-paced thriller catches literary fire, crackling along with a nicely meshed Jason Bourne–*I Know What You Did Last Summer* vibe.... Abbott, a deft and nimble writer, skillfully steers us through small-community pettinesses and pressures, as well as, yes, the dark evil that lurks—all too often, it seems—deep in suburban territory."

—*The Seattle Review of Books*

"*Blame* is a thriller with a story that becomes more fascinating as it unfolds."

—*LA Review of Books*

"Jeff Abbott bundles raw emotions together and lights them on fire in his intense and superbly executed thriller *Blame*.... Riveting."

—Shelf Awareness

book makes me have to use a word I hate: *unputdownable*. I loved it." —Alison Gaylin, *USA Today* bestselling author of *What Remains of Me*

"Jeff Abbott...is fantastic."
  —Meg Gardiner, Edgar Award–winning author

"From the moment I set eyes on the viscerally magnetic Jane, I was spooked and positively riveted. Jeff Abbott proves, with this richly satisfying novel, that he is a master of suspense and tension."
  —Sara Blaedel, #1 internationally bestselling author of *The Forgotten Girls*

"Adrenaline junkies take note: The new Jeff Abbott novel, *Blame*, unfolds in totally unexpected ways—just as his fans have come to expect." —*Bookpage*

"Gripping...The story is filled with action and surprises that people will not see coming. Readers will not want to put this novel down, until they have the answers to the mystery of what happened that night."—*CrimeSpree Magazine*

"Jeff Abbott is one of the most versatile authors in the crime fiction genre, and his broad storytelling talents are on full display in his latest thriller. The deeply psychological *Blame* has it all—a cast of fully realized, complicated characters with plenty of secrets, and a tightly wound suspenseful plot with so many twists and turns that you'll never see the ending coming....This is one of those books that will keep you up at night—first you won't be able to put it down until way past your bedtime, and then you'll lie awake trying to puzzle out the characters' secrets and the plot's riddles.... Rest assured that when you finish his latest, you'll be hooked."　　　　　　　　—MysteryPeople

"Not only is Jeff Abbott's *Blame* the most addictive thriller of the summer, it also happens to be an astute study of the corrosive nature of blame and the destructive power of its sibling emotion, guilt.... With domestic suspense, pacing is so important, and Abbott really hits the sweet spot here. This book belongs on that short list of novels that demand to be read in one sitting. When your boss asks why you are late for work, blame Jeff Abbott—because he is no doubt culpable of keeping you up all night with this winning thriller.... This is a novel that will live on in readers' minds for a very long time to come."　　　—BOLO Books

"Abbott's *Blame* is every bit as good [as Harlan Coben's *Fool Me Once*] and packs even more surprises along the way, leading up to a shocking ending that nobody, not even veteran readers of the genre, will ever see coming. Abbott's lightning-quick pacing and constant twists and turns make his latest offering impossible to put down. A one-sit read that'll have readers up way past their bedtimes, *Blame* is Jeff Abbott's best novel so far—and a strong contender for best psychological thriller of the year." —TheRealBookSpy.com

"Abbott is a master craftsman, an architect, Racehorse Haynes building a case for reasonable doubt, brick by brick. *Blame* left me shaking my head in admiration for his mad skills."　　　　　　　　—Lone Star Literary Life

"Abbott expertly weaves an intricate, intense, and complex thriller that gets more exciting and addictive as you go along. His twists are chilling and completely unexpected....I will definitely seek out further reads by this talented writer." —TheMysterySite.com

"[The] characters and storyline continue to stick with me. Abbott turns the trope of the amnesiac into something far more haunting and tragic....I am picky as hell about psychological suspense, but this book is excellent."
—The Crime Lady

THE FIRST ORDER

"This is a thoroughly riveting addition to one of the most compelling espionage series in modern fiction." —*Bookpage*

"Will leave readers breathless...Buckle up and hang on to the end of this electric read!" —BookReporter.com

"Fast paced and just plausible enough to satisfy readers who demand realism in their adrenaline-fueled thrillers, the book should definitely appeal to action fans. Each novel in the series can be read as a stand-alone, which means newcomers can plunge right in. Go for it." —*Booklist*

"Abbott loads his story with entertaining plot twists....The bond and betrayal between the two brothers add emotional depth to the action." —*Kirkus Reviews*

"Fast paced, high-octane...plenty of twists."
—*Publishers Weekly*

"Compelling stories and characters that keep readers on the edge of their seats." —*Crimespree Magazine*

"Inspired by Shakespeare's *King Lear*, this action-packed, bicontinental tale of revenge...is a tightly controlled roller coaster of a narrative, goosing the reader forward with almost every paragraph." —*Austin Chronicle*

"One of the best ongoing series in the thriller genre. Readers will be hooked from the start....*Inside Man* jumps into the action right away, and the last 100 pages are downright terrifying. Abbott has a gift for creating great character-driven thrillers, and readers will clamor for more, especially given the cliff-hanger ending." —Associated Press

"The most layered and personal of any installment in the series...*Inside Man* is not a book to be taken lightly and clearly sets up the next thrilling chapter in Jeff Abbott's winning series." —BookReporter.com

"Thriller Award–winner Abbott draws on Shakespeare's *King Lear* for his outstanding fourth Sam Capra novel....Abbott injects enough of Sam's back story to make his intricate plot believable, judiciously spices his tale with tasteful but usually interrupted romance, and convincingly makes Sam a genuine contemporary 'chevalier.'" —*Publishers Weekly* (starred review)

"Exciting and imaginative, full of action and intrigue... Abbott's writing raises the pulse, taking readers on a wild adventure." —*Fredericksburg Free Lance-Star* (VA)

"Think of it as *Homeland* meets *Miami Vice*: a South Florida bar owner named Sam, who happens to be an ex-

CIA operative, tries to avenge the death of one of his regulars by going undercover in the mysterious and powerful Varela family."
—*O, The Oprah Magazine*

DOWNFALL

"A must read."
—Associated Press

"Abbott knows how to slowly ratchet up the tension while maintaining great characters and terrific plot twists."
—*Washington Post*

"Abbott packs a lifetime of thrills and suspense into a mere five days.... Abbott excels at spinning complex webs of intrigue combining psychological twists and abundant action.... Sam is both pawn and knight in an exciting chess game."
—*Publishers Weekly*

"Action-packed, never-stop-for-a-breath storytelling."
—*Dallas Morning News*

"Filled with action, intrigue, twists, and a variety of locales...It's perfect for a summer weekend's reading pleasure."
—*Fort Worth Star-Telegram*

"[A] whirlwind ride...*Downfall* moves like a juggernaut out of control and is impossible to put down....A torrid read that grabs the reader by the throat and never lets up."
—BookReporter.com

"Often wildly entertaining...a ton of action."
—*Austin American-Statesman*

"A pulsing adventure...The narrative shocks, repels, intrigues, and ultimately draws the reader in....Another Abbott thriller that packs a punch."
—*Fredericksburg Free Lance-Star* (VA)

THE LAST MINUTE

"An explosive cocktail." —*Washington Post*

"[An] adrenaline rush that won't stop."
—*San Antonio Express-News*

"Abbott is one of the best thriller writers in the business, and he delivers action and complex characters....The next Capra novel cannot come fast enough."—Associated Press

"This is the second in the Capra series, and he hasn't slowed down. It has killings, betrayals, big-time conspiracies, and action galore." —*Oklahoman*

"Gripping...edgy...a breathless suspense novel...As a writer [Abbott] is fluid, smart, witty, and easy to take."
—*Dallas Morning News*

"Like *Adrenaline*, this is a fast-paced thriller with a likable, morally conflicted hero. Sam is in a difficult situation, seemingly forced to commit murder to find his son, and—this is a testament to Abbott's skills as a storyteller—we really don't know whether he will follow through....Let's hope Abbott isn't through with Sam. He's a very well-drawn character, and it would be nice to see him again."
—*Booklist*

Capra is the heir apparent to Jason Bourne....The most gripping spy story I've read in years....It just grabs you. Great read!"　　　　　　　　　　　　　　—Harlan Coben

"Exhilarating...keeps the intensity at a peak level... *Adrenaline* proves worthy of its title." —*Columbus Dispatch*

"[A] complex, mind-bending plot...If Sam improves on his parkour skills, the future thrillers will spill over with nonstop action, just as *Adrenaline* does."
　　　　　　　　　　　　　　—*San Antonio Express-News*

"This is a wonderful book and the start of one of the most exciting new series I've had the privilege to read....Sam Capra is now on my short list of characters I would follow anywhere. *Adrenaline* provides the high-octane pace one expects from a spy thriller, while grounding the action with a protagonist that anyone can root for." —Laura Lippman

"This one hooked me and didn't let go....Abbott does a great job with pacing and switching perspectives."
　　　　　　　　　　　　　　—*Seattle Post-Intelligencer*

"*Adrenaline* lives up to its name. It's pure thriller in pace, but Abbott manages to keep the book's heart anchored in the right place. The characters aren't cardboard action figures, but people under incredible stresses and strains. I read it in a big gulp." —Charlaine Harris

"A white-knuckle opening leads into undoubtedly the best thriller I've read so far this year....*Adrenaline* will surely vault Abbott to the top of must-read authors. The relentless action will hook you from the heart-stopping opening to a conclusion that was as shocking as it was heartrending."

—*Ventura County Star* (CA)

"Nail-biting." —*Austin Chronicle*

"*Adrenaline*, like its namesake hormone, is all about pace, and a high-speed pace at that. A word of caution: don't start reading [it] just before bedtime!" —*BookPage*

"Engaging from the first paragraph, terrifying from the second page, *Adrenaline* accomplishes what most modern thrillers can't. It makes us care about its characters even while we're speeding headlong down the ingenious rabbit hole of its plot. Well done!" —Eric Van Lustbader

"Engrossing…flows rapidly from page to page… definitely a page-turner…wonderful descriptive writing… Abbott's demonstrated ability creates a highly recommended 5-star book." —*Kingman Daily Miner* (AZ)

"The title of this book pretty much sets the pace for this action-packed thriller. Within its pages are all the best aspects of a very enjoyable good-versus-evil plot: intrigue, spies, double crosses, foreign locales, technology used for nefarious purposes, a good-hearted hero, and the obligatory nasty bad guys." —*Suspense Magazine*

"Sam Capra is the perfect hero—tough, smart, pure of heart, and hard to kill. And *Adrenaline* is the perfect thriller. Taut and edgy, with breakneck pacing and perfect plotting, it's a breathless race from the shocking, heart-wrenching opening sequence to the stunning conclusion. Jeff Abbott is a master, and *Adrenaline* is his best book yet." —Lisa Unger

"Hero Sam Capra likes to unwind with parkour, leaping from building to building, clambering up walls and hurtling through space across the urban landscape.... The sport's a fitting metaphor for Abbott's style, tumbling from page to page with the frantic inevitability of Robert Ludlum.... It all works beautifully."   —*Booklist*

BLAME

ALSO BY JEFF ABBOTT

BLAME

JEFF ABBOTT

GRAND CENTRAL
PUBLISHING

NEW YORK   BOSTON

Copyright © 2017 by Jeff Abbott
Preview from *The Three Beths* copyright © 2018 by Jeff Abbott

Cover design by kid-ethic
Cover photo © Shutterstock.
Cover copyright © 2018 by Hachette Book Group, Inc.

Grand Central Publishing
Hachette Book Group
1290 Avenue of the Americas, New York, NY 10104
grandcentralpublishing.com
twitter.com/grandcentralpub

Originally published in hardcover and ebook by Grand Central Publishing in July 2017
First mass market edition: September 2018

Grand Central Publishing is a division of Hachette Book Group, Inc. The Grand Central Publishing name and logo is a trademark of Hachette Book Group, Inc.

The publisher is not responsible for websites (or their content) that are not owned by the publisher.

The Hachette Speakers Bureau provides a wide range of authors for speaking events. To find out more, go to www.hachettespeakersbureau.com or call (866) 376-6591.

ISBNs: 978-1-4555-5844-5 (mass market), 978-1-4555-5845-2 (ebook)

Printed in the United States of America

OPM

10 9 8 7 6 5 4 3 2 1

For Holly Frederick

1

TWO YEARS AGO

WHAT SHE WOULD never remember: their broken screams starting with *I love...* and *I hate...*, the sudden wrenching pull, the oh-no-this-is-happening-this-can't-be-happening feeling of falling as the SUV rocketed off the road, the horrifying downward slope of the hillside in the headlights, his hands tight over hers on the steering wheel, the smashing thunder of impact, the driver's-side airbag exploding in her face, the rolling, the lights dying, the unforgiving rock, and then the blow to the head that undid her and wiped her clean and made her new.

The old Jane died; every version of David died. The new Jane, product of a dark night's fury and tragedy, knew nothing more until she woke up four days later, remembering nothing, not her name, her mother's face, the crash, what had happened to her in that hospital bed, or any of her past seventeen years. Slowly the memories began to seep back: her birthdays when she was a child, cake sweet and soft on her lips; the smoky, rich aroma of her grandfather's pipe matched with the woolly smell of his tweed jacket with leather elbow patches; her mother's favorite lavender soap; the notebook she'd filled with short, odd adventure stories one summer and proudly read to her dad; the faces of her teachers; the smile of the librarian who'd give her stickers during the summer reading program; the feel of her hand in her father's palm; the faces and the laughter of her friends when they were kids.

Sometimes the memories felt immediate; sometimes they felt like something she'd seen in a film, present but distant, nothing to do with the person she was now.

Except for the past three years.

Jane was seventeen, but as the memories surged back, she was stuck at fourteen. Those last three years were gone, all the joy and all the drama of her high school life, lost in the damage and the trauma. Including those mysterious, unexplainable final hours, when she was with a boy she wasn't supposed to be with, when she was out doing no one knows what. The girl lived and eventually limped back into the bright sunshine, and the boy died and went into the cold ground, a secret sleeping with him.

And so the world she knew turned against her.

Except someone watched, and waited, and wondered how much of that night Jane Norton really remembered.

2

JANE NORTON WONDERED what it would be like to remember a single detail of the biggest moment in her life. Today was the second anniversary of the crash. She lay in bed, staring at the ceiling, as if waiting for pictures to appear. But the ceiling above her was only a screen empty of images.

She got up at six fourteen, alone, glancing at the other unoccupied bed in the dorm room—Adam had once again spent the night at his girlfriend's. It was best to get ready before the dorm's residents did. She put on a robe and gathered a bag of toiletries and opened the door a crack, peering down the empty hallway. She walked down to the dormitory showers in her robe, like she belonged, stood under the hot spray, and brushed her teeth. The bathroom was empty, so no odd looks from the other girls in the mirrors. Done and back in the room, she changed into the last clean set of clothes in her backpack. She would have to figure out where to wash clothes soon; too many students lingered by the machines in the basement here, trying to make conversation. She didn't like conversation.

She went down to breakfast, selected her items, and made sure she went to the older cashier, who recognized her and smiled. She used her old student ID Adam had hacked for her to pay for the meal—it withdrew money now from his account, making it look like he was steadily burning through his meal plan. Other college students sat together, chatting amiably at the round tables. She sat alone in a corner with her scrambled eggs and bacon and coffee. Other early-rising kids who sat alone stared into their smartphones as if the answers to the world's riddles lay there. She didn't; she didn't want to fill her unsteady brain with memories from looking at a screen. She looked out the window, at life, at St. Michael's professors and students walking by, at the warming sky, at the tree branches swaying in the November breeze. She ate in silence, trying to push back the emotions of the day, then went back to Adam's room. When the bells of St. Michael's began to sound, she opened a window and slid out through it, leaving the window unlocked, lowering it so it was barely open.

You could go to his grave, she thought. *You could take flowers.*

It was a mild fall morning in Austin, the sky dotted with clouds against a bright-blue vault. She walked to an American history class where the professor never seemed to notice her erratic attendance. She'd taken the same class last year, but with a different professor.

She could always find a seat in the front row, and it was daring and bold to sit right under the professor's nose. The actual students brought sleek laptops, but Jane took notes in a thick sketchbook designed for drawing, not writing. But she liked it. Once, the notebook had been the journal she was supposed to fill with her recovered memories and the events people had told her about that she didn't remember. Her Book of Memory. It had been Dr. K's idea, and she'd abandoned it, except for when she went to a class. Sometimes during the lectures, she doodled on the new pages. Often she drew endless mazes and ornate Gaelic patterns, labyrinths impossible to escape, and she would think of stories where interesting characters were trying to escape the mazes she'd lay out, like heroes trapped in a video game. Today she did not draw; her mind was full of David. Her hand shook a little.

The lecture today was on early New England funerary customs; she didn't have a syllabus, of course, and she thought, *Thanks, fate*, and she bit her lip as the professor began a slideshow of worn tombstones from Massachusetts. So often they were for children or those who died as teenagers, angels' wings attached to skulls. Gruesome and lovely, all at once. Twice she saw David's name on the engravings. Her heart tightened in her chest. She blinked and David's name was gone from the picture of the tombstone on the screen. She started to feel like she couldn't breathe. She left halfway through the lecture, ignoring the glances and the one stray laugh that accompanied her out the door. The professor paid her no mind.

She stopped outside the building, blinking in the bright sunlight, breathing in the fresh, cool air. She fumbled in her backpack and slipped on the sunglasses her mother had given her. They had round lenses, with metal edging, ugly, but they kept out the light that sliced hard into her eyes and her brain. The sunlight was harsh today, like a judgment.

She could go back to Adam's room, pull the curtains closed, and sleep off the rest of the day. She had some pills hidden under the mattress, pills she'd stolen from her mother when she'd left home. You couldn't take sedatives while living on the streets, it was too dangerous to be that vulnerable. And amnesiacs often had insomnia, as if kept awake by what they couldn't recall. But she was safe here. Pills it was.

Back at the dorm Jane walked past the front door, around the side of the building and to the window she'd left cracked, which faced onto a small, grassy area. She pulled herself into the room and fell onto the floor.

Adam walked in, freshly showered, wearing a robe. "Hey, graceful," he said. He shut the door quickly behind him.

"Hey." She pulled herself to her feet and turned away from him as he dressed, the way she would for a brother if she'd had one. She busied herself lowering the window shade.

"How's Bettina?" Jane asked. She was his German graduate-student girlfriend at the University of Texas, a few miles to the north. Adam often spent the night at her apartment, which made it easier for Jane to hide out in his dorm room.

"Fine. Hey, I didn't realize today was, you know, today. I should have been here this morning."

"Adam, I don't need coddling."

"Good, as I'm hardly a coddler."

But you let me stay here and you pay for my food and you've never asked for anything in return...except that I put my life back together. "I'm totally cool."

She avoided looking at him by checking her phone, as if she regularly received calls from anyone other than Adam. One message from Mom: Are you all right today? I don't know why I pay for this phone, you never call me. I love you, sweetheart. Let me help you. At least let me know how you are.

Jane deleted the text and collapsed on the spare bed. She wanted to go to his grave, suddenly. She had never been because she could not face it. But she missed him.

"I'm decent now," Adam said. He collected his gear for class. He'd pulled on jeans and a T-shirt that promoted the St. Michael's robotics team—he wrote software for the robots. "You know it's OK not to be OK today."

"Gag, you sound like a therapist." Jane hated therapists. They wanted to crowbar open your brain and peer around inside, giving you false hope.

He sat next to her and he hugged her. Gently. She didn't like that at first, but it was Adam, her pretend brother, and so she let him and then the hug felt reassuring, like she wasn't so alone in the world. He hugged her a moment longer than she liked, his face closer to hers, and she scooted back. Then he went all brotherly tough love.

"You have to get reenrolled. If you can sit through one class, you can make it through five. But if the administration realizes you're camping out here, they could deny you readmission forever. Not to mention the trouble I'd be in."

"Are you kicking me out of your room?" She would have nowhere to go. Except home. That was not an option.

"I don't mean to sound harsh, Jane." His voice softened. "You know I only want what's best for you."

"I don't want to talk about this today." And she knew the way to shut him up was to focus on the accident. It was pure magic, the way it silenced everyone. Jane got up and went to the iPad he kept on the desk.

She opened up an Internet browser and typed in the address for Faceplace, a social-media site she'd used before the accident, and briefly afterward, as she tried to remember and understand the lives of her classmates at Lakehaven High School. People whose faces she saw every day but didn't really know.

"What are you doing?" Adam said, watching the screen, realizing. "Let it alone."

She signed in to Faceplace, pausing to remember her password—which was *password*. She had an unfounded terror of her amnesia suddenly robbing her of current memories, her damaged temporal lobe sabotaging her, so she went with the obvious. She had not signed in to her page for ten months. Jane's page appeared, with its old profile picture, smiling at a Lakehaven High School football game. A few days before the accident. The last good picture of her. Her mother had claimed if she replaced it with a picture of her in the hospital, fresh from the coma, people would be nicer to her.

She had no new friend requests. Adam was pretty much it on the friend front. She went to the search field and typed in "David Hall." The first result gave her David's page. His parents hadn't taken it down.

"Jane, don't do it." Adam leaned over her shoulder. She clicked on the result.

Many new posts were already on his page today. Flowers, photos of David throughout his life, an animated banner ribbon that read, "We Will Never Forget You." Hundreds of likes. Posts from names she knew—people who were once her friends.

David, we will never forget you. Will love you always.

David, bro, missing you still. Thinking about you and all the good times.

The world is emptier without you, David.

Cannot believe it has been two years. Know you are at peace in the company of Our Lord.

"Don't," Adam repeated. But he didn't move to shut down the iPad or take it from her.

Jane read the rest of the kind tributes to David, and was relieved no one mentioned her by name. Adam leaned into her shoulder. Then she went back to her own page. At the top was a new posting, from today, from a user name she didn't recognize: Liv Danger. A tickle in her brain. Was that a person's real name? On the posting it read,

I know what you claim you don't remember, Jane. I know what happened that night. And I'm going to tell. All will pay.

"Is this a joke?"

"Who is Liv Danger?" Adam asked. "Is she someone you know?"

"I have no idea." A thought, unformed, danced at the edge of her mind. Like a memory that could never take form. Jane's hands started to tremble. Suddenly her guts twisted. She bolted down the hallway to the bathroom. She was sick, twice. She washed her face, staring into her dark-circled eyes in the mirror. She brushed her teeth and came back to the room. Adam looked up from the iPad.

"This Liv Danger looks like a fake user. Account set up last month, friends with mostly other accounts that have huge friend numbers."

"I haven't approved any new friends."

"Then someone hacked your page and approved her."

"Hacked me?"

"Your password is *password*, Jane." He rolled his eyes, but his voice was calm. "But they could also buy your password off a hacker website. They get account information on thousands of users when there's a breach on one site, so they'll just try the same passwords on all your sites: banking, social media, online stores, and so on. Is your password 'password' everywhere?"

"Yes. It's easy for me to remember," she said defensively. "I don't have to worry if my memory slips again."

He softened his voice. "This is just someone trolling you, Jane. Unfriend and delete."

She didn't; instead she read the message again. There

were people, Jane knew, who thought she should be punished for the accident. "Liv Danger," she said. "It sounds like a joke name."

"Google it," Adam said.

Jane did. There were two other social-media accounts using that name—she guessed it was a play on words for "live dangerously." These all had the feel of pseudonyms, not real names. She clicked on the "about" tab for the various accounts. One lived in California, another in New York. No one she knew here in Austin.

Jane inched down her own Faceplace page. No postings to her page from anyone for months. Then, two years ago, many posts that started with Thinking of you, Praying for you, Jane, and Get well soon, but soon devolving into memorable tidings such as YOU'RE A LIAR AND MURDERER. Written by someone she didn't even remember from high school, because she didn't remember high school before the crash. The accident had taken care of that.

That was when she'd left Faceplace. Jane hadn't deleted that post when she saw it, not because she thought she shouldn't but because she thought her friends would rally. A couple of people had said, in the comments below, that nothing was proven, expressing concern for Jane. The final comment, from Adam, read, Say it to her face. Or to mine. Leave her alone.

Adam touched her shoulder. "You should delete this account. There's nothing to be gained from keeping it except to paint a target on your back."

Jane stared at the words:

I know what you claim you don't remember, Jane. I know what happened that night. And I'm going to tell. All will pay.

Tell who? she wondered. Tell what? And "All Will Pay"—what did that mean? She felt cold.

Adam's voice went soft. "You know, if the near impossible were to happen and you did remember something, anything, no matter what...you can tell me. You can tell me anything."

Even if it's the worst thing I could know about myself? That maybe everything they say about me is true? She shook her head. "No. Nothing to tell. But maybe someone knows something I don't know. Someone saw something..."

"There were no witnesses to the crash. Someone would have come forward." Adam touched Jane's shoulder. "Forget it. Erase it. At least change your password."

"No. I want to see if they say anything else." She logged off Faceplace before Adam could take the tablet and start deleting. She stood up. "I keep thinking," she said, "that whatever happened, it's still stuck in my brain somewhere, and I just have to work it loose."

"You know that is not how amnesia works, Jane."

She knew he didn't mean to sound patronizing, but he did, and she turned on him. "Adam. I live with this every day." She'd read it described in one amnesia memoir as "the burden of uncertainty." It was so true. "I know what you mean. I'm saying I cannot shake the thought that I will remember this."

"It's been two years. Most memories, if they're going to return, do so in six months."

"But what we don't know about the brain is equal to what we do know." That was what Dr. K, her neurologist, had told her, lighting a candle of hope that never burned very brightly.

"Don't you see how that holds you back, Jane? This pointless hope."

She turned away from him, a flush flooding her face.

"You tell yourself the only way you get whole again is by remembering. I'm telling you, that isn't going to happen. You better find another way to pull yourself together."

She pressed her fists to her eyes.

Adam's voice broke. "I'm sorry. I don't mean to be a jerk; I'm just trying to help. I'll skip class today. I'll stay with you."

"I love you for that," she said, and suddenly tears, which she hated, were in her eyes and she wiped them away with the back of her hand. "But no. Go to class. Be brilliant. I'm…"

Going to David's grave. Maybe it would loosen a memory. As if being close to him would work a bit of magic on her mind. "I'm going to rest," she lied.

"I could find out who it is," he said. "Ask my hacker friends."

"All right," she said. "Let's find out." What scared her was the end of the posting: And I'm going to tell. All will pay. Like there was a score to be settled.

He nodded. "I'll start after class."

Adam gave her another hug and left.

She didn't drive anymore, but there were the ridesharing services, and her mother let Jane use her PayPal account for payments. She didn't use it often, because she didn't want her mother to know where she was. She crawled out of the dorm room window and walked across the greens and the college's parking lots toward Congress Avenue, tapping a request into the app once she was a few blocks away from the school, biting her lip, sick with nervousness at the thought of seeing David's grave.

3

AFTER GRANTING HERSELF a good cry as soon as she awoke, Perri Hall showered, still sobbing under the spray. When she stopped, she told herself, *There, that's done, no more.* Then she felt ready to face the terrible day. She pulled chilled spoons from the freezer to ease the puffiness of her eyes, resting on the couch with the spoons curved against her eyelids, the bright chatter of the TV morning-show hosts a garble of voices in her brain. She chose to wear a modest dark top with slightly patterned gray slacks, and a silver necklace that David had picked out as a Christmas gift when he was in middle school. Perri carefully applied her makeup. She looked, she thought, somber but elegant. Now she had to be strong. For David's memory, for everyone who expected strength from her. She watched herself in the mirror and made sure her bottom lip had stopped trembling.

She and her soon-to-be-ex-husband Cal met for breakfast at The Baconery, an iconic Lakehaven restaurant that served all-day breakfast and was always busy. There were always some of her friends here in the morning, after school started: community groups meeting; committees of volunteers to support football, volleyball, choir, band, robotics, science clubs, and more at Lakehaven's schools. It was an exemplary school district, nationally ranked, and the parents volunteered many hours to support the teachers and coaches. Supporting it had once been her life. After she and Cal ordered at the counter, they walked into the dining room and, in a slow ripple across the room, heads turned. Perri took a deep breath and steadied herself for the litany: *How are you* (like she could ever get better), *You look so lovely* (did not matter), and the dreaded *He's in a better place* (that doesn't matter to me, I want him back). Perri believed they uttered those platitudes as much for themselves as for her. *I'm sorry* was sufficiently graceful and could never wound, could never subtly suggest that her grief made them uncomfortable or that thank goodness it wasn't their family, their kids were alive while her handsome, smart, generous son lay in a grave.

Ronnie Gervase, a local luminary who was a fundraising powerhouse in Lakehaven, embraced them both and dropped two of the three platitudes that Perri expected.

"I'll see you at the gala meeting next week," Perri murmured, eager to be left alone.

"Of course," Ronnie said. "Be strong, darling."

They sat and ate. Cal didn't look good, tired and worn, but he took her hand while they finished their coffee. The hand where she'd already taken off the wedding ring.

After breakfast they drove to the cemetery. Cal, a big, strong, determined guy who'd played football in college and then made a fortune in business, always seemed to have trouble walking toward the grave, as if he could not bear to get close to David. He tottered on the grass. Perri tightened her grip on his hand and led him along.

At first when she said, "There's something on the stone," he said, "No, that's just the light" because a tree branch did create shadow on the granite. But when they stood in front of his grave, she saw the words smeared on the tombstone, in white chalk: *ALL WILL PAY.*

"What is that?" she gasped. The words were small, neat, above his engraved name: David Calhoun Hall. Cal knelt.

"Chalk…" He scraped at it with his thumb.

"What does it mean?" A cold anger stirred in her chest, eclipsing her grief.

"It's just someone being stupid," he said. She ran back to the car and got a water bottle and paper towels—still prepared as if she had a kid to clean up after—and washed the words into a snowy smear.

"I should have taken a picture." He looked around. "It's not on the other graves. Only David's." He embraced her and she hugged him hard.

"What does it mean?" Perri kept her voice under control.

"Thoughtless kids, probably. I'll call the management and let them know. Let's have our visit." Trying to make the morning normal again.

"Hello, sweetheart," Perri said. She laid fresh flowers on the grave, with the kind of gentleness as if she were putting a blanket on his sleeping form. She ignored the white smear. She talked to David for several minutes about what had been going on in their lives, not mentioning the pending divorce. Cal, she knew, could not do this, could not speak to David as if he were still alive. Her own mother had done it at her father's grave and she didn't know what else to do. Not talking, the silence, was worse, the hush from her boy being gone.

She finished her monologue and Cal coughed. She reached for his hand and after a moment he took hers.

What else was there to say? The glue that kept their marriage together was buried at their feet. After a moment he let go of her hand and mopped at his eyes and his face with his handkerchief. Monogrammed, with David's initials. Perri had gotten the linen cloths for David when he finished Cotillion, a Lakehaven tradition of dance lessons and etiquette that he had hated but endured with his usual smile. Cal had bought him video games. Her gift was better; it could still be used.

"You don't want to be here," she said to Cal as if he were betraying her with his hard breathing and his unsteady stance.

"I don't think this will ever get any easier."

"It's not supposed to be easy." Her voice rose.

"I know that, Perri, for heaven's sake. Could you let me grieve how I want? Not everyone is you."

Perri couldn't believe he'd snapped at her, today, here, with the awful desecration of his son's grave.

"I don't want this divorce," he said, his voice barely louder than the breeze.

"Not here. Not now."

"Why not, you like to talk in front of him. Shouldn't he hear what's going on in our lives? Do you think this divorce is what he'd want?"

"Stop, please, Cal." She began to hurry back toward the car. She got in. She thought she smelled a perfume different from hers, a scent of lavender, still lingering in the passenger seat, and her stomach clenched. But she had asked for the separation and then the divorce and if he found comfort with someone else—she could not complain. But she hated him a little bit, for being able to move forward.

"Just take me back," she said as he got into the car.

"I hoped we could spend the day together," he said quietly. "I didn't want to be alone."

The lavender tells me you're not alone, she thought, but today was not the day. "I just need some time alone. I'm sorry." *Why am I apologizing?* she thought. She had nothing to be sorry for. The shock of the graffiti turned to a primal rage.

All Will Pay? There was only one who needed to pay: Jane Norton.

She tried not to think of that girl, ever. But to pretend Jane Norton no longer existed was impossible: the Nortons lived next door.

Well, Laurel Norton still did. Jane was gone into the wind, supposedly sinking into insanity, living on the streets of south Austin, according to the Lakehaven gossip chain, a communications network unrivaled in both speed and inaccuracy. Perri had heard several wild rumors about Jane's current situation. Laurel could not seem to bring her home. Jane's dad, Brent, had died three years ago, a year before the car crash, so there was no other family to help. Laurel Norton rattled alone in that big house she refused to sell. Now Perri would rattle alone in hers, next door.

Once, both families had been so happy, so whole...now, both houses felt haunted by their losses. Somewhere today that reckless little bitch was breathing, she was walking, the sun on her face, not lying cold in a grave that could be desecrated.

"Perri." Cal hadn't started the car. "I am so sorry. I am sorry. I am sorry." He had his face in his hands. Not crying, but barely keeping tears at bay.

"You don't need to..."

"I didn't keep our boy safe. I moved us back to Lakehaven. If we'd stayed in San Francisco; if we hadn't come back here; if I had put him in private school; if I'd just—"

"You can't blame yourself. No one knew she would try and hurt him."

"I know. But I feel I failed him."

"I used to imagine the worst," she said slowly. He turned to face her. "The worst. That he would be caught in a fire, or an accident, or come down with some horrible disease. And you see, I believed, really believed, that because I imagined these terrible things, they would never happen; my thoughts were a shield for David. I never could have imagined to keep him safe from someone who decides to kill herself and him along with her."

He stared at her, his expression softening. *He still loves you*, she thought. *He loves you and you're pushing him away. You lost your son and now you're handing off your husband*. But there was nothing left to feel. This had ended her heart. She looked toward the grave. Her anchor, her compass.

Perri said, "I'd like to go get my car. Come over and have dinner about six, will that work?"

"Yes." He cleared his throat. "I think I'm going to set up a mentorship program in David's name. Something to help kids from disadvantaged backgrounds get into the software business." He had been the CEO of two software start-ups, one that had succeeded and one that had failed, but he had recovered quickly from that business setback. She had been scared they'd lose the house, but Cal quickly found a new calling. Now Cal worked independently, did private venture-capital investments across the country. He said that was where the real money was. If David had lived, his father's solo investment practice could have been his. She looked out the window again. So much squandered, so much gone.

"That's a lovely way to remember him." She told herself
not to cry.

He pulled up next to her Lexus in the Baconery parking
lot. "I'll see you at six. I'll bring some wine."

"That sounds fine." She leaned over and hugged him.
She hoped he wouldn't see it as encouragement for more.
He didn't really hug back. Then she got into her car and
waited for him to drive off.

She didn't drive back to the house they'd once shared.

She stopped at a store to buy cleaning supplies and then
drove back to the cemetery.

She returned to David's grave and knelt on the cool
grass. She sprayed cleaner onto the stone and began to
scrub away at the smear left by the unwanted words.

"Baby," she whispered to David as she cleaned. "I miss
you so much. What is this, this garbage written on your
stone? Who did this?"

She felt better with the stone clean. Perri spoke quietly
to the grave, about her days, about what his friends were
doing—although she heard a bit now and then about Kamala Grayson and Trevor Blinn and a few others, she found
if she thought too much about the joys of their ongoing
lives in college, the knot in her heart started to tighten.

She heard the car approaching, resenting its intrusion,
then she glanced up. A sedan drove on the road that lay par-
allel to David's grave on the right, slowing, then speeding
up, and in the backseat window she saw Jane Norton staring back at her.

Something broke in Perri.

Jane leaned forward and spoke to the driver. The car
zoomed forward, but to get out of Memorial Heights, it
had to follow a U-bend, and Perri found herself running
to the left, intercepting the car as it snaked in its turn to

leave. She reached the one-way road before it did and she stood square in the middle, hands up. The car slowed. The driver—an older woman with curling gray hair—leaned her head out and said, "Excuse me, ma'am."

Jane Norton had no reason to see what her stupidity, her thoughtlessness, her recklessness had done. Perri stormed toward the car, fury in her face. She opened the door as Jane tried to lock it.

"Why are you *here*?" she screamed at Jane as she pulled her from the car.

"I'm calling the police," the driver yelled, holding up a smartphone.

"No, don't," Jane said, and Perri wasn't sure if the girl was yelling at her or at the driver. Perri thought, *She looks horrible. Maybe she really is homeless.*

"You want to see him? You want to say something to him?" Perri said. "Were you here already, writing garbage on his gravestone?"

Jane's face was pale. "What? Please, just let me leave…"

"Oh, no, come say hello. Come see what you did." She had one hand in the girl's hair, one on her arm, and she hauled Jane across the cool, immaculate grass toward David's grave. "Honey, look who's here: Jane. You remember Jane. She killed you."

"Mrs. Hall, stop it…" She had the gall to try and pull away.

Perri struck Jane's face with a slap without thinking, shoved Jane to the grass.

"I didn't know you would be here…" Jane said.

The words were like a blow to the face. "Where else did you think I would be? Manicure? Shopping? I am here even when I'm not here. He's never far from my thoughts. You took him from me, and you didn't think I would be here, especially today?"

Jane had her palms pressed against the grave, heaving, and then she glanced back over her shoulder at Perri, tears streaking her face. "I'm sorry...I can only say it so many times."

"Is that what your mother told you? If you said sorry enough, I'd forgive you?"

Jane said, "What do you want from me? I can't bring him back. Can't we both just miss him?"

Shuddering, Perri turned and staggered away from Jane. She fell to her knees on another grave belonging to someone else's child, mother, sister, loved one. "Please, don't ever come back here again. I don't want you here."

"The police are on their way right now!" the driver screamed across the quiet of the graves, still holding the phone, aiming it at them.

Perri Hall froze. *What...what am I doing? Laying hands on a brain-injured young woman on David's grave.* The fury began to fade but not the hate. It was like a seed she could feel planted in her, a dark vine that would grow, take on its own life if she let it. It was a hatred that could blossom into obsession. And for an awful moment, she wanted to let it. Jane had never paid for what she'd done to David. Never.

A siren sounded in the distance.

"Mrs. Hall." Jane stood over her, eyes reddened.

Frozen spoons will fix that, Perri thought.

Jane's hair was more disheveled than before.

Did I do that? Perri wondered. *Oh. Yes, I marched her by her hair.*

Jane picked up the ugly sunglasses that Perri had knocked off her face and put them back on. "The police will be here in a minute. I'm going back to my ride to wait for them. I have a witness. I could press charges."

Perri said nothing. She just wanted to cry, curl up, and wait to die. She had been so careful and controlled this morning. Jane had undone her.

"*Could* press charges. You get me?"

"Just go," Perri said.

Jane stood up and headed back toward the car. Now a patrol car, its lights flashing, pulled up next to the driver, who was waving it down and pointing at the two of them.

Slowly Perri got to her feet.

"Ladies," the police officer who was getting out of the patrol car said, taking in Perri's perfect suit and Jane's rumpled clothes, "what's going on here?" The officer was young, female, hair pulled back in a severe bun.

"That crazy woman," the driver said, pointing at Perri, "attacked my fare. She dragged her from my car."

"A misunderstanding," Jane said. "She doesn't want me visiting her son's grave. So I won't. And if you're not arresting me, then I'm leaving." Jane got into the car, the driver followed, and the car zoomed off. The officer didn't stop them.

Perri watched them go. She shivered. The fury was gone and now there was just the emptiness, a hole in her heart.

"Ma'am," the officer said, "are you all right? Do you need me to call someone?"

Perri straightened her suit, inspected her fingernails, and brushed her hair back into place. "I'm all right," she lied. She forced a calm expression onto her face. "Thank you for your prompt response." As if she'd been the one to call the police.

"Ma'am, I don't know what the history is between you and that girl, but you cannot be dragging people from cars."

"They told me my son lived for another two minutes once they got him out of the car," she said. "They tried to save him and they couldn't. I wonder, could they have tried harder? Do you ever think that, officer? That you could try harder?"

"I try hard every day, ma'am."

"I'm sure you *think* you do," Perri said. "I mean no disrespect. But if that was your child lying in the wreckage, how hard would you try? Do you ever think that?" Her voice wavered. "I mean, you can try...to make sure your son doesn't go around with a girl like her, who decides to end her life and instead ends your child's..." Her voice faded. "I will always blame her. Always."

"Ma'am, I am very sorry for your loss."

"It's not like it's your fault. It's her fault!" She pointed in the direction of the departed car. "She's horrible. My son—"

But there was nothing the officer could say, no way to make it right.

ALL WILL PAY. If only that were true. If only she could make it true. But she couldn't.

Perri turned and walked with dignity back toward her Lexus. She got into her car, her hands shaking. What if Jane told people about Perri attacking her? She had made such a show of not ever saying anything bad about Jane to people. She had felt so superior in her graciousness. People thought Perri was a saint for this kindness. *That driver has a video of me dragging her from the car. I hit her. Not that hard. But still.*

It wouldn't matter. In Lakehaven, Jane Norton was a pariah. A cast-out killer. And Perri was always That Dead Boy's Mother. That was why Perri hated Jane Norton— she had stolen not just David but her normalcy. Perri had defined herself as a mother from the moment she knew David was growing inside her, and Jane had stolen who she was.

She had done more than kill David. She had murdered the person Perri used to be.

4

An explanation for whoever reads this: my memory has been
returning slowly since the crash, except for the past three
years, so I'm a seventeen-year-old who feels like a fourteen-
year-old, and Dr K said I should write down what I remember,
that this would help me. Because my amnesia, she says, might
have two causes: the physical damage and the emotional
shock. MIGHT HAVE. We don't know definitely. If there is
emotional shock that is blocking my memory [*here several
words are scratched out*], then writing might help me remember.
Work through my issues. Kamala makes an air quote when I
say "issues." So grateful she is standing by me.

Also sometimes when amnesiacs can't remember, they
make up stories to fill in the blanks, this is called "confabulation" and so I record what I remember to be true so I don't fill
in the blanks wrong. I could lie to myself and never know. Dr
K doesn't want me confabulating.

So: I remember most of the big details of my life up until
I was fourteen. My family, my friends, school. But high school
years are a blank; I don't remember my dad dying when I was

a freshman. I don't remember how I felt after he died. Apparently I had some "issues." Dr K thinks losing Dad and the crash are sort of bookends of my lost years. Sometimes from that lost period...there will be a fleeting image, a blip of memory, I don't always know what it means or what I'm remembering.

So I am supposed to write down important moments in my life that I do remember, and if I have memories that return, write those down as well.

Dr K told me to write down this journal instead of talking into a digital recorder on my phone since I like to write (although I think Mom probably bragged about being a writer, too, because she always says it's genetic, that I'm not at all like my dad). So. Here are some things that I remember.

1. Must always remember the look on my mother's face when she realized, after I woke up, that I didn't know who she was. You don't want to see a look like that again. Regaining all memories of her (up until I was about fourteen) took a few weeks. My first returned memory of her was her reading to me, me sitting on her lap, her mouth close to my cheek as she held me and read. I have some other memories, of her writing her "mommy blog" about what it was like to have me as a kid, but those are mostly of embarrassment. I might write about them later. But I looked at my own mother like she was a stranger. I'm sorry, Mom. No one knows how to act as an amnesiac at first. It's so awkward. I pretended I remembered her in a few days after I woke from the coma. It was our first little lie of our new lives. No doubt she blogged about it.

2. Mom says that Mrs. Hall—Perri, I had just gotten old enough where she invited me to call her Perri—came and sat with me while I was in coma, the day after the crash. She said to Mom, "Our babies. Our babies." And they cried and they held each other. And then the note was found in the crash debris, and they didn't talk much again. Of course the first time

I saw Mrs. Hall, I had no idea at first who she was. You cannot imagine. I can't even write about it yet.

3. I learned to ride a bike when I was six. Dad was gone a lot and Mom didn't like bikes (you can find her articles on her mommy blog complaining about bike safety—until she got a bicycle sponsor), so Mrs. Hall and David taught me. Mrs. Hall gave me lemonade when we were done. It was hot, summertime, and I was afraid the pavement would burn if I fell on it, so I decided I would not fall.

4. My favorite teacher in middle school was Mrs. Martinez, for English, and she came and visited me in the hospital, during the coma and after. I did not remember her—the world and everyone in it was a stranger—and she tried not to cry but she did. When I remembered her, weeks later, I knew she encouraged me to be a writer. I filled notebooks full of bad stories when I was a kid, but I loved writing them. I'm not sure I could ever be a writer now.

You have to understand people. A lot of that died in me.

5. Trevor says he kissed me when we were in first grade and we pretended to get married at recess, but I think he's just saying that to make me feel better since nearly everyone hates me now. The level of hate is like a fog I walk through every day. He told me this in the cafeteria two weeks after I came back to school. And then he walked away. He is so weird. He's a football player and I'm just going to assume there have been some concussions. (Like I can talk.)

6. Kamala was my best friend when we were seven. She and David were dating when he died. She could hate me but she doesn't. She is sticking with me and helping me at school. I need to write down a bunch of memories with her.

7. My favorite movie in high school was *Casablanca*, but I saw it during the time of my life that's lost in the Black Hole. A poster for it hangs in my room still. I haven't bothered to

watch it again. That other girl I was liked it. What if I don't? I don't have anything to put up on the wall in place of that poster if I hate it.

8. I don't remember my dad dying. That is still in the Black Hole. So what Mom told me: He killed himself, but it was an accident. With a gun. His business was having problems. He was an accountant and he was starting a new business, setting up offices to do bookkeeping in underserved neighborhoods. (All these words are not mine, this is from a printout of his website that Mom showed me.) He had a gun and he was handling it and it went off and he didn't realize it was loaded. But he was alone when it happened. So. People said things. That he killed himself. Mom stopped writing the mommy blog for a while and started writing a widow's blog, but the sponsors weren't as good and it was just so depressing.

I should say a lot more about my dad, but not now. I know when I was little he smiled a lot and didn't seem sad enough to take his own life. But over the past few weeks I remember him from when I was younger: how excited he was when we moved into the house on Graymalkin Circle, how hard he took it when the company he started with Cal Hall failed. They were business partners first, then neighbors, and Mom and Mrs. Hall were best friends, maybe they were too close. Love and hate, two sides of a coin. The hardest thing is not remembering losing Dad. But Mom said I've been through so much, to think of it as a blessing. Mom means well.

9. I only remember David up to eighth grade. In high school he got tall and he got hurt-my-heart handsome. The braces he got early were gone. Mom had a picture from last year of him and me after the musical, both of us still in costume, in the chorus of concerned parents of River City who knew how to spell "trouble." I look mad and not really happy to be there and of course I don't remember why I didn't like

being in *The Music Man*. He is of course beaming. Mr. Popular. So I'm told. But he was already setting the seeds for
that in middle school: football star, class president, academic
achiever, soloist in the winter choir concert. I looked in the
yearbook for pictures to see if I was ever around him in high
school. I found one: I'm behind him while he's singing in front
of the choir and I am watching him. Not looking at the audience. Looking at him. Mortifying. We are together in twelve
pictures in our last year in middle school. Inseparable. Then
down to one in high school. Try to remember: things change.

10. I remember summers: school years run together but
the summers came back to me. I would walk to the library,
often alone. Past the baseball fields; I would see David and
Trevor there. Sometimes Kamala walked with me and we
talked books we loved. We would (or I would, if I was alone)
stay in the cool of the shelves, reading, checking out books.
Madeleine L'Engle, I loved *A Wrinkle in Time* so much Dad
bought me a copy so I wouldn't wear out the library's (I would
just sit and read it if it was still on the shelf, all day, and if it
wasn't, I read the rest of the Time Quintet and the Vicky Austin
books); Edward Eager; Lloyd Alexander; Ursula K. LeGuin;
then later I binged on British mysteries (I was never into
Nancy Drew or the Hardy Boys). I was competitive about the
summer reading challenges and when I came out of the coma
and came home, Mom showed me, tucked under my bed, all
these posters, colored and filled in with stickers, of the summer reading programs I had finished. I had done them all.
There was a jagged tear in one corner that Mom said Kamala
tore in my poster because she was mad I finished and she
didn't and she doesn't like to lose. Then she said she was so
sorry and she had taped it up and then I remembered those
summer days in the library, all up until high school, and then
I asked Mom if I had still participated, and she said I was

too old. Then she cried over the posters. In the corner of one David wrote, *Stop being such a bookworm, Jane, come out and play*, in his small, cramped handwriting. I knew it was his handwriting, he didn't sign it. He had come to the library after playing basketball in the heat with his friends. To see me, to find me.

11. Lakehaven has two middle schools: Hilltop and Ridgeway, and they both feed into Lakehaven High. I went to Ridgeway and so did David, Kamala, and Trevor. Most of my friends are Ridgeway. In high school I made some new friends from Hilltop, in French class (I don't remember any of my French) and in choir (I don't remember any songs). But those new friends were gone from my memory. Including the one and only Adam, who had to reintroduce himself to me, and never gave up. Everyone liked David, and after he died I turned radioactive.

I could have fought or begged to keep a friend. I'm the biggest coward around. I didn't have the bravery to have a friend, to confide. I didn't tell Kamala or Adam the truth about my memories, how lost I felt. It felt like part of my brain was gone. My heart, too. Gone. Memories are the engines for our feelings.

5

***

YOU WANT ME to take you back to Saint Mike's?" the rideshare driver asked Jane. She had pulled over to the side of the road, a half mile away from the cemetery.

Yes, that would be great, Jane thought. *I have a bed I can hide under.* But she made her hands stop shaking. *You can hide later. See this through.* "Do you know where High Oaks Road is?"

"No, I can find it on the GPS, though..."

"It's not far. I can just tell you."

"I took a video of her attacking you after I called the police," the driver said. "Do you want it in case she comes after you again?"

After a moment, Jane said, "Yes."

"Give me your e-mail address and I'll send it to you."

Jane did. "Thank you."

Jane gave the woman directions to the crash site. She had been here only once before, a few weeks after she came home. She had stared at the evidence of what she'd done: the spray-paint signs on the road, to indicate the direction and estimated velocity of the car; the lack of skid marks; the torn ground along the steep hill; the shattered oak saplings and cedar and ripped grass and the heavy rock where the front of the car had smashed. Just once. The doctors had said perhaps it would help prod her memories—but it had done nothing. Mom had watched her, as though expecting a dramatic returning of memories in a rush. She had stood in the sunlight, waiting for the miracle of memory. But nothing. The sides of the road rose and fell steeply, too steep for easy building of houses. There were only three houses, all palatial, but on the opposite side of the road from the crash site, and among them, only one person had heard the crash, a resident named James Marcolin.

The road curved and went back down the hill past the Marcolin estate, intersecting again with Old Travis Boulevard, the main thoroughfare for Lakehaven that stretched through the whole town and into Austin, south of Lady Bird Lake. High Oaks had many bends as it wound up the cliffside, and its two endpoints, separated by a mile, both dead-ended into Old Travis. Sometimes, during rush hour, it would be used as a cut-through. Most of the time, the road was lonely and quiet.

Jane wondered, *So why were David and I here, on this empty stretch of road? We knew no one here. Where were we going, hours after school let out, when we should have been home doing assignments or waiting for early college-admissions decisions or looking at our friends' pictures on social media?*

The rideshare driver dropped her off; Jane gave her an extra-big tip and a five-star rating. The woman said, "You sure you'll be OK out here?" Jane nodded and she drove away.

High Oaks Road was narrow, surrounded by oaks and

cedars, undeveloped. The road ran west to east. The land north of the road where the three remote houses stood rose in a steep hillside, the south side began a slow then steep descent, tumbled down to boulders and more oaks and cedars and then finally a cliff's edge. There was still a cleared path where her small SUV, two years ago, had torn through the growth. Here she walked down, through the shade of the trees, the wind gentle against her face.

No reason for her and David to be here. Unless they'd driven up here to be alone, or if the suicide note was accurate and she'd tried to drive off the cliff. But she hadn't reached it. Of course maybe David, realizing her intent, grabbed the wheel and they fought for it and the car spun and crashed into the rocks before it could plummet over the edge.

She didn't like to think about that.

Old bunches of flowers rested against one of the trees, part of a solid grouping of oaks close to where Jane's SUV had come to rest on its crushed top. A large rock face, rising from the grass, was where the SUV's front had impacted. If they had slid another twenty feet, they would have gone over the edge into a forty-foot drop into rock and cedars and oaks below. A bunch of deflated silver balloons lay by the flowers, still tethered together with strands of ribbon, the colors faded by the sun. Last year's remembrances? Or for David's birthday?

She sank to her knees.

Remember, she told herself. *Remember*. She made her own thought intense, commanding, stern. Willing her brain to give up its secrets.

She dug her fingers into the dirt. Like she could pull the secrets out of the ground. Or David. David had died here. Memories of three years of her life had died here.

She rose. She walked to the edge of the cliff. She felt vertigo but she made herself peer down. If she had wanted to end her life and David's, like the note suggested, then...this would have been a good choice.

She knelt again and she cried. Silently. Despite the bright light she pulled off the steampunky sunglasses that guarded her eyes from the sun-spiked headaches and she let the tears fall from her face and water the rough stone.

"Oh, Jane. Are you all right?" a young woman's voice said behind her.

Jane jerked, turned, slowly climbed to her feet—realizing how close to the cliff's edge she was. An attractive young woman stood between her and the road, clutching a bunch of flowers and a football. She had black hair pulled back in a tidy ponytail, high cheekbones, a small, neat bud of a mouth. She wore expensive jeans and a black top, nicely fitted. Kamala Grayson. Her mother had been a beauty queen from India, fourth runner-up in a global pageant twenty-five years ago, and had used her scholarship money to get her medical degree here in Texas. Kamala's father was from an old Lakehaven family.

Her smile was warm, compassionate, and caring. Jane nearly screamed.

* * *

Four days after Jane woke up from the coma, this lovely girl had come into her hospital room carrying flowers, smiling at her, saying, "Hi, the doctors say you may not remember me. My name is Kamala Grayson, we're like sisters." And Mom, gushing, happy to see a smiling face from Jane's social circle, who had been fewer than Mom would have liked, saying, "Hi, Kamala, it's so nice to see you,

Jane's memory isn't quite back, forgive her." As if Jane had committed a social blunder.

"So I heard," Kamala had said. "Do you remember me?"

Jane shook her head. "Sorry," she had said. "I don't." Her voice was very small. Every interaction felt like a test she was failing.

"Well, we've known each other since second grade. We went to middle school together, and now high school. We suffered through Mrs. Montoya's Spanish class together."

"OK." Jane said this a lot. It seemed an all-purpose answer that never upset anyone.

"Kamala, would you like a Coke? I was just going to get one," Mom had offered.

"I don't want to trouble you." Kamala didn't look at Mom. Only at Jane.

"Maybe you talking to Jane will help," Mom had said. "She just doesn't remember anyone so far, but I know she'll be better soon, the more friendly faces she sees." Jane could hear a strain in her voice. "I'll let you two talk while I go get us some Cokes. I find this hospital air to be very drying. Is it me?"

"No, ma'am," Kamala said. "I agree with you. My parents say it's always so in medical offices. Mom says you really have to moisturize."

"Yes, absolutely," Mom said, as if moisturizing was the biggest medical imperative.

"How do you feel?" Kamala asked after Mom left. She set the flowers down alongside the others that had been delivered.

"Sore. Everything hurts."

"But you can feel, can't you?"

"Yes."

"That's good. To still be able to feel." Kamala stood close to her bed. "Your poor arm is broken."

"Yes."

"I'll get everyone to sign your cast when you're back at school. And you remember nothing?" Now she touched Jane's shoulder carefully. "I want to hug you but I know you're hurting. And... you truly don't know me, right? It's not an excuse."

"I'm sorry I don't remember you."

Kamala just watched her for a moment, as if Jane's face were a map.

"You seem a little emotionless. I guess that's a side effect."

"OK," Jane said again.

"Have you had a lot of friends visit yet? That must be awkward. I mean, since you don't remember." Kamala watched her.

"No. Not really."

"You don't really have a ton of friends."

Her words had jolted Jane, but Kamala had said quickly, "Oh, I don't mean that badly. You tend to go your own way. I always admired that about you. What can I do to help you?"

"I don't know. Tell me who everyone is. I have no idea if I'll even go back to school."

"You will. We'll get through this together." Then she asked, "Why were you and David together in your car?" Kamala sat on the edge of the bed.

Jane twisted the sheet in her hands. "Who is David? They keep mentioning his name and no one tells me who he is."

"Are you sure you're not lying, just a little? You can tell me. C'mon, amnesia? It's so, I don't know, nighttime soap opera." She said this very gently, almost kindly.

"I really don't remember."

"David's not the kind of guy you can forget." Kamala had settled her stare back into a smile. "But your face isn't hurt. That's nice. You're pretty enough." Kamala ran a hand through her glorious black hair. "I heard David's face was badly damaged. The service was closed-casket."

Jane had scrunched down farther in the bed, watching her. Service?

"I don't know how amnesia works. Do you remember basic knowledge from the culture you live in? You know what a funeral is? What 'closed-casket' is? When someone dies, we put them in the ground. The casket is what holds the body. 'Closed' is when the body is so ruined, so destroyed, that no one can bear to look at it."

Jane couldn't speak. Ever since awakening she had felt like she was in a haze, but she knew that if she pushed the button on the bedside control, the nice nurse would come, and the nice nurse was a big-shouldered guy, about six-three, who could pick Kamala Grayson up and carry her far, far away. Her hand inched toward the control. Kamala's hand closed on hers, almost gently.

Kamala leaned close and brushed her lips against Jane's forehead. "I'm just a little raw right now. But we've been friends forever and I love you. When you remember what happened with you and David...talk to me. And no one else. I promise it will be all right."

Mom reentered, holding two Cokes. "I thought you might want one, Kamala."

"Did I...kill this David?" Jane asked her mother in a hoarse whisper.

"I'm sorry, Mrs. Norton," Kamala said. Her voice was soft and consoling. "Jane got agitated...I tried to calm her down. I should have just rung for the nurse. I mentioned David without thinking, I'm so sorry."

"Who's David?" Jane's voice rose. "Did I kill some-one?" Laurel rushed to her side.

"Jane, I'm sorry, it'll all be OK..." Kamala backed away from the bed. "I should go. Please, call me, if there's anything that I can do for you, Mrs. Norton. I'll be happy to help Jane fit back in if she returns to school." And with that Kamala was gone, scooping up the Coke Laurel had set down as she tried to hug Jane, and took a long sip from it as she left the room.

Jane had to be sedated.

* * *

And Kamala had been good as her word. Oh, what a help she had been.

Now she stood before Jane, close to the edge of the cliff, and Jane's first thought: *We're alone here. No one else is around. Just her and me, and a long drop down.*

Kamala smiled. Then Jane saw, up the rise, on the side of High Oaks Road, a car parked, a girl watching from the window.

"How are you?" Kamala asked. "I've been so worried about you. I heard you flunked out of Saint Mike's."

"You heard wrong," Jane lied. "Thanks for your con-cern. How's life at UT?"

"Let's not compare our lives right now, Jane. I've heard you're not doing well. How can I help you?"

She took a step toward Jane. Slowly Jane moved away from Kamala, up the hill, away from the ledge.

Kamala shook her head sadly. "I wish you would let me be your friend again."

"Just stay away from me."

"Jane. How will you ever get better if you don't take responsibility for your life?"

"I know what you are behind the smile, and behind the gentle words, and behind the fake caring," Jane said.

Kamala just kept smiling and shaking her head. "I forgave you. I guess you can't forgive yourself."

"You sound like a therapist talk show."

Jane turned to head up the steep hill.

"Jane, I so want to help you," Kamala said to her back. "Why won't you let me?"

"I finally figured you out," Jane said, turning back to face her. "All this hating me behind your sugary smile and your fake concern is just a drama, with you as the star. Messing with me, ruining me, it's just about you. Did you bring your friend along to watch, so she could tell the really good sorority how kind and noble you are?" Her words sounded so harsh in the quiet of the breeze. While Kamala just kept those gentle, pitying eyes on her.

"I didn't just lose David," Kamala said. "I lost you, too. I just don't understand why you hate me so."

Kamala. She had to be this Liv Danger, who'd left the creepy Faceplace message. It was entirely the kind of bullying stunt she would pull. *All Will Pay.* Especially for killing Kamala's boyfriend. Jane turned and started to walk back up the hill.

"We're not done," Kamala said. "You're not well, Jane. Don't you realize that I care, your mother cares, we just want you to get better."

Jane stopped and turned back to the young woman who had been her best friend for years. "You don't get to call me crazy. Not you!"

Jane stumbled up the steep incline of the hill, back to

High Oaks Road. A BMW was parked along the side of the road, and by it stood a young woman, who stared at Jane.

"What are you looking at?" Jane snapped at the girl, who said nothing, but got back into the car.

Oh, great. Jane realized she was going to have to stand here and wait for a rideshare car to respond to her request on the app. She could not bear it if she was still loitering by the side of the road when Kamala left.

Kamala, who had been popular, and was so beautiful, and salutatorian at one of the most competitive high schools in Texas, and perfect. If she tried to hug Jane, Jane thought she would punch her.

Nowhere to go. Then, farther down the road and to her left, she saw a gate to a driveway. That house, she knew, belonged to the man who had heard the crash and had called the police. She knew from the newspaper accounts of the crash that his name was James Marcolin.

She started walking before she could think. The driver could pick her up at the Marcolin residence. It would be an address on the GPS, and even a hundred yards between her and Kamala was better than nothing.

She was halfway there when she heard the BMW's engine start.

She studied her phone, a camouflage she knew to be lame but she couldn't help herself.

The BMW pulled even with her. Kamala was in the passenger seat.

"You don't drive, of course, do you? Let us give you a ride. Is there a homeless shelter you're staying at?" Kamala asked.

Every word a jab of the knife. Jane kept walking.

"Jane, are you homeless? I want to know the truth."

Jane stopped and leaned down toward the window.

"Let's talk truth. Do you know what kind of monster you have for a friend?" she said to the other girl, who was driving. "I was in a hospital, with brain damage and no memory, and she started a campaign to turn the whole school against me. She pretended to love me and she made my life hell."

"Oh, Jane." Kamala lowered her voice. "You're confused. Are you high? Are you on street drugs? My mom can get you into a clinic by this afternoon. Let me..."

Jane closed her hand into a fist. "If you don't get away from me..." Then she turned and picked up a rock and raised it as if to smash it on the pristine black hood of the car.

Suddenly the other girl sped the BMW past Jane, while through the rear windshield Jane could see Kamala turning in the passenger seat to watch her.

With a momentary smile.

Jane wanted to throw the rock at the departing car. Tears sprang to her eyes. She could imagine Kamala saying right now, *You see, I tried to help her. I tried to be there for her, even after she killed David. I tried. But she can't be helped.* She kept walking, trying to shove the words out of her brain. She wanted to tell Kamala's friend, *She'll make you think you're the center of the world, sisters, bonded in blood, your friend you can tell anything to, and then she'll watch you die from a thousand little cuts. And she made them all.*

Jane stopped. *Forget Kamala. Think about the crash. Remember.* She looked down the road again and back to the crash site, where the car had veered off so wildly. Not a bend. Not a curve.

What were David and I doing here?

She reached the gated entrance for James Marcolin's property. The gates were large, ornate steel, taller than she was, automated and elaborate. The street number was artistically part of the gate. Nothing to stop her now from opening the rideshare app and giving them this address.

She stared up at the huge house. It was elaborate—three stories, Tuscan architecture, truly stunning. She stood before the gate's panel, which had a security touchpad and a speaker box, hesitating to ring the bell. Just to ask him what he heard, what he saw that night. Thank him for calling and saving her life. He was likely at work now.

Her finger inched toward the buzzer for the gate and she glanced toward the house. A camera watched her and moved, slightly, into a better position. Her hand stopped above the buzzer and stepped back.

She gave a little wave. The camera watched, unmoving.

"Hello?" a voice called to her. A man dressed in jeans and a nice T-shirt approached the gate. He was fortyish, with dark hair and eyes and a narrow smile. He held a giant sponge dripping with soap, and she could see he had been washing a sports car in the driveway.

"Hi. Are you Mr. Marcolin?"

"I am."

"I'm Jane Norton. Um, this sounds weird, but I was in a car crash here two years ago. You were the one who called the police." Realization dawned on his face and he nodded. "I wanted to thank you. You saved my life."

"It's nice to meet you." He didn't seem to know what else to say. His voice was soft, with a slight accent she found hard to place: Spanish, perhaps Italian. "Are you recovered now?"

Recovered. What a lovely word. "I lost my memory. Well, part of it. The three years before the crash..." She hated explaining. To so many people, amnesia seemed like something from a movie. So rare that they would never forget meeting her, like meeting quintuplets or an astronaut. She fell back on her lie. "I go to Saint Michael's. I'm a sophomore there."

"Ah," he said. "Perhaps visiting the road will help you remember."

"I'm sure," she said, because it was too hard to explain that wasn't how it worked. Hollywood had trained audiences to expect amnesia to be temporary, like a cold. "I just wanted to ask you if David, the boy who died, did he suffer? You saw us, right? You came down to the car." Her voice had gone very soft.

He pressed a button and the ornate gate slid open, nearly silent. He stepped out to stand closer to her. "He did not suffer. Please put your mind at ease about that."

His kindness—compared to how the rest of the morning had gone, with anonymous threats, with Perri pulling her from a car, with Kamala's poisonous smile—nearly made her cry.

"Thank you for calling. I just wondered..." And despite her certainty that Kamala was Liv Danger, the words *I know what you claim you don't remember. I know what happened* rang in her mind. "...This is a dumb question. Did you see anyone else that night, here? Another person, another car?"

"You mean another witness? No, I was alone. I was just back from a business trip overseas, only for an hour or so, when I heard the crash."

"I meant did you see anyone else near the crash, or on the road..." The question sounded stupid, as if someone was waiting for them to come to that road. Were they? Were they supposed to meet someone here on that dark stretch above the cliff?

He shook his head. "No, I didn't see anyone."

"You said you travel?" She glanced up at the gorgeous home. "What do you do?"

"Ah. I work in international finance. I took today off as I've been traveling so much. Which I am glad of, since I got to see you, and see that you are doing better, and hopefully answer your question."

"All right. Thank you again." She turned to walk away.

"Ms. Norton?"

She stopped and looked back at him. "I wish you well. I hope you get your memories back. Even the painful ones." Marcolin offered a tentative smile.

"Thank you."

He glanced down the road. "No car? You didn't drive yourself?"

"I don't like to drive much anymore since the crash. I use rideshares."

"Would you like me to take you where you need to be? I can finish washing my car in a few minutes. You could have a cup of tea while I finish."

"No, sir, thank you. I appreciate it, though."

"All right. Good luck to you." He stepped back onto his driveway and the beautiful steel gate began to close. Jane used her rideshare app to summon a car to his address. He watched her for a few moments and then waved and stepped out of view.

Of course there was no one else. Liv Danger was a lie, designed to upset and scare her on a day that was already difficult. She was going to prove it was Kamala, and if it wasn't, then she'd find the guilty party and make them look her in the eye and confess.

The rideshare soon arrived, and as she headed back to St. Michael's, she realized that tracking down Liv Danger was the first real sense of purpose she'd felt in months.

6

———

Jane? Jane Norton?"

Jane was walking toward Adam's dorm. She had thought of going to her house—of running home to Mom, and whatever comfort she might be offered—but she couldn't bear to see the Hall house, next door, and the chance of meeting Mrs. Hall again. She had to figure out her next move, to prove that Kamala was behind the Liv Danger posts. But she needed to eat her lunch off Adam's meal plan; she didn't have much cash. Near the dorm entrance—which she planned to walk past and use the window into Adam's room, as she usually did—stood a young man, late twenties, smiling uncertainly at her, walking to intercept her, calling her name.

"Aren't you Jane Norton?" His accent was soft, not quite British, something else. He stepped a bit closer to her, still smiling. Dark skin and hair, bright smile. Handsome.

"Yes," she said. Bracing herself.

"Hi. I'm Kevin Ngota." He offered his hand but she

didn't shake it. After a moment he lowered his hand but he didn't look offended.

"Am I supposed to know you?" She studied his face. It was disconcerting when people she might have gone to school with but not known well came up to her. Sometimes it felt like they were testing her, trying to catch her in a lie.

"We've never met, but I know who you are. I'm doing a graduate thesis in counseling here at Saint Michael's. My particular interest is in memory recovery after accidents."

"And of course you'd pick today to talk to me." She turned and walked away. Fast.

Kevin Ngota hurried along beside her. "Yes. Because I thought today might be difficult, so you'd be open to a new approach."

"Please leave me alone."

"I believe I can be of help to you..."

At that she stopped. "Oh, thank goodness. My hero. You're who I've been waiting for. Everyone else has tried to fix me and has failed. But, hurray, here you are." She threw up her hands in celebration.

"I mean no offense. My understanding was you are not currently seeing a therapist."

She took a step back. "So a counselor *and* a stalker. You're a double threat."

"No, no, I just asked around. I've never done this before. I'm botching it quite badly and I truly do want to help you." He had a charming smile. Jane could see that but was not swayed by it.

"I'm not interested."

"Talking it through could prompt memories..."

"And by that you mean it would give you quotes for your master's thesis." She turned away and then stopped, turned back to face him. "How do you even know about me?"

"I learned about your accident when I started looking for people in Austin who had traumatic amnesia. 'The Girl Who Doesn't Remember.' I read those articles."

"Yeah, not a fan of those stories. Matteo Vasquez got addicted to that headline."

"Well, I read his articles on you. I learned you were a student here."

"You can understand why I don't want to talk about this. I think it's unethical that you approached me." She had found that nearly any shrink or doctor flinched, automatically, at an accusation of being unethical. It would normally deflect them and put them on the defensive, and then she got her way.

"It's only unethical if you're currently seeing a therapist, and you're not. I honestly believe I could be of help to you. Your friend, Adam, he told me that you were no longer in therapy. This could be a new start for you." Kevin handed Jane a note with his e-mail and phone number. "Think about it. It's just you talking and me listening."

Adam. Trying to help, and making things worse. She appreciated everything he did for her but sometimes she wished he'd just back off. "What, so your ears are better than anyone else's? The doctors said if I haven't gotten all the memories back by now, I'll probably never remember."

"That might be true of a physical cause. But yours could be an emotional block, because of losing your friend, and the period of your lost memories begins soon before your father's death. Many amnesiacs regain those lost memories. In London I successfully worked with a man who had lost ten years. You only lost three years."

He managed to make her condition sound mild, and normally she would have gotten angry, but now she laughed.

After her morning with Perri Hall and Kamala Grayson, she laughed.

Bolstered by her smile, he continued: "And the memories could return if you're emotionally repressing them, Jane. It might not be the physical damage. Wouldn't you want to know?"

"I don't remember," she said, her voice flat as stone. "You can pretend my memories are going to pop back into place, but they haven't. They won't."

He lowered his voice. "Jane, people said the crash was an attempt to kill both yourself and David Hall. Because of this note, in your handwriting, that was found in the debris. That you must have written it earlier that evening and then acted upon it."

She stared at the ground. She could just walk away, but she had to find a way to discourage him. "I obviously have no memory of writing that note. No matter what anyone else suggests."

"That's still OK, Jane." Kevin Ngota used her name, again and again, like it was a tip he'd gotten from a book, to create a connection. "We could try a range of approaches. You could talk about the experience of not remembering. How your amnesia affects your life, your choices..."

"There's nothing you could do for me."

"Hope is scary, isn't it? It can crush you as much as lift you up."

She didn't answer.

"Contact me if you would like to try."

What was she going to do after she proved it was Kamala harassing her? What was the next step in life? Couldn't she try again? It wasn't like her calendar was full. "Sure. I'll try."

The bell tower chimed noon. He didn't make a big show

of her saying yes. Mr. Persistent had turned into Mr. Cool.

"Three o'clock today, will that work? I'm in Fletcher Hall, room two-eleven."

"Today I went to my friend's grave. I went to the crash site. There were...people there who don't like me at all. They still blame me. They think it wasn't an accident. One of them tried to hurt me. The other is smearing me online." As soon as she said it, she knew she sounded paranoid, she could hear the insistent fear in her words.

Kevin Ngota's smile had narrowed. "Then let's talk about that, if you like."

She nodded. And then he turned and walked away.

If you like. Maybe she'd go, maybe she wouldn't.

Jane pulled herself through the window into Adam's room. He was at class or at lunch. She lay down on the bed, and Kevin Ngota's words sent her to shivering.

Hope is scary, isn't it? What could he know, with his nice smile and his intact brain, his sense of self never disturbed, about hopelessness?

She took off the sunglasses. She put them carefully on Adam's side table and put her arm across her face. Beautiful darkness. No one looking at her. No one pointing.

No one blaming.

Jane opened her eyes.

Hope. Hope can crush you.

7

JANE'S BOOK OF MEMORY, WRITTEN IN THE
DAYS AND WEEKS FOLLOWING THE CRASH

This is about my first night home in my old room. It was like
sleeping in a hotel where you have never been, and the walls
are weighted with pictures from someone else's life. But it's
your life. So they tell you. But do they edit the story for you?

I remember there was a reporter named Vasquez, a
young, geeky man from the Austin newspaper waiting for
us outside the house, asking if I had remembered anything
more about the accident that had killed my next-door neighbor, and Mom got out of the car and screeched at him that
he was trespassing and she would file a restraining order,
and my head hurt so bad suddenly, I thought I would have
to crawl to the door. The pain was blinding. I'd just made
a brief reentry into this world and now I was going to leave
it. I went to my knees. Vasquez said to Mom, "Ma'am, your
daughter is fainting," so then she had to stop yelling at him
and help me. She kept bellowing at Vasquez, although it felt
like nails in my brain when she did that.

Vasquez asked her about the suicide note. That had become a story because they hadn't found it right away, the

police had only found it the next day. It was in police custody as evidence and not to be discussed, but then the story leaked. This crash had been all over the news. Lakehaven kids. Kids of parents prominent in the high-tech community, Austin's business jewel. A famous so-called "mom blogger" who had once drawn hundreds of thousands of daily readers a few years ago. Next-door neighbors. Childhood friends. Vasquez ended up writing three articles about me, a newspaper series he would call "The Girl Who Doesn't Remember." This was when all these book titles with "girl" were big and I guess he was trying to ride the wave. Or score a book deal off my misery. I'm sure he's nice, to the people who know him.

We went inside and Mom slammed the door. More nails in the brain. I didn't recognize anything. It was terrifying. My memories of my early life had only just begun to return, rising like scant bubbles to the surface of my mind. I (sort of) knew my mother now, and she had told me my father had died—after I had remembered him and asked for him twice.

I stared at the stairs and the walls. This was just a new place that wasn't the hospital. Mom started babbling. "This is the window where you used to wait for your father and me to come home from our jobs. We had an au pair then; she was from Sweden. Do you know that there's a country called Sweden?"

I probably nodded.

"And here was where you fell down the stairs and bumped your head . . . I wrote a very popular piece about that on the blog when it happened . . . oh, gosh, do you think you hurt your brain then, maybe that's why your memories aren't coming back now, oh, I need to tell that to the doctor, I completely forgot"—like she was the one with amnesia—"so does any of it seem familiar?" So much expectation in that last word.

"A little," I said, because it seemed to mean so much to her. Dr. K warned me not to lie about memories, but she needed to try living with this "Mom" person, who was constantly demanding that I test my memory, which was like catching smoke. Mom went to the window and looked outside, peering past the curtain to see if the reporter was still there.

"I don't like him. Not at all," she said quietly.

I wanted to ask about the note. I decided to wait until we were settled.

I stood in the den. Looked around. Suddenly I could picture toys on the floor and a Christmas tree in the corner, a hazy image . . . but I didn't know where my room was.

I wandered into the kitchen, to the breakfast nook. This seemed more familiar—the smells of food, me sitting at the dinner table while Mom typed in her office—yes, there it was, through the French doors, her antique table and her computer. I remembered her office. A little swell of joy opened in my chest.

"Do you still write the mommy blog?" I wasn't asking from memory; she had talked about it while I lay in the hospital bed, working it into conversations with an odd pride.

"You always called it that. Never just 'the blog' or by its title, *Blossoming Laurel*." An edge in her voice.

"Sorry. The blog." I thought the title a bit too cutesy, but I didn't want to hurt her feelings.

"Not since the accident. Too many people felt I hadn't been a good mother . . . " Then she stopped. "I'm tired of writing it. Of writing about you. You didn't like it as you got older."

I felt a vague unease when I thought of her blog, but I didn't know why. That was for worrying about later. I went back to the front; the reporter was still out there, but standing away from our yard.

I took a step toward the stairs and Mom realized, maybe, that I should be the priority. I looked at her and wondered if she'd slept at all in the past week.

She enclosed me in a hug. "You remember your room, I'm sure. Let's go see it." I followed her up the stairs. I paused at the family photos on the wall. Me, as a baby, as a toddler, as an elementary school student. And a man.

"Is that Dad?" I asked. She hadn't yet shown me a picture. She didn't have one on her phone, hadn't brought one to the hospital.

She nodded. "Do you remember him?"

"I knew it was him. Before I asked. But...I don't see him, like in a movie of my memories, doing anything yet."

My dad. He had a blondish beard in some and was clean shaven in others.

"Jane? Do you remember me yet, or do you call me Mom because I told you to?" Her voice was tense.

"I remember you, Mom," I lied, because it seemed to matter, and she was all I had right now, and with time, little moments of the past with her were beginning to take shape, to clearly appear. Her office, the smells of dinner in the kitchen. But only scattered bits.

"Tell me something you remember." She sounded insistent.

I grabbed at the smoke in my brain and came up with: "You sitting at your desk and writing *Blossoming Laurel* on your computer while I ate dinner."

It was vague, but it was enough. And apparently accurate. Mom tried a bright smile, and then trudged ahead, determined to get me to my room.

You'd think the place I spent the most time would send a resounding boom of memory through my head. It didn't mean much. The room was medium-sized, with a bed and movie posters. I remembered where the bookshelf was. The movie posters on the wall meant nothing to me.

"You like movies," Mom said. "You said you might want to be a screenwriter one day. Or write for video games or television.

You're a very gifted writer, Jane, like me, and you will be again."
As if any gifts I had might be lost along with the memories.

"You mentioned that," I said. It was weird that I felt like I
had to keep her calm, when I was the one in crisis. There was a
movie poster from *Casablanca* (a black-and-white movie, how
odd), from *The Piano* (a musical, maybe?), from *The Hours*,
with three women staring back at me. I knew none of these
films. I wondered if I would like them now. Would my tastes
change if I couldn't remember what I liked?

I had not remembered the room's location, but I immediately recognized my bedspread. The arrangement of books on
one shelf, unchanged from when I was younger. I knelt and
studied the titles. I recognized them all. I realized, with a jolt,
that one was missing. My favorite: *A Wrinkle in Time*. How
could I remember that book but not all my friends or my own
father's passing?

But the book was gone. Was I imagining that I thought it
should be there? It was an odd thing to notice, but I was cling-
ing to any recognizable sign that this was the home I knew.
Why was it so important? Why?

"Where's my copy of *A Wrinkle in Time*?" I asked.

"I don't know, honey, I'm sure it's around here somewhere.
You remember that's your favorite book?" Hope sweetened her
voice.

"Yes. Meg and Charles Wallace and Aunt Beast and Cama-
zotz. I remember the whole story."

I thought she was going to cry, maybe in relief. If I could
remember fictional people and places, more memories of what
was real would surely soon return.

Below the shelf of books was a line of video games: more of
the puzzle-solving variety than first-person shooters. I pulled
one out at random, with two cartoonish, big-eyed girls on the
cover: *SPYGIRLZ!* I smiled.

"You and David used to play video games together," she said, then bit her lip.

I stared at the game. *Remember*, I told myself. *Remember. You played it with David.* But nothing. I put it back and moved away from the games.

On the shelf were sketchbooks. I pulled one down. It was designed for drawing but I'd filled it with stories. Several pages were full of three-panel comic strips with sarcastic teddy bears. "You and David made comic strips just for fun, when you were little. He drew the pictures and you wrote the stories. I wanted to send them to the newspaper, they were so cute. He drew very well, he wanted to major in art, but Cal and Perri would hear none of that." I studied the drawings: cutesy bears, confident superheroes. He was talented.

I moved to the other side of the room. Photos of me, with other kids, were stuck on a blue corkboard above my desk.

And a picture of my dad. Dead from a gun accident. Now Mom had to tell me twice that he was dead. She carried a heavy load, I was aware now. I wondered how she would get through this nightmare—and what I would do if she didn't, if she couldn't cope. Her strength seemed, well, as variable as the wind.

"You made me buy blue, although I wanted to get you pink," Mom said, pointing at the corkboard. "You might like the pink better now." As if my amnesia was a good way to enforce her decor choices.

"The blue is fine," I said. I didn't want her to alter anything in this room. This was a moment of my old life, untouched since the accident. This was a map to me and my past few years. The last time I'd been here I'd had no idea that my life was about to evaporate. I looked at the pictures on the shelf. The framed ones seemed to be reserved for adults. Me and Dad. Me and Mom. Not Mom and Dad together. I wondered,

What was their marriage like? Did they love each other or did they have troubles? I have no idea. How odd not to know. Then to the blue corkboard. Most of these were with high school friends. Standing awkwardly in a group, the girls in pretty dresses, the boys in suits or ties, all of us by a pool.

"Homecoming," Mom said. "Do you remember that?"

I knew the tall, broad-shouldered blond boy next to me was named Trevor Blinn, he'd come to see me once in the hospital after I woke up. He seemed quiet and slightly scared of me, like he didn't know what to say, but he had brought flowers and I'd watched him give my mom an awkward hug. I didn't want anyone hugging on me. I was still physically so sore from the accident. An old friend, although he'd certainly gotten taller and bigger since I remembered middle school.

But he made a memory tickle.

"Husky jeans." I pointed at Trevor. "When we were little. A girl with a big red bow in her hair made fun of Trevor having to wear husky-sized jeans, and I was so mad at her, we got into a fight on the playground and I snatched that bow right out of her hair. I got sent to the principal's office and the boys teased Trevor about me fighting for him. Fourth grade?"

"Yes," Mom nodded. "You remember."

"Well, I remember that one incident. Don't get too excited. You picked me up at school." The words came in a rush. "You took me home and talked to me about it and then wrote about it in your blog. But you got me pizza for lunch, and Trevor's mom called to say she was sorry I'd gotten into trouble." A memory, slick and clear and newly born. "And David and I did a comic strip about a girl who fights bullies and called it *Bowsnatcher!*" I thought I would faint. Memory, bright and clear and full. Overwhelming.

"And you still hate giant bows." Mom pressed her hands to her mouth in happiness.

I didn't recall my feelings on that important fashion issue. I looked closer at the homecoming picture. Adam was on the other side of the group, smirking; I knew his name from his hospital visit but remembered nothing about him. How could I forget that handsome smirk? He had announced, as if nothing was wrong with me, "I know you don't remember me, but you will, I'm your friend who's a bit of a jerk."

The pretty dark-haired girl next to me was Kamala. Our heads were nearly together, our smiles matching. [*Written in the margin in a different color of ink:* In two more weeks many more childhood memories of Kamala and Trevor would start to rush back, but I didn't know that then.]

And then the boy I'd killed. David. He was in two pictures. One, when we were young, maybe eight, smiling, his front teeth missing. We were both in matching blue-and-white football jerseys. He had a cowlick in his dark hair, I had on a thin matching ribbon in mine—decidedly not a bow—that went with my jersey. I looked real cute. I remembered this. It didn't come like an electrical shock. The memory was just there, as if waiting for me.

"We played flag football together. The team was the Lions."

"Yes! When you were little, for one season. You wanted to do it because David did it and you hated to stay on the sidelines." Mom nearly clapped her hands together. Every new memory felt like a yard of land won in a battle.

"One of the other moms didn't want me to play," I said. "She wanted me to be a cheerleader instead."

Mom nodded.

"You and Dad politely told her I would play and that was the end of that."

Our smiles were huge. But then I thought of David, dead, and the smile faded.

"There don't seem to be a lot of recent pictures of me." The ones with me and Kamala smiling, being sisterly, were all when I was a few years younger.

"You stepped back from a lot of activities after your father died. You felt depressed."

Depressed. Who had I been, what sort of young woman had I been before the crash? And who was I going to be now?

"Mom, what is this suicide note the reporter talked about?"

Her face went to stone. "Never you mind that, it's a mistake."

"Mom. Tell me."

"Let's look at your clothes. And your playlist. I bet those will jog your memories."

"Mom, tell me."

She sat on the bed and gestured me to sit next to her. I did. She took my hand. Her own was cold yet slicked with sweat. I wanted to pull mine away but I dared not. She put her fingers under my jaw and turned me to face her. "Baby, they found a note, so they say, in the grass down the hill. Like it came from the car, there were odds and ends in the back—you know, our reusable shopping bags, a canvas folding seat I take to the football games, a couple of books . . . and a bunch of it spilled out as the car rolled and the windows smashed, and this note was in it. Written by you, they say. I saw it and it sort of looks like your handwriting, but none of you kids use cursive anymore, you all print the same to me, so who's to say."

"What did the note say?"

She pulled a piece of paper out of her pocket. "This is a copy they gave me. So, as they said, I can get you help if you need it. Not the original. The police have that. Or the investigator working for their lawyer, he's all cozy with the cops, he's the one jabbering about it."

"Lawyer?" I was waiting for her to hand me the note.

"Never mind that." I had noticed Mom had a habit of mentioning unpleasant subjects, nestling them in your brain, and then telling you not to worry about them. "I think this note could wait until you're further along in your recovery. That damn reporter. I hate him for yelling that at you."

I held out my hand, the one that wasn't in a cast. "What does it say?"

She seemed to take my measure. She put her gaze to the note, and read aloud:

I can't do this. I can't. I wish I were dead. I wish we were dead together. Both of us.

She folded the note. "Obviously this is a fake."

I stood because I wanted to get away from the words. Then I sat down again on the edge of the bed, my legs, my brain, my heart all like water. "So. I had that note with me and I crashed my own car…"

Mom's hand closed hard around my upper arm. "You listen to me, Jane. It's not a suicide note. It cannot be. It just isn't."

Was I supposed to sleep in this room with the photo of the boy I killed looking back at me? I ached, everywhere, my head, my guts. I got up and I took down the pictures of David.

"What does that mean?" Mom asked. "Jane?"

"I think I need to lie down," I told Mom.

"Yes. Of course. I'll go see about dinner. People brought food here while you were recovering…before they heard about the note…"

And then they stopped was the rest of the sentence, I guessed. "People think I killed David trying to commit suicide." The words felt like ash in my mouth.

She nodded and I lay on the bed. I thought the phone might ring, friends or neighbors calling about us, but it was quiet. I looked at the picture of my friends and wondered if Kamala and Trevor would come see me again. If anyone ever would. Finally, I slept. When I woke up I felt no mad surge of memory. I wasn't a cursed princess waking up from a dream, back into the life I knew. I could hear Mom's voice outside, talking with a neighbor. Loudly. Later Mom would tell me it was Perri Hall, telling Mom to tell me to stay away from her family.

8

I'M GLAD YOU agreed to meet with me," Kevin said. Jane sat across from him, in a research room in the counseling department. "I'm going to be blunt with you. You're a mess. You're nearly homeless, you've been accused of an attempted suicide/murder, and your once-promising life is a shambles."

"You should work with children," Jane said.

He didn't smile or laugh at her joke and she thought, *Well, he doesn't care about spending six weeks building rapport with me.* Kevin leaned forward. "May I make a guess; you tell me if I'm wrong. The reason you don't like therapists is because they have tiptoed around you. About the accident, if it was an attempted suicide and David Hall paid the price. I don't think I will tiptoe around you. I take a more direct approach."

It was like he'd sat in on her useless former therapy sessions. "OK," she said, now hesitant, waiting to see what he'd say next.

"Maybe you are repressing the memories due to intense

emotion. I think you have to be willing to explore that possibility, that it's not purely physical."

"I had a SPECT scan." She waited for him to not know what it was.

But he said, after she paused, "Single-photon emission computed tomography. Measures the amount of blood flowing to different parts of the brain, to see any reduced flow to injured areas. And?"

"I had injury in my temporal lobes."

"Where long-term memories reside. Yes. But your memories of your first years did slowly return, correct? At least that was what it said in Mr. Vasquez's newspaper articles about you."

"Yes."

"Ribot's Law. Simply put, the oldest memories tend to be the safest."

"Yes." She knew the name Ribot from Dr. K. Ribot had been a French psychologist who studied memory.

"Except your high school years."

"Yes."

"So that could be either emotional or physical. You lost your father?"

"Yes."

"And that is when the amnesia begins, when you entered high school, a cushion of time before his death, and it includes the crash and David's death. You are spared the memories of two terrible tragedies."

Jane said nothing.

"So. What do you want from our work together?"

No one had asked her that in so long. She almost shivered under his stare. "I want to remember. I want to know that I didn't kill David on purpose. That it truly was an accident. I want to be able to cope," she said. "I want to finish school. I want to be self-sufficient. I want David..."

"David is gone."

"I want David to not haunt my thoughts so much. I don't want to be blamed anymore for this. In the suburb where we lived, the school we went to—I am hated. I have exactly one friend left. If it was an accident, I could be forgiven. A suicide attempt isn't forgivable."

"People are always going to blame you. We could come up with some strategies to help you cope with that and not let it define you. To find a safe place for you."

"That's a big promise, Kevin." Because she had never learned to cope with the blame. Just shove it in the back of her mind, where it writhed, angry and restless.

"You have a big problem, Jane. I don't think we should think small."

She rubbed her palms along the arms of the chair. "OK, so how do we start this? Do you analyze me from when I was born? I had a nice, boring childhood."

She studied the shoes on his feet. They were worn, scuffed. Grad students never have money.

"Tell me about that day of the crash. I know you don't remember it, right?"

"Is that a trick question?"

"No. But you must have been told some of it."

"David and I left school that day at four fifteen. We were seen leaving together. He texted his parents that he was staying to work with a friend on a school project and they'd grab some dinner. We took my car."

"Did you have a homework project with him?"

"Apparently not. We only had two classes together, choir and entrepreneurship."

"Entrepreneurship's a high school class?"

"At Lakehaven it is." She paused. "A friend, Trevor Blinn, saw us leave together."

"You were next-door neighbors. Couldn't you simply have gone home and talked?"

"Sure. But we didn't."

"And there was no text or e-mail communication between the two of you that day? I understand this is how American teenagers make their plans." He gave a gentle smile.

"No." Jane shifted in her seat. This had started to feel like an interrogation. Most therapists tried to soften the blows of their questions. Maybe this was his style. "A girl named Amari Bowman said he passed me a note in entrepreneurship, because she sat between us. I mean, note passing isn't something people do when you could text each other, but in that class, I'm told, we had to turn in our phones at the beginning of class and got them back at the end. We each had a slot for our phone."

"What did the note say?"

"I didn't keep it. I don't know." Her gaze had gone to the floor.

"You don't know where this note is now?"

"I presume I threw it away. Or it was lost at the hospital when they cut my clothes off me." She kept staring at the floor. "It probably said, 'Meet me after school.' Since that's what we did."

"So for six hours, the two of you were out and about, and no one knows what you were doing. How difficult that must be for you." Finally, his tone of voice softened.

"We were seen around town in the course of that evening. Once at dinner. Once at a hardware store. Buying a crowbar. The receipt was in David's pocket."

"A crowbar." Kevin tented his fingers below his chin. "Why would you need a crowbar?"

She shrugged. "It wasn't found in the car with us, so I don't know where it went. And that's all I know. Four days later I woke up in a hospital. I didn't remember anything. My memory began to return in the next week, though, memories up until I was fourteen. After that, nothing."

"Nothing at all. No fragments, no bits." His gaze met her own.

"Nothing that I could recognize as a memory." Her stare didn't waver from him.

He didn't say anything, as if he was waiting for her to confess, *Oh I'm just kidding. Of course I remember details, I've just kept them to myself.*

"What is the last thing you recall before the accident?"

"Before high school started my dad and I went on a trip. Mom was working, she couldn't go. Just the two of us, to Disney World. We had a wonderful time." Her voice was soft. Not defiant. "David was so jealous. He wanted to go, but his parents hate theme parks. I brought him back a book on Walt Disney's art. He liked art. He liked to draw."

"I'm glad your last memory is a happy one. So nothing of your freshman year?"

"Not really," but her gaze slid away from him.

"Forgive my bluntness, Jane. You don't remember anything that would support this suicide note being legit?"

"No."

"Have you been told of anything going on in your life that would have made you suicidal at that time?"

"No. I wasn't in therapy. The school counselors didn't have a record that I was at risk. I guess at Lakehaven they monitor such things, especially after a parent dies."

"Were you with your father when he died?"

Jane ran her hand along the arms of the chair again. He'd read the articles about her, he must know what had been reported about her father's death. But she pretended like she didn't realize this. "He was at a house he owned over in central Austin, it had been his uncle's, he'd inherited it, and Dad was going to put it on the market. My uncle kept guns—a rifle and several pistols. Dad was handling one and it went off and killed him." She picked at a spot on her palm.

"I'm sorry."

Jane shrugged. "I don't remember it. I think that's hard on my mom."

"And so I guess you can't tell me how you reacted."

"It's in Vasquez's articles. I went wild for a while. Drinking mostly, but I apparently straightened out."

"Was there any suggestion your father had committed suicide?"

Jane stared at him. "The police investigated. It was an accident."

"And then your suicide note. I mean, people must have jumped to an unfortunate conclusion."

"Like father, like daughter." She stopped worrying the flesh on her palm and got up and paced over to the window. "My mother was famous—well, Internet-famous—for chronicling her every decision as a parent. She lost her husband and then nearly lost me. I heard people say she hasn't been the same since."

Kevin was silent for several seconds. "Let's go back to the day of the crash. Any communications from David? He hadn't sent you an e-mail or a text that would suggest what you two would have been doing?"

"No. My mom looked through them all, then I did, trying to jog my memory. We didn't e-mail, or text, or have lunch together. We weren't close the way we once were."

"And I presume his parents checked his e-mails?"

"I presume. His mom would leave no stone unturned if she could prove it was my fault. But they've never come forth with any proof like what you're asking."

"Do you remember anything about his parents?"

The question surprised her. "That they were nice to me growing up. Until the crash. His mom hates me now. She attacked me this morning at his grave." She related the story.

"And how did you feel?"

"I wanted to hit her. I'm horrible. She's a grieving mother. But I just wanted her to leave me alone."

"Do you want to prove to her you're innocent, at least of the suicide attempt?"

"I don't care what she thinks." She sat back down in the chair, sighing as if bored.

"I wonder if this might be helpful. Could you write out a detailed time line for me of that evening, what is known? You gave me an overview, but I'd like to see actual times— what is known, from witness testimony or the accident investigation? Surely your mother must have papers."

She felt a hot flash pass through her. "I've never wanted to look at that night. I thought the memories would just come..."

"Let us," he said, "try to impose some order on that hazy night. Perhaps it will tell us. You were not off somewhere being unhappy and suicidal, yes? You were doing something. A crowbar implies activity. Purpose. And this was secret. He told no one, you told no one."

She stared at his cheap shoes.

"So, we have two notes. The note he passed you, which you do not remember, and the note found at the scene. What did it say?"

"*I can't do this. I can't. I wish I were dead. I wish we were dead together. Both of us.*" It was like a morbid poem she had memorized.

"What is it you 'can't do'?"

"Algebra. Eating broccoli. Gardening. I don't know."

"The note says nothing to you."

"It upsets me," she said. "Because I cannot imagine writing it."

He switched topics. "After the crash"—she noticed he wasn't calling it "the accident" anymore—"you must have finished high school? Did you get your GED?"

"No." Now her gaze met his. "I went back to Lakehaven High School. I graduated."

He looked at her with frank surprise. "Why not attend another school?"

"I thought about starting over. But I only had a semester left…and I still had friends there. I thought they would help me through it. Some did. And my mom thought…if people saw how pathetic I was, maybe they'd feel sorry for me. And in turn feel sorry for her. She was losing friendships, her standing in the community. She wanted it back."

Kevin cleared his throat, as if embarrassed. "But you wouldn't have remembered your earlier course work."

"I managed to wing it. Relearn what I had to know to keep going. And I think they mercy-passed me. Keeping me back for a year wasn't an option for my mom. But I wasn't really prepared for Saint Michael's. They were kind to honor my admission still."

He looked at her with new respect. "That must have been difficult as well from a social standpoint, not remembering many of your friends or your teachers."

"It's harder when you kill the boy next door and the whole school wishes you'd killed yourself instead."

He looked up at me from his notes.

"Would you give me access to your medical records? I'd like to understand the extent of your injuries."

"No," she said.

"Why not?"

"I don't want to. I said I'd talk to you, not unlock my life. You're not a doctor."

For some reason she thought she saw a flash of frustration under the surface of his face. Then the neutral expression back in place. "Would you describe your injuries, then?"

"I was in a coma for four days. I had a broken arm and a fractured collarbone. I had a severe concussion and slight brain damage in the temporal lobes."

"David's injuries?"

For a moment she couldn't speak. "Both his arms and legs were broken. His face was badly lacerated. Broken ribs. His back was broken, and a lung punctured. He died at the scene."

"Why were his injuries so much more?"

"The car tumbled as it went off the road and a steep drop to the cliff's edge began. He was on the side of the car that smashed into a rock face along the hill. The car bounced off it and came to rest. And..."

He waited.

Jane said, "David didn't have on his seat belt."

"Did he normally ride without it?"

"Who could stand that constant pinging? The suggestion was he undid it..." She stopped.

"To stop you from driving off the road and then off the cliff?"

"That," she said, "was one popular theory, thanks to the suicide note." She took a drink of water.

"What was your first memory on awakening?"

Jane got up and paced the floor again. "Is this OK? I don't feel like sitting."

Kevin nodded.

"I was in the hospital room. I don't remember being afraid, just confused. I didn't know I'd been in a coma. I didn't recognize my mother, who was in the room with me. She said, 'Oh, Jane,' and started to cry because I was awake. I didn't know it was my name. It was as though I'd just been born in the world.

"The doctors came in and checked me and asked me questions. What did I remember, where did it hurt? I panicked because I didn't remember anything. Then they started testing me, asking me the year, my name, who was the president, where did I go to school. I watched this woman—my mother—I watched her heart break."

"Did anyone suggest you lied about your amnesia?"

"Yes. Mrs. Hall. She thought I was faking it. To avoid responsibility. You know, someone is taunting me online that they remember what I don't." She explained about the Faceplace posting. "It's my sore spot. I know they have to be lying, but it enrages me."

"Are you lying about your amnesia?"

Her gaze met his.

He continued: "Because if you are, I would understand. It would be a defense mechanism. You can tell me, no one will know, our sessions are privileged." He leaned forward. "If you were lying, I'd be impressed you've kept it up for two years. But what a heavy burden."

The silence became uncomfortable. She finally said, "No, Kevin, I'm not lying about my amnesia."

"All right."

She wasn't sure he believed her. "This person who

threatened me online, who screws around with an amnesiac? Who wants to pretend that they know something I don't remember, when there's absolutely no way that they could?"

Kevin frowned. "First, it could be a harmless—in their eyes—prank or joke. Second, it could be someone who believes you do in fact remember and is trying to provoke you."

"Why would anyone think I faked this for two years?"

"They think you know something from that night. And the amnesia is a cover-up. Do you know who is taunting you?"

"I have a suspicion." *Kamala*, she thought.

"Who?"

"I'd rather have proof before I say."

"It's all confidential here."

She shook her head. She didn't trust him quite yet.

He didn't press her, but he made a note in his papers. "Do you miss David?" Kevin asked.

"No one has asked me that. I don't think I'm allowed to miss him." But she didn't answer the question.

"All right. Before we meet again, will you work on that time line for me?"

"All right. What do I do about my harasser?"

"I would ignore them. If you try to engage them, you give them power, you give them your attention, you validate them. You want peace, you want forgiveness? Practice it."

"Maybe I'll tell them to go ahead and tell the world whatever it is that they know." She stood and put on her backpack. "I think I'm done for the day."

"Jane?"

"What?"

"Is there any chance, from anything anyone has said to you since, that someone else was involved?"

"What do you mean?"

He hesitated. "That another car ran you off the road, or veered into your lane and you swerved off to miss them, or was racing you, or...pursuing you. Do you ever feel like someone is after you? Or wants to hurt you?"

"Why would anyone want to hurt me or David? We were just high school students."

"I'm sure no one wants to hurt you, Jane."

"Do you think that's what happened?" she asked him. Why would he ask her this?

Instead of answering her, Kevin looked at his notes. "Shall we meet in two more days?"

9

THAT NIGHT PERRI poured a glass of sauvignon blanc before Cal arrived. She'd spent the day taking phone calls and answering e-mails. She was grateful to those who reached out to her, but at the same time it felt like a bit of a burden to respond. She could have gladly spent the entire day alone, in silence.

Cal texted that he was on his way. She checked the dinner in the oven and sat down at the granite countertop of the kitchen island with the glass of wine. She took a deep breath and opened up her laptop and jumped to her Faceplace page, finally ready to read it today. Lots of notes of condolence, lots of "thinking about you" private messages. A reminder from Ronnie Gervase about the gala volunteers meeting, and sending her a virtual hug. She felt grateful. Then she saw:

Mrs. Hall, I wonder if we might talk. I know it's the anniversary and it's a hard time for you, but I'm thinking of writing a follow-up piece on the loss of your son and Jane Norton's amnesia. I apologize but I don't have a current e-mail address for you. I'm not at the newspaper anymore, but you can reach me through my Face-place account or at mv@now-mail.net. Thanks, Matteo Vasquez.

Perri didn't feel like being on display again. Seeing another article about her son and still having it be mostly about the poor murdering so-called amnesiac who still hadn't recovered. And if she talked about Jane, Jane would talk about her actions at the cemetery. And she had a witness. So she clicked, wrote No thanks, and hit Send.

She closed the laptop—she didn't want to look at the words anymore—and took her glass and went upstairs to David's room. She had kept it just as he had left it, as if it were a room encased in amber. The only item she had removed was a photo of David with Jane Norton, fourth grade, in their flag-football uniforms. They'd played on a coed team. David had been the star and Jane had been the pity player, but you couldn't see that in the photo, in their white jerseys, Jane smiling in surprise, the participation medal on her chest, the same with David but also with a trophy for, what, most improved player? Best sportsmanship? Yes, that made sense. David was driven by such a sense of fair play. She'd taken down the picture because she could not bear to see Jane Norton's face during the times she came alone into this room to lie down on David's bed and let the grief and the loneliness fill her.

She sat on his bed and let her gaze roam over the room. Pictures he'd drawn, he was so gifted. Books on a shelf, novels and instruction guides on drawing. He had been a talented artist, although she and Cal felt it was important to gently push him toward something practical. Art made for a nice hobby, but David was used to a certain standard of living.

The wineglass broke in her hand. She jerked so that the wine didn't spill onto the floor but stayed in the now-stemless bulb. The stem had broken cleanly but she couldn't set the wineglass down, so she gulped down the entire serving of sauvignon blanc. It coursed through her and she hurried to the restroom and blotted a dot of blood from her hand. She threw the broken wineglass away.

She fought down a sob. So what if he'd become an artist, if that was what he wanted to do? He might have been a very successful one. He might have been happy. What was wrong with her and Cal that they hadn't told him, *Yes, be what you want to be. Be an artist. No, you don't have to be a business tycoon, a tech giant. Be yourself. Go draw superheroes. Be one.*

She washed the blood off her hand, making sure no particle of glass was in the wound. She put on a Band-Aid that came from a box he'd kept under his sink. His cologne, his aftershave, his razor, his toothbrush, all still here. She should throw them away. But she hadn't.

She went back into his room, the blood welling up under the bandage.

He had gotten an iMac computer a few months before he died and she woke it from sleep with a touch on the keyboard. She knew his password—that had been a condition of her buying it, she wanted to give him his privacy but was unwilling to give up access to where he browsed and his e-mails—but he had never given her a real moment's worry. The dock along the edge of the window appeared on his Mac's screen and she opened up Faceplace, his password already entered in by default.

She went to his page. Tribute after tribute. She read of his friends, scattered now all over the state, and the country, to college, keeping David in their thoughts. There were fewer tributes than last year, and a hard little knot formed in her chest. Fewer people would remember him as time passed. He would further recede into memories. Lives would go on.

Except for his.

She wanted to send notes to some of the girls, and to David's fellow football players, who left the most touching tributes. But she would do that from her own page. It was too strange to do it from David's page, creating the illusion that he was still alive.

She typed into the Faceplace search bar: Jane Norton.

Perri clicked.

The top posting was a new one. From someone Perri didn't know, named Liv Danger.

I know what you claim you don't remember, Jane. I know what happened that night. And I'm going to tell. All will pay.

Posted today. She stared at the words *All will pay*. The same three words that had been scrawled on her son's grave.

Her eyes scanned down the page. Jane herself had posted nothing since a few days after the accident, when she and her mother claimed that Jane remembered a deer bolting out in front of the car. Considering the fact that Jane could remember nothing else of the tragic night, and that there were no deer tracks or signs in the bushes or the damp ground of the too-steep hillside, this story did not hold up. Nothing on her return to Lakehaven, nothing about her time at St. Michael's. Nothing on Christmas or birthdays or anything, although it looked like a few people had reached out to her. It was as if, like David, she had died. No photos of herself at college, no interactions with friends, no likes of photos or videos or other people's postings.

And then the postaccident torrent of inevitable garbage commentary on a newspaper article in which someone had so thoughtfully tagged Jane:

They found a suicide note in the debris. She wanted to die. She wanted them both dead. Can u believe?

It was just two rich Lakehaven assholes, who cares?

Her heart felt like it would explode in her chest.

Jane's father died and it was suicide people said and now she tries to kill herself and David dies instead. We'll miss you David.

You know she was in love with him and he didn't love her so she tried to kill them both. She must have thought she was driving off a cliff but it wasn't. Stupid selfish bitch one day she'll fry in hell

How is she not in prison, why did the Halls drop their wrongful death suit, I smell a payoff!!!!!!!!!

Her mom writes one of those mom-blogs and has a lot of views and so they must be rich so she'll get probation and then go off to some rich bitch school up north and that's that.

Wow that mom of hers wrote about her all the time when she was a little kid and she and her dad both were suicides I guess a blog where you dissect your family life is a bad idea LOL too bad for the idiot in the car with her

I blame the parents. Both sets. They shouldn't have been out drinking and driving, kids do what they see at home if you ask me. Bad examples!! Bad parenting!! You don't get in a car with a drunk kid you'll DIE!!!!!

No evidence they were drinking, dumbass, but thanks for playing.

The news covers up for them, your the dumbas!s

Try reading the article. I know it has words of more than one syllable but try.

Perri Hall stopped. Closed her eyes. Her son's beautiful life, his tragic death, dismantled and discussed—with no knowledge of him—by strangers, who felt they could yell and argue over her son's dead body, figuratively. Who felt that just because they had a keyboard, they could and should say whatever they wanted.

She toggled back to the top of the page. She clicked on Liv Danger, who claimed to have a better memory than Jane's. The account had only a few friends, a few of which looked like fake spam accounts, and only one she recognized: Jane Norton.

So it was a fake account? Someone just messing with Jane and with her and Cal as well. Desecrating his stone was much worse than posting on Jane's social-media page. What if this Liv Danger was telling the truth and knew something about the crash that wasn't known?

All will pay.

I could try and find out who this is, she thought.

The doorbell rang.

You have to be better than this. You can be better than this. She went downstairs.

* * *

She cooked a favorite of David's: baked chicken breasts stuffed with feta cheese, wrapped in bacon, with quinoa and salad with homemade lemon-and-shallot dressing. Cal brought a cold bottle of Grüner Veltliner wine from Austria and, without being asked, poured a hefty glass for her and then one for himself. He hadn't realized she'd already opened a bottle of wine, which was now tucked in the fridge door, and she thought, *Well, this will numb us.* She took a long, gulping drink and then set the wineglass down and stepped into his arms. He was surprised. He didn't hesitate to fold her in his embrace, kissing the top of her head.

"The cemetery management is going to increase security. There shouldn't be further issues with David's grave."

The oven chimed. She turned away and busied herself,

feeling the wine kicking in hard, and he finished making the salad. Just like he still lived here.

"I spent the day outlining that mentorship program for David."

"Alone?"

He nodded, surprised.

"You said you didn't want to be alone today and I thought," she said, thinking of the perfume in his car, "that maybe you were seeing someone."

"I'm not," he said after a few moments of silence. "I would tell you if I was."

She started to clean up and he said, "No, I'll do it, you cooked," and so she sat back down with her wine while he cleaned and then he came and sat by her and refilled her glass and his own with the cold Austrian white wine. Two glasses were her limit, and he'd chosen what he nicknamed her big "book-club glasses," which she could normally only drink one of. She didn't trust open bottles of wine tonight. It would be too easy to dull the pain, get too lost, and she'd feel sick and tired tomorrow.

He took her hand. She let him.

"What do you know about Jane Norton these days?" she said.

She felt his hand stiffen and then squeeze her fingers with just a bit more pressure. "Nothing. Unlike you, I prefer not to think about her."

"It was why you dropped the lawsuit, you felt sorry for her." *And that was the first crack in our marriage.*

His glass paused on the way to his mouth. "Do you think bankrupting my best friend's widow with a brain-damaged daughter would have brought back our son? No."

"But it could have gotten us to the truth. Forced an investigation into whether or not they were lying about her amnesia, or maybe encouraged a witness to come forward."

"Perri." He sounded exhausted.

Fine, she thought. *I won't tell you about my scene with Jane, or this Liv Danger person. You wouldn't do anything about it anyway. I know you. You give up too easy, Cal. You accept.*

"I love you," he said. "I always will."

"I know." But she couldn't say it back.

A resigned pain crossed his face. He told her he was tired and he left. She closed the door. Picked up her glass of wine. She went back upstairs. The Faceplace screen was still up. She clicked on Liv Danger's link.

I'm going to find out who you are. Perri sent a friend request.

10

BRENDA HOBSON COULDN'T sleep. Numbers danced in her head: the amount she still owed off her husband's credit card debt, the college payment that would be due soon for her son. Sometimes when she closed her eyes she could see the numbers sliding around on the ceiling. She'd worked hard after Rick died to pay off the debts he'd left; the insurance had covered some but not all. He liked her to have nice things, he just didn't like paying for them.

She'd erased forty thousand in debt—ten thousand still left. But Hunter was starting at the University of Texas at San Antonio, studying accounting, and he wasn't on full scholarship, and Lindsay was coming up two years behind him, and she wanted to go to art school. Considering how little artists were paid, you'd think art school would be cheap, but it was the opposite. She hoped it was a phase and Lindsay would want to make a more practical choice. But she hated to tell either of her kids no—they were not spoiled, but they'd lost so much when they lost their dad. Her life had turned into one giant making of amends for her husband's death. The debts. Not all of it had been credit card debt; she didn't want the kids to know that some had been to people he made bets with. Those she had paid off first, trembling when she met one bookie's representative in a department store parking lot to hand him five thousand in cash. Rick had gambled because he firmly believed life was short, and then his heart conked out, far too early at age forty-four, and proved him right.

The dark days were behind her. She'd gotten slowly back on her feet. Last year she'd bought the small house here in the new development on the outskirts of San Antonio suburbia, a new start for her and the kids, and more importantly, one that she could afford. Austin had been too expensive for her, after she lost Rick's income and with his debts, and too full of bad memories. Soon enough the houses on each side of her would be sold—it seemed like everyone was moving to San Antonio—and the new, better memories would start here. She had bought the first house built on this street.

It's small, Lindsay had said, frowning.

Cozy, Brenda answered, thinking, *An artist's garret is going to be even smaller, honey*.

She turned her face toward the pillow, did the math in her head; she could just squeeze out the tuition and the mortgage. The car was old but serviceable. She could even watch YouTube videos on how to repair it herself. She turned over. Two a.m. Then she did the math for how much sleep she could get before her next shift as a paramedic. The bed still felt empty without Rick, but she had, finally, gotten used to his absence.

She closed her eyes, the torture of the math done for the night, and fell asleep. She dreamed of walking through a vast glass house. She reached for a sculpture of delicate crystal, glowing with light.

She heard the sound first, the breaking of glass, and thought she was still in her dream. Brenda Hobson sat up; no more sound. A distant shattering, maybe next door. The empty, new, unsold houses. She'd heard people would break into them to steal the copper wiring and resell it. They weren't her houses, but this was her neighborhood, her new best hope, and the thought of thievery on a house belonging to a future neighbor made her mad. She'd call the police—

The smoke alarms blared.

She opened her bedroom door.

Flames were spreading across the den's carpet like wind surging, and the window beyond the fire was shattered. On the other side of the room was the staircase leading up to her children's bedrooms.

"Hunter, Lindsay!" she screamed. She couldn't get through the fire to them. She ran back into her bedroom, forced open the window, climbed out into her front yard. A strange calm kicked in; her training, to do her job in the midst of chaos. She picked up a heavy white stone from the edge of her planned flowerbed, and lobbed it at the upstairs bedroom window. Hunter's. After a moment he came to the window, his face twisted in panic.

"Get your sister and climb out onto the roof," she screamed. "Now. You can't get down the stairs."

He nodded and vanished back into the rising smoke. The smoke. It would all be rushing upward, toward her kids, choking them, suffocating them...

She turned and ran along the length of her house.

She saw a flash of light in the windows of the house next door. Fire. Her mind registered it: the house next door is on fire, too. Nothing to be done for that—Hunter and Lindsay were her only focus.

She ran around to the back, to the garage. She heaved it open and pulled out a ladder. It felt like it weighed nothing in her arms. She ran with it back toward the front of the house.

The house across the street—also empty—was burning as well. Flames burst from its upper windows. Again she registered it but kept her focus. She shoved the ladder against the house, by the window. She ran up its rungs, crawling across the roof. No sign of her kids, smoke pouring from the open window. *No, no*, she thought. Then she saw Lindsay coming through the window, coughing, gagging, Hunter sliding out behind her. They both rolled onto the roof, racking coughs. She pulled them to her, hearing a loud explosion inside the house.

"Hurry, hurry!" she screamed. Lindsay went down the ladder first, falling the final few feet onto the new grass. Brenda sent Hunter, but he was coughing so hard—he had gone after his sister in the thickening smoke—he fell from the ladder, sprawling on the lawn. Brenda could feel the fire raging, rising, through the roof. Hunter lay curled at Lindsay's feet in a fit of violent coughing and vomiting. Brenda rushed down the ladder and started protocols on her son.

"Mom!" Lindsay screamed. "All the houses are burning!"

The houses around them—all five of them—were ablaze, flames licking out their empty windows. The For Sale signs in every yard glowed as the flames rose. No neighbors to call 9-1-1. Her phone was inside, and her son was choking to death.

She began to pound on her son's back, trying to drive the smoke from him and the life back in, willing him to breathe, while everything she'd worked for burned.

11

The most ill-advised Faceplace posting in the history of Faceplace postings, courtesy of my mother:

Jane now remembers a deer running out in front of
the car.

This was Mom's big, nasty, Lakehaven-unforgettable lie.
She said it, I suppose, to lessen (futilely) the evidence of the
suicide note. And I went along with it, because the world
seemed to not like me much once the news of the suicide
note spread through Lakehaven, except for Mom. (It wasn't
initially in the news reports. The Halls' investigator found it
in the debris field of the crash the next day, gave it to the
police, who didn't release it to the press, ever, it was part of
the investigation. Then, in performing some forensic test on
it, the note got ruined. Destroyed. But the lawyer's investigator, a guy named Randy Franklin, or the Halls, leaked the
news of the note's existence to a few people in Lakehaven,
and then word of mouth took over, and that was that. I was
damned.)

You'd think, given Mom was a widow and the mother of

an apparently suicidal amnesiac, that people would be more forgiving. Some were, but many were not. If she had stayed quiet, maybe it would have been better for me and for her—Lakehaven can be a very generous place. But this one, stupid lie seemed to change something between us and the town, forever. What do they say about sports and celebrity scandals? The lie is worse than the cover-up.

Plus, there was the sense she was protecting her own interests. Her blog, *Blossoming Laurel*. She'd made a name on the Internet for being a stellar mother and sharing her insights. All the entertaining, oddball moments of my youth—which normally would have been told only to family or close friends over coffee, at reunions, or on holidays—were instead written up in her breathless prose and posted for the world. Every moment when she had faced an "Important Choice" as a parent. And then each thing was commented on. She finally shut them off when they turned cruel or twisted. I had become vaguely aware of her blog as my memories of her surged in like a slow tide. And then I read a few entries the day after I got home from the hospital—at the suggestion of Dr. K, that it might help prompt memories—with a kind of detached numbness, like I was reading about another girl, a stranger. In the blog I was "The Blossom"—never referred to as Jane. That was her idea of protecting me: changing one detail, not using my name. Some entries were funny, others touching—her love was clear. But it was strange to see my life laid out like a novel, available to anyone who wanted to read about it. She had written about my first crush, my first period, my first failing grade. Had she ever asked me if that was cool with me?

Back to the deer, Mom's last "Important Choice"—a choice to lie.

Deer running out from the oak and cedar into the streets

in Lakehaven were a real threat. There were more deer than coyotes, and despite the growth in Lakehaven and beyond as Austin's population boomed and real estate prices soared, deer bounding across major thoroughfares, especially at night, were a problem. A few DVCs a year resulted, usually not fatal except to the deer. (DVC means "deer-vehicle collision"—I looked it up online—nationwide, on average, a couple of hundred people die in them a year, and they result in a billion dollars' worth of property damage, which seems awfully high to me.) There had not been a fatal DVC accident in Lakehaven in twenty years.

Until me and David—according to my mother, the storyteller, who could not sell this story to Lakehaven.

"You just tell people it was a deer," she told me in a strict voice. It was my fourth day back from the hospital. The first three I'd spent alternately resting and walking and picking up things because Dr. K said my memory could be prompted by physical contact with reminders from my life. We had lived in this house since I was really little, so Dr. K was hopeful that I would have a wealth of physical reminders to help my memory. I didn't see how that was supposed to work if my brain was physically damaged. But then I didn't question Dr. K— she was a neurologist, and she was right: already I had started to remember times from my early childhood. They came, at times, like a rush of dreams inside my head. I would have to stop and focus and then the memory, like a scratchy film, would come. Playing flag football with David, a Christmas with Mom and Dad opening presents under the tree, running through the house laughing, singing along with Disney Channel musicals with Kamala. We knew every word, every inflection.

"I don't remember a deer," I said. She had made me lunch, a ham sandwich she claimed I liked, but I was not so sure. I was wondering if my taste buds could have been changed by amnesia. "Did I say there was a deer?"

"Yes," Mom said, voice booming with certainty, rinsing a dish. "While you were in your coma. You opened your eyes and you said, 'It was a deer running in front of us, Mom,' and then you closed your eyes again. You woke up the next day."

"Was a nurse or a doctor there when I said this?"

"No. Just me. Dr. K had just left." Her gaze held steady into mine. "There must have been a deer and you swerved to avoid it. That's the logical explanation. Your brain knows it's true."

"What difference does a deer make? David is still dead. And that note..."

"You did not. You could not. I see one thing you haven't forgotten is your argumentative attitude." But she folded me in a hug when she said it.

"Mom. OK, if you said I said it was a deer, then I believe you." I said this because I wanted to believe her.

"Yes, and I am going to post it to my Faceplace page. And my blog, which I haven't written in a few weeks, since you asked me to stop for a while. I am going to tell people at church, and some of the more sympathetic parents, and I'm going to tell the Halls so they will stop this campaign against us."

"Campaign?" I didn't like the sound of that word; it seemed so organized.

"Oh, they're upset. I understand. David was their son. But... obviously, honey, there has been some bad-mouthing of you. Not so much by them. By friends of theirs, but it's like wildfire, it spreads so fast. Whole group texts going over days and days, forwarding lies and misinformation. I feel the Halls could stand by us and put a stop to it."

"But I don't remember anything, and yet I'm going to re-member this deer?" I felt a cold panic.

"Of course. It was the last thing you remember. Memory is selective."

"Mom. I don't know if people will believe us."

"But it's true." [*A note added in blue ink:* Reading back on this, I am sure Mom convinced herself that this was true. She believed it, heart and soul, rather than believe I would have killed myself and left her alone, with no family remaining.]

"Is this because of Dad?"

"You're being silly. Two different accidents."

"I can't lie about this, Mom, I can't."

"They will crucify you at that school. David was a very popular boy, Jane, and they've already buried him, so the grief is turning to anger. Real anger. I saw it when I went to the grocery store. People staring at me. One mother told me it should have been you...well, never mind. I got asked to resign from every volunteer position I'm in. Your circle of friends is close, but, forgive me, honey, it's small. And David was a big deal. I wasn't like you in school, I was popular, I would have known how to cope. But people are going to believe the worst of you."

"Why was I with this superpopular boy if I'm such an outcast, Mom?" This was the first I was hearing of our respective social standings.

"You didn't run in the same circles anymore. And you withdrew from your friends, a lot, after your dad died. You changed." She coughed, as if those final two words choked her.

"Changed?"

"You stayed away from people. You dropped out of extracurriculars. You didn't hang out so much with your friends." She gave me a reassuring pat on the shoulder. "I'm going to go post this about the deer on Faceplace. I'm going to make some calls."

"Mom, I won't be able to keep the story straight."

"Of course not, you have brain damage," Mom said, as if it were an advantage.

I wanted to cry, and really, I was so sick of crying. I was cried out. I just felt dazed and frightened and tired, all the time, and it was starting to scare the hell out of me. I couldn't sleep. The whole world seemed alien to me. I felt I didn't know the rules. When you are sick, aren't people supposed to be kind to you, support you? I was sick and Mom said people hated me. A fear from deep down inside me, curled along my spine, a realization of how much my life had changed. "No, Mom."

Mom leaned down close to me. "You remember that flash at the moment of the accident. The deer, running out in front of you and you trying to avoid it. Repeat it after me."

I said it. "There was a deer. It ran in front of us. I don't remember anything else." The whole time I felt like a noose was slipping around my neck.

"Yes. You tell that to Kamala. She'll tell the kids who matter."

"Mom..."

She sat down at her computer and brought up Faceplace and wrote this short status about the fragment of deer-filled memory that magically absolved me from suicide. She tagged me so it would appear on my Faceplace page.

I should have written an apology to the Halls for the accident. But I didn't. So the first public statement I gave the world was an excuse, a cheap lie told by my mother.

Of course Mom didn't consider that the investigator working for the Halls' lawyers, Mr. Franklin, and the sheriff's accident investigation team would look at the damp earth around the crash site and not see a single trace of deer prints. She didn't realize it was standard operating procedure, for a one-car accident in the hills, to look for signs it was a DVC. There was no sign any deer had been through there that day on either side of the road. Not to mention that their consulting neurologist discounted my magically intact single memory.

But then, once the investigator's report disallowing the presence of deer got to the Halls, I wasn't just a loser who had wrecked her car and killed David Hall, I was a liar. Nail me up.

They told everyone that we had lied.

12

PERRI HAD PUT "Office Mom" on her business cards because she didn't care about titles, and there was a certain
pervasive wry humor at Hylist Software. And she was still
a mom, in her heart, in her mind—that was an unchanged
image. Hylist was a start-up company, ten months old,
thirty employees strong, in an office overlooking a bend
of Lake Austin. From her boss's office Perri could see
the soaring arch of the Pennybacker Bridge spanning Lake
Austin along Loop 360. But the new HR chief, a prim-
mouthed woman named Deborah, who seemed to lack any
sense of fun, had told Perri that it was unprofessional and
to replace her cards and use the title "Executive Assistant
to the CEO." Perri had smiled tightly and said, "All right."
She knew she could go to her boss and keep the original
card, but that wasn't how she wanted to start with Deborah.
Here she would pick her battles.

She worked, officially, for the CEO, an old high school
friend named Mike Alderson she'd grown up with in Lakehaven. She and Mike had been the less fortunate kids at

what was often seen as a rich-kid school: he lived with
his grandparents in an old house, one of the first built in
Lakehaven, back when it was country and not suburban;
she and her mother had lived in one of the few apartments
in Lakehaven's school district. Her mother cleaned houses
and eventually started a housecleaning service that had a
dozen workers. Mike had gone on to Rice, at full scholarship, for an undergraduate computer-science degree and
then an MBA, while Perri, also on scholarship, stayed close
to home at Texas State and got an English degree. She
started teaching middle school, but then met Cal, who was
a friend of Mike's, and married him six months later. They
moved to San Francisco for his first start-up company, and
after a few more years she decided to stay home when she
got pregnant with David and they moved back to Austin. So
this had been her first out-of-the-home job in many years,
and she loved it. Basically, she took care of the office.
There were four execs—Mike, the marketing/sales, engi-
neering, and HR vice presidents—but most of the employees were software designers, grinding out code to finish
their first product release. They were building a product
to simplify the integration of company-issued cell phones
with computer networks, to make them easier to manage
and to share information securely. Many of the developers
were young, and they worked long hours. Perri often felt
tender toward them. Aside from managing Mike's schedule, she stocked the refrigerator, had dinner brought in
when lots of the "kids"—she knew she shouldn't think of
them this way, but she did, some of them were barely older
than what David would be now—were working late, and
coordinated the Friday-afternoon beer break that was one
of the rewards of working for a driven yet more casual
company. She had taken two of the developers who were

in sore need of fashion advice shopping for clothes suitable for high-level meetings with customers. She'd helped two engineers who'd moved here from San Francisco find places to live and a preschool for another family. She kept things running smoothly, while Mike and his execs wooed potential customers and the programmers coded and drew incomprehensible diagrams on whiteboards and lived off the pizza she ordered.

Perri had needed this, after David died. Activity and chatter to fill the empty hours. She liked the people, and she knew they liked her. She was valued.

She had gone in extra early the morning after the awkward dinner with Cal, ignoring the wine headache gently throbbing in her head. So she was productive about what needed to be done: she brewed two pots of coffee (the developers usually did this themselves because they drank it so fast), stocked the fridge with new cans of soda, cleared the conference rooms, reordered supplies.

"Good morning," Mike Alderson said as he hurried past her desk. He was a nice-looking man, tall and trim, brown hair thinning, divorced for several years, with soft brown eyes and a bold smile. She had talked him into a more stylish pair of eyeglasses. He kept trying to talk her into dinner, a kind of dinner that seemed between more than friends. It was a side effect of long friendship and loneliness, but she could not encourage him. At least not now. She was deeply fond of Mike, but she wasn't ready. "How are you?" he asked. "I'm sorry I was gone yesterday. You and David, and Cal, too, were much in my thoughts."

They walked into his office together. She closed the door. "I'm fine. I don't want to make a production of it here."

"Of course."

"But I do need your help. I want to unmask an anonymous Internet user." Mike Alderson had been David's godfather. Mike would want to rage at this person's cruelty, fix the problem, take care of it for her, but he was busy launching what could be a hugely successful company. She didn't want him involved.

"Is someone bothering you?" He took a step toward her.

"No, it's nothing like that." She said nothing more and he waited and she still said nothing.

Mike hesitated. "Is Cal being difficult?" Mike had kept his opinion about their separation to himself.

"Of course not. So who would you suggest?"

"At ferreting out someone who wants to be hidden? Maggie, I'd say."

She gritted her teeth, but she put a bright smile on her face. "Thanks, I'll ask her."

"Is there anything else I can do to help you...?" He flushed with embarrassment. Mike had been a wonderful godfather to David, remembering every birthday, always encouraging him in his art and his sports and his studies, coming to his football games, laughing at his drawn comics. She would not tell him about the "ALL WILL PAY" written on the stone.

"If you feel up to it, could we have dinner this week?"

Perri hesitated for a moment, then said, "Sure." *He's being your old friend and your boss. He's worried about you.*

"How about tonight?" Mike asked.

"OK, but late this afternoon you've got that conference call with the San Francisco product testers, they're two hours behind us, and they always run long." He was notorious for not remembering his own schedule. She smiled. "But dinner with a *friend* sounds good." He seemed not to notice her emphasis.

"You have the phone conference call in ten minutes with Brad—he's calling you," she reminded him, and he nodded. She closed his office door behind him so he could prepare his notes in peace.

Maggie. One might expect or hope that two women over forty working at a software company full of twentyish programmers would be fast friends, but she and Maggie had virtually nothing in common, and Perri found Maggie distant and odd.

She walked down the hall to the darkest office, where the lights were kept dim and the reclusive programmer typed by the glow of her monitor. From the computer, an Eddy Arnold song from the 1960s softly played: "Make the World Go Away." Maggie Chavez had interesting tastes and did not bother with headphones, but she kept the music low and unobtrusive. The song choice, however, didn't make Perri feel more comfortable in knocking on Maggie's open door.

"Good morning, Maggie."

Type, type, type. Maggie didn't glance up from her screen. Apparently she didn't react to greetings, but awaited further data.

"I have a technical question for you."

"Did you try restarting the system?" She still didn't look up.

"No, I know how to fix my own computer." She moved a towering stack of Java and Python programming books, topped by a massive tome on regular expressions and algorithms, off Maggie's spare chair. Maggie, she was sure, kept them there to discourage visitors from sitting down and chatting with her. Most of the other programmers didn't keep libraries of books; Perri had seen them looking up code examples online, in a corner window of their screen. But then, Maggie had been programming longer.

Eddy Arnold gave way to Patsy Cline's "Crazy" on her computer speakers.

What a self-descriptive playlist, Perri thought. She sat. She waited. A minute ticked by.

Maggie Chavez kept typing in code, but realized Perri was not going to leave. "Sorry, OK, what? Does Mike need something?"

"How would I find out who created an account on Faceplace? They're using a fake name."

Maggie stopped typing. She actually looked away from her computer screen to focus on Perri. "Is this a fake account using your name?"

"No."

"Are they bullying you?"

Perri explained. Maggie listened with a surprising intensity.

"So how can I find out who Liv Danger is?"

"You need to set a little trap for your target."

Perri waited and Maggie sighed that the explanation wasn't obvious. "You need to get whoever is posting as 'Liv Danger' to click on a link. It will take them to a custom-designed page, a trap containing code that gathers data about their computer."

"I sent 'Liv' a friend request, but she, or he, hasn't answered it yet."

"Well, if they do, send them a private message with that link. Of course you could just ask them who they are, but they might lie."

"I don't think she'll be dumb enough to click on a link. Won't she be suspicious?"

"You give Liv Danger a great reason to click on it."

Perri could not think of such a reason, but pushed the thought aside. "And once they visit this site..."

"The customized page harvests information about the computer looking at the page. It could tell you if it's being accessed by a computer or a phone, the operating system, the IP address..."

"The what?"

"IP address. Each device accessing the Internet has a unique address. The same computer doesn't always get assigned the same IP address from the service provider, but the provider would know which computer had a certain IP address at a certain time. Getting them to share it with you is another matter."

"And that would tell me who was accessing the page? It's like a Social Security number?"

"Well, the service provider would then know the physical billing address for the account, which might be the same as where the computer was accessing the Internet. They might not share that with you, but it's enough to complain to Faceplace that Liv Danger is an imposter account. Then you can request the information, such as who created it, what time they did so, the IP address of the computer they used, and so on."

"And that would be definitive?"

"I would think." Maggie started to turn back to her computer, wisdom dispensed, ready to start coding again.

"Wait, where can I get this code...how would I set up this trap page?" She was embarrassed that she knew nothing about how to set up a website.

"Oh, you want to do that?" Type, type, type. "I thought you just wanted information."

"No, Maggie. I want to know who is saying this about my son. Please." Her voice cracked on the final word.

Maggie stopped typing again and looked at Perri as if for the first time. "Sure, Perri, I can do it for you. I can help you craft the message, too, so this Liv Danger will want to click on it."

"Thanks. It means a lot."

"It would be helpful if I could sign into Faceplace as you, if Liv responds."

"Sure." Perri wrote down her account name and her password on a sticky note.

Maggie tucked the note away. "I'll have something for you by tonight. Is that OK?"

"Yes, Maggie, thank you." She couldn't help herself, she came around the desk and gave Maggie a quick hug. Maggie said, "Yeah, whatever, OK," but in the reflection of the monitor Perri could see a little smile from her.

She went back to the desk feeling better; Maggie would find this prankster. Perri turned to her computer, to answer the five e-mails from different parties begging for Mike's time that had arrived while she was gone. She was good at e-mail. She always sounded warm and cheery. So while she wrote e-mail answers with a tempered verve, she thought about what she would say—or do—to the defacer of her son's grave.

13

JANE SLEPT IN the bed that should have been assigned to Adam's roommate. The new semester would soon be here and St. Michael's would likely assign a new student to share the room. She had a sense of a clock ticking, that the existence she had made for herself here, this limbo, could not last. Adam, forsaking the German girlfriend, was typing on the computer, trying to figure out who had created the Liv Danger page, when she finally fell asleep.

When she woke the next morning, he was already awake and showered. The local news played on the TV. Jane sat up in the bed and noticed a cup of coffee and a plate of bacon and toast that Adam had brought to her from the commons.

"Breakfast in bed. I'm touched," she said. "Thank you."

"So what do you do today?"

"I'm going to go to my mom's house and see what files she has on the crash. What the investigators said." She ate the bacon and watched the news. The anchor started talking about a bizarre arson case in San Antonio, ninety miles away, five homes, just built, gutted by fire. One family had already moved in, and they interviewed the woman, upset and distraught. Her name across the bottom of the screen: Brenda Hobson. Her son was in the hospital with smoke inhalation and she was begging if anyone had any information on the fires, to please contact the police.

"That is just straight-out crazy, burning down all those houses," Adam said.

I know her name, Jane thought. Blinking, staring.

She'd compiled a list of names of people who had helped her after the crash, when she wanted to write thank-you notes, but Mom said it wasn't necessary. Brenda Hobson was one of the paramedics who had responded to the crash.

"I'm going," she said, full of resolve. "To San Antonio."

"What?" Adam said, who had stopped typing on his computer to watch the news story.

"That woman was a paramedic at the crash, her house and every house around her burns down, and now someone is saying 'All Will Pay' on my Faceplace page? It can't be a coincidence."

"You don't have a car, and I have class today," he reminded her. "And I don't know if talking to her is a good idea. She's not going to be at her house, how will you even find her?"

"My mother has a car," she said. "You have a car you could loan me, you know, if you were like a really good friend to me."

"No, Jane. You don't drive anymore," Adam said. "Bad idea."

She let it go for the moment. She had an idea. She got dressed as he turned away, pulling on jeans and a long-sleeved T-shirt, and she grabbed her backpack and headed out the door.

* * *

Rather than hike across south Austin into Lakehaven for two hours, she took a rideshare car from a few blocks away from St. Michael's, so her mother wouldn't see she was still on the campus, to a shopping center near her mother's house. She had decided it would be better to approach it on foot; that way she could make a better case for borrowing her mother's spare car to take to San Antonio to see Brenda Hobson. She would look needier. After the rideshare car pulled away, she started her short walk to her mother's house.

Lakehaven hadn't changed much. Lava Java was still in the main shopping center; there was still a line of cars with high school parking stickers working their way through the drive-through at McDonald's (there was no golden-arches sign, though—Lakehaven had strict signage controls, so the fast-food joints were tastefully marked with subtle letters against cool marble). It must have been a late-start morning; she remembered the joy of those infrequent days in school, when the teachers had meetings and the school didn't start for two extra hours. She walked past signs urging either a yes or no vote on a massive school bond. She kept her eyes to the sidewalk, not wanting to look up. She had felt nervous passing the sign that read Lakehaven, Pop. 3,975.

This was where she grew up, but now it felt like enemy territory.

She walked into an older neighborhood not far from the high school. Two turns down was the cul-de-sac, Graymalkin Circle. She stood at the circle's entrance.

She hadn't been back since last Christmas. The houses lay ahead, both of them. Norton. And Hall. She thought of the line from Shakespeare's Romeo and Juliet: *Two households, both alike in dignity, in fair Verona where we lay our scene*...she had had to reread it to catch up for her classwork her senior year, having read it as a freshman, to finish a senior thesis for honors English on Shakespeare. She had no memory of having read it before or having watched any of the film versions, from the classic one with Leonard Whiting and Olivia Hussey to the modernized approach with Leonardo DiCaprio and Claire Danes.

And suddenly David, walking next to her, laughing on this sidewalk, his smile bright as the sun, walking her home not because he was her boyfriend but because he was her neighbor, braying out words from the prologue they'd studied that day as freshmen: *Ancient grudge! New mutiny! Civil blood! And fatal loins! Not just loins, Jane, but FATAL loins! Poisonous loins. We'd all better be careful. Did you think we'd hear about loins in English today?*

She put her hand over her mouth. David was gone.

It was a new memory. Did that really happen? Or was it her imagination stretching to bridge the gaps, the ever-dangerous threat of confabulation? She had no idea. She stood on the sidewalk, shivering, his words and laughter ringing in her ears. It would have been freshman year, right on the twilight where she began to lose her memories.

Did this mean she was breaking into the borderlands of the memories she'd lost?

If it was an emotional block, was it crumbling, now that she was confronting the crash? Or just a strand of memory, easing back into place, not to be repeated.

Oh, please, she thought. *Please come back to me.*

She stared at the two houses at the end of the cul-de-sac. "Bury their parents' strife," Shakespeare had written. That hadn't happened.

Both yards were on an incline, studded with oaks. The houses were large even by Lakehaven standards, two stories. Her mother's brick house had a wraparound front porch, empty now. The Halls' house had a limestone exterior; it was a bit larger. Jane walked toward her house, but she kept her gaze on the Halls' front door. If Perri came out of it toward her, she would be ready.

She walked past the parked car and glanced in: a backseat with blankets and duffel bags, in the driver's seat a man working on a computer tablet. She walked on and she heard the car door open behind her.

"Jane?"

She stopped, turned. Her breath caught in her chest. Matteo Vasquez. The reporter. The last time she'd seen him here at her house was when her mother was bringing her home from the hospital. They'd cooperated with his first story about her, but not the last two in his "Girl Who Doesn't Remember" series.

"Hi. Do you remember me?"

"Yes," she said. "I remember you. What do you want?"

"I'm writing a follow-up story on you. It's been two years. I would love to interview you for it. See how you are. People would like to know how you're doing."

"I doubt that. Get away from my house."

"I'm on the street; it's public property," he said, trying to smile. He looked bad, she realized, red-rimmed eyes, in need of a haircut.

"I don't want to talk to you."

"Where are you living?" he asked. "You're no longer enrolled at Saint Michael's. I called."

"Here."

"I've been here for two hours and I didn't see you walk out."

"Can't you just leave me alone?"

"I'm not at the paper anymore," he said. He had a thin, reedy voice, a habit of his tone rising at the end of sentences as if he was always interviewing, always asking a question. "I'm freelancing. So, you know, a story like yours, I can sell it to a much bigger paper."

"I'm not that interesting."

"Did the memories ever come back?"

She decided to answer. "Not all of them. Not the past three years."

"So your memories only go back to when your dad died. See, that's what makes it so great. It's such a good framing device, your two tragedies..."

At that point she turned away. He hurried after her. "I don't mean to upset you, Jane."

"Well, you have. I don't have anything to say." But then she realized, yeah, she did. What if she told Vasquez about Liv Danger, and Brenda Hobson? Of course Brenda's misfortune might be a coincidence. She had no idea, and if she was wrong, she would sound crazy. It was better to wait. That would be so satisfying, to send a reporter after Kamala, hiding behind the Liv Danger name. But she didn't—she couldn't, not until she had proof.

"What if I talk to Perri Hall? Wouldn't you want to tell your side of the story?"

"I'm not interested in what she has to say."

"Kind of amazing you've both stayed in your houses." Trying to provoke her, she thought. If he was camped out here, maybe he was waiting for Perri Hall, too. "You know, another article on you could be a big help."

"How? You wrote my dad killed himself and he didn't. You wrote I tried to and I didn't. You told the world I was awful."

"I never made a judgment about you," he said.

"You told. You made so many more people hear about me..." As if he had exposed her, naked, to an unkind audience.

"Jane. Lots of movies come from magazine articles. *Saturday Night Fever*. *The Fast and the Furious*. If I can tell the end of your story, that you rose above what happened, then there could be real interest from Hollywood."

If I rose above what happened. Above David's death and losing my memory and walking around homeless with a brain that won't always help me. She wondered what he would say if she told him she'd just recovered a memory. She stood still while he approached her and handed her a business card. The name of the Austin paper was scratched out, a cell phone number and an e-mail address written in by hand. "If you change your mind," he said.

"The sunlight hurts my head. Excuse me." She walked across her front yard and up onto the porch.

She hesitated at the front door. She sensed the weight of Matteo Vasquez's stare on her back. This was still her home, right? She shouldn't have to ring the doorbell to go inside, although she knew that was what Mom would prefer. Mom would be annoyed with Jane if she just let herself in. But. But. This was Jane's house, the one she had grown up in. She still had a key and she hoped it would work. She felt a brief terror that Mom might have changed the locks. She had threatened to before, saying, *You're living on the street, with a key and a driver's license that could bring some street lunatic straight here? No!* But the key worked.

She opened the door. There was no *ping-ping-ping* of the alarm system; so Laurel Norton must be home. She glanced back at Vasquez, who stood by his car, digging through one of the duffel bags in the backseat, glancing up at her, watching her, hopeful.

Like a guy who needed a movie deal? What did "freelance" mean for him? He'd lost his job? She knew the guarded look of homelessness; was Matteo Vasquez living out of his car? He might be more desperate for a big story than ever.

She slammed the door.

"Mom?" She called. Loudly. "Mom?"

No answer.

"Mom?" she yelled up the stairs. No answer.

Jane wandered into the kitchen. She was thirsty. She poured herself a glass of water and drank it slowly. There wasn't a lot of food in the refrigerator—half a casserole, a few half-full jars of condiments. Four bottles of white wine, chilled. That seemed a lot for a person living here on her own.

She spotted her mom's Filofax on the kitchen counter. Laurel had always kept a paper calendar. She thought it more elegant than always tapping at a phone screen, "like a woodpecker," as she once put it. Jane looked at today's date. Mom had an appointment and she would be back in an hour. The handwriting was neat and small. She flipped through the previous few weeks and the approaching weeks. Her mother had a few business appointments, usually marked with initials of the person she was meeting. In addition to writing her mom blog, she had run a charity for the past several years, helping deserving students overseas get needed books and supplies. Jane wondered exactly how much money her mom had raised. When she had been a volunteer supreme at Lakehaven's schools, she'd been very good at getting people to donate money.

She went into her mother's home office. Once, before everything fell apart, when her blog was getting nearly two hundred thousand unique visitors a month, it had been featured in an Austin design magazine. The antique desk gleamed. Books filled the bookshelf. There were very few papers on the desk; before, it was always full of file folders related to her volunteer work for the school district. Or she volunteered to help other charities. But Laurel didn't seem to volunteer anymore. There had not been a single such entry in her carefully maintained calendar. Now there was only her charity.

Of course not. No one wants her around. You made sure of that when you crashed the car.

Jane opened the elegant wooden file drawer (Laurel Norton never would have had a metal file drawer in the house). The top drawer was full of printouts of her blog postings; she liked having a paper copy to read through when she wanted to revisit an article. Jane went through the drawers, and in the bottom one, stuffed at the back, was a file labeled Accident. It needed no further explanation. She felt a sickening sense of relief that it had been so easy to find. Initial news clippings, sparse on details, then "The Girl Who Doesn't Remember" pieces by Matteo Vasquez. There was a sheaf of notes from the lawyer her mother retained when the Halls temporarily sued the Nortons (Cal Hall then dropped the lawsuit, suddenly, and at his lawyer's advice settled immediately for the proceeds from the Nortons' insurance company, with no punitive damages) and a set of medical reports and photos.

There were no transcripts of police interviews with Jane, because her mother had refused to allow them. As a minor, and under the protection of the Fifth Amendment, Jane could not be compelled to talk to the police. Not that she knew anything helpful to say to them anyway. There was also a complete file of Jane's social-media postings, presumably pulled by lawyers for both the Halls and the Nortons, to assess whether or not Jane was suicidal or violent or lying about her amnesia, even though she was hardly on social media after the crash. She read through her scant postings before the crash: chatting with Kamala (who kept encouraging her to find a boyfriend), a few postings with Trevor and David about falling behind on a school group assignment, a single post with David about "working on their secret project." Whatever that was—something for school, she guessed. No sign of depression, no drunken posts or selfies. No venting, no anger. Nothing to indicate she was thinking of taking her own life, or felt a desire to kill David Hall.

Jane took a fresh piece of paper from the drawer.

She wrote out a time line for Kevin from what she had been told, from the investigator's reports and phone records, from the newspaper reporters who had talked to students at the high school and at least two people who had seen them out in Lakehaven that evening, and from the investigator's more detailed notes of how the evening unfolded.

3:00—During our entrepreneurship class, where we had to turn in our phones for the class period, David passed me a note via Amari Bowman, who sat between us. I read the note and did not write a note back to him, but Amari, who was watching, saw me nod at him. I don't know where this note is. After the crash, Amari told this to her parents, who then contacted the

Halls. (This according to a note in the investigator's file.)

4:05—School ends.

4:15—Trevor Blinn told police he saw David and me leave school together, in my car. He saw us walking to my car and he started to walk over to say hi to us but we appeared to be arguing or having an emotional discussion; this kept him at a distance. Before driving off in my car I apparently texted my mother from the car, telling her that I was studying with friends at the Lakehaven library and then going to a group study session for math, which I was having trouble with. These were both lies. Presumably whatever we were doing had to do with the note he passed me.

4:20—David texted his mother saying he was staying after school and playing basketball with a friend and then working with another friend on a science project, and would grab some dinner out. I don't play basketball and we don't have science together, so that was a lie.

4:30—Neither David nor I respond to after-school texts from Kamala Grayson. Kamala told the investigators that this was unusual.

6:00—David texted his mother that he was fine but might be late (not home until ten on a school night). He did not mention my name. Where we were for nearly the past two hours, I don't know.

7:30—We ate dinner at Happy Taco off Old Travis, there was a cash receipt, time-stamped, found in my wallet. I paid for dinner. We ordered a taco plate, an enchilada plate, and two sodas. We sat in a back booth. Later the investigator got video from Happy Taco that showed us entering and then leaving

shortly after 8 p.m. (Investigator took statement from
HT manager Billy Sing.)

7:40—Kamala Grayson got a text from Amari
Bowman (yes, same classmate from entrepreneurship) that David was with me at Happy Taco. The
investigator had the texts in his report to the Halls:

David is here with Jane, they are sitting on the same
side of the booth, whispering. Jane looks like she is crying.
David is stroking her hair! WTH!

Kamala's answer: I'm sure there's a reasonable explanation. They're old friends.

7:55—**Kamala texts David:** Babe what's up?

7:58—**He responds to Kamala:** Nothing. Helping a
friend with a project.

8:00—**She responds:** Not what I heard.

8:03—**He responds:** I'll talk to you tomorrow.

8:04—**She responds:** No, David, we'll talk now. You,
Jane, Happy Taco?

8:06—**He responds:** Tell Amari I can see her texting
you. Good night. I'll talk to you tomorrow.

She attempted to phone him, leaving seven voice
mails (the last at 9:00 p.m., he never responded).

8:10—**David gets a text from Trevor Blinn:** Hey
what's up? Need to talk to you.

David never responded to Trevor's text. Trevor did
not call back or text him again.

8:15—I text my mother that library has closed but I
am going to study at Kamala's house.

8:43—In David's pocket there is a cash receipt,
stamped with this time, indicating that we bought a
crowbar at Tool Depot in Lakehaven. Crowbar not
found in car. Why did we buy a crowbar and where
did it go?

10:12—9-1-1 receives call regarding car crash. Police and ambulance dispatched. No one saw the actual crash, but a man named James Marcolin living on ridge above High Oaks Road heard it, wasn't sure at first if it was a crash, and after several minutes went across street down the hill and found the car. Only two other houses along ridge above road—one neighbor out of town, other neighbor did not hear. David died at the scene, half in, half out of the car. I was still in the car, buckled in, unconscious.

Ambulance arrived and crash investigation team arrived, I was taken to hospital. My mother and the Halls arrived separately at the scene, then Mom went on to hospital. I remained in a coma four days.

Six hours. What had we done? Where had we gone? Jane thought. According to the paperwork: Eaten a tearful dinner, bought a crowbar. That left a lot of time. An hour and a half later we were in the crash, heading away from home, heading to nowhere.

She kept writing, mostly from the investigator's report:

Items found at the scene: My phone, just outside the car, screen broken. David's phone, in his pocket, neither phone was making a call at the time of the crash. Also found: backpacks from school, a folding stadium seat, reusable shopping bags, empty bottled waters, library book. Found next day: suicide note that looked to be my handwriting, along with loose change from tray in car, this was down from the crash site, not noticed during the night.

She thought there would be more. There wasn't.

The roads were dry; conditions were fine for driving. That said, thirty-nine percent of the fatal auto accidents in Texas involved only one car. Thirteen hundred dead a year. Jane's accident was in that large group.

The suicide note pretty much sealed the deal in terms of Lakehaven opinion.

The suicide note also meant people might well slam doors in her face. People weren't just going to open up to her after two years. The case was closed. She would have to think about how to find out what she wanted.

She finished making her list of people to talk to: witnesses like Trevor Blinn; the lawyer for the Halls, Kip Evander; and his investigator, Randy Franklin. Maybe they could help her. They would likely say no, but she had a sudden urge for action.

She paged through the rest of the file. There were mostly printed e-mails from her mother's lawyer, strategizing before the Halls surprisingly dropped their case. At the back of the file was a plastic bag, taped to the inside of the heavy manila cardboard of the file. She froze: It looked like there was blood along the edge of the paper. Brownish now, not red, folded so she couldn't read what was on the paper. She pulled it free of the file and carefully unfolded it. It was very fine, thin paper torn along one edge, but not from a spiral notebook:

> *Meet me after school in the main parking lot. Don't tell anyone. I need your help but it concerns us both. I'm in bad trouble. Will you help me?*

It was in a plain, blocky, noncursive handwriting; like most kids their age, Jane and David hadn't learned cursive, because they were on keyboards and screens so much, and his printing wasn't so different from the penmanship of their earlier school days. Or hers, for a matter of fact.

I'm in bad trouble.

For a moment she stared at the note as if it was a bizarre artifact. The note David had passed to her in class? It must be. And it had blood on it...from the crash? Her blood?

How did her mother have this and why had she never shown it to her? Or to anyone?

It concerns us both. What did that mean? It was formal, but that was how David talked even when they were little, pleading his case to a teacher or coach. He was serious, thoughtful.

Jane folded the note back into the plastic sheeting.

She heard the garage door opening. Mom, home. She quickly tucked the plastic bag, with the note inside, into her front pocket and stuffed the file back into the drawer. She folded her time line and stuck it into her other front pocket.

She called, "Mom, I'm here," as she walked from the office into the kitchen.

"Sweetheart!" Laurel Norton stood at the sink, tentatively sipping a glass of water. She was dressed in a stylish blouse and blazer and a pair of slacks, her hair immaculate, her makeup perfect. She set down the glass and hurried to Jane and gave her a gentle hug. Jane could hear the soft sniff of her mother, checking her for odor.

"I wanted to see you. Where were you?"

"I had a meeting for my charity. If you had called on that phone I pay for, I would have canceled it to be here." Laurel intensified the hug, presumably to take the sting out of her words.

"Sorry," Jane said. Laurel released her and studied her daughter's face.

"Well," Laurel said. "Are you here to stay?" She could hardly keep the tension, and the hope, out of her voice.

If Jane confronted her mother about this note, she might not get the car. And she needed the car. She wanted to ask, but she decided to play out the moment, see what happened, see if they could have a normal conversation. This would be good practice, she thought, for interrogating her witnesses.

"I told you I would call you if I didn't have a safe place to sleep at night. But I do. OK?"

"OK. You appear to have a relationship with soap and shampoo, so I believe you." Laurel ran a hand through her daughter's hair.

"I agreed to help a psych grad student who is studying memory loss. He's trying a more direct approach with me than the first therapists. I had a memory. One that I didn't have before, of David and me walking home from high school. Maybe I'm starting to remember." That was overselling it a bit, but there might be an advantage to her mother thinking she was getting better.

"Oh, honey." Laurel sighed. "That's wonderful."

"That is not permission for you to write about it."

Laurel managed to look hurt. "Baby, I'm taking a break from the blog. Who is this student?"

"His name is Kevin Ngota."

"What kind of name is that?"

"He's from England."

"If you're back in therapy, why not get an actual doctor instead of a student?"

"This is free. He's writing a paper."

"Just what we need, more articles written about you." The irony was lost on the blogger. "But I hope he helps. Are you hungry?"

She was always hungry but a contrary tug in her chest made her say, "No."

"You look skinny. Have you had lunch?"

"No."

"Well, at least have a peanut butter sandwich." Laurel turned to get the fixings from the pantry, not waiting for Jane to say yes or no to her offer.

"I can make my sandwich. I can make you one, too," Jane said. It would be a nice thing to do, what with the lying she was doing right now.

"I'll do it," Laurel said. "Let Mama take care of you."

Jane sat down. Laurel set down the sandwich and a glass of iced tea. Jane ate, and Laurel watched.

The price of the sandwich became clearer. "If you're in therapy, then maybe you should consider, you know, a more permanent situation. With an assortment of actual doctors. And being off the street."

"I don't need a psychiatric hospital, Mom."

"It's not just the amnesia. It's the depression. It's the self-destructiveness." Laurel raised a finger for each malady. Then she closed her hands and put them over Jane's. "You could come home, be off the streets, or wherever on South Congress you are"—she had been monitoring the rideshares. "They could give you the help you need." Jane waited for her to mention taking rideshares to the cemetery and High Oaks, but for once her mother decided not to say anything.

"I'm staying with a friend and you don't need to worry about me."

"Of course I worry. I want you home and safe, where I can watch you."

The unsaid words: *because you're broken, damaged, aimless.* Jane finished the sandwich. "You know my price."

Laurel's mouth twitched. "This is my home, our home, Jane, and I'm not selling it. The Halls can sell." Jane could see her mother's jaw shift into a teeth-gritting position.

There was nothing more to say. So Jane finished her sandwich. "When I was unconscious after the wreck and you were staying in the room with me, did I ever say anything, you know, while I was not conscious or asleep or anything?"

"Other than mentioning the deer?" The lie her mother would not let go of, even now.

"Anything about David being in danger?"

A pause. Laurel Norton's mouth quivered slightly, then settled. "No, you said nothing more. Why do you ask?"

"For the new therapist. He asked me." Little white lie number one.

"Well, I'm not sure what a good idea this grad-student therapy is." Laurel air-quoted "grad student" and then folded her hands. "I want you to come home, please."

I see a therapist, I make progress maybe, and suddenly she wants me home. Jane felt a shifting inside her chest.

"Mom. No. I can't live next door to them. I don't know how you bear it."

"You don't know what I've beared. Borne. Whatever the word is."

"No, I guess I don't," Jane said. "Because I can't live here with you while you stay here, and so I can't be around you, and you don't care about me enough to even find out where I'm living."

Laurel said, "That's so unfair. You know I care. It's your choice not to come home. This house was what I have left of your father and you—the you that you were." Her voice trailed off. "I'm sorry, Jane. I didn't mean it that way."

"I'll go up to my room for a bit, then I'll get out of your hair. Thanks for the sandwich."

Her mother followed her up the stairs to the room, as if worried a memory might jump out and surprise her. She went into her room; it was clean, tidy, had been dusted, but was otherwise unchanged from when she had left it to go first to St. Michael's, and then, when she flunked out and couldn't bear living next to the Halls, out onto the streets. A stack of books at the bedside—last summer she had finally worked up the courage to read memoirs of people who had entirely lost their memories: a Texas housewife who had a ceiling fan fall on her head, an Arizona businessman who slipped in an office bathroom, and a Norwegian man who had fallen from a ladder. These seemed ludicrous ways to get a devastating amnesia, but they were heartbreakingly real. They never remembered anything from before their accidents. Sometimes their lives healed and their families stayed intact, other times they did not. She wondered how her story would end.

She sensed her mother follow her into the room. She nearly turned and asked her mother, *Why do you have that note? Why didn't you ever tell me? Do you know what kind of trouble David was in?*

What if she knew and she had never told Jane? Why, to shield her? As if things could be worse. Laurel's attempts to protect her—the lie about the deer running onto the road—had backfired badly.

"You see the room's ready for you," her mother said. "I want you to stay. Isn't this a nicer option than a hospital? You can pretend the Halls aren't next door. We're all very good at avoiding each other."

"I figured it out," Jane said, turning to face her. "Something went out of you when Dad died. It died in you, too. And I guess you feel I've exceeded your amount of grief you expected to have in your life, and I'm sorry for that, but as much as I hate not having my life be what I thought it was going to be, I can't stay here with you. I can't live next door to the Halls. I'm sorry you're choosing a house over me." *Burn it down*, she thought. Burn the house down, then Mom would have to move. It was insane, but at times, the thought seemed to make perfect sense, and that frightened Jane.

She walked past her mother, and Laurel said, "I'll give you money if you'll go into that hospital. If you let them help you."

"A hospital won't fix me."

"You're depressed because you're homeless," Laurel said. "You won't be homeless at a hospital. You could write your stories. I'd visit every day. You could get your life back on track."

Jane pivoted the conversation. "You know what you could let me have? The Toyota." It was a car she bought Jane when they were optimistic she would soon drive again. "I could use it right now."

"For what?"

She didn't want to explain herself or the Faceplace page. She didn't want Mom looking at *that*.

"I thought, now that I have a place to stay, I might try to get a job. I would need a car." The lie slipped out, so easy, so bold, and would surely be Laurel-approved.

"I sold the Toyota. We didn't need it, what with you not driving and not living here."

Great. Jane started down the stairs.

"You're telling me a white lie, Jane. You're not thinking about a job. Why do you need a car?"

Jane didn't answer. She walked to the garage. Yes, there was only her mom's aging red Volvo there.

"If you can't get your head together, I'll have to take action. Jane, I would have you committed rather than see you on the street." Laurel said this to her back, iron in her voice.

Jane turned to face her. "You would really do that?"

"For your own good. No school will take you again until you've gotten your life back on track. What will you do without an education? You're one hit off a crack pipe from turning into a street whore or a druggie or I don't know what." She stopped as if aware she'd taken a step too far.

"The vote of confidence is inspiring." She went out the front door. She wanted the fresh air. Matteo Vasquez was gone, and she wondered for a moment if her mother had seen him, sitting in his car. She thought not. Mom would have mentioned it.

"Jane?" her mother called to her.

"What?"

"I love you. Please don't go. Please." But she didn't step forward, she didn't chase Jane down the driveway to embrace her. "Everything I've done. Or am doing. Is to protect you."

Doing? "I love you, too, Mom, I really do," she said. But she thought: *I don't trust you.*

David's note meant *something*. It had to, tucked away, protected, preserved. She wasn't ready to tell her mother she had it. Perhaps it could be leverage with the people on her list. A passport, of sorts. David had been in trouble and she meant to find out what kind of trouble it was.

14

SHILOH ROOKE HAD finally picked out the ring. He'd stopped by the jewelry store three times, summoning his courage. Buying the ring was as good as asking Mimi if she would be his wife. It was a step you couldn't take back. Once the ring was in his pocket, then soon it would be on her finger, and then it would be forever. One woman, forever. He liked the novelty of that.

He went inside, the saleswoman smiling at his now-familiar face. He bought the ring, put it into his pocket with a shaking hand.

"She'll love it," the saleswoman said. "You made a thoughtful choice."

"Thoughtful." It wasn't a word applied a lot to Shiloh and he liked the sound of it. He didn't even wink at the saleswoman, which would have once been his standard response. Marriage changed a man in the best way, his father had told him, and now Shiloh wanted to believe that. He stopped at a high-end grocery, where he never normally shopped, picked up the customized picnic lunch he'd ordered—Brie, flatbread crackers, peeled shrimp and re-moulade, roast beef sandwiches with horseradish, potato chips that were somehow artisan, and a bottle of rosé wine that was pink but the catering lady promised it would be delicious and not sweet.

He and Mimi both worked crazy schedules, but they both had today and tonight off, so...Here goes. He drove over to Mimi's apartment, knocked on her door.

She answered the door and he raised the basket over his face, then lowered it with an excited grin. She looked furi-ous. Beyond furious. He tried a confused smile.

"Hi, babe," he said. "Am I late?"

"You're right on time," she said, "for me to tell you to get the hell out of here. I never want to see you again."

"Meems?"

"I know about all your other women," Mimi said. "I saw your sex tapes."

He thought the earth was going to open and swallow him up. He tried to speak and it came out as an awkward laugh, and from her expression that was fire on gasoline. Deny? Accept? How could she know? He tried another dodge. "What's happened?"

"What's happened is that someone sent me a flash drive with your little sex tapes, Shiloh. We're done."

But I have a ring for you. I love you. "Mimi, no, wait, that's all over..."

"So you admit it."

He knew his next words would make or break him. "I wasn't used to dating just one woman. OK? And I made some bad choices, but I love you, Mimi." This couldn't be happening. It could *not* be happening. "I brought all your favorites. I brought this pink wine..."

"Choke on it. You screwed around and you recorded

yourself with these women. Did they know they were having sex on camera? I bet they did not."

"Please. I bought you a ring. This morning."

For a moment her anger ebbed, and then the fury surged
back. "Then you're in the return-policy window. Don't ever
call me, or text me, or contact me again."

"Who sent this to you?" Shiloh could hear his rage and
grief exploding from his voice. He would kill whoever it
was. *Kill them.*

"It was anonymous. Good-bye. Have a nice life." She
slammed the door in his face and then he could hear her
sobbing on the other side of the door. He thought of kicking
in the door, to plead for forgiveness again. Instead he
leaned against the door as if all the strength had fled from
his body.

How could anyone have the recordings? He planned
to get rid of them once Mimi said yes. They were in a
lockbox under his bed. Someone had to have known about
them. But he had never told anyone, and none of the twelve
women had known.

"This isn't over!" he screamed at the door.

He left the picnic basket behind, like a pathetic peace
offering, and stumbled back toward his car. He had taken a
dozen steps, when he heard her door open, and two more
steps, when he felt something hit the back of his head. He
stumbled, looked down at the ground. The wheel of Brie.
Next she threw the box of ridiculously expensive flatbread
crackers, next the bottle of wine. She had a good arm and
the bottle of rosé exploded across his car's hood.

He got into the car. She ran toward him, throwing the
basket, and it landed on the hood of the car. He drove away,
with the broken bottle and the basket skittering off the hood
and into the road. He made it two miles before he pulled

into an office parking lot and pushed back the tears. In their place he let a hot rage build.

Who could have done this to him? He had no enemies. Well, just guys he'd tangled with over the years, but they were all morons who couldn't pull this off. He had stopped dealing the black-market prescription drugs two years ago, and he hadn't worked as muscle for any of his friends who dealt in a year. He could not imagine any of the women he'd seen while dating Mimi betraying him with this level of sophistication. It had just been screwing around, nothing more. And he was sure they didn't know they'd been filmed.

Someone hated him enough to ruin his life.

But he would find out, and he'd find a way to make them suffer.

15

JANE'S BOOK OF MEMORY, WRITTEN IN THE
DAYS AND WEEKS AFTER THE CRASH

What I wasn't prepared for was disbelief. Not about the suicide note. Not about Mom's ill-fated deer story.

About my amnesia.

Every day was a gauntlet.

A girl, stopping me and Kamala on our second day back at school (Kamala had been assigned to help me, since we had several classes together and she assured me we had been good friends forever, and yes, she and David had dated, but she was sure that suicide note was some kind of misunderstood bit of scribbling, and after that first day I was just so grateful that she was standing up for me, her, the person who could have hated me the most). But I couldn't help that people were staring at us walking together. I saw hands cupped over whispering mouths, gossiping heads touching each other. Everyone knew me, and I felt like I hardly knew anyone.

"This is so generous of you, Kamala. Hi, Jane." The girl who spoke to us had warmth in her voice for Kamala and a coolness for me. I could hear the drop in her voice. "Do you really not remember things? Like Jason Bourne in the movies?"

"Of course she's lost her memory," Kamala said. "Most of it. It's coming back, slowly." She put an arm around my shoulder. She did this a lot when I first came back to school, as if she could cocoon me from the painful uncertainty, the stares, the whispers. And to send a signal, I suppose, that I had her loyalty.

"Really? I heard, but I didn't think it was true."

"I remember my childhood years," I said. My voice sounded so dry. "Not so much high school."

"You think it would be the reverse," the girl mused. "I don't remember what I ate for dinner last week."

"Morgan." Kamala sounded like her patience was wearing thin. "She doesn't know you. Or anyone she didn't know in elementary or middle school. It's like she's still fourteen. I thought name tags, for our classmates, might not be a bad idea."

Forcing everyone to wear name tags. Morgan had spoken to me, but a lot of kids just glared at me. Because of David, of course. He was dead and I was alive and compared to him I was a nobody. I suddenly, very badly wanted to go home. But I had to do this. I had to.

"Name tags," Morgan said. "That would be a great service project for me." And she left, like she'd been given a job.

There was more of the same as we navigated from the student center through the hallways.

"Jane, this is Claudia Gomez. She went to middle school with us."

I nodded. But Claudia had changed so much; she had gone from being kind of mousy to vibrantly pretty with a kind smile. We transform into new people in those years from middle to high school. "I remember. Hi, Claudia."

"Hi. Did you really lose your memory?"

No, I just thought in the aftermath of our friend's death this would be a great conversation starter. Or a funny joke. Ha, ha.

"Yes. The last three years."

"Wow. I'd like to forget freshman year." And Claudia moved on, as if I were contagious.

Kamala eased me out of the hallway traffic. I could feel stare after stare after stare. Like rocks being thrown, or bullets. "I'm embarrassed for our classmates."

"I'm not optimistic about this."

And I shouldn't have been. The variations of greetings I got:

"Of course you remember me!" (Yes, but the last time I remember you, we were in eighth grade.)

"Jane! This amnesia thing is a rumor, right?" (No. It's a curse. I am like Snow White, except the curse continues after I wake up from my sleep.)

"Jane, sweetheart! Hey, baby, how you doing?" ("Baby"? Is he an ex-boyfriend? He was kind of cute. But I also thought Mom or Kamala would have mentioned a boyfriend, or that he would have shown up at the hospital.)

The rest of that charming hallway scene went this way:

Kamala: "She doesn't know you, Parker." (Her voice coated in ice.)

Parker: "Well, Jane, we've been dating awhile." (Leaning close.) "More than dating. Meet me in the parking lot after school and I'll show you what you like." (Lowers voice.) "Because you're not going to get many other offers these days."

Me: (Speechless, confused, and angry at myself for being speechless.)

Kamala, shoving him: "The concussions have caught up with you, moron. Get away from her."

Me, standing, shivering, realizing, You are at the mercy of all these people. And some of them are going to think it's a joke.

Parker: "I'll give you something to remember, Jane." (Wiggles his tongue at me.) "You won't forget me." (And then laughing and high-fiving with his friends, like he's accomplished something of lasting value.)

The hot little rage demon in me that Mom had warned me about decided to dance out of the bottle. "I do remember, Parker!" I yelled at him. "I remember how tiny and quick it was. Thanks for the reminder."

Kamala's jaw dropped. I shrieked this down the hall at Parker, LOUD, and he froze, and then he came back toward me, muttering "you little murdering whore" and then this big blond wall of a boy stepped between us, put his hand on Parker's chest, and told him to stop it. It was Trevor Blinn, the boy who'd visited me in the hospital but seemed to have nothing to say.

Parker tried to dodge around Trevor and then suddenly Parker was pushed up against the wall and Trevor was whispering in his ear, low and soft and even in the sudden hush that fell across the gathered students, you couldn't hear it. I noticed Trevor was wearing a knee brace, but he didn't seem bothered by it in pushing Parker into the wall.

"Get off me," Parker said when Trevor was done whispering, and then Trevor stepped back and Parker eased away from him. He stared at me and then went back to his friends. I kept staring at him. *Murdering whore*. I still felt weak from the wreck, but at that moment I could have punched him, again and again. It was an awful thought and I wondered if it was a thought the old Jane would have had.

Trevor looked at me. He said nothing. Then he looked at Kamala, like he was angry.

"Thanks, Trev," Kamala said. "Thanks for standing up for her." I realized she had her hand on my arm.

"What are you doing, Kamala?" he asked her. As if I weren't there. "What are you doing?"

"Helping our friend," she said, her voice suddenly icy. She put her arm around my shoulder. "She needs me right now."

Then he gave me a long look. I said, "Thank you, Trevor." He just nodded and walked on, limping slightly with his leg brace, settling his backpack more firmly on his shoulder.

"He got bigger from when I remember him," I said. "What happened to his knee?"

"Football." Then Kamala said, "Yeah, I figured you really do remember." Only after a moment did I realize she thought I actually remembered an encounter, ugh, with Parker.

"Gross, no, I don't. I just wanted Parker to shut up."

"But your memory about the deer, that's true," she said. "Right?"

And so this was a big moment about lying, and I made my choice, because I'd realized something.

If information was power, then they all had sway over me. I didn't know before two minutes ago that Parker was vicious or that Trevor was the kind of friend to truly stand up for me.

"Yeah," I said. "It's hazy, but yeah."

"Oh, good. You let me know what else you remember."

"I will." I wished I remembered more recent memories of Trevor. I needed my friends. But he didn't seem interested in renewing our friendship.

"Forget Parker," Kamala said. And then she said, "Oh, I did not mean that word choice."

"I know."

"You remember me, right, Jane?" an anxious-sounding girl said, stopping and staring into my face. "We met freshman year."

"She doesn't remember," Kamala said, already tiring of the novelty. "She does not remember, OK?" Raising her voice in the hallway. The bell sounded; we were late, the gawkers were late, teachers coming into the hallways to see why kids were not hurrying in, still talking about the fight that almost was over the school's biggest mental freak.

"I'm sorry," I said to the girl. I would later decide I needed a button to wear, pinned to my shirt, because the answer would become so rote. *No, I don't remember you.*

But many kids did not even look at me beyond a first awkward, painful stare. No, not a stare, a glare. An actual glare.

"I'm not very popular," I said after she and Kamala sat down in class. This was a shock to think about; I had not really considered the possibility of open hostility and physical threats.

"People are upset about David."

"I get that," I said, and my voice trembled. "Is anyone happy I survived?"

"Oh, Jane," she said, giving me a mournful smile, "of course we are."

16

<hr>

JANE RECONSIDERED HER plan: San Antonio, and interviewing Brenda Hobson face-to-face, would have to wait until she could find transportation. She should start with people she could find on her list. So she picked Trevor Blinn, although other than his one visit to her in the hospital—where she did not remember him at all—he had mostly avoided her. She had found his Faceplace page on her phone; he was attending Travis Community College, probably trying to get basic courses knocked out and a GPA high enough to transfer to the University of Texas or St. Michael's or Texas State. It was a common strategy. She could probably get readmitted to St. Michael's if she got her head straight, but it might be less stress to try starting again at Travis CC. That could be her gambit in talking to him if he was reluctant.

Because they weren't still real friends.

His Faceplace page told her Trevor was working part time as a barista at a locally owned coffee shop in Lake-haven called Lava Java. It was in a big shopping center, anchored by a large Italian chain restaurant and an organic grocery. She'd seen it when she'd walked to her house this morning. She saw a big black truck parked near the coffee shop and she remembered she'd seen Trevor driving it after she returned to school.

When Jane stepped inside, it wasn't very busy with the early-afternoon crowd: an older woman typing on a laptop in a big leather chair, two young women talking at a table, another man, frowning at his tablet screen. Trevor was hard to miss: a big blond guy, wide shoulders, big arms, military buzz cut. He towered over the other barista, who was a small woman who looked to be in her forties. She was clearly in charge and she barked out a couple of annoyed orders to Trevor, who was staring at Jane and seemed not to hear. Then he nodded, and vanished into the back of the store.

Jane stepped up to the counter. The woman's demeanor instantly changed from irritated to a warm, welcoming smile. "Welcome to Lava Java, what may I get you?"

Jane asked for drip coffee, decaf, with room for cream. Jane paid and the woman handed her the coffee with a smile.

"Is that Trevor Blinn who just went into the back?" Jane asked.

"Yes." The woman's smile didn't waver.

"I went to high school with him, but I was in a very bad car accident and I had amnesia. I haven't really talked to Trevor much since the accident. I would love to say hi to him."

An admission of amnesia usually brought a nervous laugh, or a blink of disbelief, or a look of immediate pity. She got the last from the barista. "Oh, OK." She didn't say more and she didn't move to summon Trevor. Jane sat down with her coffee and pretended to check her phone.

But she decided she was not going to just sit here and meekly drink her coffee and not talk to him. She had to get him to agree to talk to her, later if not now.

Trevor reappeared and the barista stopped him in the doorway. She whispered to him, and Trevor's gaze went to Jane.

Jane raised a hand in a shy wave. The barista whispered to him again and Trevor shook his head. The older woman said something again to him and his mouth tightened, but he came over toward her table.

"Hey, Jane," he said.

"Hi, Trevor."

"Um, did you get more of your memory back?" He had a deep voice, a little scratchy, with a Southern drawl.

She shook her head. "But I still remember you when we were younger. In elementary school." She thought, *He knows that; I don't need to tell him. I can't be this nervous. I can do this.*

"My aunt says I can talk to you, but if we get busy again..." He was giving himself an escape route.

"Sure. Thanks." She forced a smile, steadied her voice.

"Do you want a refill?" He nodded toward her cup.

"No, thank you." He sat down.

"What can I do for you?" Jane thought he had a nice face; plain but strong, his mouth firm, his eyes a light blue. He needed a shave; the bristle on his chin was reddish-gold. She tried to think of him in a Lakehaven Roadrunners football uniform, like David had worn, but no picture came to mind.

"I want to ask you about the day of the crash."

"Jane. I really don't have anything to say to you about it."

"You stood up for me that day in school."

"What, Parker? I would have done that for anyone. I don't like Parker."

"What's he doing now? Going to charm school?"

"He got a football scholarship at Tulane," Trevor said tonelessly. "Look, I don't have long to talk." His voice was low, like he didn't want the other customers to hear. "What do you want from me?"

"If everyone could stop hating me, maybe just for a minute, it would be so great."

He looked away, back toward the coffee counter. "I don't hate you, Jane. I just have nothing to say to you. Why would you even come here?"

"It was an accident. I swear it was. I couldn't have hurt him."

A hardness came into Trevor's kind, plain face. "David was my friend. My best friend. And you..." He looked at her, the years behind them, and she thought, *He lost me, he lost David, I wasn't always good at thinking about other people's pain.*

"Wasn't I your friend, too?" Jane asked quietly.

He looked down at the table.

She tried to offer a cute memory like it was a gift. "I mean, we 'got married' in first grade. And I beat up that mean girl for you in fourth."

Cute memories did not work. "Jane. Everything changed." He looked at her and then looked away. Miserable.

"What happened, Trevor? You come once to the hospital to see me. You stop a guy who's threatening me. But you don't talk to me, you keep your distance from me. When I needed my friends so badly."

"I was your friend, Jane. You don't have to ask. But I can't be now."

Seeing him was so much harder than she thought it would be. The thought that everyone from her childhood— the time she did remember—could think so poorly of her was hard to bear. *This is why you stayed away from them all*, she thought. *You were afraid of total rejection. It was easier when you turned away from them.*

"Look at this," she said. She pulled the note from her backpack, still in its clear plastic envelope.

Trevor read it through the plastic. "What is this? Is that blood?"

"Yes. Mine. It was in my jeans pocket when the crash happened. It's David's handwriting, isn't it?"

He read it aloud. "Meet me after school in the main parking lot. Don't tell anyone. I need your help but it concerns us both. I'm in bad trouble. Will you help me?"

"Is that his handwriting or not?"

He studied the note. "Yes, it looks like it."

"None of us know the truth about that night. There is a big secret here and I'm going to find it out."

"Jane, this isn't a movie. If he was in trouble, he would have asked me or Kamala. He didn't have a lot to do with you in those days."

"We grew up next door to each other. We were like brother and sister."

"I don't think that's quite accurate," he said in a flat tone.

"He wrote, 'It concerns us both.' So what were he and I involved in before the accident?"

"I don't know." But she thought he was lying. She lied her way through her days and she knew the betraying quick flick of the gaze.

"He didn't want you or Kamala or Adam or anyone else to know. Just me. Something affecting me as well."

"If he was really in trouble, David would tell me."

"He gives me this, and then that night he dies? Trevor, please, maybe someone ran us off the road. Why would we even be on that road? Or maybe we were chasing someone, or someone chasing us…"

He leaned back suddenly, pale, his mouth twisting into a frown. He rubbed his hand along his unshaven chin, like an old man. "This is an awful big jump, Jane," he said. "This is crazy."

"Tell me about the last time you saw us."

For a moment he didn't answer. She glanced over toward the coffee counter and saw a young woman idly watching them; no, watching Trevor. An odd little bolt of anger surged in Jane's chest. Finally, he spoke: "You were walking to his car together in the school parking lot. I started to say hi, because you both went past me, about twenty yards away, and I called hey, but neither of you looked at me. You were arguing, I think."

"He was upset?"

He looked at her. "No, you were. He was calm."

"But he was the one in trouble."

"He stopped you and I started to walk toward you to see what was wrong, I wasn't trying to be nosy, but I thought, hey, something's wrong with my friends… and I heard him say to you, 'This concerns more your dad.'"

The words were a slap in her face. "My dad? Why would he and I be talking about my dad?" She blinked. "Did I talk about my dad a lot?"

"No. Never. It was clearly painful for you. I lost my mom, too, cancer, a year before your dad died." He cleared his throat. "We knew how much it sucks. It made us closer." And his face went a little red. "Everyone thinks they know what it would be like to lose a parent. Everyone is wrong. Until it happens—"

"Trevor!" The other barista—his aunt—called.

"Stay here." He got up, worked the line that had formed, smiling, making change, dispensing coffee. Jane sat, wondering, *What would David have possibly known about my dad?* When the line was served, Trevor hurried back and sat down.

She told him, then, about Liv Danger.

He shook his head and lowered his voice. "It's someone jerking you. Delete and forget it."

"I'm going to figure out who it is." She wondered if he would suggest the obvious, that it was Kamala.

"It's a misguided friend of David's. Just a kid holding a grudge."

She looked at him.

"It's not me," he said quickly.

"You'd be surprised how quickly people believe the worst of you."

"I don't have time to torment you online, Jane. I work, I go to community college."

"I guess you weren't going to play in college." As soon as she said it, she regretted the words. The stress, and having not dealt with anyone but Adam and her mother and people who hated her, was making her thoughtless. She told herself to do better.

His expression went blank. "The week after your crash, I hurt my knee. Was out for the season. No college stayed interested in me."

She remembered the brace on his leg when he'd stopped Parker from bullying her. In that awful daze of running the school gauntlet, she never asked him about it. The accident eclipsed everything else in her life. She had been a bad friend. Football had always meant so much to him. She wanted to reach out and take his hand. But she thought he would pull away. He didn't want to be her friend.

"It was that week of the accident. I was distracted from the game with thoughts of you. And David. Whole team was. I didn't pay attention and I got hurt." His mouth narrowed. "It's no one's fault but my own."

"I'm really sorry."

He shrugged.

"I'm going to find out what was going on with David. Especially since you told me he said this somehow involved my dad. You can help me or you don't have to. I really wish you would."

He didn't say yes, but he didn't say no. "You still have your old cell phone number?"

"Yes."

"You're at Saint Michael's, I heard?" Like it was unfair that a brain-damaged amnesiac was there at an expensive, selective school and he was grinding it out at a community college.

"I flunked out. I couldn't handle it, academically. But I live on campus. In Adam Kessler's room, so I don't sleep on the streets. I sometimes go to classes; the bigger ones, where I won't be noticed." She had not confessed this to anyone. Only Adam knew. "I am pretending to have a life. So finding out the truth matters to me, OK, I need this. Mock it all you want."

Trevor stared. "I am not mocking you. I never would." She waited for him to say more, but he didn't.

She stood up. "Thanks for talking to me."

"Sure. Jane?"

"Yeah?"

He swallowed. "I'm just sorry about everything."

She turned and left before anything else could be said. She walked down Old Travis, the traffic thick, heading to the next name on her list.

17

Perri?" Maggie said. "We need to talk. Um, about that trace you wanted me to do."

Perri glanced up from her desk. "Already?"

Maggie was giving Perri a look that she didn't quite care for. "Mike made me go to this superboring meeting, so I turned my attention to your problem. Liv approved your friend request about two a.m. So as you, I posted a link on her page to a quick memorial I created about your son. Liv clicked on it. But I added in trap code that would give us Liv's IP address, and then I called the ISP and found out the billing address. We've been working with a few of the big service providers on security issues and one of my buddies there was willing to share."

"So who does the account belong to?"

Maggie said, "You."

"What?"

"It was posted from your computer." Maggie stared at her. "So, either you wasted my time because you thought you could get away with this or someone has access to your computer that you don't know about."

Perri was stunned. "That can't be. I wouldn't have asked you to trace it if I'd written it."

Maggie kept a neutral expression on her face. "I'm going to assume you're not harassing yourself. Does anyone else have a key to your house? What about your ex-husband?"

"He's not my ex, the divorce isn't final. But he gave me back his keys when he moved out and I changed the locks. But Cal would never do anything like this."

"A neighbor?"

"No. But I leave a key under a potted plant in the backyard in case I get locked out."

"Who would know it was there?"

"No one." She realized it was the same hiding place where she'd kept a key when David and Jane were little, and she and Laurel had both told each other where the emergency key was. Laurel's was in one of those fake rocks. Laurel.

"Wait, are you saying that someone was in my house at two this morning?" A sick panic rose in her chest.

"Or your system could have been hacked and someone is accessing it remotely. You could bring it to me and I could check." But Maggie's voice, never warm, was strangely flat.

"Oh, I will. Thank you." Maggie nodded and left. And Perri realized, with a jolt, that Maggie was wondering if Perri was capable of posting that awful garbage on the Faceplace page of a girl who'd killed her son.

18

JANE'S NEXT STOP was an open-air office park built of limestone, sprawling across a half acre. Freelance investigator Randy Franklin had an office nestled in among several real estate agents, mortgage brokers, and clinical psychologists. There were so many counselors on the wealthier side of Austin, it made Jane wonder—in a way she never had before—if money could not buy happiness.

She thought of knocking but instead she decided to try the door. It was unlocked. There was a reception desk with no one sitting at it, but she could hear the steady clack of typing in the inner office.

"Hello?" a deep male voice called to her.

"Mr. Franklin?"

He stepped out of the inner office. He was a big, broad man, with short, thinning hair and the solid, no-nonsense look of a former police officer. He wore a good-quality suit, no tie.

"May I help you?" he asked, friendly at the possibility of a client.

"My name is Jane Norton," she said.

"Oh," he said. Maybe he hadn't recognized her face at first. But she heard the reaction to her name in that one syllable.

"I was hoping I could talk to you about a case from two years ago. I was involved. You were the investigator for an attorney named Kip Evander."

"Yes. I remember it. You crashed a car and killed a young man." His voice now was flat.

She decided to be as blunt as he was. "You found a so-called suicide note the day after the wreck? And gave it to the police?"

"I don't think it's appropriate I speak with you about this."

"Please," she said.

"Since you and your mother refused to talk to the police about it," he said, "I don't see why I should talk with you. The door's behind you, use it. Good day."

"I would like to hire you," she said. She had gotten better at lying when she'd lived on the streets. *No, I'm not homeless. No, I wasn't sleeping behind that Dumpster, I was just looking for shade. I have a razor in my sock and if you don't leave me alone, I'll cut you.*

He blinked, and then he smiled. "Hire me for what, Ms. Norton?"

"Someone has been harassing me online. Claiming they know what I don't remember, and that I'm going to 'pay.' I would like to hire you to find out who it is."

"You're hiring me, or your mother?" He remembered Laurel. *Well*, Jane thought, *Mom is hard to forget.*

"Does it matter who is paying?" She had no idea where she would get the money, but maybe, if he thought there was a job in it, he would talk to her. Tell her something useful. "You'd be paid."

His mouth narrowed. "Have your memories returned?"

And then she decided to lie. What good had being the amnesiac done her? She was "the girl who doesn't remember." And she was so tired of it.

"Yes." Not a lie; she had remembered talking *Romeo and Juliet* with David, and that was new, and the more she thought about it, maybe that was not a touch of confabulation. It was real. It had to be. "More has started to come back. Yes. I think there was much more to that night than people realize. And I'm starting to remember it. So. Rates? How does this work?" She would figure out the money later. There would probably be a retainer fee.

"I'm not going to work for you, Jane," he said. "You wrote that note, you killed that boy trying to kill yourself."

"No one ever thought I was suicidal," she said.

"Your father..."

"An accident." She made the words sharper than she intended.

"Your family has more than its fair share of accidents, then," he said. "I'm sorry."

She wouldn't give up. "David passed me a note in class. That was in your report."

He blinked, as if recalling the detail.

"I found that note. David wrote in it that he was in trouble. He was in danger. Real trouble. Maybe someone wanted to hurt him. Does that put a different spin on the case?"

He seemed to study her face for evidence she was lying. "Where is this other note?"

"Someplace safe, and if you work for me, I'll tell you. I'm just thinking maybe you have some professional pride and you don't want to be played. And you got played. That suicide note was a fake."

He shook his head with a slight smile. "It wasn't. We got a sample of your handwriting, had it analyzed and compared. You wrote the suicide note."

Her heart jolted in her chest. "Analyzed? Why wasn't that in my lawyer's report?"

"Because Cal Hall dropped the lawsuit and settled for the insurance proceeds before we went to document exchange. So his lawyer didn't have to tell you about the analysis of the note. And the police weren't eager to tell you anything after you and your mother wouldn't cooperate. Once the note was destroyed during the testing and they decided not to charge you, well, it didn't matter to the cops. And the Halls had settled. End of story."

Her hand clutched at her stomach as if she'd taken a punch. "But it makes no sense," she said.

"You were in love with David Hall and he wasn't in love with you. Simple."

"He had had a girlfriend for two years. She and I had been best friends for most of our lives. If I was so eaten up with jealousy, why then? Why that night? What happened to make me crack?"

"I don't know and I don't care." But he glanced away from her.

"You didn't buy it. The suicide note. I mean, it's awfully convenient."

He sighed as if in pain, and kept explaining. "A note like that is only evidence if it is contemporaneous with the writer's mental condition. You have to write it and then act immediately afterward for it to be a factor. The note wasn't written immediately prior."

"How do you know that?"

"Ask the Halls."

"But the Halls let everyone think that I'd written it that

night." A storm of emotions surged through her. "Which is crazy. Who writes a note while driving? Or did I write it and convince him to get in the car and look for the nearest remote spot to kill us both?"

"People have actually done such things, Jane. You could have written the note, gotten him in the car, and then looked for the nearest place where the fall would kill you both."

"Why did you tell me this?"

"The note analysis isn't privileged information. Now, go get whatever help you need and put your life on track."

Jane sank into the chair, and Franklin surprised her by getting her a glass of water. She drank it down. "Please. I have to know. This analysis. What did it say?"

"Your handwriting. The paper came from a Japanese notebook, a manufacturer called Tayami, known for very high-quality paper. And the ink was at least two years old."

"You mean I wrote it long before, or the ink was old?"

"It was written at least two years before the crash."

"How can they tell?"

"Some pen companies put chemical markers in the ink, so the forensic analysis can show how old the ink is if needed. But then Mr. Hall dropped the lawsuit."

"If they had told people the note was that old, no one would have believed it."

"That was about the time David Hall and Kamala Grayson started dating. You might have been on a slow, angry burn that whole time. Written the note then and only acted later." He said this like it was a suggested theory.

"Let me guess. That's what Perri Hall thought."

He said nothing.

"A two-year-old note? I kept it on my person? In my schoolbag?" *Someone left it*, she thought. *I wrote it long before the crash, I didn't destroy it, someone else got hold of it and then they planted it at the scene. That's one possible explanation. Stop dancing around whether you wrote it or not.*

Franklin said, "It was your handwriting. The analysis doesn't try to guess the motivations of an angry teenage girl."

Someone framed you for this. Someone you trusted. Someone who could have known about that note, maybe written for another reason or out of context, and they decided to crucify you the morning after the crash.

Why? Why would you need to frame me? Why blame me? Because it was murder.

The thought bolted through her brain.

"Thanks." She got up and without further words she left. She walked past the counselors' offices, and she hardly blinked at them, but then she saw one with a series of names and the unusual arrangement of letters jumped out at her: Dora Principe/Kevin Ngota/Michael Todd.

But... Kevin was a graduate student, working on his master's. There was a master's degree abbreviation following his name on the sign. How many Kevin Ngotas could there be in Austin, and how many of them worked as counselors?

And how many of them were a few doors down from the office of a man like Franklin, who was intimately involved in the investigation?

Why was Kevin, who had an office down the walkway from the PI who had investigated her, saying that he was a graduate student and offering her free therapy?

Kevin. What was his game?

She knocked on the door. No answer. She tried the doorknob. It was locked.

She stepped back, and then she saw Randy Franklin hurrying out of his office, a cell phone pressed to his ear.

He'd told her all this, why? What did he have to gain? Hoping to scare her? Or did he have another reason?

She turned and she ran.

19

THERE'S A SECRET here. Something terrible happened that night.

Perri Hall, attacking her for even showing up at David's grave. Cal Hall, suddenly dropping his lawsuit against her and her mother. Both of them, smothering the proof that could have cleared her of penning that suicide note on the night that David died. Kevin Ngota, misrepresenting himself to her. Trevor Blinn, holding back some truth of that night. Kamala Grayson and her unrelenting sugar-coated hatred— the girl who had once been her best friend. And her own mother, who had a note that showed David and Jane feared a danger and had apparently never bothered to show it to anyone, and seemed ready to commit her to a hospital.

She walked along Old Travis to the next name on her list.

Happy Taco's customers, after the midday rush, were a few people working through their solitary lunches, chowing down a taco with one hand while tapping at tablet computers with the other. Another table held a woman writing on a laptop, a finished lunch plate pushed to one side.

At the counter, Jane ordered the cheapest taco they offered and a glass of water. She went to the back booth where she and David had allegedly sat and eaten David's last meal. A chill settled on her; she pressed her palms against the table. When the cheerful attendant brought her food, she said, "Is Mr. Sing here, by chance? It's personal."

"Let me check."

She ate her taco. Four minutes later a spare young man, in his late twenties, with a goatee and a Happy Taco ball cap, came out. She stood. "I'm Jane Norton."

"Billy Sing. I recognize you."

"Really? You remember me?"

He nodded. "Sure. It was a weird night and then you hear about the car crash and I had to talk to the police and all the memories sort of get set in stone." His eyes widened. "Oh, sorry, that was thoughtless. Do you still have amnesia?"

"Yes. But I'm so glad you remember. Can you tell me what you know about when we were here?"

"OK. You came in, you ordered, I saw the two of you sitting back there. You were upset. Crying even, once. He was trying to comfort you. He looked upset as well. I tend to notice anything that looks like it could lead to an argument or a disturbance. Because, we're, well, Happy Taco."

"Do you know what we were arguing about? My memory of that night is still gone."

"I came toward you to see if you were all right. If you needed anything, but I was trying not to insert myself into whatever your drama was. So I cleaned the table next to you and eavesdropped." He bit at his lip. "David Hall had his arm around you, and he was bent more toward you, trying to reassure you, and I heard him say something about getting out of town."

She had no idea what that meant. "Leaving town?"

"Yes. He had a laptop open and he was showing you a travel site. Places you could go. I thought, it was odd, you know, like maybe teenagers eloping. But kids don't elope these days, do they."

"Where were we going to go?"

"He said Canada, because you both had passports, and maybe they wouldn't make a fuss about you being minors. And you said, 'What, sneak across the border?'" He coughed. "It was the weirdest conversation I ever over-heard in the restaurant. But, I remember, because the police came the next day and I had to tell this to them."

But their going to Canada was something she hadn't heard. It must have been a story that withered in light of the discovery of the suicide note. It also seemed very out of character; she would never have left her mom alone like that. Would she?

Who had she been then?

While Billy Sing had talked, she'd pulled out her list of items recovered from the crash.

There was no laptop listed. So where had it gone? And why would they have been running to Canada? The police didn't tell her any of this, confront her with it, because her mom shielded her. But had her mom known about this wit-ness interview?

"I guess the police came and talked to you."

"Yes, a couple of days later. I guess kids had told them that they had seen you and David here and they found a re-ceipt on one of you. I didn't know your names before this. They wanted to know if I thought you might have been sui-cidal, like that was something I could tell. I told them you were upset, but not in a loud or aggressive way, but you two were talking about running away, but I didn't know if it was serious. I don't know if they thought you talking about running away to Canada was a sign of, um, instability. Or being upset. They asked for the video when you were here. I gave it to them."

"A security video? You don't still have it, do you?"

He bit his lip again. "Before I turned it over, I made a copy of it. I also wanted to have my own proof that you hadn't been served beer or wine here. We had a problem with that once before, one of our servers was a Lakehaven student serving beers to his buddies but ringing up sodas. I thought I better have a copy in case there were any further questions. But I might have thrown it out when I last cleaned my office."

She felt a tickle of hope. "Can you show me that video, please?"

"You have to fill out a form for our downtown office…but I can give it to you if I still have a copy."

She nodded. "Please."

She waited. What did any of this mean? She was crying, they were planning on running away to *Canada*, it was insane.

He brought back the form, which she signed, and he slid a DVD to her. "I burned a spare one for you."

A thought occurred. "Thanks so much. Did anyone else ever ask for that video? Maybe the Halls' lawyer, or my mom's lawyer?"

"Hold on. I might still have the forms." He left and returned with a folder. "Hey, how was your taco?"

"Very good, thank you."

"OK. There was a request from Randy Franklin; my note here says he was the investigator for the Halls' attorney. That reporter did. Matteo Vasquez. I gave him the video, but I didn't do an interview with him. It seemed wrong to talk about your problems." That was why none of this Canada detail had been in his articles.

"Thank you, Mr. Sing." She slipped the DVD into her backpack.

"I hope you get your memories back. Is there any chance of that?"

"Maybe," she said, and she gave him a smile. He smiled back.

She walked home—it took about forty minutes—and let herself in. Her mother wasn't there. Jane was still hungry, so she ate a bowl of cereal and slipped the DVD into the player on the TV. The surveillance footage was in color—she had expected it to be in black and white. She took the remote and sped it up a bit. The video switched from the counter and the register to the various corners of the restaurant so that the whole room was covered. She thought of fast-forwarding through it, but then she thought, *This is an actual record of something I don't remember and it's a memory laid out for me*.

So she started again at the beginning and she watched. A slow but steady march of people—some she recognized from school, sometimes kids on their own, sometimes with their families—came up to the counter, sat at the tables and the booths, and ate and chatted. Ten minutes in she saw herself and David enter the restaurant.

He was carrying something, she couldn't see what it was, until they got closer. It was a laptop, a thin black one. They used iPads and Macs at school and she could see it wasn't a Mac. He tucked it under his arm. She looked distraught, like she was just holding it together.

Wait. Wasn't he the one in danger? Wasn't he the one asking her for help? They looked reversed. She looked troubled. He looked grim, but he also looked worried about her.

They ordered food. They sat across from each other at the back booth. The camera switched away from them for a few seconds. Then went back, her leaning over her plate.

David was holding her hand. He crossed and sat next to her.

Switch again.

David put his arm around her. Comforting her. He put his lips close to her hair.

In another corner, Jane saw a girl—that would be Amari Bowman—turn and look at them. Stare. She was the girl who texted Kamala.

They ate, David one-handed, keeping his arm around her, then him opening the laptop, showing her something.

She was shaking her head.

She saw Mr. Sing walk past them, glance at the laptop, hover near the conversation.

Jane got out of the booth and walked out of sight, toward the restroom. David pulled out a cell phone and made a call. He was on the phone for only ten seconds and then he hung up.

When Jane came back into the frame, David was standing by the table, ready to go. He hurried her out.

Jane didn't stop the tape. She wanted to see what Amari Bowman did. Amari kept texting. Billy Sing walked past and went behind the counter.

Four minutes after she and David left, Adam Kessler entered. With Trevor Blinn. They walked in together.

She froze, watching, her fingertips suddenly reaching out to the screen. *Why are they there together? Right after we were there?* Adam, who knew nothing about that night, supposedly.

Adam. Who had given her shelter, gotten her off the streets. They had talked about everything. But not this. Never had he mentioned this. She felt sick, cold, a shiver prickling her skin.

Then Trevor left, glancing back. Adam went to the counter and bought a drink, bringing his phone up to his face. Amari Bowman walked out a few moments after Trevor, oblivious to anything but her phone screen, perhaps still texting the scandal of Jane and David to Kamala and her gossipy friends.

The video ended.

She watched it again. Maybe Adam and Trevor were hanging around together that night. Maybe they got hungry. Maybe it meant nothing.

She went up to her room and looked at the yearbook, a document she never much cared to consult, finding Amari's senior tribute card, which said she would be going to UT. Jane could call her.

She sat on the floor of her room, the photos from her life on the walls, and once again, nothing was as it seemed. Her mother, her friends, her counselor—they had all lied to her. Lies of omission. Go back to what Trevor had said about seeing her and David. A mention, from David, of her deceased father. David comforting her while she cried at the restaurant. Thinking about her father would have made her cry. And there was something else going on, something so bad they considered running away to Canada, which was lunacy.

But there was nothing to connect these thoughts or fears. Nothing to tie the events, these scraps of rumor, together. If she went around proclaiming what she'd learned, with no evidence to back it up, she was simply the damaged girl trying to avoid responsibility for her own recklessness.

She needed to figure out how to get to San Antonio and talk directly to Brenda Hobson. She wasn't ready to confront Adam about why he had never told her he, too, had been at Happy Taco that night; if he threw her out, she had no place to stay (her mother, at the moment, felt like no improvement on the deal); and if he threw her out, she could learn nothing more.

When she had awoken in the hospital, and not known her own name, or any face around her, or where she was, she had felt like a shell with the soul ripped free. At first she felt almost numb with shock—she knew words, she could speak, she could feel fear—but when she realized she was a person with no past except what others told her, the dread and the terror had felt like a physical presence in her body, there as much as tissue, blood, and bone. The fear only started abating as her memories seeped back.

And now...so many lies. So much hidden from her. She could go back and hide at Adam's or her mother's, or she could push the fear off her and do something.

Choose, she told herself.

20

⎯⎯⎯⎯

THE AFTERNOON PASSED, and night fell. Jane waited. Her mother didn't come home. Jane watched the video a few times, she used her mom's computer to track down Amari Bowman's home address, and called. Amari's mother answered and politely agreed to take a message, although Jane could tell from her initial hesitation that she recognized Jane's name.

On Faceplace she found Brenda Hobson's page, and an announcement from Brenda that she was staying at her sister's house. Her son was still in the hospital. She sent a friend request to her, then, impatient, posted a message on Brenda's page, asking if she could talk to her, that she might have information about the fire. There was no immediate response.

She tried Kevin's number. To her surprise he answered. Counselors, she had learned before, loved voice mail and usually let calls roll over to that.

"Hello?"

"It's Jane Norton. I had a memory return today. From

the time I've lost. Freshman year. Walking home with David Hall. He was joking around about a school assignment."

"I see," Kevin said. "That's very promising, Jane."

Why are you lying to me? she thought. "I'm wondering why it happened now. Do you think it's because I started therapy with you?"

"It might be. Or were you in the same spot where the memory occurred?"

"Yes."

"That might have been the trigger. The anniversary of the crash has put that time at the forefront of your thoughts. You've been treading water, Jane, and now you're swimming."

She wondered if counselors had a phrase book of reassuring metaphors.

"Perhaps," she said, "we should increase the frequency of my sessions or perhaps we could visit some of the places related to the crash together. Having you with me would be so helpful, I think."

"We could try that. Where are you now, Jane?"

"I'm at home. My mother's home, I mean."

"I'm glad you're not just wandering the streets, Jane. I think that you had a memory return with the return of structure—being at home, having counseling sessions. That is a clear sign that structure would benefit you enormously."

"I'm putting together that time line you asked for. I found notes from the Halls' private investigator that were shared with my mom's attorney." She waited for a reaction from him.

"And?"

It wasn't much of a reaction. What if it was just coincidence? There were a dozen counselors in that office park. "Well, I'll have it the next time."

"Why don't we meet here at Saint Michael's, assuming you're coming back here."

"I am. I can't stay in this house for long."

"All right. We'll look at the time line and then we'll figure out where to go to prompt your memories. I'm so pleased, and a bit surprised, that you made such good progress."

She hung up. *You should have just asked him about the office. About why he lied about being a graduate student.* But, she thought, if she watched where he led her therapy, maybe she could find out if he did indeed have an agenda. He had mentioned structure. Her need for it. And he'd agreed to visit places on the time line. She would watch him like he watched her.

Jane took a bottle of water from her mother's refrigerator and twenty bucks she found in the drawer her mother used for petty emergency cash. She wrote "Sorry" on a sticky note and left it in the drawer. She took a raincoat from the closet her mother would never miss, stuck in the back, and walked out the door into the rain, which had started and grown heavier in the past hour. It would be a two-hour walk to St. Michael's, or she could call Adam or the ridesharing company, but then she thought a walk might do her good. Clear her head. She had learned so much today and she needed a plan. She could always call a car if the rain got too heavy.

She walked past the other houses on the cul-de-sac— all lit with a warm, homey glow—and glanced up at a car turning into Graymalkin Circle. A Range Rover that she recognized as Cal Hall's. She stood in the wash of his headlights—he had stopped, dead ahead of her—and she felt a bolt of terror as he got out of the car.

Why is he stopping? She felt a sudden, sharp fear of having to deal with him after being attacked by his wife.

"Jane?" His deep baritone voice rang out in the darkness. "Is that you? Are you all right?"

She shivered and stood there as if mute.

"Jane?" Cal left the car running and stepped toward her. The rain pounded. "Are you OK?" he asked again.

"Hi, Mr. Hall. I'm fine, thank you for asking." Politeness was such a refuge. She half expected him to run toward her, grab her hair, and haul her out of the neighborhood the way his wife had seized her at David's grave.

"What are you doing walking in the rain? Have you moved back home? That will make your mom happy."

As if he could care about that. "I'm walking back to school."

"To Saint Mike's? That's miles."

"Yeah, well, I better get going." She dodged around him, keeping his big car between her and him, and headed down the sidewalk.

"Jane. Stop. Let me drive you."

She glanced back at him. "Why?"

"Because no matter what, your father and I were friends, and I don't want you hiking across Austin in a storm in the dark. If you won't ride with me, let me pay for a cab at least."

A cab was such a dad offer. "You know what happened between me and Mrs. Hall at David's grave."

"No," he said. "What happened?" She could hear the slow dread in his voice.

"She hates me so much."

"She's hurting. Get in the car and tell me." He was getting wet, standing there.

She scrambled into the passenger seat, grateful to be out of the rain. He climbed back into the driver's seat and the rain hammered against the roof. She told him about the cemetery incident. "It was stupid of me not to realize she might be there. I should never have gone. But..." Her voice broke. "I miss David, too. I know I have no right. But I do miss him. I do." She fought back the sob. She felt raw after the events of the past two days.

"I know you do. I do, too," he said quietly. "I'll take you to Saint Mike's." Cal turned the car around in the cul-de-sac.

"Sorry to keep you from getting home," Jane said.

He said nothing until he'd stopped the car at a stop sign. "I don't live there anymore. Perri and I are separated and we're divorcing. I was just stopping by to see how she is."

Jane's stomach twisted. The Halls' marriage was next on the list of casualties from the accident. "Sorry," she said. But then she thought, *Surely they'll sell the house. I could come home. They'll be gone.*

"It's not anyone's fault. It's her and me. I'm trying, but she doesn't love me anymore, not like a husband."

She didn't know what to say. She shivered.

"Are you cold? Do you want a coffee? We could stop. My treat."

"Yes, please," she said. Why was he being nice to her? She thought of Kevin, of Adam, of her mother, of their secrets she'd learned. But he had always been nice. David's dad, easygoing and thoughtful. David's death had not changed him the way it had Perri. But the note. They'd tested the note; they'd known the truth of it. Maybe Randy Franklin called him and told him about Jane's visit. Did Franklin still owe the Halls a warning, as a former client?

He stopped on South Congress, not far from St. Michael's, at a trendy new coffee shop. She sat in a back corner while he got their drinks, texting on his phone while he waited at the counter, eyebrows raised in apology. He brought her a decaf, and one for himself. He sat across from her.

She took a warming sip. "This is weird," Jane said. *Please don't talk about David. Or the crash. Tell me a dumb joke, the kind dads always know. Just tell me no lies.*

"Jane, it was an accident," he said.

She could hardly look at him. *OK, so no dad jokes.*

"An accident," he said again. "I think Perri and Kamala and some of the football players had a hard time accepting that. We like to think—especially in a town like Lakehaven—that we have such good lives, they couldn't be broken by a bad moment. But life is fragile. We're all hostages to fate. Blaming someone makes us think we have more control than what we do."

She wondered if he would bring up the suicide note, the one he knew was written long before the crash. The one he and his wife let Lakehaven think she'd written that night. *So*, she thought, *let's see what he says.* "I do blame myself. I was at the wheel."

"But you don't know what happened. You don't. Maybe there was another car, maybe someone ran you off the road, being stupid or drunk or reckless." He studied his coffee. "Or maybe you took your eyes off the road, or maybe my son did something stupid and distracted you. He wasn't perfect, despite what his mom and Kamala would say."

"The suicide note. I spoke to Randy Franklin today."

Now his gaze met hers. She thought, *He's actually bracing himself for this.*

"He said there was an analysis done on the ink. That the suicide note wasn't written that night of the crash, that it was much older. He said you knew that."

Cal Hall's gaze didn't waver from hers. "Yes. But that was when I decided to drop the lawsuit. We thought maybe you wrote it with an old pen, or the analysis was wrong. But it was your handwriting, Jane."

"Why would I have had an expired suicide note in the car?"

"I don't know. You hadn't been well since your father died. You pushed everyone away. I don't know. But it didn't matter. The note made no difference."

"The difference it made was to me," she said. "What people believed about me, what they said about me, how they treated me. And you let them think this." And now that she had thrown his cruelty back in his face, her complaint sounded so petty. David was gone. Would telling the school that the suicide note was old have made a real difference to the Kamalas and Parkers of the world? She realized it wouldn't.

"I don't know what to say, Jane." He wasn't going to say he was sorry, she supposed. That was a bridge too far.

"Did the police ever tell you that David and I were thinking about running away?"

He made a face. "There was something said by that manager at Happy Taco, but that can't be right. It would have been utterly unlike you both."

"David had a laptop at Happy Taco. It wasn't in the car inventory. Do you know where it went?"

He looked uneasy for a moment. "That inventory must be wrong," he said. "I remember. He did have a laptop in the car and it was ruined."

Tell me no lies, she thought.

"There has to be a reason we did what we did. Those missing hours."

He stared at his coffee.

"Someone claims to know the truth. Someone named Liv Danger." On her phone she showed him the Faceplace page. "Do you recognize the name?" she asked as he read it.

He shook his head. "It means nothing to me. But the words 'ALL WILL PAY' were written on David's tombstone when we visited his grave yesterday."

Jane remembered now, the cleaners, the cloths, by the grave. No wonder Perri had felt so raw and angry. She told him about the fight.

Cal said, "Who would do this? Who would know something? Maybe we can contact Faceplace, see who posted this, who created the account."

"I think it's Kamala Grayson. She still hates me."

He shook his head. "She wouldn't deface David's grave."

"She would do just about anything to make me look bad," Jane said. "Don't be fooled by her sweet exterior."

"Jane..."

"Look, I'll tell you one more thing. Did you ever meet the paramedics who responded to the wreck?"

"Meet them? No. I didn't talk to them. I don't know their names."

"Mom found their names out for me because I wanted to write them notes of thanks. I remember seeing the list." She explained about Brenda Hobson and the strange arson that had torched her neighborhood. "This is on the same anniversary of the crash. That was why I came home. To get a car and drive to San Antonio. But mom's sold the Toyota and I didn't want to tell her this, it would upset her. I want to see if Brenda Hobson knows anything. I sent her a note."

Cal frowned. "Has she responded?"

Jane checked Faceplace on her phone. There was a message from Brenda. Yes, I'll talk to you. I sent you my address. Jane checked the messages and there was the address.

"I have to get to San Antonio to talk to her. It's not something I can do over the phone."

"What's the address? I'll go."

"It's not your problem, Mr. Hall, it's mine."

"You don't have a car. We'll go right now."

Jane was stunned. "It's a ninety-minute drive each way. We can't go tonight."

"Why? Don't you want to know? And I don't think you should go by yourself."

She sipped at her coffee. Three hours round-trip in a car with David's father. It would kill Perri Hall. But going back and confronting Adam did not appeal to her either. She nodded. "All right. Let me send her a note." She did so.

He finished his coffee. "Let me make a pit stop, get us a couple of coffees to go, and we'll head out."

She nodded while he excused himself. Brenda responded: Yes, we can meet tonight. I don't sleep well anyway and am anxious to hear what you have to say.

Her phone beeped. A text from Adam, asking where she was. She opened up a text and sent it to Adam: I'm off to San Antonio with David's dad, to talk with that paramedic.

21

Cal drove onto I-35 south, the interstate that snaked through the heart of Austin. The traffic wasn't bad at night, although it seemed like Austin was expanding south and San Antonio was expanding north. Much of the country-side was turning into an endless landscape of shopping centers and housing developments. Cal drove just below the speed limit, which meant every other car blasted by them in the left lane.

They were quiet for several minutes. She felt a sick exhaustion. Her phone buzzed. Probably Adam responding to her text. She didn't feel like reading it.

"How is it going at Saint Michael's?" Cal asked, breaking the silence. "Has your amnesia affected your studies? I think it would be so hard."

She glanced over at him. "I flunked out. I'm sleeping at a friend's place. I don't know how to be me anymore."

"So move home." His voice was quiet.

"That's not really an option for me." She couldn't say to him, *I can't bear being next door to you, and Mom won't*

*sell the house, and your wife won't sell, and I don't blame
her, she doesn't want to leave a house full of memories of
David.*

"Are you in counseling?"

"Yes." *Until I see my counselor and he can explain his
lying self.*

He tapped fingers on the steering wheel. "I went to a
counselor for a while after David died. I didn't want to
at first. I thought it was for weak people. I didn't want
to 'work through my grief' or 'find closure.'" She could
hear the air quotes around the phrases when he spoke. "I
pretty much just wanted to die. But the counselor made
me see that my life was going to go on and I could either
live it in a way that made David proud or I could curl
up and do nothing. I could let him go and love the time
I'd had with him or I could hate you. I decided not to
hate you."

His voice caught at the end and he wiped at his right eye,
quickly, with the back of his hand. It felt like her chest was
going to explode. She couldn't speak.

"I just wish you could remember. I wish you could tell
us. So we could know his final hours."

"I'm sorry. I know Mrs. Hall thinks I'm faking it, but
I'm not…"

"Nothing's come back?"

And here she had suggested to a few people that memories swirled around her, trying to form. "I remembered
David being silly about a school assignment when we were
freshmen. That's all." Him braying the lines from *Romeo
and Juliet.*

He veered over into the next lane, jostling her. "Sorry."

It wasn't the same as a memory, but she could show him
David's note. It was in her pocket. But she decided to wait,

to see how this evening went. She decided to play another card.

"David was overheard saying to me, that night, that whatever he was upset about was connected to my dad."

Now he glanced at her. "What?"

"I guess something my dad did before he died."

"Jane, that can't be right. When he passed, he was going to open his own CPA start-up. It would have been lucrative and steady. I can't imagine any way remotely dangerous that his and David's lives intersected. Who told you this?"

"Trevor Blinn."

"Well, I don't know what he's talking about."

"We've never talked about you finding my dad dead." It wasn't a statement; it was a request for him to repeat the memory she didn't have.

"We did when you had your memory. More than once, didn't your mother tell you?"

"You tell me." Her voice sounded small. Like a child asking for a story heard many times.

"Your parents both went to run errands, but separately. They left you at our house because you and David loved to draw comics together. And you had one you were working on, so you were going to stay with us for the day because you didn't want to go with them."

"Did he say good-bye to me?"

"Of course he did." Cal's voice nearly broke. "He loved you very much."

"How did I find out?" Her mother had told her, but she wanted to hear his version.

"He didn't show up for dinner. Your mom was back and was worried. He wasn't answering his phone. So Perri and I went looking for him. He had mentioned he was running by his uncle's house to do some work on it before putting it on the market. I found him there. In a back bedroom."

"His uncle's gun in his hand?"

"Yes."

"And no note."

"No note. He was handling the gun and it went off."

"You and my mom aren't keeping something bad from me, are you? That there was a suicide note? Because people talked. I know they did."

"I swear, there was no note."

"So what would David have learned that he would tell me that day about Dad?"

"I have no idea, Jane, I truly don't. We weren't business partners anymore. Obviously our business failing had been hard, but we were both going to land on our feet. And he was the most decent man I've ever known, integrity above reproach, and he was excited for his life and his family and his future."

"Mom said once that when Dad died, she was too wrapped up in her own shock to be of much comfort to me."

"You took it very hard. You were not yourself. Terribly depressed. You went kind of dark in your clothes, your hair, your whole look. I think your friends were not of much comfort because they didn't seem to understand—so you thought—what you were going through. You were drinking. David was constantly worried about you."

She thought of the video at Happy Taco, David trying to calm her.

Because she didn't agree with Cal: She thought Trevor was telling her the truth. Even if her father's death was an accident—and it had been investigated and found to be so—then maybe he still knew something, had something, that

David had somehow found or learned or known and told her about the night of the crash.

Where did Dad and David's lives overlap? she wondered. "I'm sorry David was so worried about me. Tell me what was important in David's life before...the crash happened?"

Cal waited a moment to answer. "School. Football season, although he was hurt, so he wasn't playing, he hated that. He wanted to get healthy again, so he was resting a lot, working on school projects."

"Did he have a job?"

"No."

"Did he ever get in trouble no one knew about? Did the police ever bring him home?"

"What a question, Jane." For the first time Cal sounded irritated with her.

"I..." She changed her mind on showing him the note. "My memory...I sometimes see fragments. I don't always know what they mean." *Liar, liar, pants on fire but so what*, she thought. This man was being somewhat nice and helpful, but that didn't mean she trusted him. He might run back to Perri and tell her everything she said. "And David passed me a note in class. He said he was in big trouble and needed my help. I don't know why he didn't ask you or Mrs. Hall or Trevor or Kamala, but he asked me."

"How do you know?"

"My mother kept the note he'd passed me. Did she never tell you and Perri?"

He sighed. "No, she didn't. If that was the last thing he ever wrote, I sure would like it back."

"I understand," she said. But she didn't offer to give it to him.

He was silent for a long minute. She thought he

wouldn't speak. He finally said, "Most people have believed the simplest explanation for that night: he spent six hours trying to talk you out of suicide and failed."

"Would David have gotten in a car with me or let me drive if that were true? He would have called you, called my mom."

"Not if you begged him not to call. If you asked him to let it be the two of you, just talking. Because he would have been sure that he could save you."

"Is that the kind of person I was?"

"I don't know. You didn't like to share him." He said the last sentence like it was a painful admission. "In high school, you and David drifted a bit. Still friends, but not like how you'd been. He started dating Kamala. I wondered how you felt about it, because I sensed you cared for him. That he was more than a friend to you. But you adored Kamala and so you seemed OK with them being a couple. After your dad died, you withdrew. Dark clothes, dark fingernail polish."

Such a man, Jane thought, *to focus only on the exterior*. "I withdrew."

"From everyone. Except David could still talk to you. Kamala tried. She'd be at our house crying because you wouldn't let her in the house, you wouldn't talk to her. I think that was when she and David got much closer."

Wasn't that nice of me, Jane thought.

"You started to get back to normal...I mean, not normal, but back to being, you know, happier. Adjusting. Being the Jane we knew."

"You don't adjust," she said. "There is no closure. There's only learning to live with the loss."

"That's true," he said. "So true."

"Your wife attacked me at David's grave. I have a video

of it. She's proof you never adjust." Now she watched him. "Why are you helping me?"

"Because if someone is posting about knowing something about my son, I want to know. And *ALL WILL PAY* sounds like a threat."

She said nothing further about suspecting Kamala. No one believed Kamala could burn down a house. But Jane did.

22

Pᴇʀʀɪ's ᴅɪɴɴᴇʀ ᴡɪᴛʜ Mike had not gone well. She was distracted by Maggie's news that Liv Danger had somehow accessed her computer, and Mike was trying to be more than a friend, more than a boss. She could see it in his smile, his tender solicitude, an unsettling hope in his gaze. At the car she was afraid he would try and kiss her and she couldn't handle that right now. But he only walked her to her car, thanked her for a nice time at dinner, and told her he'd see her tomorrow.

Her phone vibrated. She'd set her mobile Faceplace app to alert her if there was a posting from Liv Danger. She pulled out the phone.

The new posting read, LOOK IN DAVID'S ROOM FOR THE ANSWER YOU SEEK.

She felt faint. Was this person already coming into her house to use the computer or to plant evidence in David's room? Or while she had been out at dinner with Mike?

Maybe Liv Danger was in her home right now.

She drove straight home. The lights she'd left on downstairs and upstairs were aglow. She parked and walked across to a neighbor's house. She told her neighbor, John, that she was worried someone had gotten into the house. He agreed to walk in with her and search the rooms to make sure they were empty. The house was fine; no intruders. She thanked him and he left. In the backyard she found the spare key. She pocketed it.

Look in David's room.

Fine, Liv Danger, I will.

Perri started with David's desk. She found a handful of flash drives, a couple with tiny labels of symbols: books for homework, a treble clef for music. She remembered he was always losing these when he used them for backup for his schoolwork. She slid an unlabeled one into the port but it was blank. So were the others. She tried the music one. It was locked with a password. She always kept her passwords on sticky notes in her desk drawer, but there were no notes in the drawer. She tried the school one. There were folders for math, English, entrepreneurship, physics. She opened each folder, feeling a bit foolish. Nothing suspicious jumped out at her. It was all assignments and notes he felt important enough to back up onto this drive. He had been writing a paper on John Milton; had notes for calculus, along with links to study guides (math was his least favorite subject); in government he'd been working on a paper about James Madison; in entrepreneurship he had what looked like a first-draft business proposal for a video-game company, with a placeholder for the company name of D+J DESIGN.

She went through the other drawers. A stack of sketchbooks. He was such a good artist, and she felt a pang in her chest again as she thought of the hours she and Cal had pushed him in sports and academics, instead of art. This was something he'd loved. She looked through the sketches. He'd drawn Jane a few times: frowning, angry, shrugging with indifference. Not posed, remembered. A picture of his father, staring out the living room window on the east side of their second house on Lake Austin; she recognized the curtains. David nearly drowned there, on the lake, as a child, and she hated going to the house and rarely did, but David and Cal loved it, so she let it be their retreat for father-son fishing and boating. She studied the picture of Cal; the next one was of him on the pier at the lake house, smiling and waving, a wonderful rendition. A drawing of herself, caught with laughter, happier than she'd looked, well, in forever. She had to close the sketchbooks. No more.

She put them aside. Below them lay a few loose papers and notes. One, titled "Pro and Con," said, "Be direct. Tell her how you feel. Tell her it will be OK. Not telling her is worse. Life will go on. She needs to know the truth." All these were on the pro side. Nothing on the con.

Was this something he'd written about Jane? If she had loved him and he hadn't felt the same about her. It had been the reason supposed by Kamala and others that she might attempt the murder/suicide.

Had he followed this list and died?

The other drawers were empty.

She searched the shelves. A long row of video games: everything from gentle games like *Animal Crossing* and *Pokémon* to shoot-ups like *Call of Duty* to fantasy epics like *Assassin's Creed*. Below them, a few books. She ran her finger along the spines, leaning close to take them out to see if anything was hidden behind them. The Ranger's Apprentice series, The Hunger Games trilogy, all the Harry

Potters, The Maze Runner books, *A Wrinkle in Time*. She
remembered that had been Jane's favorite book—she'd
broken the spine of multiple copies and her devotion to the
book was a running joke among their circle of friends, Laurel called it "Wrinkles Come in Time"—but she couldn't
remember ever buying the book for David, especially in a
hardcover edition. He liked action stories, and *A Wrinkle in
Time*, which she had read and loved as a teacher, was a bit
more philosophical. She opened it.

Jane's name, carefully written in pencil on the inside
cover. This was Jane's book, why was it on David's shelf?
Had she loaned it to him and never gotten it back? She
didn't want anything of Jane's in the house. She set the
book down on his desk, slamming it, thinking she'd take it
downstairs in a few minutes. She didn't want to see Laurel
but she could return the book. Or just throw it away.

Or maybe it had been left here. For her to find. A
taunt, that Jane or Laurel had been in her house. Accessing
her computer, leaving something in his room. The thought
made her ill.

She picked it up and thumbed through it. It opened to
page ninety, where a deep fragment of blank paper was
lodged in the spine. Maybe a bookmark? She pulled the paper free and held up the torn edge to look at it. It was like
the paper had been violently wedged into the book and then
torn. The torn edge wasn't a straight line, it was jagged at
one end, slightly, like the outline of a mountain. A stray
thread of ink at the bottom.

She put the book, and the slip of paper still inside it,
back on the shelf.

She searched the closets. Clothes: She remembered buying each item for him. She spent a few moments looking
at the shirts, leaning into the fabric. They didn't smell of

David—the soap he used, the regrettable body sprays, his shampoo—only now of dust. The top shelf in the closet held forgotten trophies and ribbons from youth sports, a deflated football, and a stack of board games, worn with use. She pulled down the trophy box. She hadn't touched this after he died. Her heart swelled in sorrow as she looked down at the wrinkled ribbons and the dusty athletic figures on the trophies, frozen in timeless runs and jumps. The hours he'd spent. The joy he'd had in sports.

She set the trophies down. What would happen to his stuff when she and Cal were gone? There was no one else who would want his memories. They'd go into a trash fill, she supposed, and it was silly to be upset, but she felt a chasm open in her chest.

She looked up. Bringing down the trophy box had left a vacant stretch on the shelf. Peeking out from behind the stack of board games—Life, Monopoly, Stratego—she saw the edge of a notebook. She pulled down the board games, fighting back memories of the hours she and Jane and David had played them—Cal was gone so often on business—and stacked them on the floor. She pulled down the notebook. It was thin, with fine paper, stamped with a Japanese logo. She'd never seen it before.

She opened it. Inside were more of her son's sketches. These featured detailed drawings of a young woman in a form-fitting red jumpsuit, as if ready for action, with a bobbed haircut of white hair and purple eyes. She turned the page. The next drawing was a close-up of the young woman's face, and her cartoonish eyes were enlarged. Perri could see that the black pupil was oddly shaped, not a circle but a raised fist.

She turned the page. The next had huge, stylized letters above the same figure:

LIV DANGER!
SHE NEVER RUNS FROM A FIGHT!
THIRSTY FOR ADVENTURE AND INTRIGUE!

(Artistic Concept by David Hall, Game Story by Jane Norton, Game Prototype by D+J Design. All rights reserved. Do not steal this idea, Jane will cut you!)

23

JANE AND CAL drove to Brenda's sister's house on the north side of San Antonio. A woman in her late forties stood in the driveway, in jeans and a UTSA sweatshirt with a roadrunner's profile above the letters, her hair pulled back in a ponytail.

They made quick introductions. They followed her through a small and neatly kept house. She had made a pot of decaf and they accepted her offer of a cup. They sat out in the quiet of the patio and kept their voices soft. The night breeze felt good against Jane's face.

"I'm sorry to bother you so late," Jane said. "Is your son going to be OK?"

"Yes, he'll be fine. I wanted to spend the night with him at the hospital, but he'd said he'd rest better if I came home." She knotted a napkin, unknotted it.

"I'm glad he'll be all right," Jane said.

Brenda said, "I haven't told the arson investigator that you called. This better not be some kind of prank."

"It's not. And I'll be happy to talk to them," Cal said.

"But we're not at all sure these two incidents are related."

"The investigators haven't told me much." Brenda knotted one of the napkins. "They think the fires have to do with my financial situation."

Cal and Jane glanced at each other; better to let her talk.

"Why, when your own son was hurt?" Jane asked.

"My husband died several months ago. He left a lot of debts. I've been slowly paying them off. Some were gambling debts. The house was fully insured, I made sure of that. They think that I did it for the insurance, to pay off the gambling debts. Which is crazy." She glanced again at Jane, as if recognizing something in her face. "It's like whoever did this knew how much this house meant to me, that it's a fresh start, and they took it away."

"Do you know someone named Liv Danger?"

"No."

"Mr. Hall's son and I were involved in a car accident two years ago. The anniversary was yesterday. He died and I lost my memory of the previous three years, including the night of the accident and what specifically happened to us. Someone posted on my Faceplace page, using this Liv Danger name, a message to me, that they knew what I didn't remember and that they were going to tell—that 'all will pay.' I took it as a threat. You were one of the paramedics who worked the crash."

"How weird." Brenda Hobson shifted in her seat.

"The accident was in Lakehaven. On High Oaks Road," Cal said.

Her gaze jerked over to Jane. "You. You're the 'memory' girl."

"You remember her?" Cal asked.

She nodded. "I mean, we work so many emergencies,

but you were in the paper, and they wrote about your amnesia." She paled. "What does this have to do with me? I did nothing wrong. Why would someone try to hurt me?" Her voice rose in the quiet of the patio. She stood. "My son is in the hospital because of that fire."

"Look, whoever did this, they're crazy," Jane said. "They targeted you. They targeted me. They wrote this 'ALL WILL PAY' threat on Mr. Hall's son's headstone. So please, try to remember. Did you see anything unusual at the crash site? Was there another witness, maybe? Someone on the road, or someone close to the wreck who might have seen it?"

"It was"—Brenda hesitated, looking at them both— "bad. It was a miracle the car didn't go over the edge. Your son died a minute or so after we arrived, Mr. Hall. There was nothing that could have been done, and I'm sorry."

"I know you did everything you could for him," Cal said, his voice soft as a whisper. "Thank you."

"Please try to remember," Jane said. "What did you do, step by step?"

"The call came in, we headed toward High Oaks. I don't think I'd ever responded to a wreck there. I guess it's not a busy street. Saw the car, down the hill. You couldn't have seen it from the road if there hadn't been flashlights, it was pitch-black, I guess whoever called it in was there with a flashlight for the police and the emergency crews so they could find it. I remember. He lived on the street."

James Marcolin, Jane thought.

"I went to the passenger side, my partner went to the driver. I remember because I hurt my knee, kneeling on a cell phone that had been thrown from the car, I guess. I kicked it aside and we got him out. He passed. We then focused on you, you were still alive and not as gravely injured."

Jane closed her eyes. She could feel the tension coming off Cal, sitting next to her, hearing David's death described in a clinical, two-word sentence. "A cell phone? Thrown from the car?"

"Yes. I remember it because it had an orange plastic case, like something a child would pick. And plus, we're not supposed to move anything that could be evidence. I mean, obviously to save someone, we do. I just moved it out of the way with my foot so we could get your son out of the car."

"I didn't own an orange phone," Jane said. "I don't think I did. Did David?"

Cal shook his head, pale. "No. His cell phone was found in his jeans pocket." He looked like he was fighting to maintain emotional control, and losing. Jane reached out and took his hand.

"I saw the inventory. An orange phone wasn't on there." Jane squeezed Cal's hand. "Someone took it."

There was another, unexplained phone at the crash scene. Did that mean they'd had a phone no one knew about, or that someone else had been at the scene and left it there? "Did you see this orange phone again?"

Brenda shook her head. "My focus was entirely on saving you and getting you treated."

"Thank you," Jane said. "David didn't suffer, did he?" She glanced at Cal; his eyes were closed. She had asked James Marcolin the same question. She couldn't bear the thought of him suffering.

"No, he didn't. He was unconscious. It was over very quickly."

"Excuse me." Cal got up and went out farther into the yard, breathing heavily.

"I know that's upsetting," Brenda said. "Once the boy passed, I started to help with you. I wasn't even sure you would live. I'm glad you did."

Jane found her voice: "The witness...Mr. Marcolin, who called the police and the ambulance? Did you talk to him?"

"I wouldn't have. He would have spoken to the police. So I don't understand why anyone would want to hurt me or my family now, I was just doing my job." Her voice went jagged.

Jane lowered her voice. "There was no other sign of another witness."

"No. I think once we all arrived, no one could have stayed hidden on the hillside. Wait. When we turned onto High Oaks, we were coming from the north, so we turned in at the entrance that was farthest from the crash. There's a stop sign there, and another car was stopped. It pulled off as we pulled in. I remember it now."

"What kind of car?"

She closed her eyes, willing to remember, and Jane wondered what that was like, to be able to summon any memory on demand. "I'm sorry. I don't recall. You work so many accidents."

"But this one, this one you remembered the orange phone, you have to think, Ms. Hobson, please, please. You're brilliant. You can remember when I can't."

She concentrated, and with so much at stake—perhaps catching the arsonist who had nearly killed her child—Brenda Hobson's eyes opened. "It was a truck. Black, tinted windows. Clean. Not like it got used for working a lot, you know. There was a streetlight and it gleamed on the black paint. I mean, it was dark, so I couldn't describe it more, but I saw the gleam on it. Shiloh Rooke, the other paramedic, was driving the ambulance, so he was focused on the road and we were just trying to get there. But Shiloh, he said it was a beauty ride."

A black truck. "And you saw no other cars?"

"No."

"You mentioned Shiloh. That's the other paramedic."

"Shiloh Rooke." She gave a little shiver. "And he's crazy. Glad I'm not working with him anymore."

"Crazy how?"

"Honey, don't you go talk to him about any accidents. Stay away. He's very bad news. Our bosses thought he might have been dealing prescription drugs. Every crew member had to keep an eye on him, but no one could ever prove anything." She frowned. "If anyone burned down *his* house, Shiloh would hunt them down and set them on fire himself."

Cal Hall returned to the table. "I'm sorry, I just needed a moment. What's happening?"

"We're leaving," Jane said. "Ms. Hobson, thank you and I'm so sorry. I hope your son is all right."

"This isn't good-bye. I want answers. I want whoever did this to pay..."

"I'll call the lead investigator on your case tomorrow," Cal said. "Or my lawyer will. We'll share our info."

They walked outside.

"What else did she say?" Cal whispered. "I'm sorry, it was hard. I was there soon after the crash, Perri and I both were, and it was awful. I try my hardest not to think about it."

"She remembered a black truck turning off High Oaks, but it might not mean anything. She said you couldn't see the wreck from the road, with the headlights out." She also told him about the other paramedic, and that Brenda had warned her away from him.

"If this is someone who hates me," Jane said, "they're just using words against me, but they are actually hurting someone like Brenda, who was an innocent bystander. Why? Why not come after me?"

"Maybe Brenda knows something she doesn't even know she knows, and she's a threat to this person. She mentioned the truck. I don't remember a truck in the report."

He was right. She didn't remember one either.

"Let's head back," he said. They walked back to the Range Rover.

* * *

"I never encouraged David in his art." Cal's voice grew bitter. "I feel bad about that. I should have encouraged him more. But I wanted him to be like me. I wanted to build a venture-fund business where he could work with me side by side and then he could take over. It's so old-fashioned. It was a mistake. I loved that he wanted to be an entrepreneur, like me, like your dad. I thought art wasn't the right thing for him to study, but if he wanted to study computers, that would be fine, as long as he got an MBA afterward. You don't want to just write code forever; you want to run companies."

She wanted to say maybe you could have just let David be David. But now, it just sounded cruel. So she said nothing.

She texted her mom. Know it's late, can I stay at the house tonight. I'll be there in an hour or so. And the answer: Of course, please do.

She dozed the rest of the way home. It was odd to think she could sleep after the long day, but her brain wanted rest and took it.

Suddenly, rising from the mist of dream: headlights, bright in her eyes. Terror. Was she looking at a mirror or straight ahead? She needed to get away from those headlights. She knew it. Life or death. The headlights could not catch her. She opened her eyes and the image faded, like the afterimages of a light flashed in her face. She shivered.

"Are you OK?" Cal asked.

"Yes. I remembered something."

He glanced at her. "What?" Surprise on his face.

"From the night of the crash. Another car. Behind us. Chasing us. I don't know."

Pieces of a puzzle that did not quite fit together. She thought of the jumble: the orange phone, the black truck, the headlights that she had to escape. Then her head and David's head, close together on a summer porch, drawing teddy bears, her putting the words into the speech bubbles he drew, crayons scattered between them.

24

So, Perri thought, *Liv Danger was a secret. A secret that only David and Jane knew*.

But someone could say you knew, too, she realized. Someone could accuse you of being her. It's your computer used to post her rantings. It's your house with the notebook with the character sketches. She felt cold. Someone was framing her and that someone had to be:

Jane Norton. Who else would know?

It explained so much. If no one knew the character—hidden in a notebook—that only Jane and David had worked on, then Jane was Liv Danger. The amnesia was fake, or this memory had returned. And for some reason she had decided to use David's creation as her camouflage.

Jane really was crazy. How could she have hacked Perri's computer? If it wasn't her or her nutcase mother just finding her hidden key and trespassing in her house, then she'd hacked Perri's computer. Well, she must know someone. She was friends with that Adam Kessler and he was certainly an oddball, and he had been a computer geek. She

went to Adam's Faceplace page. Yes, the About section
listed him as being in the honors Computer Sciences program at St. Mike's. As far as hacking went, a phone and a
laptop and a social-media page weren't exactly like breaking into a bank or a government agency.

Who else? No one had gone into the room in months but
her, and Cal had moved out and he'd only been in the room
with her. Kamala had come over a few times, to say hello,
but she hadn't gone up into David's room...and there had
been no one else.

Her phone rang. "Yes?"

"Perri? It's Ronnie Gervase." One of the leading lights
of Lakehaven, the woman who'd run a lot of the volunteer
programs for the athletic department, a queen of the football
moms. She'd been one of the people she'd seen yesterday at
the Baconery, who'd offered kind condolences and a hug.

"Hi, Ronnie, how are you?"

"More like how are *you*?"

"Me? Um, I'm all right..."

"I was just on Faceplace updating our football-moms
page and I saw this on your page. This video. You screaming at and assaulting Jane Norton."

That had not been up there earlier this evening. "Oh.
I...I was upset."

"You hit her, Perri. I mean, I understand that you blame her,
but, well, look, I'm not trying to judge you."

*Of course you are. We all are. With every breath, and we
lie and we say we aren't.*

"But maybe take down that video," Ronnie said. "It is
not a good look for you."

"Who posted it? Jane?"

"Someone named Liv Danger. I don't know her. Is that
a real name?"

"Thank you for telling me, Ronnie. I have to go."

"Perri…"

"Yes?"

"Maybe get some help? You know, we all love you."

"Yes, Ronnie, I'll think about that. Thank you again."
She felt like she was thanking her for a blow to the guts.

Her hand trembled as she drank more wine.

She went to the Faceplace page. There it was, under:
Jane never paid, did she? Neither did the others. I know how you
hate them all, Perri. Isn't blame an ugly thing?

And then the video, originally shared from the driver's
account where Jane had been tagged and then Perri had
been tagged, thirty seconds of awfulness where she acted
like a maniac and not the refined, controlled person she had
always seen herself to be. And the rideshare driver, narrat-
ing for the audience: *This lady attacked my fare, dragged
her out of the car, hit her, pushed her, and I guess that is
her son's grave and she's upset, but damn, lady, this is not
the answer.*

Then the comments, over thirty of them: Perri, call me.
Perri, are you all right, I'm worried about you. Did she hit her hard
enough for assault charges? Perri, I know a good lawyer.

And then in the midst of the concern and judgment, a
comment from Liv Danger: Don't delete this video from this
page, Perri, or I'll post worse. I know what you did that night.

What did that mean? It couldn't mean anything. There
was nothing worse. She swallowed, her throat feeling like
stone. She hadn't done anything wrong that night…ex-
cept not hunt for her son. Not go out looking for him
when her instincts told her he was lying to her about his
whereabouts. But the message made her inaction sound
far worse. She had said as much in Vasquez's articles:
that she wished she'd gone out looking for David. Per-

haps he would still be alive if she had. The thought wrenched her.

If she unfriended the stalker...she couldn't post anything more to the page, right? She hesitated.

I'll post worse.

She should call the police. And they would do what? Nothing.

She left the video up and wrote in a comment: Whoever you are, you're not a well person to post this. I'm sorry I lost my temper, but my son's headstone had been defaced and I was deeply upset. It bothered me that the girl who is responsible for my son's death came to his grave. I apologize for losing my composure. If you have any decency, you'll take this down and leave me alone.

She got up and paced. The front porch light at the Nortons' was on. She stood, watched to see if Laurel came out. Perhaps she was expecting someone.

She couldn't sleep, her mind racing. She tried Cal; he wasn't answering his phone. Maybe he was off with the girlfriend who smelled of lavender.

So she sat in the front dining room she didn't use that often—David used to spread out his projects on the dining room table—and drank a book-club glass of wine and watched the empty street. And waited.

I know what you did that night.

A car entered the cul-de-sac. She tensed, but then realized as it headed under a streetlight that it was Cal's Range Rover. Relief swept over her. It didn't even matter he was coming here so late at night. She'd talk to him about Laurel, her online conversation with Liv Danger, her awful discovery, the cruel video. The car aimed for her driveway, then pulled slightly to the side. Toward the Norton house. And then the door opened, and in the light she could see Cal at the wheel and Jane Norton getting out of the passenger side.

Perri made a noise in her throat.

This couldn't be right. No. She watched Jane speak to Cal, illuminated by the car's inside light, and then Jane closed the door, quietly. Jane walked up to the front door in the wash of headlights—Cal ever so thoughtfully left them on for her—and then she unlocked her door and went inside.

Cal backed out and drove out of the cul-de-sac.

Perri Hall stood at the window for a long while, the oversized wineglass cool against her forehead, but feeling like she had a fever. It couldn't be what she thought it was. That was madness.

Fine. She would do this alone. Cal had gotten her pregnant. But she alone had pushed David out into the world, and she alone would find justice for him from this crazy girl and her mother. And from whoever was trying to ruin her life.

She went upstairs. She was going to need a good night's sleep. She went into David's room. She touched the space bar, waking his iMac from sleep. She refreshed the Faceplace page. There was a new posting from Liv Danger:

It feels awful to be blamed for something, doesn't it? I know what you did while your son lay dying. All will pay.

It was a lie. She had done nothing. Nothing. She nearly screamed, shoving her fist against her mouth.

25

RANDY FRANKLIN AWOKE to darkness. His mouth tasted metallic—oddly of copper and silver, as though money had been dragged across his tongue. Where was he? For one awful moment he thought he had gone out drinking, had a blackout after five years of sobriety, and it made his chest hurt with anger and disappointment in himself. But no, he hadn't gone out drinking. He remembered: Jane Norton had come to his office, and he'd left for the day, calling the temp agency to arrange for a receptionist to come tomorrow, because he wanted layers between him and that girl. Her case, and the others', had been nothing but trouble for him. He wanted out, and he wondered if she might be his ticket.

Then he'd headed to a junkyard east of Austin, found the wrecked car on his newest case. It was a late-year-model European sedan, driven too fast by an Austin engineer, who had run a red light and T-boned another car, one with an older couple inside. They were both badly injured and were suing the engineer. The engineer claimed he had applied brakes and that they had not been responsive as quickly as they should have been. Franklin's boss—representing the engineer—had dispatched him to the junkyard, where both cars were interred, to check the so-called black box, that would measure and record the engineer's car's data—speed, application of brakes, and so forth—for the last five seconds before the crash. In inspecting the black box, Franklin had "accidentally" erased it. Oh no. How awful. It happened now and then. If at the moment of impact, the car suffered a power failure, then the reserve electricity went to deploying the airbags and didn't salvage the final seconds of data. Sometimes Randy used a magnet, or if he could restart and move the car for five seconds, the data could be overwritten, depending on the damage. Lawsuits were war. Now it would be easier to blame the automobile manufacturer than it would be the inattentive engineer. This wasn't uncommon. Franklin worked both sides of accidents; if he had been employed by the lawyer for the plaintiffs, then he would have downloaded the information first to ensure against such interference from the opposing investigator. Now, if the opposing investigator bothered, he'd find the black box's data damaged, perhaps from a power failure tied to the crash. No way to prove otherwise, when Randy was careful. Fortune favors the bold.

Had he interfered with the computer systems in the Jane Norton crash? He thought not. Her suicide note was enough to veer a judgment toward his clients.

Then he remembered heading toward his car, and spotting a fat wallet lying on the ground close to it. He'd bent down to pick it up, curious, and then a rush of movement from the other side of his car, then the momentary sting of a needle in his neck. Then a delicious floating nothingness.

He'd been drugged.

The relief that he hadn't gotten drunk lasted all of three seconds, displaced by bold terror that he had been injected by someone and tied up and left in a coffin-like darkness.

He realized he was gagged, a neat plug wadded into his mouth. He tried to move and he couldn't, arms cocooned to his chest, legs bound together.

He explored the space with his feet. He was in a car trunk. He could hear the distant sound he recognized with a chill, of metal crushing.

He was still in the junkyard. Hadn't someone seen him taken and tied up and placed here? It was a huge operation. Wouldn't there be security cameras?

Data could be erased. He knew that well enough. His chill turned to a feverish flush of panic.

The loud grinding roar that rendered wrecked autos to scrap, sold and recycled, got louder. He'd heard it in the background as he'd fixed the computer readings in the wrecked Euro sedan to his liking. Then it was just background noise. Now it was closer.

He kicked at the trunk. Just to get his captor to open it. He could talk his way out of this. Offer money. Anything could be negotiated. That was all that happened in the aftermath of car crashes. It was all negotiation.

The mechanical noise got louder and louder.

There was no answer to his kick. He was gagged and he began to kick hard at the trunk's lid, trying to scream past the gag. *Please*, he thought. *Please*. The trunk's release cord was gone, cut or removed. He writhed in the space, panic bolting through his bones.

Sweat broke out on his forehead. He could feel the jerk of movement; the car sliding forward. He tried to pivot, trying to kick open the access port to the car's backseat. It had been sealed, reinforced somehow, and then the terror set in deep because he heard the metal grinding and he realized that the compactor that reduced the cars to scrap was *here*.

He raged, he fought, he thought of everything he wished he'd done in his life, in a rush, as the fear blinded him.

He would be crushed to death.

The trunk opened. Hands pulled him up and out and dragged him along the ground. He heard the smashing grind of the car being crushed, felt his bladder loosen.

"You listen to me," a voice whispered. It was gritty, lowered, a harsh, camouflaged rasp. He was sick with terror and he froze.

"I just did you a favor. You do me one. You are going to get out of town for a while. You will go straight to the airport or bus terminal and you will get the hell out of Austin. Do not go home. Do not pack a bag. You have your parents, go see them for a week. Maybe two. Nod once if you understand."

He could hear the death grind of the car being flattened. He nodded.

"Good. And you'll get a phone call at your parents' house when it's fine for you to come home. I know where your parents live, Randy. If you tell anyone about this, I will know, and I'll flip a coin and one of them will die. Heads your mom, tails your dad. I will kill one of them because you can't keep your big fat mouth shut. Do you understand me?"

He was too terrified to move.

"Nod if you understand me, Randy," the voice said with infinite patience.

He nodded for all he was worth.

"All right. You have a nice trip."

He felt a knife cut through his bonds. He stayed still.

"You count to three hundred. If you get up before that, a

friend of mine who's keeping an eye on you will shoot you in the head. Enjoy your visit with your folks. I know how much you love them."

Randy Franklin counted to three hundred, slowly, carefully, as if it was the most important task he would ever fulfill. He then pulled free of his bonds and took the cloth sack off his head. He lay next to his car. His keys lay on his chest.

He got into his car and aimed it, east, toward the imminent dawn, Austin in his rearview mirror.

26

At least once a week since the separation Cal drove over to his old house and jogged the three-mile circuit through their neighborhood that he had run nearly every day since they moved to Graymalkin Circle. At first Perri was sure it was an excuse for him to see her—as arrogant as that sounded, you got to think such things when your spouse didn't want the divorce—but then she realized he just liked the route. He didn't even try to talk to her, unless he needed to borrow the restroom after his run. Sometimes she would wait for him, with ice water or iced coffee, just to say hi, and then she'd wonder again exactly what she thought she would gain out of no longer being married to him.

She didn't wonder that this morning.

He parked and she waited to see if he would start his stretches, or if he'd go over to the Norton house for a word with Jane. He started stretching.

Perri came out of the front door and hurried toward him.

"What is going on with you and Jane Norton?" she asked. "I saw your carpool last night."

"Let's talk inside," he said. They walked back into the house and he shut the door. He explained running into Jane, their talk in the rain, and their visit with Brenda Hobson.

It had moved beyond taunts and videos. "Why would someone burn down this woman's house?"

He watched her. "Someone who blames her for our son's death."

The silence grew thick. "What, me?" Perri finally said. "Are you crazy, you know me, you know I would never—"

"I didn't think you'd ever hit and drag someone, even Jane, but I saw the video."

"Cal. Cal. Come on. You know me."

"And I saw the new posting. What were you doing when David died, Perri?"

"I was here. Waiting for him to get home. Here. Trying to find him after Kamala called and said he'd taken off with Jane and they weren't studying."

"You didn't go anywhere?"

"No. That post is a lie. I felt guilty I wasn't out looking for him. I know I said that to people. But this person is trying to make it sound like I was a horrible mother or somehow to blame."

"So what does Liv Danger know that she threatens to say?"

"It's all a lie." Her voice broke. "This is some horrible person hiding behind a name our son created!" Her voice rose in a scream. "And you would believe a liar who hides behind a name, a perversion of something David made, rather than me."

It was like she opened a crack in the world. The anger, the fury between them that had been smothered in politeness.

"You're divorcing me because we lost our son," he said.

The words tumbled from him as if penned inside for a long time. "That's the only reason. Nothing else. Because you hurt so much you can't bear to love anyone. Well, I hurt, too. But I'm not angry at the world because he died. You said you wanted a divorce. I didn't want it, but I said fine, whatever makes you happy. As if giving you whatever you wanted would make you happy again.

"But you'll never be happy again. Because the grief has burned you down, Perri, and I can't do this anymore. I loved you. I loved you so much. And now I just... now I'm the one that wants the divorce." He said it, almost in triumph. "How does that sound? I want it right now. And you can blame Laurel and Jane or the world, but..." His voice trailed off. "I'm not going to tell you how to feel. You tell yourself that." He went to the door.

"Cal, wait." His words had rocked her; he had never spoken that way before to her. "Listen. The original postings from Liv Danger came from my computer. I had Maggie, a friend at work, trace it. But I swear, it's not me. If it was, I wouldn't tell you this. Someone hacked me or got into the house. Help me. Please, help me. I swear to you, on David's life, it's not me."

She could see the words leash his fury for a moment. "Then who is it? It's not me. Who would want to frame you?"

"Jane. Or Laurel," she said. "You know they hate me."

"You hate them. You hate them like nothing I've ever seen. You know, it's weird how you think that everyone else changed after David died but you didn't."

The words were like a blow. "Cal."

"I mean, video doesn't lie. You attacked her."

"She was at David's grave."

"Her being there is understandable to everyone but you. She started to leave when she saw you there, didn't she?"

After a moment Perri nodded.

"And you pulled her from the car and dragged her over to the grave that you were so desperate she not visit." He shook his head.

I will not cry, Perri thought. *I will not. I will not.* The tears, unshed, felt hot as flame.

"You have to help me, Cal, find out who this Liv Danger is," she said. "Liv Danger was a cartoon character Jane and David created. I found a sketchbook with all their notes. It was hidden in his room. He never showed it to me."

Cal studied her face as if looking for proof of a lie. "He never showed it to me, either," he said.

"So. Liv Danger knew it was in his room. Then it has to be Jane. She's trying to make me look bad. It's revenge. She wants to blame me for all her problems the way she thinks I blamed her for David's death."

"The way she thinks. You do blame her for David's death. You do. You always have. Have you ever talked to her? Really talked to her since the accident?"

"No. I don't need to talk to her. It wasn't an accident. She tried to kill herself and she killed David."

"That note was old."

"That doesn't matter. She wrote it." She made her words into a counterpunch, she saw the spittle fly from her lips. "She had been thinking about it." This was a certainty, and she refused to let it go.

"That girl is the same girl who's lived next door to us for years. We know her. She doesn't even have a car. Now you think she went down to San Antonio and burned down a bunch of houses to make a point?"

"Maybe she did. She has friends, they could have helped her."

"With arson?"

"Well, are you accusing me? Why would I do this?"

"Do you think she knew you were going to be at the cemetery and that the driver would happen to record you freaking out? She's not making you look bad, you're doing that yourself."

"I can't believe you are taking her side. How did Liv Danger even get that video?"

"The rideshare driver posted it on her own page and tagged Jane, so it appeared on her page. Liv Danger has to be watching her page. And other people started to share it."

"It proves that it's her. Or Laurel."

"No, it doesn't. I am not taking a side," he said with infuriating calmness. "Maybe it is Laurel. She's an obsessive. But I don't think it's Jane. She told me she was starting to get some of her memories back."

Perri gave a little gasp and stepped back.

The doorbell rang, twice, then a fist pounding on the door.

Cal opened the door. A compactly built man stood there, in black T-shirt and jeans, eyes rimmed red, bristly dark hair shaved close, a rope of tattoos curving up his thick right arm. "You Mr. Hall?"

"Yes."

"My name is Shiloh Rooke." His voice was low, menacing, yet playful in a way. "I understand you visited my old friend Brenda Hobson after her recent misfortune."

"Um, yes."

"I've had a recent misfortune as well, Mr. Hall, a real bad one. Now, I guess it's not a coincidence that Brenda and I were the two paramedics who tried to save your boy. I called her when I saw her name in the news this morning and she filled me in on your talk with her." He strolled in past a shocked Cal, giving Perri a measured look.

"You can't just come in here…"

"I tried to save your son's life, you could show a little gratitude," he said. "Be friendly and all."

"What do you want?" Perri said.

"I want to know who came after me and Brenda. Was it you? You mad we couldn't save your boy?"

"It's not us," Perri said. "I swear."

"Did someone burn down your house, Mr. Rooke?" Cal asked calmly.

"No. They came after my fiancée."

"How?" Cal asked. Perri found herself dreading the answer.

Shiloh's face flushed with anger. "They broke into my house, stole some things she didn't know about, and sent them to her." He took a step toward Cal. "Now, Brenda wanted nothing more than her house, a fresh start, and I wanted nothing more than Mimi, and someone's taking her away from me. This Liv Danger. I looked on your Faceplace pages after Brenda told me. You and this Jane Norton, there's a lot of hatred there. I don't appreciate it spilling over onto me."

"We have nothing to do with this."

"Bull. You blame that girl. Maybe you blame me and Brenda, too. That it? We didn't do enough to save your kid?" He glanced at Perri, gave her a measured look. "That your problem, sugar? You want some kind of sick revenge?"

"Please leave," Cal said.

"Last chance. Confess to doing it and I'm not going to go to the cops. I'm sure they'd love to talk to you about Brenda's house." He glanced around the entry hall, the nice painting on the wall, the sculpture on the marble-topped antique counter, the fine furniture in the living room.

"We don't know anything about you or Brenda's arson," Cal said. "Now, get out of here."

"Fine, don't be helpful." His gaze went between them, lingering on Perri. "Weird, though, that you and Jane Norton came together to see Brenda, isn't it? Sorry to have bothered you." He turned and walked back out the open door. Cal shut the door and locked it. Perri went to the window.

"He's walking to the Nortons' house," she said.

Cal opened the door. Perri slammed it. "They're not our problem."

"What has happened to you?" he said, pushing her aside and opening the door. "Do you honestly see Jane or Laurel Norton burning down the house of the woman who helped save Jane's life? Or taking on that thug? If you target these people, you'd have to learn about them. Do you see Laurel wanting to provoke someone like Shiloh Rooke?"

"But you see me doing that." She steadied her voice.

"I don't know what you might do right now," Cal said.

She followed Cal onto their front steps, her heart pounding at his words.

But Shiloh Rooke, glancing back and seeing Cal follow him, veered off from the Norton house and got into his car. He started it up and drove away. It was an unexpected retreat.

Cal turned to Perri. "If you know anything about this, you better tell me, right now."

"I don't." Some of her shock had been replaced by anger. "The same goes for you."

"I don't know anything."

Perri said, "What do we do?" But she was thinking, *You know what you have to do. You have to prove it's Jane or Laurel. And then you have to end it. Not with an arrest and a trial that could go wrong. End it, forever.* That second thought made her tremble.

Cal said, "I need to talk to the arson investigator in San Antonio and tell them what we know. I promised Ms. Hobson that. And I think we need to find out more about this Shiloh Rooke guy. Will you be OK here alone?"

"I'm not afraid of him," Perri said.

"OK. Have a good day. I'm going for my run now." And off he went.

She had to get ready for work. But she had a new purpose: find out how Laurel and Jane could be responsible for what had happened to Shiloh and Brenda Hobson. She could call Randy Franklin, hire him again.

Or just talk to Jane. She had to come out of the house at some point.

Maybe there wasn't a need for a lot of subterfuge. She texted Mike that she had an emergency and would be a bit late to the office. She went and poured two cups of coffee. She went outside and crossed the driveway and, taking a deep breath, rang the doorbell, thinking, *Beware of grieving mothers bearing gifts.*

27

JANE HAD SLEPT in her own bed for the first time in months, and slept late, a combination of exhaustion and the unexpected comfort of being home. Mom had been asleep when she got home from San Antonio. One of the wine bottles was mostly empty. Jane put it in the recycling and went to bed.

When she woke up, Laurel was gone, a note left at Jane's bedside:

You know you are welcome to stay here as long as you need. You can stay here forever. I'll take care of you.

Jane showered, dressed in some spare jeans and a favorite black T-shirt still in her closet, and checked her phone: Amari Bowman, the student who had seen them at Happy Taco and passed David's note to her in class, had left a voice mail for her while she was in the shower. Amari said, *I really have nothing to say to you. Don't call me back.*

Jane thought, *We'll see about that.* She ate a quick bowl of cereal, and when she was washing her bowl, the doorbell rang.

She opened the door to find Perri Hall holding two cups of coffee, and Jane thought, *She'll throw one in my face.*

"I would like to talk to you," Perri said. "Calmly."

"No slapping, no hair pulling? The coffee is not poisoned?" She kept her voice steady.

"No," Perri said. "If I said I was sorry, you wouldn't believe me. So I'll say I was deeply upset by what had been done to my son's grave, and I wasn't thinking straight."

"That's actually fair. Your husband was very fair to me last night."

Perri waited. *You want to be accepted, forgiven. I hope I can sell you on this.* "Might we talk? About what's going on? Please?"

"Come in." Jane held the door wider and Perri came inside.

"Is Laurel here?"

"She is not," Jane said.

Maybe Laurel was spending her time and resources playing the Liv Danger role, Perri thought. Burning down houses and upsetting thugs.

They went to the kitchen table, just off the entrance to Laurel's home office. Perri set down the cups of coffee. Jane picked up one. "Hazelnut, not arsenic?"

Perri ignored the comment. "I've seen the postings on Faceplace from this Liv Danger," Perri said. She had to be careful. She needed Jane to make a slipup, so she could not be threatening. "That must have been very upsetting for you."

"She seems to be blaming you."

Hence, it's you or your mom, Perri thought. "So. Who do you think this is?"

"Someone who hates me. Or you. Or both of us."

"You understand that Brenda Hobson wasn't the only target. The other paramedic was targeted, too." Briefly Perri explained about Shiloh Rooke.

"Brenda told me he's dangerous."

"I would say that was fair. After accusing us, he headed toward your house, but Cal followed him and he got into his car instead. He might still bother you. Or your mother. I thought you should know."

"Thanks." It felt strange having this conversation. Because this was a war against Jane, too, and she could think of only one person willing to wage it: Perri.

Perri took a deep breath. "If this is just someone who hates you, then why involve innocent people? These people were only doing their jobs."

"'All will pay.' Someone is mad at the people involved in the crash. All of them."

"And you think it's me?"

"I don't know. I wouldn't have thought you capable of it, but the accident changed everything for all of us." Jane took another sip of the coffee.

"You'd have to be unbalanced to burn down the house of a woman who saved your life, Jane."

"True. I wouldn't. So if it's you or Mr. Hall doing this, then stop it."

"Us?" The shock went through her like a knife. "Us? You can't be serious."

"Mr. Hall being nice to me aside, you two have the greatest motive for revenge."

"But this isn't revenge." Perri shook her head. "Shiloh loses an engagement; this Brenda Hobson loses her home. Both are terrible. Neither equals losing a child. I have no quarrel with either of them. That's a petty revenge."

"You take what you can get. Not telling everyone that suicide note I wrote was old isn't really a revenge either, but it seems to have worked for you."

Perri's mouth worked. "Maybe you shouldn't have lied about the crash. The deer."

"We were desperate. You were turning the whole town against us."

"Why don't you take some responsibility for what you did?"

"I do, every single day," Jane said. "It will never be enough for you."

"If you know your mother is behind this, I will go with you to the police," Perri said. "I will hold your hand while you tell them everything you know. I will stand by you."

The only sound was the odd tick of an antique clock in Laurel's office.

"Take your coffee and go," Jane said, her voice shaking.

"I know about Liv Danger. You know where the name came from, Jane. You told your mother. Fine, whatever. But now you've got this thug Shiloh angry. I know arson is a serious charge, but your mental history, they'd have to take that into account. Your mother made you do it. Her highly dramatic nature is all over this. Has she written her blog post yet about it all, painting herself as the victim? Did you pay off that driver to make the video? It was all staged, wasn't it?"

"Get out of my house," Jane said.

"There isn't going to be another chance."

Jane slapped her hand, sending the coffee flying. The mug shattered on the tile, the java sprayed the floor and the walls and Perri. She cried out in shock.

"Get out of my house," Jane said. "I saw what 'Liv' posted to you. You know something from that night. I don't know anything. I couldn't know anything. So 'Liv' isn't me. She's you." She jabbed a finger in Perri's face.

"It's beyond amnesia. You are truly crazy." Perri started to collect her broken mug.

"It's broken, you can't fix it. You can't fix what's broken! Get out! Get out!"

"I wonder what people will say when they arrest you and your mother both for this," Perri said. She turned and stumbled out the door. She started to say something else, but Jane shoved her off the porch and down the steps.

"If you come near me again," Jane said, "you will regret it. Oh, and by the way? Your husband believes me. He knows it was an accident. He told me so. He's lucky you're divorcing him. Because you're the one who's crazy."

And she went back inside and slammed the door.

Perri got up from the steps. She hadn't fallen far and there was just a slight scrape on her palm. But she thought maybe the eyes of her neighbors were on her, and she shivered as she went back to the house.

Matteo Vasquez, she thought. *I could get him to write about her. But how do I explain knowing who Liv Danger is? How? What if Maggie comes forward and talks about my computer being linked to the postings?*

It was not her proudest moment, but she began to think of a plan.

Her phone went off. She glanced at the screen.

A text from her boss, Mike: GET TO THE OFFICE. NOW.

28

THE DVD FROM Happy Taco was playing when Adam Kessler followed Jane into her living room. The television was a large one, and as Adam walked in the video version of Adam was walking into Happy Taco, trailing Trevor Blinn.

"What's that?" he asked, his eyes turning to the screen.

"The night David died. You were at Happy Taco right after we were."

He turned to her in shock. "Where did you get that?"

"That's the first thing you say to me, Adam?"

He didn't answer, he looked back at the video.

"The police and the investigators weren't interested once David and I left. I was. You know how I always stay at the movies until the credits play."

His handsome face twisted into a helpless smile. "Well, so, I was there. It's a popular place."

"You could have mentioned to me that you were there right after I was."

"What difference does it make?"

She pointed at the screen. "You come in with Trevor. You look around. You don't order. You're looking for someone. Is it me?"

Adam sat down on the couch. Staring at his sneakers. Then he looked up at her. "Yes."

"Why?"

"I stopped by your house. You weren't there. Your mom asked me to find you. She didn't believe your texts that you were studying with a friend."

"Why didn't she come looking for me herself?"

"I don't know." Adam put his face in his hands. "I don't know."

She sat next to him. "So, what, you and Trevor were both looking for me?"

"I don't know why he was there. We both arrived separately, I said hi to him, he almost ignored me. Then we walked in together."

She thought of Trevor, watching her and David's exchange in the parking lot. "Was Trevor looking for me, too? Or for David?"

"You'd have to ask him."

"So, all this time, after the crash when I was trying to piece together my memories, you never felt you should tell me this?"

He tried to take her hand and she pulled away from him. He folded his hands back in his lap. "What was the point? I never saw you that night. You didn't even remember me as a friend. I was a stranger to you in those early weeks."

Then she wondered if he was lying. It was only a matter of minutes between her departure and his arrival. Did he see her leaving with David? Did they encounter each other in the parking lot? If so, why would he still have entered the restaurant?

"OK, you never saw me. You still could have mentioned it."

"I don't know what the point would be, we didn't see each other. And any mention of that night seemed to upset you."

"I mean you could have told me," she said, her voice tight with anger, "that my mother had you out searching for me. Is that what you harboring me in your room is? Do you report back to my mom on my moods, what nights I stay, how crazy I am?"

"Yes, Jane," he said, "I spy on you. That's why I risk getting thrown off campus so you can sleep there at night, or risk getting into trouble for hacking your dining-plan card, and why I spend nights away from my room so you can have privacy. All so I can spy on you for your mother."

The sarcasm hit her like a fist. "All right," she said after a moment. "I realize that sounds a little paranoid."

"I don't have warm feelings for your mom, to be frank," Adam said, softening his tone. "She's done nothing really to help you or to get you off the streets." He stood up.

"You give a lot and don't ask for anything in return."

Something dark flashed behind his eyes. "The curse of the nice guy," Adam said. "I have a girlfriend, thanks. Who is not that patient with me spending so much time around you."

"Adam..." Her reflex was to say *I'm sorry*, but she wasn't. She had no reason to be.

"Fair enough. I guess I should have told you. But I never found you that night, I never saw you or David"—here he got up and turned away from the images playing out on the TV—"and..."

"You know something." A prickle of dread touched her spine.

"Your mom was afraid you might hurt yourself. But she didn't tell me that until later."

"Because of the suicide note. But Mom has always denied that the note meant anything. Always."

Adam said nothing. "Look, I was worried about you, regardless of what your mom said. You were full of secrets back then. We told each other everything, it seemed, but you were keeping stuff from me. And I think it had to do with David." His voice dropped to a sneer. "Mr. Perfect."

"What?"

"I don't know what you two were doing. If I knew that, I would tell you."

She sat down on the couch and paused the video. "Supposedly we were running away to, like, Canada."

He laughed, and then saw it was not a joke. "What? Why would you?"

"You've never heard that as a rumor?"

"No."

"How do you know my secrets were about David?"

"You were with him that night, it must be."

She thought of what Trevor had said. "Did I talk much about my father and his death?"

Now he tried to take her hand, to comfort her, and she pulled away. "Jane, don't."

"Did I?"

"No. It upset you too much. You didn't like to talk about him."

But David had brought him up.

"So you, what, decided to look for me?"

"I came over, that wasn't unusual, your mom let me in and wanted to know where you were. I don't think she believed your texts. She and Mrs. Hall were both here."

"Doing what?"

"I think maybe having an argument. I don't know about what. It felt like I had interrupted something between them. But I don't know why they would argue. She asked if I'd go look for you, see if you were at any of our usual haunts. So I went to the Starbucks, I went to Happy Taco, and I ran into Trevor there, looking for you and David."

"Why was Trevor looking for me?"

"Well, he said he was looking for David and that you were with David." He rubbed his face. "I mean, the whole thought of going out to look for someone is so ancient. We have cell phones. But you wouldn't answer again."

"Did I owe you an explanation for where I was?" Something here was off. He wasn't being entirely truthful.

"No, you didn't," he said evenly. "And after the crash, you didn't even remember me. At least you remembered Kamala and Trevor and David. But we didn't know each other except in high school. You had to get to know me all over again." His voice softened. "You were my best friend, Jane, it was hard to lose you. It was hard not to help you. I'm glad you've let me help you now."

The curse of the nice guy, she thought. "All right. I forgive you."

He started to speak and then simply said, "That's great. Your forgiveness. Did you bring me over to see this video or did you need my help once again?"

Later she wished she had recognized the bite in his words. But, preoccupied, she didn't. "I need your help. Will you drive me?"

29

—————————

SO YOU'VE HAD an interesting morning," Adam said, his voice dull, as he drove her to the office park where Kevin Ngota and Randy Franklin both had office space.

"Yes." Jane's voice sounded dead. "Because I think I just saw the soul of Perri Hall, and it was cancerous."

"Um, she's been accusing you of murder since David died. This is not new behavior for this woman."

"This Shiloh guy..."

"Now him, he sounds dangerous," Adam said. "Maybe call the cops on him."

Jane said nothing.

He parked where, from his car, they could see both office entrances. "What are we doing here?"

"Waiting for them to show up." They sat in the car, with coffee and apple fritters they'd bought from a little bakery on the way. Adam had treated by way of apology.

"Can I tell you something?" she said quietly.

He nodded, chewing his fritter. "You know I eagerly await your every pronouncement."

"When you lose your memory, it's a chance for the people around you to rewrite history."

Adam stopped chewing, stared at her. He wiped glaze from his mouth with his fingertip.

"They all get to tell you what *they* want you to know. What they want you to remember. They reshape you. No one has ever told me a bad thing I did, or David did. Were we bad?"

He stared at her, then out at the parking lot. "Jane... don't."

"I think maybe you and my mom have tried to make me into a better person than what I was." She watched him. "Who was I, Adam? Was I any good?"

He put his hand on her shoulder. "Of course you were good."

"How?"

"You were good to me. The best. People were crappy to me at that school when I started. I never fit in." His voice broke. "But you weren't. You were my friend, from instant one. Even before I blossomed into the incredible stud you see before you." He tried his smile on her.

She didn't say anything for several seconds and then she locked her gaze on his. "My dad, it wasn't suicide, right? He wouldn't have wanted to leave me, right?"

"Oh, Jane. You were so close to him. He was such a good guy, he just wanted the best for you. He was funny, he would feed us all, let us jump in the pool, tell the requisite lame dad jokes." Now Adam looked like he might cry. She knew his own father wasn't around much; Mr. Kessler had remarried and had a new set of twin toddlers with a younger wife.

"So why would David be talking to me about my dad's death? In secret. Away from everyone."

Adam set down his coffee into his cup holder. "You think David knew something about your dad's death."

"What if it wasn't an accident? Or suicide? I sound like I'm talking about the crash." Her father's death, her terrible night, all seemed to be part of the same echo reverberating inside her head.

"Your dad wasn't murdered, Jane. The police investigated. They're not dummies."

"I know. It's not a movie. But why does David say anything to me about my dad, in secret, and then we vanish for hours and then a man overhears us planning to run to Canada? There was something in what David knew that was big and awful and so bad that we thought of running away from it."

Adam bit at his lip. "I swear, I don't know. Neither of you ever confided any of this to me. I wish you had."

She set down her coffee. She steadied her voice. "Here comes Kevin. If anyone comes to Franklin's office, text me."

"I'm actually sitting here on a stakeout," he said in mild disbelief.

"Yes, and don't be looking at your phone, you'll miss seeing something important. Keep your eyes open."

"Yes, bossy." But he said it like the rift was now healed between them.

She got out of the car. Kevin was fumbling at the door with the key, then dropped it, trying to hold a Lava Java cup and a satchel and a file of papers.

"May I help you with that?"

Kevin glanced up at her and the surprise spread itself across his face. "Hello. I didn't expect to see you here."

"I just couldn't wait for our next session. It's funny that you're not listed on this practice's website."

He kept his smile in place. "I'm new."

"And yet they got your name on the door before the website?"

"We're not very tech-y here," he said. "You seem different today."

She ignored the comment. "It's a little weird. You're two doors down from the PI who investigated my car crash on behalf of my accusers. You volunteer to be my counselor. Just a coincidence?"

"Let's talk inside," he said quickly. The office was empty; it was early. He gestured with a nod of his head toward a closed inner door. She followed him in and sat down. The room was calm greens and grays, the only decoration an antique painted map of his native Tanzania, framed and matted behind his desk. Next to his university diploma and a graduate degree.

She pointed at the framed vellum. "You're not a grad student."

He smiled. "But I am. I'm getting an additional master's at Saint Mike's and I'm not taking on new clients until it's done." It sounded so reasonable and for a moment her resolve wavered. "Are you upset I didn't tell you I have an office in Lakehaven?"

She took a measured breath. "It's just that you were very careful to present yourself as a regular graduate student. Someone desperate to make his mark and I was your project. I was the one you needed to help. You made no mention of ties to Lakehaven. Or being Randy Franklin's neighbor. Did he hire you to spy on me? Is Perri Hall behind this?"

He gave her a confused smile. "I didn't think the fact that I just, two weeks ago, got an offer to join an office here was pertinent to us working together."

"You being in Lakehaven is pretty pertinent to me. Is Lakehaven why you had the interest in me? Heard all the rumors about the Norton girl?"

"No. Your memory condition was. I am only trying to help you."

"Maybe your job is to prove I'm faking amnesia."

"No," he said. His mouth twitched.

"Then who sent you? Someone did and don't lie to me, not if you want to help me. Who?"

"Jane, really..."

"I don't like this coincidence. I will go to the graduate dean and report you for lying to a patient unless you tell me the truth. Tell me."

He hadn't even set down his briefcase yet, but now he did, and arranged his jacket on the back of his chair, and then sat across from her. He gestured and she sat, perched on the edge of the chair. "Your mother," he said.

She stared at him. "My mother."

"She called me. I don't know how she found me, but she knew I had joined this office in Lakehaven and had just started graduate work at Saint Mike's."

Mom knows where I'm living, she thought. *How does she know? I don't tell her.* She had made sure the tracking on the phone Mom gave her was turned off. But the rideshare charges: too many landing close to the campus. It wasn't a hard guess. Or worse: Adam.

"And she paid you to prove I'm faking? Or see if you could get me to remember."

"She believes you're in danger, but she said you wouldn't listen to her."

"Did she mention having me committed to a facility?" Her mother, yesterday, coolly saying how better off she'd be in a hospital.

"Just generally. To keep you off the streets and to get you into intensive therapy."

"And she paid you what for this service?"

A momentary biting of his own lip. His voice choked with shame. "Jane..."

"How much?"

"Twenty thousand. I would not have done it if I had not desperately needed the money. And, more importantly, she said you desperately needed help."

Jane stood up and began to pace the room.

"Jane." He made his voice a soft cajole. "I truly want to help you. Your mother only wants to help you get your life back on course so you can be whole and happy."

"But you were eager to take her money."

"You know what school costs. My family came from nothing in Tanzania, I came to the UK and then here, but the accreditation...I had to have more schooling. The rents in Austin...the money would have gotten me established."

"And you write a diagnosis of commitment, and she gets what she wants. Draw up the papers to have me involuntarily committed."

"It would only be a recommendation..." His voice trailed off and then he cleared his throat. "And unnecessary if you would fully embrace treatment."

"How do you report to her?"

"I text or e-mail her."

"Text her. Tell her you must meet her. Face-to-face."

He stared at her.

"Do it," Jane said, "or I'll sue you, and even if I don't win, no one will hire you. And don't you dare warn her that I know. I'll go to the state licensing board."

She knew how to scare a therapist. He stared at her and then got out his phone and wrote a text message.

Her own phone buzzed. Adam, texting her: A woman just went into Franklin's office.

"You call me when you set up the meeting. I want to be there. Maybe I'll have commitment papers drawn up for her."

Kevin nodded, miserable. "I sincerely want to help you. So does your mother."

"You have an odd way of showing it." And now he looked stricken. She thought maybe he'd been played, too. Her mother, pretending yesterday at lunch that Kevin wasn't qualified enough, being doubtful of his therapy, which of course would have made Jane take his side in reaction. Her mother really was sharper than anyone realized.

She walked out of the office and to the car, fighting down a surge of nausea.

Adam rolled down the window. "A woman went in. She knocked, then she dug a key out of her purse, and opened the door, and called in, like she wasn't sure she could just walk in. Then she went inside. As you can see I was not staring at my phone."

"So not a client," Jane said. "Maybe a temp? He didn't have a secretary on duty yesterday."

"Well, I don't know. A temp, I think. She seemed a little hesitant about just rushing inside."

"I'm calling you and leaving my phone in my pocket. You listen in. I need to get into Franklin's files and I might need a diversion."

"Are you crazy?" He grabbed her arm.

"Let go, Adam."

"Jane. Consider what you're doing, this is breaking the law."

"Kevin just told me my mom is working on having me committed to a facility. I really hope you're not part of that."

"I'm not. I swear." His shock looked genuine, and he released her arm.

"Help me or don't," she said. She called his number and stood staring at him until he answered it. "Idiot Friends, Incorporated," he said. "May we help you?"

She slipped the phone into her jacket. Then she touched Adam's cheek for just a moment. He had been her only friend at times and she couldn't lose him, no matter how aggravated she was with him. She went to Franklin's door and walked straight in. The young woman—dark hair pulled into a ponytail, wearing a light blouse and a dark jacket—stood behind a desk, frowning, still holding her purse, as if unsure where to put it.

"Hi, I'm Mr. Franklin's nine o'clock appointment," Jane lied. She put a touch of panic in her voice, careful not to overdo it. "Are you his assistant? Is he here?"

"Um, no, I'm his temp for the day. He's not here yet, I'm sorry. What's your name?"

"My last name's Hall," she lied again. "I was here yesterday. I'm hiring him and really..."—she glanced back out the door—"the guy I want watched by Mr. Franklin, he's here, he's followed me here."

The young woman paled. "Let me try to call Mr. Franklin."

"I don't want him to find me here." She peeked out the thin window on one side of the door. "Oh, he's going door to door. He must have seen me park here." She clutched her hands together. "I cannot believe he's turned into such a stalker."

The young woman was in a panic. "Is he dangerous, should I call the police? I have pepper spray."

"As long as he doesn't see me, it'll be fine. Can I hide in Randy's office? Just for a second?"

The effort to make a decision warred on the girl's face. *Please, Adam, just play along*. A knocking on the door.

"Yes," the temp said.

Jane hurried past her and closed Randy Franklin's office door. Then, gently, quietly, she locked it. Back corner. File cabinet. She'd noticed it yesterday.

He had a scanner on his credenza, along with a printer, and his computer on his desk. She panicked for a moment that files from a case two years old would be digitally archived instead of left in paper form. She'd try the file cabinet first. She broke the cheap lock with a letter opener she grabbed off his desk and slid the drawer marked "H–N" open. It was stuffed full of paper files.

"I'm looking for my girlfriend!" She heard Adam's voice thunder. "Is she in with the investigator? I have NOT been stalking her. She doesn't need to hire anyone. I love her SO MUCH."

"Sir, you can't just come in here. You'll have to leave, or I'll call the police."

"BUT I LOVE HER. PLEASE."

He'd for sure get pepper-sprayed at this rate. She found a folder marked "HALL, DAVID" and pulled the whole thing loose. She shoved it into her backpack. "N." She looked. Surely nothing would be under her name. But there was a name. "NORTON, BRENT." Her father. She tried not to scream out in shock, clapping a hand over her mouth. She took that file as well and shoved it into her backpack. She slid the drawer closed very quietly.

"She's not here, sir. Please leave, or I will call the police."

"Fine, then. BUT I STILL LOVE HER," he vowed.

Jane moved to the door. She heard Adam leave, heard the temp lock the door behind him. She unlocked the office door. Just in time, because then the door flew open. "He is crazy!" the temp announced.

"I really need Mr. Franklin to follow him and record him stalking me." She peered out the window, the temp leaning over her shoulder. "Oh, good, he's leaving. I'll go once he's gone."

And she did, hurrying back toward Kevin's office. She was shaking and shivering. She walked past Kevin's office, turning in to the side parking lot, out of sight of the office.

Adam pulled in his car at the edge of the parking lot and she got in.

"You have truly and completely lost your mind," he said. "I'm not tiptoeing around it anymore, Jane."

"You're such a good actor," she said. She clutched the backpack close to her chest.

"I hope that was worth it," he said. His voice shook a little.

"No, not really. Although I'll notify the Oscar committee of your performance." She made herself shrug. "His files were, like, triple-locked. I couldn't get in. Thanks for trying, though."

"So you got nothing. After I go full Matt Damon."

"Nothing," she said.

He studied her and she thought, *He doesn't believe me, but what does it matter? This is Adam. He's not going to search my backpack.*

Adam sighed. "Trevor is having a party tonight. At his dad's place. I think you should go with me."

"He didn't invite me," she said. Right now she just wanted to get away from Adam, not take these papers back to his room or her house. "Can you take me to Lakehaven Park?"

"Agree to go to the party," he said.

"Adam. Stop. I cannot go to a Lakehaven party. You know that. I cannot."

"So, you never go to another social gathering? You never get married? Have a career you want? Have kids? Are you going to deny yourself life out of guilt for the rest of your life?"

"I have too many problems to deal with to go to a party."

Adam shook his head. "Do you think, for one second, David wanted this self-imposed exile for you?"

She put her hands over her face. "Please stop talking."

He softened his tone. "Jane. You need some normalcy. You need to step up and move on. You know I care about you. C'mon."

"Is Kamala going to be there?"

"So what if she is? It's not going to be big or wild or anything. His grandmother will be there."

"Oh, it's not a college party without a grandmother."

"This will be the most Trevor Blinn party ever. A party with training wheels, which is entirely your speed. We wouldn't want you to strain yourself, you know, smiling or enjoying yourself."

Her phone buzzed. A text from Kevin Ngota. The client we discussed will meet me tomorrow at 2 PM at her office. I assume I will see you then. I can prove to you we all have your best interests at heart. I hope you will come there with an open mind.

She was going to need more help tomorrow. This time she'd ask Trevor. It, like this morning with Adam, would be a test.

30

PERRI, COULD YOU please come in here?" Mike called out to her as soon as she reached her desk outside his office. He sounded grim. There wasn't his usual smile. She walked into Mike's office.

Maggie already sat in a chair, hands folded in lap, looking miserable.

Mike shut the door behind Perri. "We have an issue."

"What's the matter?"

"A man named Shiloh Rooke showed up here this morning. He said you had tried to ruin his life and he made a scene. Loudly in the lobby. In front of a pair of potential investors."

"What? He came here? I'm so sorry."

"It really set the tone to have a raving, yelling nutcase calling for my executive assistant. Exactly the image the investors were looking for from us."

"I'm sorry," she repeated. She had never seen him so furious.

"So, given the scene, I remembered you'd asked me

for a recommendation to track someone on the Internet. So I asked Maggie what that was all about. She told me about your conversation and what she found. OK, that's one thing. But she says these threats were posted from your computer."

"I didn't write them and if I did, I wouldn't have asked Maggie to trace them, obviously."

He didn't seem impressed. "Why are you dragging my company into your vendetta?"

"'Vendetta' is hardly an apt description," Perri managed to say.

"What word would you use to describe this? This guy worked your son's car crash and now he says you ruined his life."

Perri turned to Maggie. "Did you talk to Shiloh?"

"No, I was in my office. Building security escorted him out. But Mike asked me what this was about. I had to tell him."

"It's OK, Maggie," Perri said. "I'm sorry."

"Thanks, Maggie, that will be all," Mike said, and Maggie, shooting a beseeching look at Perri, left.

"What are you doing to me? To us?" Mike leaned against the closed door.

Like this was about him, or what he thought they were going to be. She drew a calming breath. "Shiloh was a paramedic at David's crash and he's been targeted—so has the other paramedic, so have I. It's Jane Norton. She ruined his engagement, she burned down this woman's house, she defaced David's grave…"

"Jane Norton is a homeless amnesiac, not a criminal mastermind."

"I know this looks bad but…"

"Stop," he said. "Please. I beg you, as a friend, as someone who cares deeply about you. David died in a car accident and you have to accept that. For your sake. Not for anyone else's."

"She killed him. There is more to it."

"Are you ever going to leave Jane Norton alone?"

"What..."

"Maggie told me about these Faceplace postings. What if she or her mother sues you for this and it comes back to us because you've now involved my employee? You can't even see how it looks."

"I'm sorry Shiloh Rooke came here. But I'm an innocent party, Mike."

"Why don't you take the rest of the day off," he said. "Better yet, the week, and we'll let all this furor calm down."

He did not believe her. She was telling the truth and he did not believe her. The shock was like a physical force in her chest. She suddenly felt afraid for her job. "Mike..."

"I just can't have this, Perri. Can't have my company or my employees involved in your private mess. You need help. We'll work this out, all right? But go, take the time off. It's for the best."

"All right." Her voice was hoarse. "I think you're right, a break is the right idea." But she knew she wouldn't come back here again, not to work for Mike. Never again. And for a moment she saw in his face something of the acid blame and dislike that Laurel Norton had gotten at volunteer meetings, at school, after the crash, and a cold knife twisted in her heart. She got up. She checked her e-mail, responded to a couple of requests, and then sent an e-mail to the office saying she was taking some personal time; she could be reached via cell phone if there was an emergency.

She refused to show how upset she felt. She fought

down a tremble of her fingers as she typed. She thought Mike cared about her. He'd acted like he wanted to date her and now he acted like she was radioactive. In the back of her mind, once the divorce was done, she might have been interested in him, given time. Now she was the problem employee that he thought couldn't let go of her grief.

She collected her purse and went out into the hallway. She loved this job and she told herself not to think about it. She walked into the ladies' room.

Maggie stood before the mirror. "I'm sorry. I couldn't lie once he asked, Perri."

"Of course not. Did you find out anything on my laptop?"

"They've managed to hack your laptop using a method I can't detect. And I can find nearly all methods." She sighed. "Which suggests to me, both to install the hack and for the earlier postings, Liv had to have access. If not, then you're dealing with someone with top-notch hacking resources."

The key. Who knew it was where it had always been? Well, Cal, of course. And Laurel and Jane, because they had been neighbors and she'd never thought of moving the spare key after the crash. She had other things on her mind. Who else? David—which meant that Kamala might have known. Or Trevor Blinn. Or any of his other high school friends. David often forgot his key when he was a kid, before he was driving. Or Liv Danger was very, very good, and she was up against someone who could digitally destroy her life. She felt sick.

It had to be Laurel or Jane. It had to be.

She said, "Please believe me when I say I didn't do this." It mattered that someone believe her.

"OK, I believe you."

It was more credit than Mike had given her.

"But you need to stay away from this Shiloh Rooke. This guy isn't stable, Perri, please." She took Perri's shoulder, surprising her. "There was another posting from Liv Danger. I traced the IP address assigned at the time. It wasn't your computer. It's here in Lakehaven. On Old Travis, in an office park. They share a wireless network provided by the management company, but I can't tell for sure which office used it. I called the provider and they shared the address with me." She pressed the paper into Perri's hand.

"I'm sorry I dragged you into this, Maggie, you're the best."

Maggie gave her an awkward hug and walked out. Perri went down to her car before she unfolded the paper. She recognized the address, knew where it was on Old Travis, just because she knew the addresses of other businesses along there and knew the office park of small, individual offices there. It was where Randy Franklin had his practice.

A man who had worked the accident investigation for them; a man tied to them. The posting had been done in the middle of the night. When she had no alibi.

She felt a little dizzy. She headed out of the office building, across the little sky bridge that linked it to the parking garage. She walked toward her car. Her phone buzzed.

"Mrs. Hall?"

"Yes." She recognized the voice.

"Matteo Vasquez. I just received an interesting e-mail that I'd like to read to you and I wonder if you have a comment."

"From whom?"

"Someone calling themselves Liv Danger. Does that ring a bell with you?"

31

JANE'S BOOK OF MEMORY, WRITTEN IN THE
DAYS AND WEEKS AFTER THE CRASH

Good news and bad news.

Good news: kids are getting bored with me. A girl I don't remember says, "Memory back yet?" when I pass her in the hallway between third and fourth period and I cannot tell whether or not she is being mean, or is only interested enough to inquire once a day, or she's just one of those people who don't think how what they say affects you. I want to punch her in the face.

Bad news: I have to get rid of Kamala.

Because she is out to get me. I know I sound paranoid. That is not one of the mental conditions I presently have. Although I feel like the world is sometimes keeping a huge secret from me.

"I heard you remembered stuff," she said to me as we walked to class.

"Who said and what stuff?" I had learned I was often discussed in group texts, studied for any suicidal tendencies or hint that my memories had returned. I guess everyone's college applications were nearly done and the seniors had time to burn.

"I don't—" Kamala stopped herself, as if the third word was the magical *remember*. "Is it true?"

"If it was true, I would say so. I would dance down the hallway."

This was the wrong thing to say, because of David. I knew it as soon as I said it. It's like I've forgotten common sense.

"I'm sorry," I said.

"It's OK," she said. "I know you're not yourself." Every time she was nice, it felt like a small, mean shove. No one but me seemed to notice.

So good of you, I saw a passing girl mouth to Kamala. She patted Kamala on the shoulder as if giving her strength. She didn't even look at me.

"Why are you being my peer helper?" I asked.

"Don't be ridiculous, of course I was going to help you. We've been friends forever, Jane."

"Have we?"

"Yes."

"Were we still friends the night of the accident?"

"Why? Are you remembering something?" She stopped, stared at me.

I stopped. "I heard maybe we weren't as close as we once were."

Kamala put a gentle hand on my shoulder. "We did have a disagreement when David and I broke up."

"When...when did you break up?" This was news to me.

"A week before the crash." With a gentle, understanding smile. It was like seeing a snake on the floor moments before the lights in the room went out.

And then I wondered if that was true. If she said they broke up and then she still acted like my friend, it made her look good. There were no e-mails or texts to me saying, "David and I broke up, Jane, I need ice cream and movie

night with you." I had not seen a single one of those. Weren't
we best friends?

"What did you and I fight about?" David? But we weren't
dating. I didn't have a boyfriend, Mom and Adam had told me
that.

Kamala hugged me, patted my back. "Does any of this
matter? I just want you to get better."

*You were his girlfriend. Anyone else could have volunteered,
maybe they did.*

Here's the later scene at the counselor's office:

"Mrs. Coulter, did anyone else volunteer to be my peer
helper?"

"Why do you ask? Is there a problem?" I made her nervous.
I made everyone nervous. They didn't know how to act. I was
their first amnesiac. It was exhausting for them. I must have
kept them searching through reference books and websites,
trying to counsel me.

"Kamala is not really trying to help me."

"But she's so patient and understanding with you."

"I think it might be an act."

It was almost as if I had suggested Kamala was from Mars,
or that she had privately shown me superpowers. Mrs. Coulter
didn't believe me but she said, "I'll talk to her."

"No. I will. I just wanted you to know my feelings about
her. Did anyone else volunteer to help me other than Kamala?"

"Yes. Adam Kessler and Trevor Blinn. Would you like one
of them to be your peer?"

I bit my lip. Trevor had stood up for me in a way no one
else had. But Adam was a friend who wasn't particularly close
with Kamala and her crowd. She couldn't exert any influence
over him. The drawback was that I didn't remember Adam
before the accident. I had childhood memories of Trevor and
Kamala. I knew I had been close to them once. Adam was a

blank space. Maybe I needed that; someone who didn't have years of expectations and history with me. And I could trust him. "Adam, please."

"All right. I'll speak to Kamala."

"No. I will. I'll tell her."

Mrs. Coulter bit at her lip and I thought, *Are you afraid of her?* "It would be better if I could," Mrs. Coulter said.

"Let me fire her," I said. There is some social awkwardness tied to amnesia.

"Jane, 'firing' isn't really the word I'd use ..."

"I can talk to her. Please let me stand on my own feet." (Counselors love that phrase.)

And she nodded. I didn't wait. Everything was being done for me. I'd been led along, docile, trusting. So. Kamala was waiting for me at our first-period class, like I didn't know how to find my way from the hallway into the room.

"I was worried about you," she said. "You weren't waiting for me at the entrance. You know I don't like to be late." And she gave me an admonishing kind of smile, the indulgent, patronizing smile that you give a wayward child.

"I no longer need your help," I said by way of greeting. Her smile stilled and then, for just a moment, hardened into a cruel slash. Like a mask had fallen away for a second.

Then it returned with new energy, a recharged star.

"I'm assigned to be your peer helper," she said, prim as a grandmother. Now the smile was gentle, and then the bitch dusted my shoulder, like I was a disheveled toddler on the playground. "And that's what I'm going to be. I'm here for you, every moment, until we get your memory back." And then she tapped my forehead, still smiling.

I felt my skin blush terribly. I was still recovering. Physically and mentally. I was emotionally arrested—whatever leaps in maturity I'd made in high school were wiped free. Then I was mad at myself for telling her this at the start of the day rather than the end—it was Friday, the weekend could have been a needed break—and also for then not just saying that Adam would kindly take over, Kamala had already done so much, thank you, and been all diplomatic about it. I didn't know how to do that. "Not anymore. I don't need one."

"I don't think you're quite yourself, Jane. I don't think you realize what good friends we've been. You need your friends right now." Her voice lowered. More serious. As if we were still negotiating. If David had broken up with her, had he faced this saccharine resistance? That mask that slipped and showed the snarl? "I'm all that's keeping the wolves at bay." She gestured, furtively, at the classrooms behind her. "Without me, they'll turn on you. It won't be just snide looks in the hall or people not speaking to you." The half smile returned. "It will get ugly."

"Are you threatening me?" And here's the weird thing: I could hear a little hope in my voice. I *wanted* her to threaten me. I wanted all the innuendo that lay behind those sugared words and indulgent smiles to break free, like light through a long-shuttered window.

The bell rang. The hallway emptied. Neither of us moved.

She tilted her head slightly, watching me, the smile going into a tremble. "No, I'm not threatening you. Threats are for children."

And she slammed her head back against the concrete block wall, hard, screaming, "JANE STOP JANE STOP JANE NOOOOOOOOOO!" And she screamed it like she was auditioning for a horror movie.

Need I go on? She collapsed to the floor, sobbing, while I watched, saying, *Oh please*, but then it does turn out that when a girl everyone thinks is damaged goods gets accused of assault by the popular brainiac, they tend to believe the ever-smiling, ever-gentle-voiced Kamala.

Thanks to Mom's epic deer lie and the suicide note, I was what my English teacher called an "unreliable narrator."

The teacher took me to Mrs. Coulter, hustling me past dozens of staring and whispering students; they took a tearful Kamala to the nurse. Kamala kept crying out, "It's not Jane's fault. Is she OK? Is Jane all right? Did she hurt herself, too? Let me see her." I could hear her plaintive yet calculated cries down the concrete-and-tile hallways, echoing off the shuttered classrooms. Every student and teacher heard my fall from grace, like the frightened animals in Eden.

Slow clap.

Kamala's parents came. For some reason the Graysons came and talked at me. Yes, *at*.

"I don't understand why you would do this, Jane. Kamala has always been your dearest friend. A sister, even, to you," Dr. Grayson said. She had been a runner-up in a beauty pageant, whatever the big global one was with all the different countries and costumes. I only mention that because she was a very good doctor and much respected, but there was this giant picture of her in her waiting room, in her evening gown and sash, stunning, and it was so unrelated to being a good doctor. I never knew why she needed that picture up in the waiting area, why she needed to remind us all. She was gorgeous and she was brilliant and she felt entitled to give me a lecture. She even took a deep breath before she began.

I tried. I did. I waited for another deep breath. "I didn't lay a finger on her. She knocked her own head into the wall, she threw herself to the floor. Because she's mad at me. I won't let her control me."

You can imagine how this sounded, in the hush of Mrs. Coulter's office.

"How could you tell such a lie?" She actually kind of hissed this at me.

Some people, including Kamala's parents, could not stand for their child to be criticized. Mr. Grayson left to go yell at Mrs. Coulter. I wondered where my mother was. She had been called. She hadn't responded.

I looked Doctor Beauty right in the eye. "I'm not lying. I think about how she acted when we were kids and maybe I'm seeing it in a new light, all the high school years stripped away when it's easier to be allied with someone like Kamala, when you're under her protection. I lost that. I see her for what she is."

I thought she was going to slap me. She sure thought about it, I could see the decision practically inching across her brain. *Please*, I thought, *do it. Hit me. Then for a moment maybe I'll be pitied.*

But she didn't.

"We won't file charges," Dr. Grayson said. She and Kamala had the same harsh line of mouth that curled into an oh-so-kind smile.

"I would hope not, so she doesn't end up committing perjury"—well, that was what I thought of saying two hours later. In the office I just stared at my feet and wished I'd died in the crash. It would have been easier, wouldn't it? She started repeating herself in her outraged lecturing of me, so I interrupted:

"Well, it would be my word against hers. I still have a word, you know."

She looked at me like I was dirt, and since we were alone, the smile vanished. "A girl who kills a friend when she wants to kill herself."

"I wasn't suicidal!"

"How do you even know? You don't remember." And that is how you play the trump card, the unanswerable charge, the crime I can never deny. So I was the girl who killed David and attacked Kamala.

They didn't expel me; the Graysons made this huge show of pleading for mercy for me. Kamala, too. She wrote an editorial to the paper. I bet someone sent it to the Pope, to speed along her sainthood paperwork. It made them look so angelic and wonderful. I didn't have to bear the stares anymore, the sneers, the dumb questions of did I remember someone or had my memories come back. I finished my last few months working alone with a special-needs teacher, the whole day in an unused classroom. I was done at Lakehaven. I was done.

32

ADAM SAID, "I don't like leaving you here."

"You've got classes. Go. I just need to think and I want to be outside. Thanks for the help."

He could not look less convinced. "What did you find?"

After he'd kept his big secret? No, she wouldn't share this information. Not yet. She closed the car door and walked to the park bench. After a full minute of just staring at her and waiting, Adam gave her a tentative wave. She waved back, like it was all right. He drove off. The park had a Playscape, and a few preschoolers cavorted around the swings and the slides, watched by careful moms and nannies. She went to a deserted swing and sat down.

Her father had brought her to this park when she was little. She remembered him pushing her in this very swing, her scared to go up too high, him pushing her up toward the limitless sky, her laughter bubbling out of her, her feet kicking toward the clouds, which the swing seemed to put within her reach. He was a big man, tall and broad-shouldered, quiet, much quieter than her mother. He would catch the swing and lower her when she yelled, "Enough, Daddy!" letting her know she was safe.

She didn't remember losing him: the agony, the sheer pain of it. How horrible and wrenching it must have been. That was harder than not remembering the crash, in some ways. The pain of knowing she had lost him and not remembering the grief. The grief mattered: now he was simply gone, and she'd had to go through the mourning all over again, and she was sure it was a dim echo of what she had felt the first time. In a way she felt she had failed him.

She pulled the files out of the backpack. Dad or David first? She opened the file on her father with trembling hands. First she looked at a summary sheet; Brent Norton had been investigated by Franklin for a few months before he died.

First she paged through the material quickly, looking for an indication of who had hired Franklin. Nothing. If there was a client record, it was gone.

Had Franklin just done this himself? That made no sense. She paged through the reports. Franklin followed her father, writing about where he went (mostly the office and Jane's school), compiling a list of people that he had called—how had Franklin managed to get that? According to Franklin's notes, it was mostly business associates from his days as a chief financial officer for two start-up companies, including the one he'd founded with his neighbor and friend, Cal Hall.

There were certain phone numbers highlighted on the printout of his phone log. She got out her phone and Internet-searched them. One was a number tied to the Austin FBI office. Another was to the US Secret Service office in Washington, a general-inquiries number.

Why had her father been calling law enforcement, and what was the result? Nothing.

It was only one call each time, a day apart, weeks before he died. The other phone numbers were home, Jane's phone, Cal Hall, the school, his college friends. Normal stuff.

She looked at the spreadsheets. In one column were the names of what must be people or companies, but just initials: IGL was the most common one, listed several times. None of the names were companies she recognized: GM2, Alpha, HFK. In the next column were amounts of money ranging from $20,000 to $100,000. Pages and pages. A lot of money. There were no dates on the entries.

Paper-clipped to the bottom of the spreadsheet printouts was a piece of paper, with a field of flowers printed in faded colors on the background. The stationery looked vaguely familiar: written across it, printed in block printing, was a meaningless string of numbers: *R34D2FT97S*, and then *u: LDN001 p: BFH@78832*.

The numbers and letters meant nothing to her. But they had to mean something with these spreadsheets. She studied them. LDN001. She realized with a jolt those were her mother's initials: Laurel Dumont Norton.

Was this a way to access these spreadsheets?

Behind the spreadsheets were a number of PowerPoint slides that, she realized, were the investor pitch for Norton Financial. This was the company he wanted to start after he'd had a business failure with Cal. He had originally been an accountant specializing in start-up and new companies. There was a business proposal in the file for Norton Financial. The plan was to open up a network of CPA offices in lesser-served areas, with discount fees for tax preparation and basic accounting services to help small businesses start and grow, and help cash-reliant businesses with their particular challenges. There was an analysis of neighborhoods in Austin, San Antonio, Brownsville, New Orleans, Dallas, Laredo, Houston, and more, where his network would grow. She closed the proposal and looked through the other papers.

She realized, after a moment, the file was incomplete. There was no written report from Randy Franklin, no summary of the investigation to say what the whole point was. No client, no report. Just phone numbers, meaningless spreadsheets with unrecognizable names in them, and a business plan that never came to fruition because her father died.

At the back of the file were surveillance photos of her father: at his office he'd rented in Lakehaven while he worked on his new venture, leaving his office, leaving his home. One of the photos was of Brent and Jane out shopping, judging from a department store bag that Jane was carrying. Her hair was long then; she only wore it chopped short after the accident. She did not look happy, but disappointed, and Brent had an arm around her, trying to talk to her. Jane was leaning away from him. She was being awful to her dad, typical teenager stuff, and she didn't even remember why, but she felt as though she'd just been stabbed in the chest. Franklin had followed them. And then later, investigated her.

The next sheet jolted her. A photo sheet of pictures, taken in rapid sequence. She and her dad...and Adam Kessler, sitting on the patio of a favorite Tex-Mex restaurant, having lunch. Laughing. Dad joking, Adam smiling politely. Jane excused herself. Adam and Dad still talking.

Adam handing something to Dad. Dad nodding and putting it in his pocket. Jane returning to the table, unaware.

What was this? She checked the dates written on the back of the pictures. A few weeks before Dad died.

There were other photo sheets. Her father traveling, going into his business, coming home, dinners out with Mom. Laurel looking worried, tired, holding her father's hand, leaning toward him. And looking unhappy. Her father looked tired.

"You're too big for the swing," a small voice behind Jane said. She turned and saw a little girl frowning at her. "It's for kids."

"I guess you're right." Jane stood up and she walked to the park bench and sat back down. The little girl watched her, as if surprised that Jane had moved. She took the swing that Jane had vacated, empty now like all the rest, and knelt on the seat, moving gently in rhythm.

Nothing in her life seemed to be what she thought. She put away the perplexing file on her father and opened the file on David.

It was much more detailed than the file she'd found in her mom's file cabinet. She supposed that one was shared with her mother's attorney, and this was the one produced for the Halls' lawyer, Kip Evander.

There were photos, reports, and interviews with Amari (she who passed the note to Jane in class and then texted Kamala at Happy Taco), Trevor, Kamala, and others who'd had contact with her and David in the course of the evening. The time line was nearly the same as hers, with one additional fact: that Kamala had called the Halls earlier in the evening and spoken with Cal Hall. Nothing was noted as to the content of that conversation.

Did they know? Did the Halls know, before the crash, that David and Jane were together? Was that the argument between Laurel and Perri that Adam discovered when he stopped by her home?

The orange phone that Brenda Hobson remembered ly-

ing by the wreck was not mentioned in a detailed inventory
of what was recovered from the wreck site at the car. So,
after Brenda Hobson moved it out of the way, someone had
taken it. Also not listed: the laptop David used at Happy
Taco.

Or the crowbar. She and David had misplaced all sorts
of things in their secret odyssey.

Where was it all?

Unless these items had been purposefully taken from the
crash site in the chaos.

Who would have had access? Who had come to the
crash site? The Halls had both come to the accident site,
her mother. Kamala, Trevor, Adam? She realized that she
didn't know. No one had ever discussed it with her. It
wasn't a question you asked: *Hey, Mom, which of my
friends came to where I lay bleeding and David lay dead?
Did you notice?*

Could the phone, missed in the scene processing, have
been taken at the same time the suicide note was planted?
She bit her lip at this thought of efficiency.

She moved on to the report of the suicide-note analysis,
which was stamped "Confidential: Client's Eyes Only."
The paper and ink had been tested chemically. The ink
came from a Skymon Gel Pen and was two to three years
old. The ink had been on the paper for several months; it
wasn't contemporary to the crash. The paper came from a
Japanese notebook, with an unusually high fiber count—
the analyst made a note that those were expensive paper
notebooks. Jane recognized the brand name: Tayami. No
one had ever asked her if she owned a Tayami notebook.

She tried to call Randy Franklin's office. No answer.
Maybe his temp had fled once she saw his broken file cabinet. His voice mail mentioned a cell phone number. She

tried that as well. No answer. She didn't leave a message. What would she say? *Hey, I stole your files, can you answer some questions on them for me?*

She turned to the phone pages. The FBI number. She dialed it. She got an automated answer, instructing her to press the appropriate button to channel her call. She finally got an operator.

"My dad called this number before he died," Jane said, her voice tentative, uncertain. "I mean, a few weeks before he died. I'm wondering if maybe he was trying to report a crime. His name was Brent Norton. Do you know if there was a record that he called?"

"When did he call?" The operator sounded sympathetic.

She gave the date on the record. "I just don't know why he'd call the FBI." Her voice broke. "They said he died in an accident cleaning his gun and I just don't know if that's true. He tried to call the Secret Service, too."

"I'm sorry for your loss. We get lots of calls," the operator said. "What's your name and your number? I can see if I can find a record of his call in our database. And if so, we can call you back."

She gave it to her, but then she realized she had just described her father, tearfully, as if he were a crank caller: calling governmental agencies and then dying from a gun mishap. She hung up. She started to dial the Secret Service number and then she hung up, too. He had called them just once, not again. Had he lost his nerve? Why would he have only called once? Maybe these spreadsheets weren't enough proof, without knowing what the entries meant.

She tucked the files back in her bag. She didn't even know where to start with the financial files. She needed another line of attack while she figured out what to do about the spreadsheets.

Pressing Adam had already spilled some secrets about that night. She couldn't grill Trevor while he worked at the coffee shop. But she could talk to Amari Bowman, over at the University of Texas. She had her number in her phone from her earlier rebuffed attempt to communicate.

She texted Amari: I know you don't want to talk to me but I MUST talk to you. Meet me at the Littlefield Fountain at noon.

She got a fast reply: CAN'T.

She texted back: MUST. PLEASE.

Jane took a deep breath and wrote: I will camp my home-less ass in front of your sorority house. I literally have nothing to do but to bug and annoy you. Talk to me for fifteen minutes and I'll leave you alone.

Five minutes passed. Then the phone: Fine. Fountain at noon.

She didn't want to take a rideshare car to the UT cam-pus. Her mother, she knew, was tracking the charges and destinations, and she didn't want to explain. But her mother's office wasn't far from the park—a ten-minute walk—and she could borrow her car. Or take it and leave a note. Laurel seemed to spend most of her hours on the phone at the charity office. She walked, the history of her father and David thumping against her shoulder. The office of her mom's charity—Helpful Hands Reaching Out—was in a quiet park of restored bungalows that dated back from when Lakehaven was first settled.

The sign on the small pink house read HHRO. She opened the door; there was only her mother and a part-time assistant working there. Her mother had run it for nearly ten years now, as a job that still allowed her time to create her mom blog. And when Brent's business with Cal failed, it had been her mom's charity job that had kept the Nortons from having to tap into savings to stay afloat.

Laurel's assistant, Grant, wasn't at his desk but she could hear her mother's voice, talking quietly in her office. "Well, I hear Grant, back with our lattes . . ." Laurel said.

Jane waited a moment and then stepped into the open doorway.

Laurel sat at her desk, her gaze going immediately to Jane, her smile freezing, and Kamala Grayson turning to face her, the inevitable, sugared smile creeping onto her face.

33

‎

PERRI MET HIM at a bar where they'd met once before, when Matteo Vasquez had written the second of the "Girl Who Doesn't Remember" stories. That one had focused on the connections between the two families, and Perri had felt it made her look a bit petty and vindictive, when she had said nothing that hadn't been kind and forgiving. But Vasquez had a way of making one's words take on color and an edge she didn't want the world to see. Or maybe she had to be more careful about her tone. She had decided that she wouldn't help him with the third interview, but he was done with her anyway. A back part of her mind had thought he'd write about her lost boy and that rotten Norton girl forever. And of course he wouldn't. She'd had no mind for strategy back in those grief-crippled days; now her thoughts fell into place with a cold certainty. So he wouldn't be able to twist hers, or Liv Danger's, words in a way that made her look bad.

He didn't look so good himself. Vasquez sat in a back

booth with what looked like a Bloody Mary in front of
him, a notepad, and a smartphone. He had lost weight
since the last time she saw him, and back then he had
worn pressed khakis and a nice shirt, looking the part of
the polished reporter. Today he wore scruffy jeans and an
old flannel shirt and a Round Rock Express cap that had
a worn brim. He needed a shave. She realized as he stood
to shake her hand that he needed a shower. The polished
journalist was gone.

"Mr. Vasquez."

He gestured across the booth. "Thank you for coming,
Mrs. Hall."

She sat. A waitress approached and Perri glanced at his
drink.

"It's a Virgin Mary," he said.

"I'll have the same," she said. Although she had just
been sent home from her job and there was a crazy man accusing her of arson and theft and she could use a drink, she
wasn't ready to start before lunch. Not yet.

"How are you?" he asked.

"Fine. You're no longer with the paper?"

"Downsized. I'm freelance now." He said this like it
was a good thing, but she could hear a tension beneath his
words.

"What does that even mean?"

"It means I'm on social media a lot, posting supershort
news bits. Looking for a topic to write about or an interesting person to interview."

"You said you got an e-mail about me?"

"You still live next door to Jane Norton."

"Yes."

"Her memory ever come back?"

"She says not."

"I would imagine not. Liv Danger. Who is that?"

"Why are you asking me? You don't write for the paper anymore."

"But I still write, and a follow-up on the earlier stories would be interesting."

"I can't imagine that they would be."

"The e-mail I got suggested that you are conducting a vendetta campaign against people tied to the crash."

Her drink arrived and she thanked the waitress and took a sip. It was perfect and she wondered if it was the only good thing she would experience today.

"Well, that's ridiculous."

He slid a piece of paper to her. "This is the e-mail. I've had no luck tracing who sent it."

She read it:

Mr. Vasquez:

Having written so much about the Hall and Norton families you should know that I suspect a campaign is being waged against people involved in the crash by a woman calling herself Liv Danger and that woman is really Perri Hall, who blames the world for her son's death instead of blaming herself, as she should.

She attacked Jane Norton at her son's grave (see attached video, posted to Faceplace). Her son's gravestone had ALL WILL PAY written on it. I think she did that to take suspicion off herself.

Brenda Hobson, who was a responding paramedic at the crash, had her house burned down. The surrounding houses were burned down as well. There was no reason for anyone to target Ms. Hobson, and the burning of the other houses was done as a cover, easy since they were all unoccupied. Gasoline and rags in bottles are not hard to do.

Shiloh Rooke, the other paramedic, had film of an embarrassing personal nature taken from his home and mailed to his girlfriend. Again, not a hard thing to do if you follow or watch someone for a few days to determine who is important to them and what their weakness might be.

Randy Franklin, the private investigator hired by the Halls after the crash, has left town and shut down his office this week. Try calling him; his voice mail greeting now says he's closing his office. See if he talks to you. See if phone records show that Perri Hall called him this week.

You might also check her computer history to see what Faceplace pages her computer accessed at certain interesting times.

If I were Jane Norton, the person Perri Hall blames most, I would be scared.

Maybe you should write about that.

    "You can't be serious," Perri said. She took a sip of the Virgin Mary and pushed the e-mail back to him. "That's a hatchet job with no proof."

    "If I call these people and talk to them, and ask them about this, what do you think they'll say? There is a pattern here."

    "My husband talked to the Hobson woman," she said, but as soon as she said the phrase, she realized it sounded haughty, unkind—like someone who might indeed blame others for the misfortune of her life. This was a woman who tried to save her son's life. Vasquez looked at her like he was thirsty for her words. "I mean…he talked to Ms. Hobson. He drove down there with Jane Norton and talked to her. So, if I were doing this, as this ridiculous letter claims, I don't think my husband would be going and talking to the supposed targets."

"Are you still married? I heard you filed for divorce."

"I did, but it's not final yet. Nothing is final."

"Ah."

"I am not waging some battle."

"You attacked Jane Norton."

"I had no idea that she would be there. I couldn't plan that. These other crimes, they took planning. It doesn't fit together."

"That's a pretty weak defense."

"And this is an asinine accusation to make against a grieving mother." She stood. "I'm not going to listen to any more."

"I'm going to talk to Hobson and Rooke and try to find Franklin. As well as the other sources from back then. If there's no story, there's no story. But if there is, well, it's a huge one. You sure you don't want to talk to me?"

"I have nothing to say about this, Matteo." She softened her tone, although every bone in her body was thrumming with anger. "Someone is setting me up. I'm not doing this. I'm not capable of it."

"The video."

"That was a moment's madness. You don't have children; you don't know what it's like."

"I seem to remember the Nortons saying that the suicide note couldn't be real, either. Not a real indication of Jane's mental health."

She took a deep breath. "Hardly comparable."

"Oh, I think someone wants me to compare them."

A new fear crept its way up her spine. "Are you going to go to the police with this?"

"No. Not yet. I don't have any evidence of any connection. Only a pattern. A pattern's not enough." He cleared his throat. "Of course, if I found evidence, I'd have to be a responsible citizen."

"Please don't do this. Please."

"I'm giving you a chance to comment on the record, Mrs. Hall."

"Then I'll say I did not do this. I haven't."

"Then who do you think did?"

She had a decided opinion on that. "I don't know. Like you said, it would take evidence. We don't even know if there's a connection. But I'd trace that e-mail if I were you. Whoever is accusing me is most likely the guilty party. Ask yourself why they didn't sign it or send it from an account that would tell you who they are."

"Maybe they're afraid."

"Of me?"

Matteo Vasquez watched her. "May I call you for quotes if I find additional information?"

She nodded. "But this isn't anything that leads to me. You're wasting your time."

"I have a lot of it to waste."

Pay him, she thought. *Pay him not to write the story. He's giving you a hint to make this go away.* "I'm sorry to hear you've fallen on hard times."

He shrugged.

How did you bribe someone? She had no idea. Cal would know how to do this. She wanted to ask him, but she didn't want Cal to know. He'd say, *Bad idea, it will blow over.* Well, he wasn't being accused of being a nut.

He watched her. She fidgeted. "Did you want to tell me something, Mrs. Hall?"

No. She wouldn't pay him. It would only make things worse for her to offer. "No. But maybe I'll find out who is behind this, and then that's your story. Someone terrorizing a woman who lost her son. Will that get enough clicks to feed you and house you?"

He didn't answer.

She left, and tried to slam the door of the nearly deserted bar, but it was the kind that shut itself slowly. The daylight was harsh against her eyes and she stumbled to her car.

Her phone buzzed. Three text messages. All from friends, all saying, You should check Faceplace. And I'm so sorry.

Fingers trembling, she did. The video of her grabbing Jane and hauling her toward the grave had...exploded across Faceplace. What was the word she'd heard used at work: viral? Someone she knew had shared it to their page, more had followed, until a gossipy news site with ten thousand followers did so and it began to be widely shared. Blogs and online articles had been written about it, not always accurate. People had started leaving comments on her own page:

You're horrible.

Don't blame you, I'd have half beaten that girl, too, if she killed my son.

I understand she was in the car wreck with your son, but this is wrong. You need to find Jesus, He will bring you peace.

She shouldn't be visiting your son's grave, give her a punch for me.

Wrong. Even if you're grieving, this is wrong. As a mother you know this. Did it bring your son back? Did it make you feel better? Get some help.

What is wrong with you?

She trembled. The ease of strangers, commenting on her life, saying things they'd not say to her face. She could only imagine what would happen if Matteo Vasquez wrote a story about this now, and now he had even more reason to write it. To strike while the iron was hot. He'd get more views, more clicks. Wasn't that the name of the game now? Truth and nuance be damned.

Who sent that e-mail?

34

"JANE. HELLO."

"Hello, Mom." Jane's gaze didn't waver from Kamala. *What are you doing here? Why are you talking to my mom?* All those questions wanted to burst forth from her. Instead she just stared, helpless and at a loss for words. She hated the way she always seemed to freeze around Kamala, stumble for her footing.

"Jane. How are you today? Better?" Again with the Kamala-smile that seemed to fool the world. Why couldn't the world see what she saw?

Because you sound crazy when you talk about her this way. You do her work for her.

"I'm fine, Kamala, how are you?" Jane said. "Sorry, Mom, I guess I should have called first. I didn't realize you were busy."

"Kamala just wanted to talk to me about charity involvement with her sorority at UT. Doing a fund-raiser."

"I know your mom is doing such good work and I just thought maybe we could be of help to her," Kamala said.

"That's generous. Mom, maybe call me later? I'll be back at home," she lied. She forced a civil smile on her face. *She will not make me crack.* "Nice to see you, Kamala. So kind of you to help my mom."

"Well," Kamala said, modestly, "someone has to."

Jane nodded, her face burning, and she closed the door. She took a deep breath. Then she saw her mother's purse behind Grant's desk—she'd probably told him to dig the money out to pay for her and Kamala's lattes—and she, without thought, knelt, grabbed the keys to her mother's Volvo, and went out the door.

"Jane..." her mother called. Jane slid the keys into her pocket. Kamala followed Laurel out of the office.

"What?"

"Kamala and I will finish our meeting later. I can tell you're upset."

"Does everyone have to talk to me like I'm a toddler?"

"I'm not."

Jane pulled the keys out and gave them to her mother. "I was going to borrow your car, but you'll need it." She glanced at Kamala. "Are you going back to campus?"

"Um, yes, I am."

"Jane, let's talk," Laurel said.

"No, not right now." She turned her own wavering smile onto Kamala and decided to dose her with her own medicine. "Would you be an absolute gem and give me a ride to UT? There's someone there I need to see."

For the barest moment Kamala stared as if Jane had spat on her. For just a millisecond Jane thought she saw behind the smiling armor. Then Kamala nodded and said, "It would be my pleasure."

"Who are you going to see at UT?" Laurel said.

"I've had more memories returning," Jane said. "Dr.

Ngota suggested I talk to a researcher there." The lie was easier than breathing.

"Isn't that wonderful," Kamala said. "Fingers crossed that soon you'll be normal!" And she crossed her fingers and held them up and Jane thought, *They look easier to break that way*.

"Great. I'll talk to you later, Mom. Thanks, Kamala."

* * *

Kamala's ride was an Audi, new, elegant, *midnight black as her heart*, Jane thought. Kamala drove along the winding length of Old Travis back toward Austin.

"Why are you really going to UT? Did you get chased off campus at Saint Mike's?" Her voice thrummed like a wire, ready to break. The mask didn't have to stay on so securely when it was just the two of them.

She'd heard. Jane thought maybe people in Lakehaven would have found new topics for gossip.

"I didn't, but thanks for asking."

"No, really, why are you going to UT?"

"Why were you meeting with my mother?"

"We told you."

"Bull. There are any number of charities around town for you to impress. My mom's too small for your network."

"I just want to help people, Jane."

"You're an inspiration." Jane looked heavenward. "If only I could be as good as you."

"Jane, look. She sent out an e-mail to people you knew in high school"—Jane noted the word *friends* wasn't used—"because she is worried about you. She is trying to help you, believe it or not." And now, stopped at a red light, Kamala looked at her without pretense. The way she had when they had been friends, laughing, watching TV together, sharing books, doing math and writing papers and battling through Spanish. "Why don't you let your poor, scared mom do something to actually help you?"

"Like you wanted to help me."

"I'm not your mother. She'll never see you for what you are. She'll never believe you tried to kill yourself and you messed it up, so David died. She doesn't know what you really are—the piece of trash I know you to be. She has nothing left but you, and that sucks for her, but maybe you should just let her help you. Instead of wandering around Lakehaven looking ridiculous, looking like a laughingstock."

"What did I do to you?"

The world's least-patient eye roll. "You killed David."

"No. No. This is something between you and me. Has nothing to do with anyone else."

"I didn't realize amnesia sharpened intuition. It seems to dull everything else." She steered onto MoPac, the main ribbon of highway that ran along Austin's west side, and headed north, zooming over the bridge that spanned Lady Bird Lake.

"I don't remember what I did," Jane said, "and you seem to take a sadistic delight in that."

Kamala was silent.

"It's just the two of us. No one else. You can take off the mask."

Kamala glanced at her. "I don't have a mask."

It was, Jane thought, a sad confession. "You must be a little afraid of me, then."

"I'm not. I'm the one driving and the cliffs are to our west." She took the exit for Windsor, which would turn into Twenty-Fourth Street and take them straight to the

Texas campus. "Fine. You were a real bitch after your father died."

"I was grieving."

"You don't even remember it. I'm sorry your dad died. He was a sweet man. He was a second dad to me." Here her voice trembled. "David and I and all your friends tried to do everything for you. Anything to help you. You wouldn't take it. You shoved everyone away. You were horrible to me, and you can either believe that or not. Except David. You just used your father's death to eclipse everything in David's life. You just turned into this . . . huge sucking neediness and he thought he had to be the one to fix you." She wouldn't look at Jane. "Yeah, grief, whatever. Does it take over everyone else's life? My parents told me I had to be such a friend to you. I spent all this time with you and you never got better. I get it, your dad, OK. But my grades suffered. I couldn't sleep for worrying that you were going to hurt yourself. I'm not a therapist, I was a kid. Your mother was useless. It was the rest of us, trying to hold you up, and never once did you say thank you or I'll try to be happy again or anything. That's why David stepped back from you, finally." She stopped, the words at an end like she'd run out of rope.

Jane's throat felt like concrete. "I don't know what to say."

"You won't believe me, fine. Whatever. It's all done."

"Why didn't you tell me before?"

"Because you lost your dad. Because I'm not a total bitch. And because . . . it doesn't matter. You took so much from me. I lost you, and I loved you then, and I lost David. I didn't study, I spent so much time being your amateur therapist. I didn't get into Stanford. Or Harvard. I slipped from valedictorian. My parents were so upset. I'm just a checklist to them. Accomplish this, win this…and I'm supposed to take over the world and yet I'm still supposed to be your crutch, I'm supposed to still fix you. Well, fix your damn self." She stopped the car in the middle of the road. Horns honking behind her. "Fix yourself. Either put a gun to your head like your dad did or throw yourself off the cliff, but this time alone, or get off the stupid streets and make a life for yourself."

Cars honking, voices raised in anger.

"OK," Jane said, not knowing what else to say. Jane felt sick with rage, but Kamala was talking like she never had and Jane needed to press her. Kamala drove forward.

"You were trying to find us that night. I saw the text message Randy Franklin collected for his report. Did you find us?" Jane asked.

Kamala didn't answer. *She did*, Jane thought. *She did*.

"You want me to stop being such a leech and move forward. I think knowing that might help."

"Great. Let's help. I found you," she said, her voice like a dead thing. "Yep. Sure did."

"Where?"

"I found you kissing him."

"No. I don't remember kissing him."

"You took him from me and then you killed him. You screwed him when you knew, *you knew*, that I was in love with him and I'd dated him for two years and it doesn't matter that he lived next door to you or that you knew him first. What kind of friend does what you did?" She stopped; they were on the campus now, and she eased close to the sidewalk. "You don't remember what kind of person you are? That's your blessing. You were horrible."

"So why did you pretend to care? Why did you play so nice?"

"Helping you made for a good college essay. Get out of my car."

Jane did, trembling. She walked away, setting the backpack on her shoulder. She stopped and glanced back toward Kamala, but she was gone.

Was it all a lie? It would be such pure Kamala to say all that, just to be horrible.

She and David. That Kamala wouldn't lie about.

David and I were like brother and sister, she'd once said recently. To Trevor. And he'd said, *Well, that's not quite accurate*.

Had he known as well? Is that why he'd been so uncomfortable with her? Was everyone afraid she was going to remember she was in love with the boy she'd killed? Why keep this secret from her? Or did only Kamala know, and Trevor just made a comment that she was misreading?

Was that why we were going to run off to Canada? To be together, and away from everyone? Like some stupid teenager fantasy?

What kind of person was I? Well, I got my answer. You cheated with your best friend's boyfriend. She suddenly didn't want to talk to Amari. She didn't want to know more.

She hadn't noticed the truck following her and Kamala from her mother's office. She didn't see the truck illegally park in the lot across from where she stood, or the man get out of it. He wasn't tall but he was powerfully built. Shiloh Rooke watched Jane as she walked. He followed her. She walked to a big fountain with a sculpture of running mustangs, hewn in iron. Dozens of students milled about. He leaned against a wall and watched.

35

IT HAD EXPLODED at a speed Perri could not have imagined.

The captions under the video read either of two ways: She was "grieving mom" or Jane was "amnesia victim"—someone beyond her circle of friends had tied her to the accident—or she was "daughter of famed mom blogger." She could see Laurel being behind a bit of self-promotion; she had kept an eye on Laurel's mom blog in the months after the crash, alert for the barest hint that Laurel was looking to excuse Jane from David's death with self-indulgent entries or pleas for understanding.

As "grieving mom" she was trending on both Faceplace and Cheeper. Soon the phone would ring, unwanted calls. Her phone beeped. She wasn't going to answer it unless it was Cal, but then she saw it was Ronnie Gervase, who had called her before. Who had hugged her at breakfast before the cemetery incident and reminded her of the fund-raiser gala meeting.

"Hello, Ronnie."

"Hon, how are you?" *Voice soft as silk. A silk garrote*, Perri thought.

"I'm all right. This is embarrassing."

"Of course it is. I just wish I was there to give you a hug."

"Thank you."

"Listen, hon, the board of directors have called me and they are so grateful to you for all you've done for the education fund-raiser gala—you have been fabulous—but I think they think it best if you take a step back."

Such vague, inoffensive language. She closed her eyes. "This will blow over. You know the Internet. All eyes on something new tomorrow."

"I do, of course, but they don't. It's just not the look they want for a gala. You understand."

She felt hollowed out. "Do I need to resign publicly?"

"Oh, no, they'll handle the wording. We had a couple of sponsors call who got itchy about staying in, and you know what they're like. One pulls out, they all start to run. We all just want you to rest and feel better."

Like she was some sort of Victorian hysteric, or ill, when she was just mad. Why couldn't she be mad? She shouldn't have pulled Jane from the car, but why was everyone forgetting that Jane—through either intent or recklessness—killed her son?

"You know, Ronnie, whatever. Good luck with the gala."

"Don't be that way."

"Stop telling me how to be. Go run your gala."

"All right, Perri. All right. I'm so sorry."

"No, you're not." Perri hung up before Ronnie could offer another platitude.

She sat down, heavily. Her husband, siding with the enemy. Job in danger. Her volunteer career—which had nurtured so many of her friendships in Lakehaven over the years—wrecked. Lakehaven was slow to forgive; and she had taken a particular pleasure in that when it was the Nortons feeling the stings and snubs of Lakehaven.

She found her notes on the gala and ripped them from the little spiral notebook, as well as the calendar page for the gala, and she shredded them with her hands until the paper all lay like torn confetti at her feet. She deleted the board's phone numbers from her phone, Ronnie's as well, and all the e-mails tied to the event. Her breathing was harsh and sharp. Screw them. She tried to call Randy Franklin. No answer. She tried his office. Just a standard voice mail, but on it he said his office was indefinitely closed.

She could not just sit here and let the Nortons burn her life down.

Proof was a good thing, but maybe Perri could just scare Laurel out of chasing this revenge. She went and got the Liv Danger notebook from where she'd hidden it. She went back downstairs and sat near a window where she could see the garage. She began to page through the notebook, studying her son's art and Jane's storytelling, glancing up from the page every minute.

Laurel's garage was closed, but she could see Laurel, through a window, talking on her phone. Then she vanished from sight, and a few moments later the garage door went up.

Perri hurried to her own car and tossed the notebook on the passenger seat. Following Laurel wouldn't be easy: of course they knew each other's cars, and Laurel would notice that Perri left when she did.

Laurel's red Volvo drove through the circle and turned left. Perri roared out of her driveway, nearly clipping the

decorative limestone edging, and followed. Ahead she saw
Laurel turning onto Kelmont, and then again onto Old
Travis. Perri followed. There were three other cars between
her and Laurel, for which she was suddenly grateful.
Maybe Laurel wouldn't notice. Or maybe Laurel would
give up this insanity now that she must know that Perri was
onto her.

Her phone buzzed, again and again. At the red lights or
stop signs she would glance at the list of callers. Friends
and acquaintances calling, probably because they had seen
the video, some genuinely wanting to comfort her, and others, less noble, wanting to hear the tone of her voice, to see
how she was, to listen in sympathy and be secretly glad it
wasn't them. Embarrassment always drew a crowd.

Laurel merged onto MoPac, heading north, across Lady
Bird Lake, toward downtown and the University of Texas.
Perri followed, trying to keep back but also trying not to
lose her.

The phone rang again. Playing a particular piece of music. "Toxic," by Britney Spears. A ringtone tied to a number
she had never deleted from her phone. A song she and Laurel had once sung together at a mom's weekend a few years
back in Vegas, before she lost David; she'd given the six
women on the trip each a different Britney song for their
ringtone. "Toxic" for Laurel. She had no idea it was such
an appropriate choice.

She hit the icon on the car screen that answered the
phone.

"Perri, why are you following me?"

"I know you're behind this."

"Behind what? By the way, you might be hearing from
my lawyer, given your assault on my daughter."

"I don't think so. Because a lawsuit would mean you

and Jane both testifying under oath and I'm not sure you're quite ready for perjury. It's easier to prove than arson or theft."

"Your problems have nothing to do with me. Stop following me, or I'll call the police and tell them you are harassing me."

"I'm driving on a public road. I have every right."

"How does it feel?" Laurel asked after three beats of silence. "To be blamed? For everyone to mock you, to think the worst of you, to not want to hear your side of the story?"

"I knew it. This is you. You're mental. Burning down that woman's house. Destroying that man's marriage, and he's a nutcase, he'll come for you and your daughter. You have let one crazy genie out of the bottle." And then she saw the solution to her problem.

"I don't know what you're talking about. But stop following me."

"Fine. I will." And she took the next exit, into a heavily wooded older neighborhood.

"And stay away from my daughter."

"I know where the name Liv Danger comes from. Jane knows it. She remembers it. You're both liars of the worst sort."

"I don't know what you mean and you won't be able to hurt her for long," Laurel said.

"Did you just threaten me?"

"You're the one following me and you feel threatened? Maybe I'm driving to David's grave to put flowers on it. You want to come beat me up? I fight back." Laurel hung up.

Oh, I fight back, too, Perri thought. *I'm going to aim a weapon of mass destruction at you and your lying daugh-*

ter. She parked in the lot of a small coffee shop. She searched the Internet for Shiloh Rooke, found an address for him on the county's property tax rolls website, and drove to his house. It was a modest ranch house from the 1960s, in the Northwest Hills neighborhood.

It was time for them to face their common enemy.

36

UT WAS FAR bigger than St. Michael's, and Jane thought there might be a kind of wonderful anonymity here. Just so many kids, thousands upon thousands. You could hide here. Maybe she should try school again at a bigger campus than St. Mike's, where it would be less nerve-racking for her to reboot her life.

"Amari? Hi."

"Jane." Amari looked up from her phone. "Whatever this is, let's make it fast. I've got somewhere to be."

"It's about the accident."

"Did you remember it all now?" Funny how interested other people were in her memories. Or lack thereof. Or that amnesia seemed like an illness that wasn't permanent, like a bad flu.

"I wanted to ask you about that day in class."

"I don't really remember much either."

"Well, you do more than me." Jane forced herself to offer a bright smile. It didn't work. Amari stared at her. "You saw David pass me a note in class, right? But you didn't read the note."

"No, I didn't read it. Obviously."

"Then you saw us that night and texted Kamala about it."

"I thought she would want to know."

"She said they'd broken up."

"So? You were her best friend, Jane." She'd broken a code among friends: no dating the ex-boyfriend, at least not immediately.

"And David was my neighbor. I wasn't dating him." She thought she'd test Amari, see if she knew what Kamala had said.

"I know that. But you looked very intense. I mean, c'mon. I'm not justifying this to you," Amari said. "If your ex—and they'd only been broken up for a few days—was being all cozy with one of your best friends, you would want to know. Don't say you wouldn't."

"All right. Did you hear what we were talking about?"

"Uh, no. I made eye contact with David and he shot me a laser look, so I didn't."

"Did you talk to Trevor or Adam when they came in?"

"Only for a second. Adam was looking for you. So was Trevor. He was frantic."

"Frantic?"

"I guess he had something important to talk to you about. I didn't realize you two were so tight."

Why would he be upset? "Do you know why?"

"No."

"Did you ever hear that David and I were going to take off to Canada?"

Amari laughed. "No. That's a new one on me."

"Are you still friends with Trevor?"

"Sure. Yeah." She glanced at her watch. "He's picking me up in a few. I'm helping him with something."

"His party?" Jane asked.

"Yes. You coming?" She sounded a little surprised Jane knew.

"No, I wasn't invited." Then Jane quickly added, "Which is fine. I don't really go much to parties."

Amari didn't invite her, either. "Well, he should be here soon." She looked at the street, as if she had nothing more to say.

"Are you and Trevor dating?"

Amari raised an eyebrow. "Oh, no. We're just friends. My boyfriend, Derek, is at the community college with Trevor. But I don't keep a car here, and Derek and Trevor were going to pick me up so we could get food and beer and..." Her voice trailed off.

Jane pressed on: "I did talk to Trevor the other day at the coffee shop. I know we were friends when we were little. He was going to help me try to remember the night of the crash." *Yeah, big help he's been. Notice how you haven't heard from him.*

"Jane, is there anything else you want from me?" Amari asked. "If not..."

"I think I want to warn you," Jane said. "Someone went after the two paramedics who tended to David and me. The detective who investigated the crash for the Halls has gone missing. Or at least is not answering my phone calls and is not in his office."

Amari's mouth went thin in a frown. "That's crazy."

"Anyone who seems to be on the fringes of this story, they should be careful."

Amari blinked. "But I did nothing, why would anyone blame me? It was your fault."

"I think it's Mrs. Hall. The suicide note I wrote was written months before. She and Mr. Hall kept that quiet. Would that have changed your opinion about me or the crash if you knew that?"

Amari's frown didn't move. "I don't know. Maybe."

"Once suicidal, always suicidal?"

"Well, no, of course not." She crossed her arms. "You think Mrs. Hall is attacking people?"

Jane explained about Liv Danger and showed her the video on her phone of Mrs. Hall pulling her from the car and hitting her. "Oh, wow," Amari said.

"I don't think she'll bother you. But... her grief, I mean, it's consumed her. One paramedic had her house burned down. And the empty houses around her."

"You're not joking?"

"No. I'm not. She claims I'm doing this, I think it's her. I don't even have a car to drive to San Antonio and commit arson. She has the resources and the motive." She put a hand on Amari's arm. "If there is anything you remember or that you can tell me..."

"Um. Well. I stayed at Happy Taco for a while. I liked to study there. Mr. Hall came in, also looking for you and David. I didn't text him, I wouldn't have, but I think Kamala must have."

Cal must have come in after the video footage ended. "Did you talk to him?"

"No. I don't really know him. I recognized him from the football games. Kamala had pointed him out to me."

Cal Hall, also in search of them. But only Kamala had found them. "Thanks, Amari."

"Oh. There's Trevor. I got to go. Take care, Jane. I hope... I hope you feel better soon." Like the amnesia was a cold to get over. Amari hurried over to the road, where a large black truck waited for her, tinted windows, one of them sliding down to show Trevor Blinn and another guy— her boyfriend, probably—watching Amari hurry over to them.

Black truck. Large black truck. Like what Brenda Hobson had seen turning off High Oaks as the ambulance turned onto it to reach the crash site.

Trevor held up a hand in an uncertain wave. Jane stood, held up her phone, and carefully snapped a picture of the truck. Amari climbed in and Jane could see Trevor asking her a question. Glancing back with surprise at Jane. Then he drove off.

Jane texted the photo to Brenda. Is this like the truck you remembered?

The answer came five minutes later. Yes, it's that kind of truck.

There were many black trucks in Texas. But there was only one driven by someone who had been actively searching for her and David that night.

She summoned a rideshare, was told it would take ten minutes to reach her, and so she pulled the file on her father again from her backpack and looked through it.

She found an envelope taped to the back of one of the photo sheets. She hadn't noticed it before.

She opened it. Inside was a single photo of her mother and Cal Hall, kissing under an eave, standing in the shadow of a door. Her mother's hand was along Cal's jawline, and he was gathering her close to him for the embrace, his fingers tangled in her hair, pulling her close.

She stared at it for a long minute.

Where was this? She knew it but she couldn't place it. The date stamp on the picture was two months before her father died.

She stared at the picture a long time. She could go straight to her mother and ask. Or go to Cal. Or go to Perri, and knife her in the heart with it. Hurt her like she'd hurt Jane.

Instead she put it in her backpack.

"You're Jane Norton," the voice behind her said.

She looked behind her. A man stood there. Thick arms, dark hair, a mouth like a slash. For a second she thought she shouldn't say anything. But instead she said, "Yes."

"I'm Shiloh Rooke. I was one of the paramedics that saved your life." His voice was low and smoky.

"Oh. Yes. Thank you." The man Perri warned her about when she brought the coffee. She didn't want to thank him, didn't want to talk to him, but it seemed rude not to and she could tell he expected it from her.

"I appreciate your kind thanks," he said. "But I've had some misfortune that seems tied to your bad experience."

She shoved the file back into the backpack, zipped it closed. "I have to go, a ride is coming for me…"

"I can give you a ride. We can talk about Cal and Perri Hall."

"I don't really have anything to say…"

"Weren't you asking that girl about the Halls? The night of the crash?"

She realized with a shock that he must have sat close to them; with so many students walking by, she hadn't noticed. "You think Mrs. Hall burned down Brenda's house. You think she ruined my engagement. You think she made Randy Franklin disappear."

"I don't know what she's done."

"You showed that girl something on your phone. What was it?"

"Mrs. Hall attacking me at her son's grave." She rallied

her courage; she did not want to look into those eyes of his anymore. There was nothing looking back; under the muscle and the strength she could feel the emptiness of him.

"Show me," he said.

"My ride is coming..."

"Show me, Jane, please."

She did. He watched the video in silence. "Well, she seems not well."

"David's grave had been defaced with the words 'ALL WILL PAY,' she was upset."

"If she's come after me, and Brenda, and this investigator dude, like you said, where do you think she stops? Who is she warming up for? Who gets it in the end?"

Jane stuffed the phone back in her pocket.

"You? Your mama? They sure hate your mama."

The rideshare car pulled up. "I have to go," Jane said.

"They're coming for you, Jane," he said. "Maybe you and I can do something about that. Don't you want to make that bitch pay?"

"Pay?" she asked, her hand on the car door.

"I read the articles. The 'Girl Who Doesn't Remember.' I read how she treated you and your mama after the wreck. Outcasts in your own town. Blamed, suicidal supposedly, her boy a saint, you a waste. Wouldn't you like to make them pay for what they did to you?"

"I just want to remember. That's all I want. Just to remember." Jane opened the door.

"They'll come for you. 'All will pay,' right? How are they going to make you pay?" He leaned close to her as she got into the car, holding the door before she could shut it. "What more can they do to you? They've taken everything from you. What's left?"

She felt cold and sick. The pictures of Laurel kissing

Cal swam up before her eyes, and she slammed the door and the driver pulled away from the curb. Jane looked back through the window.

Shiloh Rooke was watching her, his hand held up to his face, miming a phone.

37

———————

Jane waited for Kip Evander, the Halls' attorney, in the parking lot, where she'd had the rideshare driver drop her off. She had seen his car once before, when he came to the Halls' house and her mom had told her, "That's their lawyer." She knew he had a daughter a year younger than Jane, at the high school, but Jane didn't remember her.

"Mr. Evander?"

The man walking toward the BMW, studying his phone's screen, glanced up. He had a kind face, brown hair, stylish eyeglasses, and wore a very good gray suit. "Yes? Oh. Ms. Norton." He sounded surprised.

"You know me." She risked a smile.

He smiled back, but very briefly before returning to an utterly neutral look. "I recognize you." He paused. "How are you doing?"

"I'm all right," she said. "I wonder if you could talk to me for a minute about the car crash and the lawsuit."

"Ethically, I can't really disclose anything related to a client matter."

"Please. I don't want you to tell me a secret or any-thing." She coughed, trying to cover her nervousness. "I just was wondering if you knew why the Halls dropped the lawsuit and settled for the insurance proceeds." *Because Cal Hall is kissing my widowed mother.*

"Usually I advise all my clients to do that, especially in a case like this, one involving a minor driver." He had a good voice for the courtroom, a Southern-tinged, theatrical baritone.

"I know Cal dropped it and Perri didn't want to, but I don't know why."

He looked at her with sympathy. Not pity. Those were two different states. He blew out a long breath. "Grieving parents sometimes think a lawsuit will bring justice. Then they realize it won't, because justice would be their child restored to them. I think Cal didn't want to ruin you and your mother, given what you'd already been through with your father's passing. It wouldn't have brought David back."

"I wondered if it wasn't because there was some history between Cal and my mom. Like, you know"—she let the pause carry a weight—"an affair."

"I certainly couldn't say." His gaze was steady on her. "I need to get home to my family now."

"Because my family had a note, too. One David wrote to me, expressing that he was in danger on the day he died. I haven't had it analyzed." She made dramatic little air quotes around the last word. "But maybe the Halls didn't really want the world to know that David was in a serious bit of trouble. Maybe my mom told Mr. Hall, and you, that note existed and that's why he dropped the lawsuit. Could you nod yes or shake your head no?"

He was still. Then he said, "Such a note, if it existed,

would have had limited legal value. It would have been hard to enter into evidence."

She gave a ragged, soft sigh. "See, Mr. Evander, it's a little disconcerting to know my own mother had physical evidence that could have, you know, maybe not cleared my name but it could have made all of my friends hate me a little less or even a lot less"—here her voice broke—"and she didn't let the world know about it. I'm thinking the only reason she didn't is because there was a deal. A trade-off. No lawsuit, no note." She crossed her arms.

"You really should ask your mother, Jane."

"She won't tell me. And I don't have a whole lot of peace of mind, but I would like to know the answer to this. I'm not going to do anything with it, except know it. If you can tell me. Ethically."

"I cannot say." He cleared his throat. "I could say that your mother met with Cal Hall in this parking lot before he came in to meet with me. I could see them from my office window. There was a discussion. She left. Cal stood for a long time in that lot, then he came in to meet with me. That was the same afternoon Cal dropped the lawsuit. Make of that what you will."

There was a relief in knowing. "One other question. Randy Franklin. Is he the type of man to investigate someone without a client?"

"You mean just snoop?"

Jane nodded. "In hopes of finding compromising information."

"Are you asking me if he's a blackmailer?"

"I don't know what to call it. He might call it insurance."

"Then I would guess that the rumor he has some dangerous clients is true and you should stay away from him. Just a guess."

"Thank you, Mr. Evander. Have a nice evening with your family."

"You're welcome, Jane. I hope life improves for you soon."

It was an odd parting wish.

Kip Evander got into his BMW sedan, started it up, and drove away from her in the lot, never looking back at her.

She decided she needed to get home. She had a party to crash.

38

PERRI HAD NEARLY dozed off in the car when knuckles rapped hard against the driver's-side window.

Shiloh Rooke.

"You here to burn down my house?" he drawled.

"No," she said, rallying herself awake. "I tried your doorbell and you weren't home. So I waited. May we talk?"

"What do you want?"

"I want to convince you I'm not the bad guy here. I'm not this Liv Danger."

"And why would I believe that?"

"Listen, if I were coming after you because I bore a grudge against you for not saving my son's life, I wouldn't have just stopped at breaking up your engagement. You'd have a knife in your guts." She tried to sound tough.

He laughed. "Oh, sure, Mrs. Lakehaven. You're a real badass."

"I know you think this is about you. And Brenda Hobson, and whoever else worked the crash. But it's not. It's about me. You're just an innocent victim. Like me."

He raised an eyebrow.

"I can prove it to you," she said.

"Let's go inside and talk about it," he said. "I make a real good iced tea."

She didn't want to be alone with him. He was barely taller than she was, but he was powerfully built. The way he smiled at her made her skin crawl.

"What's that?" he asked as she brought the notebook with her.

"Proof," she said.

He shrugged and walked into the house, her following. "You want iced tea?"

She didn't but she said sure. This had clearly been his parents' house; photos of the family were still on the mantel, in the hallway. The parents must be dead, she realized, and now the house was his. In a photo, a man who easily could be Shiloh's brother wore an army uniform, perhaps on a tour of duty.

She followed Shiloh into the kitchen. It was orderly, immaculate, neat as a soldier's. He poured the tea from a pitcher, then added mint and lemon when she nodded. He poured his own, added a slug of Jim Beam from a bottle on the tiled counter. He raised the bottle toward her and she shook her head.

"I drank most of that when Mimi broke off the engagement," he said. "I did not get a sympathetic vibe from you or your husband this morning, Mrs. Hall. I don't think that in this moment you realize"—he smiled again—"I am the victim here."

"I do realize that. So am I."

"Yeah, you really looked helpless beating up on Jane Norton. I saw the video." The awful little smile returned. "You sure got a lot of energy."

"I know how the video looks," she said.

"Do you?" He smiled. "Look, if it's you and the husband pulling this little revenge, tell me, and I'll concentrate on him. He's just going to drag you down."

"I've already filed for divorce," she said. Why had she told him that? It only made his smile a little sharper. "And Cal would never do this. He's a CEO, an investor, he wouldn't dirty his hands or risk his reputation." She was speaking too fast, telegraphing her nerves. He seemed like a man who could scent fear on the air.

Do this for David.

"And I am not Liv Danger. It's Jane Norton and her mother."

"And I believe you why?"

She showed him the notebook with the Liv Danger cartoon character. "Jane wrote these stories; my son drew the character. They always did this kind of stuff when they were little, I guess they thought they could design a video game around her."

"And this proves what?"

"No one knew they had done this, except Jane." She showed him the title page, where David and Jane claimed authorship of Liv Danger. "My husband and I never knew about this character. Only Jane did."

"But she has amnesia. Why would she remember this cartoon character?"

"It's a lie. Or it was a lie, until her memory came back. Or she has her own set of Liv Danger drawings and knows the name."

"Talented kids," he said, paging through the images. "Where did you find this, since only Jane knows about this character?"

"Hidden. On the top shelf of my son's room. I couldn't

bear to change anything in the room after he died. I never threw out any of his stuff. She must have thought that he had tossed the notebook."

He shut the notebook. "Or she doesn't really remember. I saw her at the wreck. Girl was hurt bad."

"Would I bring you this evidence if I was Liv Danger? It points to either me or to the Nortons. It narrows the field. I would only bring this if I'm *not* Liv." He could not find out about the postings being from her computer; it would be damning evidence.

That gave him pause. He drank his tea, watching her. She didn't like the way he stared at her; he was ten years younger than her, but he watched her with the gaze of the guy in a bar who wants to buy you a drink and you want the floor to swallow him whole.

"Or you want me to think you're not Liv."

"You could take it straight to the police."

He chewed his lip.

"Listen." She made her voice stern. "If my husband wanted revenge on you, he wouldn't steal from you and break up your engagement. He'd get your ass fired from the county; he has friends in high places. He'd plant drugs on you so you'd go to jail for a long time."

Shiloh, at this, laughed.

"But he wouldn't take your girlfriend away from you. That's small."

"Not to me it's not," Shiloh said. "So, you've had your tea and you've pled your case, Miss Perri-with-an-i. You can go now."

"I want your help proving the Nortons are behind this."

"Yeah, a girl who's got amnesia and her mother fire-bombed Brenda's house."

"Go do an Internet search on 'Laurel Norton mom blog.'

Laurel wrote this blog on raising her daughter, for years. It will show that this is a woman who is obsessed with her kid's image. And before the accident, there was another accident: her husband supposedly died cleaning his gun."

Now she had his attention. "Supposedly?"

"Did I stutter?" she said, and his lip curled for a moment. She forged ahead: "I always wondered. How low she would stoop. A woman who writes all about her child's private moments so she can sell stroller ads and yogurt coupons on her blog. And then she loses her husband, and then her daughter kills my son, and her perfect image of herself, the one she's broadcast to the world, is shredded. It's not fair. But it is what it is." She took a deep breath. "So now her daughter's homeless, a mental case, and why wouldn't she want revenge on everyone who's somehow contributed to her pain?" The more she spoke, the more convinced she became. This was the answer. Maybe Jane had defaced the gravestone and then gone to the cemetery hoping to run into Perri, or planning to wait for her to inevitably show up. She might have bribed the driver to take the video, or maybe it wasn't really a rideshare car at all but a friend ready to record Perri's grief and rage. And Perri had neatly put her neck into the noose of their making.

"So you think my next step is to read a mom blog?" Darkness in Shiloh's tone.

"Yes. It's called *Blossoming Laurel*. And then you'll see I'm telling you the truth."

"So let's say I believe you, Mrs. Hall. What then? Why are you telling me this instead of the police?" He asked like he already knew the answer.

"Well. You wanted to know. You could stop them."

"Me. Just little old me." The lip curled again. She saw

that it had been cut, as if by a knife, a thin, pale thread of scar. "What am I supposed to do, camp out on their lawn, follow them around?"

She took a deep breath. "You could scare them off from any more revenge, I could let you know when they're around."

"They could call the cops on me."

"They won't. Not if we can find evidence to tie them to the fire. Or to your burglary. Or to whatever they've done to Randy Franklin."

"And I find this evidence?"

"We do. And then we go to the police."

"I don't like the police."

She felt she'd wandered into a twilight zone.

"I don't want publicity. This would get publicity."

"Yes, I suppose."

"I'd rather privately convince them to stop."

"You won't hurt them."

The corner of his mouth went up. "Do you care?"

"Of course I care."

"I didn't get the impression you did."

A dark, shameful sensation rose in her chest, like a fist stretching, and she drank her tea and turned away from him for a moment. "I just want them to leave. Move away. She doesn't want to sell that house because her late husband bought it for her. I won't sell because of my son. Stalemate."

"This would break it. They lose something they want. And we do it so they can't go to the police."

"And no one gets hurt?"

"Yeah, sure. Hey, I save lives, Mrs. Hall. I'm one of the good guys."

"OK, so we have a deal."

He stepped closer to her again. "Shall we seal it?"

"I…I…" The way he was smiling at her. The way the T-shirt strained against his chest. The emptiness in his eyes. "I…"

"With a handshake," he said. "What did you think I meant?"

"Nothing. Nothing." *You've made a deal with a devil*, she thought. *Now you just have to be smarter than this particular devil.* "So what do we do?"

"I reached out to Jane this morning when I was sure you and your husband were the big bads," he said. "She thoroughly rejected my offer of help. I think she's afraid of me. But she's her mother's weakness, right? Let's figure out how to make that work for us."

"And no one gets hurt?" she asked again. Because she felt that he wanted to hurt someone. He wanted it badly.

For a moment she thought of David. Of what he would think of this. She had always stressed to him that catch-phrase of twenty-first-century parents, "Make good choices," and she'd said it to him so often—calling it at him every time he left the house, both of them laughing because obviously David would never make a bad choice—that it became a joke between them.

Make good choices.

Shiloh Rooke smiled his scarred smile at her again.

39

JANE HAD COME home, and spent a pointless two hours searching her parents' bedroom. There was nothing there that suggested an affair had happened, or was still happening, between her mother and Cal. She could not imagine they were still currently involved; surely the accident and its aftermath ended that. But her mother's insistence on refusing to sell the house now seemed shaded with other possibilities.

She had thought of shoving the picture under her mother's nose, saying, *You want to explain this?* Asking her about Kevin Ngota, although she thought it better to simply confront her mother at their meeting with Kevin. Otherwise, if she pushed the issue now, there would be no meeting with Kevin, and Kevin was trying to prove he was on her side. And she didn't want to explain how she'd gotten the file.

She tried Franklin's office number. No answer. She tried his cell, nervous that it would leave a record of her call. She didn't want to be tied to him. But she had to know, so she called, and there was no answer.

She left the picture in the file and hid the file in her room, in her closet, behind a stack of books on the shelf. She thought maybe it was better to wait and see what hand her mother played in this game between them, to keep the proof of an affair with Cal Hall as a trump card until she needed it.

Did Dad know? Did Dad know?

It couldn't still be going on. It couldn't be.

And snooping upstairs meant she didn't have to go downstairs and talk to her mother about what had happened this morning with Perri and Shiloh, and what else she had learned. What Adam had told her: that the night of the crash he'd found her mother and Perri Hall arguing. Was it about the affair?

She could hear Laurel downstairs, humming, perhaps delighted that her daughter had announced she had social plans. She really didn't want to crash the party, but if she could pour a beer down Trevor's throat and keep him off-balance, maybe he'd talk about his truck being on High Oaks at the time of the crash. He had been willing to talk to her at the coffee shop, but that didn't mean he didn't have his own secrets. His own agenda. His own guilt, perhaps. Now that she saw the guilt in others—she had been blinded by her own—she could see what a powerful force it was.

She kept wondering, *Did Dad know? Did he know? Did he die knowing his wife cheated on him? And did I know this and I'm just not remembering? Maybe I didn't just forget all my regular life. Maybe I forgot my secrets, too.*

"Mom?" she said, coming down the stairs.

"Yes, sweetheart?"

Start with the easy part. "Why was Kamala in your office today?"

"Look, I couldn't just tell her I wouldn't work with her sorority. I met with her. It was a courtesy. I know you don't like her, but you weren't going to be involved." She offered a smile, but all Jane saw was her mother in Cal Hall's arms, her palm against his jaw, like she was savoring his touch. Her mother paying Kevin to pretend to be her therapist, perhaps to help have her committed. Her mother meeting with her worst enemy.

If she told her mother everything that had happened, her mother would be hauling her off to the psychiatric hospital, "for her own protection." But Mom was in danger, too, from this Shiloh Rooke if he showed up again. So she had to tell her.

She very calmly explained about the harasser calling herself Liv Danger, the two paramedics who had been targeted, Shiloh Rooke following her to UT, Perri's insane certainty that Jane, or Laurel, or both were behind the Liv Danger name, Perri's attack on her at the grave. But she said nothing about sneaking into Franklin's office or his files or the photo of Laurel and Cal. She said nothing about Shiloh's offer to make the Halls pay for their supposed crimes. She said nothing about Kevin or what she'd learned from Adam. She was not ready to go there yet. As she finished, she still expected Laurel to call the psychiatric hospital and inquire about room availability. Instead Laurel stood and hugged her tight.

"Why didn't you tell me this before? I'll take care of it so this man doesn't bother you again."

"What?"

"Well, I'll call the police. He followed you. The police need to know."

"Yes, and he'll tell them what? He offered to help me tear down the Halls?"

"He sounds very trashy. This fiancée is better off without him."

"I don't want to talk about him. I want to talk about you. You had a note that proved that David asked me for help, and you didn't share it with anyone. Why?"

The answer was obvious to her as soon as she asked the question aloud. Her mother must have had a reason for keeping hidden the fact that David was in danger: because she was part of that danger.

The second thought was like hot iron through her brain. *It couldn't be.*

"He was in some kind of trouble," Jane said. "You found the note he wrote for me. This has always been a story of two notes, two messages. I had that note in my jeans and you got it and you kept it and you didn't tell anyone."

"Honey, the suicide note was the trump card. Nothing beat that. David's note was real vague. What, exactly, was I supposed to do with it?"

"Is that why Cal dropped the lawsuit? This note?" *Or that you were kissing him?* she thought.

"Water under the bridge, Jane. Go get ready for your party, and I hope you have a lovely time." End of discussion, her tone said.

Is this what hurt Dad so? she wondered. *Because of Cal Hall? You and his best friend, so he took his uncle's gun...? And then did my accident mess up your planned new life with him? Is that why you blame me, everyone else, for what's gone wrong with your life?* But she could not form the words, give them breath. She didn't want to believe it. Her father wouldn't have left her.

"I'll contact the police about this Shiloh person."

"And say what?" Jane said. "It could only make me look bad. We point them toward Perri; she blames me."

"That video has done her no favors."

"I don't want them investigating me."

"Jane?" her mother said. "Are you doing these things?"

Jane stared at her, turned around, and walked upstairs to get ready. She could answer her mother, she heard her asking the question again, but she thought, *Let her wonder. Let her not know. Let me have some secrets from her.*

At least while I find out hers.

40

JANE SHOWERED. SHE put on makeup. She hadn't worn mascara or lipstick in a long time, but she remembered how to do it. Her cosmetics were here, where she had left them when she walked away from her shattered life. She looked at herself in the mirror. Too often in the mirrors at St. Mike's she looked hunted, lost, forlorn—she couldn't linger, studying herself in the mirror, and there was nothing to see; now she looked like a well-to-do young woman, going to a social gathering.

She looked like who she should have been if the wreck had never happened. For one moment she reached out toward her reflection in the mirror. For the girl that was lost.

But she wasn't lost. The image of what she could be— hale, whole—was standing right in front of her. She only had to choose to work toward that image.

There could be another school. One far away. If she had the bravery to move, to pull up stakes. Her decisions had put her into limbo; her decisions alone could break her out of it.

Laurel stood in the doorway, watching her, an uncertain smile on her face. She pretended that Jane hadn't walked away from the question of being Liv Danger. "I think you look very nice. Are you sure this is a good idea?"

She had lied and told her mother that Trevor invited her. "Thanks and no."

"Then stay home."

She thought, *There's still one card that I could play. One that might drill a hole in the dam of lies.* "Adam told me he came here that night. You and Perri were arguing."

She shook her head. "No, we weren't. We were talking but not arguing. About schools, David having troubles with his girlfriend, small things. Adam misunderstood."

"What did you do that night?"

"I went looking for you when it became clear you had lied to me."

"Adam said you sent him to look for me."

"He offered to run by a few places where you all hung out. My gosh, you are making this into a production. Or Adam is. He does like to be the center of your world."

"And what about Cal Hall and lawsuits? You didn't answer my question."

Her mother's expression didn't change. "I don't know what you mean, Jane. If you have something to say, say it."

She took a step back. There was a look, a hard look, in her mother's eyes, one she hadn't seen before. *You've told her you know about the note. She's going to wonder what else you know.* "Did you ever have an affair with Cal Hall?"

"An affair. With Cal." And she had a look of abject shock on her face, then laughter. "Why on earth would you think that? I never would." And she took another step toward her daughter.

"Someone said." No way was she going to reveal the

picture. Not now. She needed a trump card for later. After the Kevin meeting. Or, better yet, during it. When her mother was trying to haul her off for commitment.

"Kamala?" Laurel asked.

Sure, why not. She was an easy target. "Yes. She hinted at it."

"And how did she think this?"

"I guess maybe David thought there was reason."

She watched Jane for a long thirty seconds. "I loved your father. I was crushed when he died. I have not been ready to date again and I might never be. So, Jane, the answer is no. I am not nor have I ever had an affair with Cal or with anyone."

There. The lie, like a blade cutting into her palm, slowly dragged. Finally a lie from the past that she could disprove when she needed to. She wanted to run out of the house and run and run and run. Instead she smiled and said, "OK, Mom, I believe you."

"That Kamala. Honestly." She said this with a mild frustration that she didn't fake well.

"She didn't say it meanly."

"She never does." She stepped forward and smoothed Jane's hair. "But don't listen to her. You sure do look nice. You should dress up more often, Jane."

41

LAUREL DROVE HER and dropped her off. Trevor lived a few miles from her place. There were pockets from Lakehaven's original development that were all ranch houses from the 1960s and 1970s, and Trevor lived in one of these, at the bottom of a downward-sloping cul-de-sac. Laurel said, "Call me when you want me to pick you up."

I hope that's not in five minutes. She had texted Adam to say, I'm crashing. Forgive me, meet me outside if you're already there. And she saw with a bolt of relief that he was standing at the end of the driveway. Behind that big black truck of Trevor's.

Laurel waved at Adam; he waved back. Jane got out of the car.

"Wow, you look great," Adam said. "You look..."

"Don't act shocked," she said.

"No, I'm not, it's just...you haven't looked like this since the accident." He swallowed, risked a smile. "You look beautiful, Jane."

She was sure she wasn't a beauty like Kamala or Amari,

but she made herself smile. "Thanks. Is Trevor going to kick me out?"

"Not with you looking like that."

"I appreciate the objectification." She watched Laurel driving off. Adam was trying too hard to lift her spirits with the compliments. Everyone, wanting her to be normal again. It made her uneasy.

"You look nice. That's all I meant."

"I know. I'm sorry. I'm so nervous. But I need to talk to you. And Trevor."

"Me? I told you everything." He ran a hand through his dark hair.

"Do you remember having lunch with my dad and me a few weeks before he died?"

"Yeah," he said. Blinking, trying to remember why this would matter.

"You never mentioned that to me."

"Lunch? What was there to mention?"

"Did you give him something at that lunch, when I wasn't around?"

"Oh, wow," Adam said. The dawn of the memory lighting his eyes. "How do you know? Did your dad tell you? Did your memory come back?"

"It doesn't matter, I know. What was it?"

"You tell me how you know something that only your dad and I knew about." His voice tightened.

"Just tell me." She wanted to grab his shoulders and shake him.

"I can't believe you know about this. Your dad asked if I or the guys in the school hacker club could break into a computer for him. I said no. But he asked again, and I said, well, I could give him a flash drive with a bunch of programs on it that could help him find whatever he needed on a computer: password breakers, a root kit, a keystroke monitor. But I'd have to know why he needed it."

Jane could hardly breathe.

"He said there was a laptop that had been passworded by an employee who'd left and he needed to get data off of it."

"That's not it, Adam. Was he wanting to crack my mom's computer?"

"Jane." He blew out a long breath. "He thought your mom was having an affair. He wanted to search her system for proof. He said if they divorced, he wanted the evidence to keep custody of you. I didn't want to be involved, I didn't. But he begged me, for your sake. I couldn't believe he told me this but he was desperate."

"And after he died, you didn't tell me this? Or did you?" For a moment her anger ebbed.

"He made me swear not to tell you. He didn't want you mad at me. So I didn't. And then the way he died...I thought maybe he found out stuff about your mom and this affair, and it was, you know, true. Or bad news. And he..." His voice trailed off, miserable. "The police said it was an accident. I didn't want you to think that he had a reason to hurt himself. It would have killed you."

She leaned back against Trevor's truck, her legs feeling weak.

"Did he ever tell you what he found?"

"Of course not. He never gave me back the drive, either."

A drive that could crack computers. Floating around her father's life. Never found. She said nothing for several moments. *What did he find on Mom's computer? He wouldn't kill himself over an affair, would he? Would he hurt so bad he would leave me? Maybe the answer is yes and you don't want to confront that possibility.*

"Jane."

She fought back a wave of emotion. She clutched at his hand and he closed his other hand over hers. "I'm not mad at you. You were trying to help. What did the flash drive look like?"

"Uh, it has a little musical note on it, so it will look like a music drive. I don't go around carrying a flash drive labeled 'Hacker Kit.'"

So where was this flash drive now?

"OK." She felt rocked by this. "All right. OK." She pulled her hand away from his and took a series of deep breaths. "OK. All right."

"Are you ready for this?"

She realized he now meant the party. "It's been two years, yeah, I guess I am."

They walked down the path. It was going to be an amiably boring party, she could tell, and she felt a sense of relief. Music was playing, not loudly, not even enough to bother the neighbors.

They went in through the unlocked front door, and an elderly lady, with a bright smile and gray hair cut elfin-short, leaned out of the kitchen and said, "Hey, y'all! Come on in!"

Oh yeah, Jane thought, *a real wild bacchanal*. She steadied herself. She could do this. Look at what she had accomplished in the past two days. She could handle a social gathering.

They walked through the dining room and then into the kitchen, which made Jane relieved, because most of the kids were in the big, old-style den. She had been afraid that when she walked in, all conversation would cease, they would stare, someone would say something. Or laugh. Or glare.

But they didn't. The conversations kept going, and as she and Adam loitered by the sink as the elderly lady fussed in the fridge, she saw a few Lakehaven kids she recognized pause for a second, look at her, not with scowls but at least neutrally, and then she realized half the kids here weren't Lakehaven. They must be Trevor's friends from Travis Community College. So they didn't even know about her past. She was just another guest, a young woman in a pretty blue dress. She wasn't the homeless girl, or the suicide who took down the innocent guy who was probably trying to help her, or the weirdo camped out in her friend's dorm room, eating off a borrowed meal plan.

She could just be Jane.

The thought of it overwhelmed her for a moment and then she heard the woman behind her. "Hello, sorry, had to get that pasta boiling. Hi, Adam."

"Hi, Nana. This is my friend, Jane. I brought her along but I forgot to tell Trevor, I hope that's all right."

Jane turned and the woman smiled at her. "Hi, Jane. Of course you're welcome here. I'm Trevor's grandmother, but no one calls me Mrs. Gunther, they all call me Nana."

"OK. Hi, Nana," Jane said. Nana squeezed her arm gently, welcoming. Jane felt a rush of heat behind her eyes. "I used to be friends with Trevor."

"I didn't know Trevor had 'used to be' friends," she said. "I thought he was pretty loyal to all his friends."

Jane tried to smile. "We just haven't been in touch lately. I guess we're still friends. I hope we are."

"I know Trevor will be glad you're here."

Until I bring up asking if he and his truck were leaving High Oaks after the crash.

"Yes, you must be proud of Trevor. He keeps Lakehaven fully caffeinated," Jane said, not knowing what else to say.

"I'm glad you're here, dear," Nana said. "I know you've had a difficult time. I'm glad you're letting Trevor be a friend to you."

She knows who I am. "Well," Jane said, "since I'm a crasher, I can work for my keep. May I help you with anything?"

"No, no, sweetheart, it's all under control. Go mingle. Nice to see you, and always nice to see you, Adam."

She walked out of the kitchen and among the other guests. It felt like it took every atom of courage she had. "Hi. I'm Jane," she said to a pair of chatting girls who weren't Lakehaven alums. The girls smiled and introduced themselves. She could feel Adam watching her, letting her inch out on the social ice alone, but there for her if needed.

For the next thirty minutes, she worked the room, like she was a normal person. It felt like stepping out onto a high wire strung across a canyon. The other three Lakehaven kids who were there—and at community college with Trevor—were all neutral at least, and one was friendly, asking her how she was doing. "I'm better." And she braced herself for the *Well, you're for sure doing better than David Hall* response she expected, but the boy just nodded and said, "Well, that's good, Jane."

It was like life could be normal.

She waited for Adam to get involved in a discussion about superhero movies—there was no greater distraction for him—and then she walked outside into the cool breeze. A pair of guys stood off from the patio, smoking cigarettes, deep into a discussion of a TV show about zombies that Jane couldn't stand to watch. She did not need to imagine the dead rising and shambling about the landscape. One boy watched her, gave her a slight nod and smile, and she wondered why. Maybe the dress did look nice.

"Hey, Jane," Trevor said behind her as she stood at the edge of the patio. She turned to face him and she felt an odd jolt at the sight of him.

Were we still friends the night of the accident? Or was I afraid of you?

The two smokers finished and went back into the house.

"Adam brought me. I'm sorry I'm crashing." She had not really considered the humiliation she would feel if he asked her to leave.

"It's fine, I'm glad he did. I should have invited you. Called you after I saw you talking with Amari."

"You were busy, and frankly, if you'd asked me to come, I might have lost my nerve."

"Why?" The embarrassment faded from his eyes and his gaze met hers.

For a moment she did lose her nerve. "Quite the wild college kegger," she said, finding her voice. "What with Nana here."

"With Nana here, we get much better food and my bro-dude friends don't seem inclined to trash the house or drink as much."

"I like her."

"Nana moved back in with us after my mom died. I think I would have been lost without her."

She hated to ruin the moment. Trevor, being nice and acting open with her, warmer than he had been at the coffee shop. "The paramedics who helped me were both attacked. I talked with one whose house was burned down. I asked her if she remembered seeing any cars as the ambulance approached the accident site. She saw a truck very much like yours turning off High Oaks as they turned on."

His mouth twisted for a moment.

"Were you there, Trevor?" Her voice was soft.

The smile came back on, but faded. "There are a lot of trucks like mine."

It wasn't an answer. She knew the boy he had been; she didn't know the man he had become.

"I know. But I'm still asking you. Were you there?"

Nana stepped out onto the patio. "Y'all hungry? I just pulled ribs out of the oven."

"We'll be there in a minute, ma'am, thank you," Trevor said. Jane gave Nana a smile and thought, *Maybe I'm about to upend Trevor's life. I'm sorry, Nana.*

Nana stepped back inside.

"You and Adam came into Happy Taco after we did. I saw the video, so there's no lying about it to me. He said you arrived separately, him looking for me. He said you told him you were looking for me, but you told Amari you were looking for David. Why?"

He looked at her for another long second, took a sip of beer. Like he didn't know what to say. He let out a breath, like it had been long held.

After a moment he put his blue-eyed gaze steadily on her. His awkward smile was gone. "I wasn't looking for David. I was looking for you. I ran into Adam there, in the parking lot. We didn't come together. He was looking for you, too."

She went blunt. "Did you see the crash?"

He looked stricken. "No, no, of course not. Jane. Do you think I would have driven off and left you there?"

"I don't know, Trevor. Remember, I don't remember. Why were you following us?"

"Not following, looking for you. Because I thought you were seeing David and I wanted to know if you were." He kept his gaze steady with hers. "I watched you two leave school. Clearly there was something major and emotional going on between you. I went to football practice and I covered for David, because he was skipping it. I thought maybe you were just giving David a ride home. You're neighbors, friends. Whatever. But you had totally ignored me when I called to you when you were leaving. That wasn't like you, or like David. You were both acting so oddly. Later Kamala texted me you two were being all cozy at Happy Taco and did I know why? So I went there to see you."

Instead of Trevor's face she saw headlights, in a mirror, bright, close. Following, following. She blinked the image away.

"Why would you care? Why would you try to find me and lie about it to Adam?" But then she knew. She knew it in his face, in the way he'd acted toward her at the coffee shop, tentative, shy, uncertain, a guy who had girls watching and smiling at him as he worked. And the pang of annoyance she'd felt when she noticed that. A guy who probably was normally confident. For a moment she thought she'd reached out and touched his plain, strong face along his jawline, then his blond hair. But she realized it was a memory, a shard of the past slicing through the haze, another time she'd looked at him with love. This boy she'd fake-married in first grade with rubber-band rings, this boy she'd fought a bow-headed bully for in fourth. This friend. This more-than-a friend.

"You and I had been seeing each other. No one knew. Maybe Kamala suspected. You know how her mind works."

She bit at her lip. "Why keep it a secret?"

"*You* wanted it that way. You said your mom didn't want you to date, she was still kind of mental about your dad's passing and you not being around when she needed you. I didn't like sneaking around, it felt wrong, but I didn't care, I just wanted to be with you, Jane."

She remembered the reconstructed time line. After Kamala and David's texting back and forth, Trevor had texted David, asking him what was up. David apparently didn't respond, and then Trevor did not text again.

"Kamala tried to talk to David, he put her off, then you text." She opened her eyes.

"Kamala thought you two were messing around together. Her best friend and her boyfriend."

"I thought they were broken up. She had broken up with him. That's what she told me when I came back to school."

"They had, but he hadn't told me why. He'd made a pros-and-cons list on how to do it because he thought she wouldn't take it well. It never occurred to me it was because you were in the picture—you and I were happy. So I went looking for you. I thought maybe that was really why you wanted to keep it secret—so he wouldn't know. Maybe you were seeing us both." He cleared his throat. "But then I saw how it was between you two in the parking lot...the raw emotion. That wasn't just friendship."

She didn't know what to say, so she stuck to the time line. "So you lost us at Happy Taco. We left before you got there."

He put his hands in his pockets.

"Did you find us later? You must have. You were on the road. You were following us." *The headlights. She had to get away from the headlights.*

"Jane...don't."

"I need to know. And I need to know why you have never told me any of this. You or Adam."

"Adam doesn't know any details. He left Happy Taco and I didn't see him again that night."

"And you?"

He wiped the trace of beer off his mouth with the back of his hand. "I went driving around. I felt crazy. This couldn't be. If you were with David, then you were cheating on me with my best friend and dating your best friend's ex. I didn't want to believe it of you. I couldn't believe it of you. I went by your house, David's house. No one was home at your place and I didn't want to ask Mrs. Hall if you were running around together."

"My mom wasn't home?"

"Well, I don't know. The lights were on, but she didn't answer the doorbell."

Her mother and Perri must have finished their discussion. Where was her mother, then? "And then what?"

"I knew Kamala was upset. I called her. Dr. Grayson told me she'd gone out. I asked where. And I guess her parents track her phone, because she'd gone to the Halls' lake house."

The lake house. The Halls owned another place, a large, two-story Tuscan home, down on Lake Austin. Cal and David loved it, Perri didn't, so it was a father-son hangout for them.

If two teenagers needed privacy to talk...and the parents owned more than one house...why not go there? She hadn't been there in years—that she remembered.

"Did you go there?" she asked.

Now he looked deflated and ill. "I debated about whether or not to go...I mean, c'mon, if y'all were seeing each other and sitting with his arm around you, acting like a couple, lying to Kamala, it meant you were cheating on me. I couldn't compete with a guy like David."

"Trevor..."

"Kamala texted me: They're here. I couldn't decide what

I should do, but I drove over to the lake place. Your car went past me as I headed toward the house. You were driving really fast. Like, dangerous fast. I had to drive down to a place wide enough to turn around and then try to follow you. Until I lost you."

"Lost us? But you were on High Oaks?"

"I was following you on Old Travis and I saw in the distance you had turned onto High Oaks—and then I got caught behind a car making a left turn, and there was a line of traffic, and I got caught for at least a minute. And I turned around and started to drive home. I was so torn up. I thought you must have known it was me following you but you kept going, and I finally thought, to hell with it, so I U-turned a few minutes later and I went back. I turned right onto High Oaks. I drove, but I didn't see you or your car. I looked down the hill, but I didn't see the wreckage or light, or anything."

What had Brenda Hobson said? The wreck was dark as pitch.

"I didn't see another car, or a person. So I left. I figured you had just used it as a cut-through or you just wanted to get away from me because you knew I was following you. I went home. I did see an ambulance heading toward me on Old Travis as I turned off, but I didn't realize until later they had turned onto the road."

Maybe Brenda's memory was a little faulty on that account; he might have already been on Old Travis. "So did Kamala tell you what she saw at the lake house?"

"Jane . . . what does it matter now?"

"It matters because someone is lying to me about that night. Are you Liv Danger?"

"No, of course not." His eyes widened.

"Maybe you are," she said. She took a step toward him,

her hand closing into a fist. "Did you run us off the road?" A ghost of headlights in the rearview mirror.

"No." He was pale as milk in moonlight. "Jane, no."

"But you didn't see the crashed car...what time were you there?"

"It would have been about ten. I got home about ten fifteen. I gave up on finding you."

"Is that all?"

The silence was heavy between them. "All I care to say."

She turned away from him. "Not telling me is like lying. You just hide behind no words instead of untrue words."

"Jane..." Two people started to come out onto the patio—Kamala Grayson and Amari Bowman. "Go back inside, please," Trevor said.

Kamala tilted her head in greeting. "Well. Jane. I guess you're feeling a bit more social now. Did you steal your mother's car to come over here?"

"No," Jane said. "Hi, Amari. Thanks again for talking with me."

"You're welcome," Amari said after a moment as Kamala glanced back at her in surprise.

"Kamala. Go," Trevor said.

"Well, of course. I'll give you two your privacy." She and Amari retreated back into the house.

"So, I mean, how serious were we?" Jane asked. "Were we sleeping together?"

"No. You said you weren't ready. But we kissed. A lot." He blushed in the moonlight.

She wondered if she could believe him, then she thought of him standing up for her, throwing that Parker jerk into a wall at school.

"Is there anything else?"

"Kamala wouldn't tell me anything that happened at the

lake house. I didn't see her or her car, but I didn't drive all the way down to the lake house. I turned after you pretty quick."

So why would she and David go from the lake house to High Oaks Road? They knew no one there. Maybe just trying to get away from Trevor? And then she saw it.

"You thought we were ditching you and that was what caused the wreck. Me driving fast, trying to get away from you…"

His face was pure pain. "I thought so… until they found the note. Then I didn't know what to think. Were you trying to hurt yourself and get away from me, or did you just crash the car?…If I caused it, I'm sorry, I'm so sorry." He reached for her. For a second she saw the boy who fake-married her in first grade, the boy she stood up for in fourth against the hair-bow meanie, the quietly dignified boy who had pushed the vile Parker away from her.

Then she jerked away from him as if his touch burned. "Don't. Don't touch me. Don't talk to me. You could have told me all this and you didn't."

"Your mom told me to stay away from you. You remembered nothing about us. What was I supposed to do, say, 'Oh hey, yeah, we were finally falling in love,' when the version of me you remembered was three years out of date and I was just a friend? When you didn't even know who you yourself were?"

Looking at him made a hard twist in her chest. She hurried away from him, through the house, through the kitchen. Adam was gone. He'd left. Nana was in the kitchen and glanced up with concern for Jane.

"Where is Adam?" she asked Nana.

"He left, he said he'd be back for you in a while."

"When? Please?"

"I saw him watching you all talk outside, and then he said he had to go."

What had Adam heard? Jane turned around, marched back up to Trevor, who was just coming in through the screen door. She pushed against his chest and walked him back out onto the patio. "Your truck keys. I need them. Right now."

He gave his truck keys to her. "You're upset. Do you want me to drive you?"

"No. I need to do this myself."

"Jane..."

"Why didn't you tell me?" Her voice was small. She kept her hand on his broad chest. If they were once a couple, they were a mismatched one. The football player and the creative, moody girl. He'd have to bend down to kiss her. He put his hand over the hand she kept on his chest.

His voice was steady. "Your mother made it crystal clear she didn't want me around you. I don't know why. It was as if she didn't want you remembering. It wasn't my call to say more. And you had chosen David. Not me. I thought you didn't care about me anymore. I didn't know what to say or what to do."

"There's something else you're not telling me." *I lost Trevor, too. I didn't even know I had him. I lost him. I don't remember being close to him, but I know when he's holding something back. I know him so well, yet I don't.*

"Jane, it's bad."

"Tell me!" she screamed. She pounded her small fists against his chest, his arms. "Tell me! Tell me!"

"Ask your mom for your medical files," he said tonelessly. "Ask her."

42

You can't be here," Perri said. Shiloh stood on her front porch, smiling.

"Why not? We need to talk. I've had an idea...where's the lovely Jane?"

"I saw her leave. Dressed up nicely. I guess she's moved back in with her mother and is attempting to have a social life."

"See, I've had an idea on how we can...accelerate things." Perri didn't like the tone of his voice. His scarred grin was smug. "I made a list of names and addresses..."

And then another car pulled up, catching them in the headlights. Perri blinked, turned away. The lights dimmed. Maybe it was Cal and how on earth would she explain Shiloh Rooke being here...

"Mrs. Hall?"

Oh, no. Matteo Vasquez. "I still don't really have anything to say, Mr. Vasquez."

"I wondered if you might give me a quote regarding that video. I tried your phone, but all I got was voice mail."

"I turned off my phone."

Matteo reached the porch stairs, blinking up at Shiloh. "Hello," he said.

"Hi there," Shiloh answered. "I don't think Mrs. Hall wants to talk to you."

"I know you, Mr. Rooke. I interviewed you for the articles on Jane Norton, about the crash itself. Do you remember me?"

"It doesn't matter. You're leaving."

"It's interesting the two of you are together," Matteo said, not in an unfriendly way. "Has anything else happened to people tied to the crash?"

"No," Perri said.

"You don't need to write about that. It's not really a story," Shiloh said.

"That's not what Mrs. Hall thought. I'd like to talk to you about, what was it, a theft? What was stolen? The e-mail tip I received said it was of a personal nature."

"It's a private matter, Mr. Vasquez." Shiloh's tone was cold. "I don't have a comment."

"But something was stolen from you and this happened after Brenda Hobson's house burned, correct?"

"Like I said, a private matter."

"You had an engagement that ended?" He glanced at Perri.

Perri wished that a hole would open in the ground and swallow Matteo Vasquez. Shiloh glanced at her. "Again, it's private and I don't wish to comment."

"Who do you think is behind these Liv Danger posts?"

"I have no idea."

"Anything you remember about the aftermath of the crash you want to share with me?"

"No. Are you still living in your car?" He grinned at

Matteo Vasquez. "You lost your job at the papers. These days anyone with a keyboard is writing stuff, often for free. Hard to make a living. Reporters are not the only people who can do research with a phone call or two." He gestured toward the parked car. "You sleep in the back of your car."

Perri wondered why she hadn't thought to do opposition research on Vasquez. Shiloh was smarter than he looked.

"This isn't about me," Vasquez said, his voice tight.

"It might be about your desperation to find a good story. Or make one up when there's nothing to it."

Matteo Vasquez ignored him. "So, Mrs. Hall, your husband takes it on himself to go see Brenda Hobson and you're hanging out with the other paramedic who was targeted."

"Why don't you go talk to Jane Norton?" Shiloh asked. "According to Perri, she took off dressed to the nines like it was party time."

Vasquez watched them both for a moment, and said, "If you change your mind, you know how to reach me, Mrs. Hall." He gave Shiloh a business card. "You, too, since you seem so well informed."

He got into his car but didn't start it. Perri could see him on his phone, looking down at his lap. Reading something, she thought. Making phone calls. He's on this. He'll be talking to other people. He'd said he'd talk to the other people whose lives were touched by the crash.

"You should not have come here," she said, not looking at Shiloh. "Now he's suspicious."

"What did you tell him about me?"

"Hardly anything. I was trying to get him to write about the Nortons. But someone had e-mailed him about everything that's going on—you, Brenda Hobson, Randy Franklin. It must have been Jane or Laurel."

"I can't do what I need to do with a reporter blabbering about me." A hard threat lay under the words.

A flash of coldness went across her chest. "He's not blabbering. He hasn't written anything yet." The words spilled out of her in a rush and she steeled herself. She couldn't show a moment's weakness in front of Shiloh. He fed on that.

Vasquez got off his phone, started his car, and drove away.

"I'll talk to you later," Shiloh said. "I got to go. Things to do." He kept his gaze locked on Vasquez's departing car.

"Where are you going?" Her voice rose.

"I told you, I had an idea on how to accelerate all this." He got into his car and roared off.

Accelerate? You have to control him.

He said he had a list. Names and addresses. The chill she felt burrowed into her.

She had to stop him. But she didn't even know what he was doing. If she called the police, it would be so uncomfortable. So she stood frozen, watching his taillights vanish into the night, following Matteo Vasquez, and she thought, *You're a coward.*

She sank to the curb.

43

JANE GOT INTO Trevor's truck. Started it. She hadn't driven since the wreck. She wasn't sure she even remembered how.

Ask your mother about your medical records.

She could either go find Adam or go home. She decided to go home first; it was closest, and she had an idea Adam didn't like the conversation she'd had with Trevor. Why would he have bolted from the party?

What kind of person was I before this? she wondered. A secret boyfriend. Running around with her neighbor's son, betraying her oldest friend. A mother who didn't want her to remember. Why? *Was I so awful?*

Today alone: her mother's affair, the fact that her father was likely spying on her mother's infidelities and might have turned to suicide, and now this. She had wanted to remember, and now ugly truths were showing their hideous bones, their tattered skins.

She put the truck into reverse and backed out of the driveway, slowly. She didn't remember taking driver's education, but the muscle memory remained...she could drive. Slowly she backed out and she saw Trevor Blinn standing on the porch, watching her.

You don't know him. You don't know what he was like. You don't know what you were like. But he lent you a truck, she thought. *He finally told you. That has to count for something.*

She drove home, sweat dripping down her ribs. She saw one light on in the house. She wondered if her mother was at home. She wasn't. Mom, gone again.

Where was Mom spending her hours? What if she was setting fires, breaking up engagements, making private investigators disappear? You didn't want to believe this of anyone, but her mother had a single-mindedness at times that could be frightening.

The file for the accident—which she thought at first was a gold mine, and now realized told only the barest of tales—had been in the back of her mom's file drawer. She hadn't seen a separate medical file on herself. She went straight to the file cabinet. She flipped through the collected paperwork of her family's life. Nothing on her medical records, except for a file that held the everyday receipts from doctor's visits and prescriptions, from before the accident.

Nothing relating to the crash. She closed the file cabinet. Where would Mom put such a file?

The safe. She went upstairs to her mother's closet. There was a safe behind a false cabinet panel; she had seen her mother take particularly precious jewelry out of it once, when she was still trying to hold on to her place in Lakehaven society and she still attended functions, before the invitations dried up. It was a keypad lock. She entered in the same code as the house alarm system, which was her

parents' anniversary date; it didn't work. She entered in her
birthday. No. Her mom's birthday. No. Her father's. No.

There was more than jewelry here. There had to be.

What else was an important date?

The crash. She entered in the crash date. The door
opened, ever so slightly.

It was not the Open Sesame she would have initially
guessed. But it made sense, didn't it? The defining moment
of all their lives. Her hand shook as she opened the safe.

Inside lay small boxes of jewelry, very fine stuff, but less
of it than she remembered. Papers, photos.

And in the back there was a gun. She took it out carefully.
She wasn't used to guns. She didn't know how to check
whether it was loaded or the safety was on. She had never
known that her mother kept a gun in the house. And behind
the gun, and a—what would you call it?—a full magazine of
ammunition, there lay a thick envelope, shoved into the far
back as if it were unwelcome thoughts shoved into the back
of a mind, best forgotten. Pulling it free from the safe, she
felt dread worm its way into her chest.

It was a medical file, a thick one. She opened it and
began to page through it. It was in chronological order,
from the initial ambulance report to the hospital file for
her coma, her awakening, and her recovery. She flipped
through. The pages were filled with lists of diagnoses and
observations, with lists of medications she had been given.
Brain scans and neurological assessments, insurance forms
and paperwork. She read about her brain damage, her
coma, the pronouncements of the doctors in crabbed handwriting and notes about her chances for recovery.

What was here? The initial diagnoses, the battery of
tests, the outline of her physical injuries (broken arm, fractured wrist, two broken fingers, concussion)...

Then on the third day...there was a report labeled Miscarriage.

The doctor noted an indication of vaginal bleeding on day two of the coma, and a pelvic exam. Her cervix was open; it was inevitable. Blood tests the previous day had indicated that she was pregnant...she flipped back to a blood analysis and found it, with a circle around a "Y" next to the word "pregnant," in small type. A further note indicated that the pregnancy was not far advanced, perhaps a month.

Had she known?

She felt very cold. Were we sleeping together? *No*, Trevor had said, *you weren't ready.*

The report outlined the presence of clotted material. The bleeding was stopped; she was already on antibiotics; they did not need to increase the dosage. There was no DNA analysis to tell her who the father was.

She was seeing Trevor. Had he lied about intimacy? What was the point?

But you were out with a boy who'd just broken up with his longtime girlfriend. A boy you'd been close to your entire life. A boy who had his arm around you in public, comforting you. A boy you always loved in a back corner of your heart, even if you wouldn't say it out loud.

I didn't even know I'd lost you, baby, she thought. She felt a wrenching pain in her chest, in her stomach. No one had told her.

Her mother had kept this from her.

And why...why keep this quiet? Would public opinion think she was more likely to be suicidal if she was pregnant by David or by Trevor? It seemed an old-fashioned notion—but teenagers in trouble did desperate, thoughtless things. Maybe she knew. Maybe she didn't want the nobly patient Trevor or her best friend, Kamala, to know. Maybe her mother just didn't want another angle to this already tragic story.

After a moment's consideration, she returned the file to the safe. She kept the gun.

She texted Trevor: OK now I know. Found the records. Why didn't you tell me?

Lots of reasons. I'm deeply sorry. Are you all right? I know you don't want to talk to me but if you need me, I'm here. I'll stay out of your way if that's what you want.

She didn't text him back for ten minutes, sitting on the edge of the bed. She took deep breaths and calmed herself. She needed to be smart right now, not emotional, not reacting to the increasing flood of unhappy news about her life in the days around the accident.

If Mom kept this from you, there is literally nothing else she wouldn't keep from you as well. Mom is not exactly who you thought she was. There is more there.

She gathered her thoughts and then she texted Trevor: I need your help tomorrow. My shrink lied to me and my mother is paying him to help have me committed. You want to make up for this? Be there with me when I confront them. I think my mother wants to drag me off to a mental hospital and she won't if you're there. Will you?

He wrote back: Yes. Bring back my truck tonight when you're done and we'll talk. I'll give you a ride home.

I'm not up for seeing anyone, she wrote. But that was a lie. She went back downstairs and although part of her only wanted to curl up in her bed and shut out the world, she drove Trevor's truck to St. Michael's.

The gun came with her.

44

FRIENDS, STANDING ON a porch, disagreeing.

Amari said, "Let's go. I'm done with this party."

Kamala said, "No, not yet."

"I'm tired," Amari said. Also her boyfriend, Derek, had gotten sick at the last minute and decided to stay home. She was feeling tired and spent herself, and only half of that was from dealing with Kamala's attitude.

"Then you go. I'll catch a car home."

Amari said, "You're mad at me for having talked to Jane."

"It's not the best look on you," Kamala said.

"Whatever."

"Just don't do it again."

"Kamala. Let's get one thing straight. I'll talk to anyone I decide to talk to. I don't like Jane. I think she's a loser. But if I want to talk to her, I will, and you'll keep your big mouth shut about it."

"It's great how college has given you that independence you crave," Kamala said. "You might get so independent you won't have friends left."

"Grow up. College is not high school. There are no thrones for you to sit on."

"Honestly, I thought I was doing you a favor being your friend."

There is a breaking point in friendships, and Amari Bowman reached hers in that moment. She thought of simply turning and walking away, avoiding the drama, but instead she let the words burning inside her flash into fire. "Kamala. You've never made it easy to be your friend," Amari said. "You had power, and people gravitated to that. But I'd never have called you with a problem or for a shoulder to cry on. And you don't have the power now. You're just one of many. There's a decent girl inside you and you won't let her out. And I think I outgrew you." Amari turned her back on her, went to Trevor, who was standing alone on the patio, gave him a hug, thanked him for the invitation. She gave Nana a hug as well. She walked by Kamala like she was a ghost.

Amari hadn't had a beer or a glass of wine, so she was fine to drive, but she was trembling, her chest thick with the sour feeling that comes after a fight with a friend. She regretted the fight, but not the sentiment. As she got into her car, the phone rang.

She hoped it was Kamala calling, but it wasn't. A local number. "Hello?"

"Ms. Bowman? My name is Matteo Vasquez. I wrote some newspaper articles a couple of years ago about the Jane Norton/David Hall car crash and I interviewed you then."

"Yes, I remember."

"I was hoping I might talk to you again. If you're not busy, could we meet?"

"Now?"

"Sure, if you have time and I'm not interrupting your Saturday night."

"My Saturday night flamed out. Are you writing another article about Jane? Because she seems to be doing much better."

"Have you seen her?"

"Yes. Twice today." That wasn't exactly accurate, she hadn't talked to Jane but had seen her at the party. Talking with Trevor on the patio, alone, something major clearly going down between them.

"Wow, then I really would like to talk to you."

"Maybe you could leave Jane alone."

"Are you not aware there have been unusual events— you could even say attacks in two of the cases—against people who were involved in the investigations?"

"Um. Jane mentioned that. But I wasn't part of the investigation."

"You were prominent in the case. You passed the class note, you saw them at the restaurant."

"Are you saying I'm in danger? From Jane?"

"I'm trying to figure that out, but I think you should be aware. I'm writing a new article about it."

"Can't you tell me what's going on?"

"It would be better if we could meet face-to-face." He was holding out for another interview.

Amari bit at her lip, thinking. "All right." She gave him her address. "There's a little coffee shop a block away from my apartment. We can meet at my place and walk there, they never have any parking."

"All right, I'll see you in a few. Thank you, Ms. Bowman."

Amari drove back to the campus, parked her car in the lot of her small apartment building. Thinking. Maybe it

wasn't best to meet with this guy alone. Not that she was
afraid of him—he had been polite and professional before.
But maybe it wouldn't be a bad idea to have someone else
there when she talked to him. Amari's mother, Renee, was
a lawyer so she called her and explained.

"Have him come up to the apartment and wait for me,"
Renee said. "Let's talk there and then we can see how to
proceed. I'll be there in fifteen minutes."

"All right."

Amari waited in the lot for Vasquez; he pulled in a few
minutes later, a truck driving past him and parking in a No
Parking zone, its engine idling.

"Hey," Vasquez said, walking toward her. "Thanks for
meeting me."

"Instead why don't I make coffee here, is that OK? My
mom wanted to join us as well."

"Your mom, the lawyer."

"You do have a good memory."

"Came in handy writing about amnesia." The joke fell
flat and he saw it. "And I've been reviewing all my notes.
That's fine, whatever you're comfortable with. Do you
want us to wait down here for her to arrive?"

She saw someone hurrying across the parking lot, sticking to the shadows. "Um, no," she said. "I'll put the decaf on,
if you'd like some, and I know my mom will drink a cup."

"That's fine."

They started to walk into the courtyard of the apartment.
She heard a distant noise, like breaking glass.

"Did you hear that?"

Vasquez had been asking her what she was studying.
"No, I didn't."

"Oh. Never mind." The complex was full of UT students, there was always a bit of noise happening. And then

she gave him the rote answer about her studies and her activities, the kind she gave when her parents' friends asked her how college was going. They walked up to her second-floor apartment.

"So how's Jane?" Vasquez asked. He'd try to talk to her before her mother got here.

She thought, *Jane is a pain. But I remember when I thought she was kind of cool and funny. Spoke her own mind, instead of Kamala speaking it for everyone*. But she said instead, "I think she's doing a lot better."

"Is that so? Did she approach you to talk or did you call her up for some reason?"

As they walked toward her apartment, Amari saw with annoyance that the lights along the balconies were out. All of them. *Stupid landlords*, she thought, *they need to keep this place up*. She stepped into the darkness, Vasquez following, using his phone as a flashlight, aiming it toward the floor. She passed three doors, reaching her own, close to the stairwell.

As she fumbled for her keys, she thought of times when Kamala had gone full Lakehaven princess and she and Jane would exchange the subtlest of eye rolls, and it had made Amari think that perhaps the real friend she should cultivate was Jane.

"There's glass on the floor," Vasquez said, shifting the flashlight around, and she saw it then, thought of the noise she'd heard—and some basic instinct told her to get into the apartment, now.

She unlocked her door and pushed it open, when a shadow rushed from the stairwell. She heard a hiss of air as something swung toward Vasquez, and he dropped in silence, the lit phone skittering along the concrete. A spray of wetness struck the back of her neck. She didn't scream, her focus on just getting inside and slamming the door. But then she heard the hiss again and a sudden agony exploded between her shoulders. She fell to the tiled floor of the apartment, the air driven from her lungs. She rolled, trying to face the threat, the light from the fallen phone catching the crowbar as it was raised to deliver another blow.

45

JANE HURRIED AROUND to the back window of Adam's room. Raised the window. Looked in at the stranger who was sitting on the bed she normally slept in, propped up on pillows, watching a movie on a tablet.

"Hello," she said.

"Hi," he said, looking up with a smile. "Aren't you a cute peeping tom?"

"Um, are you Adam's new roommate?"

"Yeah, just got assigned, I was in off-campus housing, put in a special request." She noticed he had a leg in a cast, with crutches. "I'm on the lacrosse team, took a bad spill during a game two days ago. Just easier to be on campus for the rest of the semester while I heal up."

"Of course," she said. Which meant now she would be on the streets, or in the house with her mother, who had kept secrets from her. "I'm in Adam's study group, I left some clothes." She pointed at the bag where she kept her gear. "Would you mind handing it to me?" She didn't want to climb through the window in her dress.

He hopped over to the bag and gave it to her with a friendly, flirty smile, and she remembered she was still in her nice dress, with her combed hair and her makeup. "I'm looking forward to meeting Adam. What's your name?"

"Jane. He's not here a lot. It'll be like having a single."

She turned and walked away, not waiting for his question on how she knew Adam's living habits.

She had someone else to go see.

* * *

Apartment 23. She knocked. She saw the dot of light through the peephole dim, and brighten again. She waited, and Kamala opened the door with a saccharine smile and an equally artificial greeting. "Did the party not agree with you, Jane? Me neither, once I saw you there."

"I never thought I'd say this, but I'm sorry. I'm sorry for whatever David and I did to you."

It wasn't what Kamala wanted to hear. "It's easy to say when you don't remember it."

"Don't you want to say anything back to me?"

"Like what?"

"An apology."

"What the hell for?"

"You planted that note at the car crash scene. My suicide note."

Kamala stared at her but took a step back. "You are legit crazy."

"No, it's the only explanation that makes sense to me."

"Nothing makes sense to you, damage."

A hot darkness rose in Jane's chest.

"The note was written long before the crash. The Halls did a chemical analysis and they kept that quiet. I didn't

write it that night. I didn't write that because I wanted
David dead, because I was pining for him. I wrote it because I missed my dad so much. So much."

Kamala started to shove the door closed and Jane
pushed in and showed her what she'd brought from home:
the gun from her mother's safe. She didn't aim it at Kamala, she kept it by her side.

Kamala froze. "Jane, oh please, put that away."

"I just want you to listen. Nod if you will."

Kamala nodded.

"If when my dad died, I wrote a note like that, and I
didn't destroy it, I wonder: Who is the one person I might
have shared such a note with?"

Kamala averted her gaze.

"There's my answer." She could barely speak. "How?"

"It was inside your favorite book. *A Wrinkle in Time.*
You always loved it, but you read it obsessively after your
dad died. Except the girl in the book loses her dad and
then wins him back." Her voice broke. "You had shown
it to me when you wrote it a few months after your dad
died. I told you to tear it up, don't let anyone see it, but
you didn't. Because it was about your dad, in a sad way,
and so you kept it."

"So you put it to"—Jane paused—"good use."

Now Kamala looked at her. "I was at both your houses
the morning after the crash. Bringing food, doing laundry
for your mom, helping Mrs. Hall. So I took the book with
the note inside from your room and then I planted the
note at the scene. No one saw me, it was easy, I'd brought
flowers to lay there. No one looked twice at me. And then
I drove back to your house, and a bunch of parents were
there cooking and cleaning the house for your mom while
she was at the hospital with you, so I went to the Halls'

and I put the book on David's shelf. I couldn't bear to keep it. We all thought you would die. No one knew you would wake up, and then you did, but you didn't remember. Then I never got a chance to put it back." Her voice was very small. "Of course the police found the note the same day I planted it. And that was that."

"How could you do that to me?"

"How could you be with David?"

"The lake house. Trevor said you went to the lake house. That's where you saw us."

Now the shame was gone from Kamala's face. Now there was only misery. "I found you both. I watched you through the window. You were crying. David took you in his arms. He kissed you, but like he'd never kissed me. He picked you up in his arms. You kissed him back. You—you wrapped your legs around his waist." Here her voice wavered. "He leaned you back against the wall...kissing you like you were everything to him and I was nothing. My best friend I'd given so much to after her dad died. The boy I still loved. I suppose if I'd stood there and watched, you would have had sex right in front of me."

The words were like a slap across the face.

"You couldn't wait to take him from me. Me, the friend who'd been best to you. Who'd let you tag along and be socially acceptable when everyone else found you a bit odd and strange and not that much fun to be around."

"Well, you've paid me back," Jane said. "Congratulations."

"Why do you think everyone believed the suicide note? Because you *were* that person. The depressive, the complainer, the nobody. Sorry your dad died, but life goes on..."

Jane slapped Kamala before she thought about it. A

good, hard slap, the kind the giver feels all the way up
her arm and the kind the recipient feels in her spine, even
though it's her face that took the blow.

"Clearly we're both awful," Jane said. "But you don't
ever talk about my dad that way."

Kamala said nothing, her shame-dulled eyes on the gun.

"So did you just walk away?"

"David set you down and went into the other room.
Probably to find a condom. I came in and you and I argued. You tried to tell me there was a good reason, you
begged me to forgive you. Like, there could be a reason
for that. I shoved you to the floor. You were screaming.
David separated us and told me I had to leave, it was dangerous to stay. Like, you know, there was something else
going on. I told the two of you that you deserved each
other. I left."

"You texted Trevor."

"I knew about you two. I thought maybe sweet, dumb
football player ought to know you were putting out for
David but not for him. And I texted David's dad. Just so his
parents would stop worrying about where you were, since
you clearly weren't studying."

"Then what?"

"I left. I went home and cried into my pillow because of
all the love and friendship I'd wasted on a whore like you
and the love I'd wasted on a jerk like David."

"Where was the crowbar?"

"What?"

"The crowbar we bought."

"I have no damn idea, and who cares?" Now the heat
was back in her voice. "Are you going to shoot me? Now
you know."

"Why didn't you tell me this?"

Kamala stared at her. "Why should I? You killed David. You took him from me and then you killed him."

"I wonder what people would think of you if they knew you planted that note," Jane said softly. "It's the kind of thing that spreads fast, like that video of Perri Hall attacking me. 'Honors Student Frames Accident as Suicide Attempt in Revenge Plot.' I wonder if the police would like to know how much you interfered with the investigation." She wanted to scream, to beat Kamala, and she couldn't. She hid behind the calm in her own voice. "I mean, I was hurt so badly in the crash, you just had to be sure I was hurt even more. Punished even more. Who does that? How did you look at yourself in the mirror?"

Kamala didn't answer, because the answer was too awful.

"'Best friends forever,'" Kamala said. "That was a mistake."

Their mutual betrayals lay between them like a stone wall that could almost be seen.

"The gun is empty," Jane said. "I didn't bring any bullets for it. But I know where the bullets are. And maybe I'm crazy enough to use them, because right now it is taking everything I have not to beat you senseless. What I did was wrong, and I'm truly sorry, but it was between you and me. You let the world think the worst of me and then you offered me a shoulder. You made a lie out of what little life I had left. There's something deeply wrong with you, and that means a lot coming from a wreck like me. You stay away from me. And from my mother." Jane turned and walked out, the gun feeling like a weight in her hand.

* * *

She had been to Bettina's apartment once in the time she'd been living in Adam's dorm room. She knocked, hoping he'd just come here.

Bettina, the German graduate student, opened the door, face bleary with sleep.

"Hi, Bettina," she said. "I'm sorry to bother you so late, but is Adam here? I need to speak with him."

"Why would Adam be here?" Her accent was heavy and she sounded angry.

"Because he's your boyfriend."

"He dumped me. Because of you."

"Me?"

"Don't play like you don't know."

"I promise you I don't."

"Well, he's not here, and he'll never be here again, because he's obsessed with you."

"That's not so." Adam was her friend. He wasn't more than that. But then she thought: the looks he'd given her, the time just tonight he'd taken her hand. Support or something more?

"You can have him, Jane." And she shut the door.

46

JANE DROVE TREVOR'S truck back to his house. The easygoing party had wound down; only a few people remained. Trevor met her at the door and said, "What's wrong?" and she said, "I can't go home right now. Can I just sit out in the backyard? Alone?" She wished her voice sounded stronger. She had felt like her legs would give way on the way back to his truck.

He nodded. She went and sat under the stars and watched the spill of the bright lights across the black sky. The party noise, now down to only a bit of stray laughter, went quiet; she realized Trevor must be easing the few remaining guests out. She sat there, sick with her own betrayal of her friend, sick with Kamala's retaliation against her, sick with the thought that Adam felt about her in a way she couldn't return. *If only I hadn't been with David. If only David and I had made a better choice. A more thoughtful choice. If only Kamala had forgiven me. If only she had never found out. If only Adam had just told me.* All the possibilities, all the decisions, all the twists of fate. Life, with a hundred different paths.

Nana came out, walked over to her, and gave her a hug as Jane stood. For a second Jane thought he'd told Nana everything, but then she knew he wouldn't. Nana said, "I'm glad you came here, sweetie. I hope you have a good night." And then she went back inside the house.

After a few minutes Trevor came back out. He carried a beer and a bottle of water. He offered both, but she took the water. He sat next to her.

She said nothing, dreading him asking questions, but he said nothing. She had never been so relieved to have a guy be silent, just letting her be.

"I made a mess of everything," she finally said. "Even before David died."

"I should have stayed home that night. Waited for you to tell me what was happening. But David was one of my best friends and you were...I just needed to know."

"Why did you even like me?" She kicked at the dirt.

"I've always liked you. Ever since you took down that big-bowed girl for making fun of me and my incredibly fashionable husky jeans." He wasn't looking at her.

She laughed. She couldn't help herself. "Yeah. Mr. Cool Football player and Miss Dressed All in Black."

"Right, I'm so cool I ask my nana to cook for my parties. It's a level of cool many dream of but few achieve."

"Smart move, it wasn't nearly as messy as it should have been. Could I sleep on your couch tonight?"

Now he glanced at her. "Sure. But why?"

"Well, Adam has a roommate now, so that's no longer an option. And I think he left here because he's mad I was talking to you." Trevor said nothing to that, and she didn't want to talk about Adam, so she continued: "I've learned just how awful Kamala and I have treated each other. I don't feel like going back to my house and confronting my mother about the miscarriage she kept from me. I just don't feel up to it."

"Yeah."

"What will Nana think?"

"She's gone to her sister's house and my dad's in Dallas at a conference this weekend. It's just us here." He didn't look at her, he didn't try to freight the words with meaning.

Finally, she said, "I know I asked you for help tomorrow. But it could be really dangerous and now I don't think you should be involved."

"I'm not scared. You're not alone in whatever this is."

He was near; she could probably lean over and kiss him if she wanted to and if he was all right with that. But she didn't. She hadn't had much human contact for a long time now; a hug from Mom or Adam just wasn't the same. But she couldn't. Not yet. Not now. There was too much to do, and she was such a mess.

"You can have my room," he said. "I'll put fresh sheets on the bed and I'll take the couch."

"I'm not throwing you out."

"You'll have more privacy. I'm not Adam or your mom. I'll let you be." The way his words echoed her thoughts jarred her. He got up and dusted the grass off his jeans. "Are you hungry? Nana left food. I was so busy hosting I forgot to eat."

"Trevor, wait." She dreaded asking. "How did you know about the miscarriage?"

He crossed his arms. "You were still in your coma. I arrived to visit you as they were treating you in the room. I heard the nurse say 'miscarriage' to your mother—they had their backs to me, and neither of them saw me. I think maybe it had just happened or it was happening. I backed out of the room, and I walked away as more nurses hurried in. But I heard them say it very clearly." He paused. "So I knew you and David must have..."

"So you kept your distance."

"I thought it was best. You didn't remember it. Or even me as your boyfriend. I wasn't going to insist you try. You had an avalanche of tragedy to deal with, I just didn't want to hurt you or to confuse you more." Now he looked at her. "And I thought, of course, that your mother would have told you."

"Are you mad at me for David, being with him?"

He let ten seconds pass. "It hurt, sure, but compared to what you were going through, my pain was nothing, Jane. I was just glad you were alive. Even if we weren't going to be together..."

"Because I cheated."

"No, because your mom told me to stay away. I tried to come by a couple of more times—you were resting. She wanted me gone. She was clear on that. It started to feel like you and I had simply never happened."

"Did she know about us?"

"I told her. I didn't tell her about looking for you or following you that night. I was embarrassed and ashamed. She said you obviously were in no condition to be in a relationship. I understood."

Mom had purposefully kept Trevor from me. Maybe she thought he was the father? Or maybe she knew David was, and that was why she was arguing with Perri that night?

"I don't know what to say. I don't know why I would throw you over for David," she said. "I don't get it."

"Well, you were in love with him for years. Or infatuation. The perfect boy next door. I think he was unattainable and then he wasn't. My timing sucked. Or we weren't right for each other after all."

"But is that the kind of person I was?" she asked. "Hurting you, hurting Kamala? I'm not sure I want to know the answer to that."

He knelt back down by her on the grass. "I think you're basically still the same person you were," he said. "Good and kind and funny. I still see the Jane I cared about in you. You'd had a hard time after your dad died. The light was starting to come back into your eyes."

"That makes me weirdly hopeful."

"Are you going to tell your mom you know?"

"I'm going to see how this goes with my therapist," she said. "I need to save my weapons."

* * *

Trevor made up the bedroom for her, left one of his oversized Lakehaven football jerseys for her to sleep in (it seemed a "girlfriend" kind of sleepwear, but she shrugged that thought off), and he retreated to the couch. She lay on the bed. His walls were still covered with photos from high school. She was in several of them, always with David and Kamala and Adam and a group of friends, but the two of them often stood together. They made an odd pair, but she thought she seemed to fit well under the crook of his arm. Then many pictures of him on the football field, with his teammates, before he got hurt. She dressed in the old, soft jersey of his and washed her face in his bathroom. For a moment she looked at herself in the mirror. She could have been a mother. She could have been so many things. She could have been with Trevor.

She could have been whoever she wanted to be.

She lay down. Sleep came in nearly an instant. But she woke up when she heard the pounding on the door.

She lay frozen on the bed; she heard voices in the den, talking quietly. She opened the door.

A man's voice: "Are you alone in the house, Mr. Blinn?"

"No. A friend of mine is asleep in another room."

"Was your friend at your party tonight?"

"Yes, she was."

"Would you wake her, please?"

She thought of going and hiding but instead walked into the den, the jersey hanging halfway down to her knees. "Trevor, what is it?"

Trevor stood in pajama pants and a Lakehaven football T-shirt, hair tousled from sleep. There was a man in a suit talking to him.

"I'm sorry to disturb you. I'm Detective Foles with the Austin Police Department. And your name, please?"

"Jane Norton," she said, feeling cold.

"Jane," Trevor said. His voice was strained. "Someone attacked Amari at her apartment. A man who was with her was attacked, too."

Brenda Hobson. Shiloh Rooke. Randy Franklin. She shuddered. "That's terrible. Are they OK?"

"They were beaten with a crowbar."

A crowbar. She sat down on the blanket that Trevor had spread across the couch. "Oh, no."

"I understand that Ms. Bowman was at this residence for a party earlier. She had told her mother."

"Yes, we're all friends from high school." He glanced again at Jane. "Did you see her leave with anyone?"

She shook her head.

"—and do you know what time Ms. Bowman left here?" she heard the officer ask.

Trevor said, "I didn't see her leave, but it was a bit before ten. I think she was tired."

"Did she have an argument with anyone here?"

"No. It was a very chill party. Jane?"

"I didn't really talk to her, but she seemed fine."

"Had you seen her earlier today, either of you?"

Jane answered first. "I did. At UT. What is the name of the man she was with?"

"Matteo Vasquez. Do you know him?"

How to answer. How long would it take them to find the connection between her and Vasquez? Not long at all. Maybe he was even there to talk to Amari about his new article. Interview her.

And someone had put a stop to that. Trevor glanced at her. Was he wondering if she…?

"I know who Mr. Vasquez is. He used to be a reporter at the paper." Jane paused. "I recognize his name."

Foles frowned. "That's right. Do you know how they knew each other? She told her mother he wanted to interview her."

"No," she said truthfully. She didn't know for sure and she saw no reason to volunteer more information. She could feel the weight of Trevor's stare. "Are they going to be OK? How badly are they hurt?"

"I don't have that information. Do you know if Ms. Bowman was involved in any suspicious activities? I have to ask. This was a coordinated attack. Someone knocked out the lights by her apartment, either before or after they were assaulted."

"She's an honors student and a track star," Trevor said. "She's a total girl scout."

"Can you give me the names of whoever else was at this party?"

Kamala, Jane thought. As soon as she hears, she'll tell all. Her or Vasquez being able to talk is a ticking time bomb for me. Liv Danger strikes again. Where was Perri when this happened? Or my mom? Or Cal? Or Adam?

"Would it be better if I write them down or text them to you?" Trevor said.

"Paper. Sure."

Trevor began to jot down names.

"Sir?" Jane asked. "Can you tell us when this happened?"

"Around ten thirty. Her mother, whom she had called to meet her, found them at ten forty."

Maybe Amari had said to her mother, *This is all about Jane Norton*. But Foles didn't seem to react to her name.

"Were they robbed?" Trevor asked.

"I can't say," Foles answered. "You can't think of anyone having a motive to attack her?"

"Maybe this was random," said Trevor.

The detective took the list from Trevor.

"Which hospital is she at? Do you know?" Trevor asked.

"Breckinridge." It was the downtown county hospital.

"But they're not dead, right?" Jane asked. She couldn't help herself.

"They're not dead, last I heard," Foles said.

"You should call her mom, Trevor," Jane said. A wave of nausea passed through her.

Trevor gave her a hard look. "I think that's everyone," he said.

"Thank you for the information. Can I reach you here at the house again?"

"Sure. Jane is staying here temporarily," he said. Jane said nothing.

Foles left. Jane folded herself on the couch.

"Jane…"

"I didn't do this. You looked at me like you thought—"

"I know you wouldn't. You couldn't."

"But they'll think maybe it's me. A crowbar, Trevor. And soon." She stood. "You should call Mrs. Bowman and go to the hospital."

"Come with me. Show everyone."

"I can't. I have to find this hacker drive that Adam gave my dad before he died. And I need to find out where the Halls were tonight. I can't just accuse them. It would point everything back at me." *My mom. Where was my mom?*

"Where will you go?" he asked.

"Home, first."

"Here. Take my truck."

"I'll drop you off at the hospital."

"I left Kamala off the list to buy you some time," Trevor said. "I'll say I forgot she was here, since I was in shock and it was so late at night."

"Thank you."

"Who is doing this? Who?" he asked.

"I don't know for sure. I thought it was Perri Hall. But I'm not sure I can see her taking a crowbar to people."

"She attacked you."

"Still."

"What about Mr. Hall?"

"No. I don't see him either…but…Perri wouldn't want Matteo writing about this if it made her look bad. She would care more."

"Could she get someone to do this for her?"

It was a smart thought; Perri Hall was the type to keep her hands clean. She thought of Shiloh Rooke, just because he seemed the type to swing a crowbar, but he had no motive; he too had been attacked. "I need to see if I can get Perri Hall to talk."

"Why would she talk to you?"

"I'll give her a reason."

47

————————————

JANE TIPTOED PAST her sleeping mother, put the unloaded gun back in the safe, and shut it softly. Then she went and sat on the side of the bed.

"Mom, wake up."

"Um. Yes." Laurel awoke with a start. She blinked at Jane. "How was your party, sweetheart?"

It was great. I found out I was once pregnant and you never told me. She wanted to scream that into her mother's face, hit her with the pillow, demand an explanation. Instead she took a deep breath—forming the words was so hard—and she said, "Where were you tonight?"

"Tonight? Oh. I went to a movie at the art house up at the Arboretum. Then I drove around, listening to Beethoven."

"You drove around, listening to Beethoven," Jane repeated in disbelief.

"It clears my head. I have to get out of this house sometimes. Why?"

It occurred to her how lonely her mother might be. She thought of the too-many wine bottles in the refrigerator she'd found when she first came home. "So no one saw you."

"No one I knew. Why are you asking?"

"I just don't know where you spend your time. Where did Dad's computer stuff go after he died?"

"Two questions, goodness. What do you mean?"

"His computer gear. His laptop, his flash drives. That kind of stuff."

"That's what you woke me up for?"

"No, I woke you for something else, too, but I want you to tell me where Dad's computer stuff is."

"I...I don't remember at the moment. Um, his laptop. I wiped it and donated it to Goodwill, I think. I gave his spare gear—backup drives, flash drives, all that to David. You know how Perri complained he was always losing his backup flash drives at school."

"I don't, but OK," Jane said. David. If David had come into possession of the hacker-kit drive, what did he do with it?

"Why would that matter in the middle of the night?"

"It doesn't. I just wanted to know." She took a deep breath. "Amari Bowman and Matteo Vasquez were attacked tonight. They're in the hospital."

There was a long pause. Laurel blinked and seemed to process the news. "Goodness. I'm sorry to hear that." But the unchanged smirk said, *Karma, such a bitch.*

"Where were you tonight, Mom? I want to see the movie ticket."

"I threw it away when I left. I don't care for your tone, Jane."

"They were attacked with a crowbar. How long do you

think it will be until the police find out Matteo's writing about me, and these other people who have been harmed, and that a crowbar features in both stories? With this video of Perri attacking me going viral, this is just fuel on the fire. Some reporter will tie it all together."

"Go back to bed, darling. I think your imagination is out of hand."

"Mom. Five people now. Five people hurt by someone who is mad about the car crash."

Laurel stared at her. "Are you accusing me? I'm your mother. I run a charity. I am a good person."

"I know you are. But you just seem to be taking real pleasure in Perri's misfortune."

"She attacked you and now she's getting what she deserves. She showed us who she is on that video. The police should question her."

"You think Perri Hall took a crowbar to two people."

"You don't remember what she could be like. I think that Matteo maybe was going to write about her now. Her, not us. I heard from Gloria..."—Gloria was an across-the-circle neighbor—"that reporter was talking to Perri and some young guy out on the porch last night. She texted me while I was at the movie. She recognized the reporter from the times he came around here when you were so sick."

Sick. Like the amnesia was a past malady she had recuperated from.

"Mom. People could blame us."

"Or blame you again," she said. "A lot of people think amnesia could make you a little crazy. Frustrated. Angry. Like you hurting Kamala in school."

"I didn't."

"I know. If you'd just let me help you more..."

"By 'help' you mean what? A facility? A hospital?" She hadn't meant to say anything about that topic, but it had slipped out.

Her mother's gaze narrowed. "I just want you to be better. That's all. You've been on the streets. You've been living a lie at the school—I know about that, Jane. At least Adam would keep you safe. But that is no long-term solution. You refuse to live here, you balk at real therapy, and you won't try to fix your life. So yes, I think you belong in a facility until you learn to cope. But I'm not going to lock you in one and throw away the key."

Jane stifled all the other accusations she could make. She thought of the pregnancy that was kept from her, the lie about the deer in the road, her mother paying off Kevin. And she wanted to give in to the rage. But no. She would wait until she had witnesses: Kevin, whom she could bend with shame and threats about ethics, and Trevor. Her mother couldn't ignore her, couldn't dismiss her in front of other people, couldn't airily go on her way. So she pushed down the anger.

She needed to find that drive that Adam had given her father.

"I know. I will," she said, to placate Laurel. "I'm sorry I woke you. Go back to sleep." She hugged her mother. She was furious with her, but she still loved her and so she banked the anger for when it would do the most good. Once Trevor and Kevin saw what had been done to her, what her mother was like around her, she could move forward. Facing Kamala and learning the truth about the note, talking to Trevor, being friends with him again, had given her a new strength.

She went back to her room and closed the door. She did not see her own mother staring down the hall at her, trembling slightly. Laurel only went back to bed when Jane turned off her light.

Jane lay in the darkness, thinking about what she would have to do. She had no choice. She'd have to make a temporary peace with Perri.

48

Cal had stopped by before Perri went to bed; he'd told her he had been in San Antonio explaining to an arson investigator the possible connection of the crash to the Brenda Hobson case. He looked exhausted and he poured himself a glass of wine without asking her if he could. She told herself she didn't mind.

"This video," he said. "I'm talking to a lawyer. We could sue the ridesharing service, except that the driver is a contractor, not an employee, and we could sue Jane, although she didn't post it first. But sue for what? It's not libel, it actually happened."

"You didn't hear from Shiloh Rooke again, did you?"

"No," she lied. Her lies to Cal during their marriage had all been of the quiet kind: *Yes, that tie looks good on you; sure, Thai sounds great; oh baby you made me feel so good then.* Never a substantial lie. Omissions, perhaps, but outright falsehoods she had avoided. "Matteo Vasquez came by. He is doing another article on Jane. I sent him packing."

"This video..."

"I'm not talking about that."

"We have to. Look, you're getting pummeled on Face-place. So stay off social media. Don't answer your phone. This, too, shall pass. Something new will outrage or anger or distract people in the next day or so. You'll be yesterday's news. Just bear down and get through this part of it."

"That's so easy for you to say," she said. "I don't need you to tell me how to handle this."

"I'm sorry," he said immediately. "I don't know what it's like and I can't imagine. But I did see some people were posting comments in support of you."

"Oh, great. Total strangers arguing about my worthiness as a person."

"Do you want me to stay tonight? I'll crash in the guest room."

She felt she should say no, but she wanted the company. Cal knew her better than anyone. "Yes," she said. "Sure." She hoped Shiloh wouldn't return tonight, but if he did, Cal's presence would deter him from lingering. Or talking to her. She hoped.

You might want to get your gun, she told herself. She'd been raised around guns—her mother, the maid, often paid in cash, kept one in her car—and her mom had taught her how to use them safely. And she'd kept the gun she'd owned when she first married Cal (he disliked guns), and after he moved out she cleaned and oiled it and went to the firing range and got her sureness of aim back. She had thought of going tonight, to blow off steam, but she didn't feel like venturing out of the house.

Cal made himself a sandwich and had another glass of wine and went to bed. Sometimes she thought she was the only one still tangled in David's death; Cal seemed to move through the world more easily.

She went and checked the gun and put it beneath her bed, on the side where she slept. Just in case. She wished fleetingly that Cal was in the bed next to her, and then fell into a fitful slumber.

She had forgotten to silence her phone. The text chirped her awake, out of a hot, thick dream in which David ran through a field, laughing, always out of reach. She stared into the darkness, startled, then saw the light on the phone screen.

A text in the middle of the night. From a number she didn't recognize. Amari Bowman and Matteo Vasquez attacked. With a crowbar. You know anything about that?

She had to blink away sleep. Amari. A classmate and friend of David's. She had seen David and Jane at Happy Taco the night of the accident. No, she texted back. Who is this?

Jane.

Why are you telling me?

Because I think you're capable of a lot worse behavior than people realize but I don't see you beating anyone into the hospital with a crowbar.

Her first impulse was to text back, *Go away*. Instead, after a deep breath, she wrote, Are they OK?

I don't know.

How do you know what happened to them?

I saw Amari tonight. I saw her earlier today, too, along with Kamala and this Shiloh nut. He approached me after I talked with Amari. I thought he was stalking me. Maybe he was stalking her?

Perri's throat went dry. She turned on the light. I don't know anything about this. Please leave me alone. Haven't you done enough to me?

I think we should talk.

I have nothing to say to you.

And the phone didn't ping for two minutes. *She's done*, Perri thought. Then the text came:

I'm going to ask you two questions. If I feel you've answered them honestly, then I'll share something with you that will change everything you think about me.

Perri almost didn't answer. Then she sent All right.

Can you come outside? Let's talk on your porch. I'm at my mother's house. If you want, we can tape me saying that I forgive you for attacking me and then that can go viral, too.

Face-to-face. The last two meetings had not gone well. Her striking and dragging Jane, Jane knocking hot coffee out of her hands and throwing her out of the house. She could wake up Cal and get him to go with her. This could be a trap. What if she was the crowbar attacker?

She decided. Meet me on my porch in ten minutes.

She went to Cal's door and listened. She heard a soft snoring. She went downstairs and loaded her Keurig with the first cup of coffee and turned on the porch light.

49

PERRI SAT ON the porch, two steaming mugs of coffee at her side. Jane walked up the steps; Perri had watched her come out of the Norton house, not turning on the outside lights, closing the door very quietly.

She held something in her hand, but it wasn't a crowbar, to Perri's relief. It was a piece of paper.

Perri offered her the coffee, hoping Jane wouldn't slap the mug out of her hand this time. Jane took the coffee and sat across from her.

"Cal's inside. I asked him to stay." Perri kept her voice low.

"I'm not here to fight with you. I'm here to ask you two questions and show you something. And it's going to cost us both a lot, but we need to know."

"You've gotten me out of bed, this better be good."

"Is my copy of *A Wrinkle in Time* on David's book-shelf?"

It was the most unexpected question. "Yes," she said after a moment. "I just noticed it was there the other day. I didn't know why he would have it, unless you had loaned it to him."

"I didn't. Kamala stole it." And she told her about how Kamala had planted the note, what her once-best friend had done that fateful night, her seeing them at the lake house, her planting the note Jane had written in the aftermath of her father's loss, and then leaving the book in David's room.

"She texted someone else. A boy who cared about me. It doesn't matter who it is; this isn't his fault. David and I were trying to get away from him, he was following us from the lake house. We lost him and turned onto that road. And then the crash."

Perri stared at her, as if trying to reconcile the fact that she was finally being given a partial story of those missing hours. "It's still your fault."

"If that was all there was to the crash, if it was simply my fault, why is someone targeting people now?"

Perri didn't say anything for a long time; it is a hard thing to have a pillar of why you hate someone suddenly stripped away. "She saw you at the lake house kissing my son? You and David..."

"Did you and my mom know about us? Adam said he saw the two of you arguing that night."

Perri cupped her hands around her mug. "It wasn't about you, no."

"What, then?"

"I had seen her eyeing Cal. She was a widow; she was distraught and she was lonely. I didn't like the attention she was giving him. I knew she wasn't thinking clearly and wouldn't have betrayed our friendship and so I told her to stop with the looks. Cal's so wrapped up in his own thoughts he never noticed. She was angry with me, denying she was after him, hurt at the accusation. Finally, I believed her. She left."

Jane whispered to herself, and later Perri would realize she'd said, "Which anvil do I drop on you first?"

Then Jane said, "I was pregnant. I miscarried during the coma."

Perri rocked in her chair, nearly spilling the coffee as she set it down, a cold agony clawing at her heart and her guts. "David?" she finally said.

"Yes. I wasn't with anyone else. I was seeing this other boy, but we hadn't slept together."

"You and David." She turned away for a moment. "Jane, when you were little, your mom and I used to joke that you and David would marry. Or date. Just joking, but you sort of hope. You were always so cute together. Inseparable. But you just say things like that... you don't really mean them." Her voice drifted off.

Jane sipped the coffee. She didn't look at Perri. "You were like a second mom to me. There's always one of your parents' friends you think, yeah, you could turn to her if you needed to. You could trust her. She would help you. You were that person for me. I thought you knew that."

Perri couldn't speak.

"I loved you. And Mr. Hall. Not just David. I lost him and I lost you both, too. Maybe you didn't care about losing me. Not a bit. I'm not your kid. David was special and I'm a screwup."

"Jane..."

"I know you had your grief. I just thought you would have sympathy or empathy or some kind of 'pathy' for me. I mean, not right away. My brain got broken and I lost the whole sense of who I was, and now I know I lost the baby..." She stopped. She took refuge in another sip of coffee.

"Why didn't you or your mother tell us?"

"She never told me. I found notes about the miscarriage in a copy of my medical file she had; she had never shown it to me. And if I knew I was pregnant, I don't remember it. I didn't tell anyone. I don't even know if I told David. But we had talked about running away to Canada. Maybe he wanted to get me away from here."

"If you had told him, he would have told me and Cal."

"Would he? Lakehaven isn't exactly a hotbed of teen pregnancy. It can change plans. And Lakehaven kids have big plans."

That truth was like a knife in the air between them.

"But he and Kamala..." She didn't finish. "I'm afraid to ask what the second question is."

"Did you ever find, in David's stuff, a flash drive with a musical-note label?"

Perri sipped the coffee; she could hardly taste it, wrapping her head around the miscarriage. David's child. Jane carried David's child. Jane cost me a grandchild, too—the thought leapt up, unbidden, and she pushed it away. She could not go there. Jane had lost as well. So she forced herself to think, and the memory came back, sharp and sudden. "Yes. A flash drive with a musical-note label. It was in a paper bag of stuff that Randy Franklin gave me. Some of David's belongings that were in his backpack or his pockets when he died. That, his phone, some cash, his keys. It was attached to his keys that were in his pocket. The police gave it to Randy Franklin when he was meeting with them; then Randy gave it back to me."

"Do you know where it is?"

"I think so." She in fact remembered clearly: she'd seen it again recently while going through his desk drawers when she'd ended up finding the Liv Danger notebook.

"Would you please give it to me?"

"What kind of music is on it?"

"It actually belonged to my dad. My mom gave a bunch of my dad's computer odds and ends to David after he died. I'd like it back. Yeah, it's just music that belonged to Dad."

She didn't believe Jane. "Why is this suddenly important?" Perri asked.

"It just is," Jane said. "It was my father's. You let me have it, I'll make a video and post it saying that you weren't at fault for what happened at the cemetery."

"I'm not sure I know where it is."

"I'll come with you to look."

"No. You stay here. I'll bring you back your book, too."

She went inside, moved silently to David's room. She found the copy of *A Wrinkle in Time* and tucked it under her arm; now glad she hadn't thrown it away. She opened the desk drawer and found the green drive in the pile of leftover red ones; she remembered he needed them for school and was often losing them. The musical note was on it.

She awoke his computer and slid the drive into the port.

It definitely wasn't music. It was a series of programs. KeyBreaker. KeystrokeMonitor. PasswordCracker. Hacking-Log.

This was stuff to help you break into a computer. Why would David have this? If it had been her father's, why did Brent have it?

And David and Brent, both dead from accidents. She looked in the operations log. It made no sense to her, numbers and ports and words she didn't understand. She ejected the drive from the computer and turned it off, and Cal said, "What are you doing?"

"Nothing," she said, slipping the drive into her robe

pocket. "I couldn't sleep. I wanted to see what the Internet was saying about me."

"That doesn't sound like a good way to go back to sleep."

"It's not. It's a terrible idea, like you said."

"On David's computer? Your laptop is downstairs."

"I know." *Why are you lying to him?* She decided, in a flash, that her dealings with Jane were hers alone. Cal would come in, take over. No. This was hers.

"Go back to bed," she said. "I'm going myself." *Please, Jane, don't come in. Don't knock at the door. Just wait.*

"You're sure you're all right?"

"I am. Like you said, best not to look. I think Jane might be willing to help me make a public apology."

"Jane helping you? I think you should stay away from her."

"I didn't expect you to say that. Don't you want us to make peace?"

"I guess so. We'll talk in the morning." He went back to the guest room and she said, "I'm just getting a drink of water." He made a noise of sleepy acknowledgment and closed the door.

She hurried down the steps and went out the front door as quietly as she could. Jane still sat in her chair, the piece of paper on her lap where Perri couldn't see what was on the other side.

"I found it. You lied to me. It has programs on it."

"Programs to hack a computer. Adam Kessler gave it to my dad shortly before he died."

"Why?"

"I don't know. Randy Franklin was following my father around in the weeks before his death. He had a picture of Adam giving this to my dad. Adam said my dad bought it

from him. He said he had a computer an employee left behind that he wanted to hack. But I think that was a lie."

"Why?" She could barely breathe.

Jane hesitated. "I...I'm trying to figure that out. It all
ties back to why people connected to the crash have been
targeted." She held her hand out for the drive and after a
moment Perri dropped it into her hand. "I've been investigating that night." And she told Perri what she'd learned:
from her taking the files from Randy's office to what she
had heard from Kamala and Amari and Adam and Trevor
and Billy Sing at Happy Taco, in piecing together that
night. She told her everything, except about the photo of
Cal and Laurel kissing—she decided to talk to her mother
first about that. Perri listened, a stunned look on her face.

"So, I have more things to find out," Jane said. She
stood.

"What's that you wanted to show me? Is that it?" Perri
pointed to the paper. It looked like the back of a photo.

"I think I've dropped enough anvils on you tonight.
Thanks for the coffee. I'll post a video on my Faceplace
page tonight. I think if you share it, since people are leaving mean comments on your page, it will put a stop to the
attacks against you."

"Thank you." Two words she never would have imagined saying to Jane Norton.

Jane stood up and left without another word.

50

So what are your plans for today, Mom?" Jane asked. She hadn't slept well and her mother was up early, brewing coffee, and bustling around.

"Um. I have some meetings at the charity office."

"On Sunday?" She kept her voice neutral. The meeting, she knew, was with Kevin.

"Yes, well, that's when people could meet," she said vaguely. "My donors tend to be extremely busy. How about you?"

"I'm going to make a video forgiving Mrs. Hall and post it to Faceplace."

"Oh, I think that's a bad idea, darling."

"Forgiveness is a bad idea?"

"Look, she's finally getting a taste of what real blame feels like. Let her taste it. Have you read the comments on her page? I wonder sometimes who these people are, who have all the spare time to hate on a stranger. We know that feeling." She bit into her toast.

Jane stared at her. "I think you wrote several times about forgiveness on the mom blog."

"I did, but that was more about forgiving one's self."

"You're good at that."

"What's that mean?"

"Nothing, Mom."

"I'm so glad you're home." She tried a smile.

"Adam has a roommate now. So I might be back on the street."

"No, you'll stay here."

She tested her mother. "I don't like being next door to the Halls."

"You are not going back on the streets, Jane. We'll find a different solution. I'll get you an apartment."

"You will? You said I had to either be in school or here."

"Well, I was wrong. I won't have you in that situation anymore."

"Thanks, Mom." She wasn't sure if she could believe this new promise.

"But don't make that video. It's a bad idea. At least not now."

Jane didn't say any more.

"How do breakfast tacos sound? I'll run over to the Baconery and get us some."

"Wonderful," Jane said.

Her mother left and Jane went straight to Laurel's computer. She awoke it and it asked for a password. She slid the hacker flash drive into the port. The windows for the various programs opened. She selected the PasswordCracker; it asked for information such as pet names, anniversaries and birthdays of family members, streets one lived on, and other common denominators of passwords. She entered all that and within two minutes the password was cracked. She went to her mother's e-mail application. Her mother had a home address; one for the charity; and a couple of others, spares Jane supposed, that she didn't seem to use much.

She searched for "Cal." She found old e-mails, from before and after her dad died, but nothing romantic. Many offers of help and solace from the Halls after Brent's death. Nothing suspicious. She searched for "Perri"—more of the same. She found a few e-mail exchanges after the crash, pleas that Jane tell what happened, angry e-mails doubting her amnesia, rejections of Laurel's pleas to publicly forgive Jane. Those were hard to read. And then nothing.

She went to the charity e-mails, paged through them. Notes to Laurel's assistant, drafts of e-mails soliciting funds. A note to a bank about an unusual deposit, her mother had to fill out some paperwork. It had been a large overseas donation.

Jane skipped to the accounts she hadn't seen before. They looked mostly like spam; perhaps these were the accounts her mom used when shopping online or enrolling in a loyalty program. But there were several from banks overseas, and they recorded deposits and withdrawals. Like the spreadsheets she'd seen in her father's file she'd taken from Randy Franklin. She even recognized some of the abbreviated names: HFK, Alpha. Those had been entries in the spreadsheets.

Were the spreadsheets in her father's file not her dad's at all but her mother's? Why?

She printed out a couple of the bank e-mails, folded them, and tucked them into her jeans pocket.

She went back to the search window and searched for "Jane."

She found two recent e-mail threads. The first was with a private mental hospital just outside Austin. Questions, arrangements, discussions about whether or not it was the proper place for Jane. How the involuntary-commitment process would work, if that was the path she chose to pursue.

She means to lock you up. Or she did.

And then the second batch of e-mails, all variations found in a drafts folder. She read them, her heart hammering in her chest:

As you know I wrote the *Blossoming Laurel: Modern Mom* blog for many years, being one of the top five parenting blogs for an extended amount of time, generating both substantial advertising revenue and readership. I wrote primarily about the challenges of raising my daughter Jane (while running a successful charity) and then later about the tragic loss of my husband, Brent. I am proposing a new book project, dealing with my daughter's traumatic accident and resulting amnesia, the crash investigation and how it made us pariahs in our small tight-knit suburban hometown. I especially wish to focus on the way amnesia patients are ignored by our medical system and how my daughter Jane was reduced to living on the streets (against my wishes), my difficult decision to commit her to a mental facility...

Jane closed her eyes. Her life, her problems, the current disaster, were fodder for her mother's career, still. And she was writing like the commitment had already happened. Like it was just a chapter. The same way she had treated the rest of Jane's life. She Internet-searched the intended recipient's name: it was a top literary agent in New York.

She went to her mother's browser and went through the

history. Many views of the video of Perri attacking Jane. Searches for names like Brenda Hobson, Shiloh Rooke, Amari Bowman, Randy Franklin…but all from the week before.

Had her mother been building a list? Jane had never checked if her mother had an alibi for the night when Brenda Hobson's home burned.

It couldn't be. Her mother. But…if those spreadsheets her father had been investigating belonged to her mother…

She thought of the odd code written in her father's file: *R34D2FT97S*. She had written it and the other odd numbers in the file down on a piece of paper in her wallet. She entered the number into the search window for the computer. Nothing. She entered it into a browser search window. Nothing.

Then she noticed the two entries under the long code. U: and P:, each with their own entry. Username and password? Typical log-in requirements if it was a website. Maybe the long code was a website address. She copied *R34D2FT97S* into the address line for the browser, added the usual ".com."

The browser jumped to a clean black page. A message on the page read, You are not authorized for access from this system. Thank you.

It *was* a website, but it couldn't be accessed. No way here to enter the username and the password. What did that mean? What was it? It wasn't the kind of website address a person would enter, just looking to see what it was. It made her uneasy.

She heard her mother enter through the garage door. Jane wiped the browser history, yanked the drive from the port, and put the computer to sleep. The stray bits of the world she knew had been shredded, and she forced a smile to her face as she walked into the kitchen. Her mother un-loaded the foil-wrapped tacos.

"Hungry, darling?"

"Yes, Mom." She sounded subservient, but for the mo-ment that was the role to play. She had to figure out a way out, a place to go where her mother couldn't find her and stick her in a padded room.

She needed a weapon with which to fight back. A secret to stop her mother cold. And if her mother was Liv Danger...she needed a way to put a stop to this now, be-fore someone else got hurt. She didn't want to call the police on her own mother.

They ate and then she went upstairs to text Trevor. She had changed her plans.

51

Sometimes small talk stuck in Perri's mind; such knowledge had been a good way to navigate the social strata of Lakehaven, to remember where someone went to school or whose brother married whom or that someone's parent worked in an unusual field. She had made small talk a few times with Randy Franklin during the investigation and it seemed a miracle that any of it had stuck in her head during the haze of David's death—but it had. She remembered once that he'd mentioned he was from La Grange, a town halfway between Austin and Houston on Highway 71, famous for its kolache bakeries—sweet and savory pastries that Czech immigrants had brought to Texas. When driving back from Houston the Halls would often stop at a certain bakery, but Randy insisted that a rival bakery a block down was better. This smallest of details had stuck in her mind.

She did some Internet searching and found Randy Franklin's parents still lived in La Grange; his father had been a coach at the high school there. She called the number she found, and Randy Franklin answered with a hesitant yes. She said, "Oh, sorry, wrong number," and hung up.

It was about a sixty-five-mile drive. She would go as soon as Cal left. He did not seem the least bit inclined to do so, standing in the kitchen showered but in yesterday's clothes, sipping coffee. He eyed her over the mug.

"What's on your agenda today?"

"Lots of errands to run. I need to get going."

He didn't take the hint. "Jane posted a video about you." He held up his phone and thumbed the control.

Jane, sitting at a desk. "My name is Jane Norton. Recently a video of me being dragged toward a grave has gone viral on the Internet, and many harsh comments are being directed toward Perri Hall, the woman in the video. Please don't hold this against Perri. She is the mother of my dear friend David, who was in a car crash with me and died. David's grave had been defaced and Mrs. Hall was understandably devastated, as any parent would be. She is a good person who has suffered a terrible tragedy. Put yourself in her shoes. Please don't post that video anymore, take it down if you've shared it or put it up. You are mocking a woman who lost her only child. I don't want to be a part of that. Thanks for listening."

Perri watched it and then turned away. Her eyes and face stung.

"Wonder why she did it. I guess it gets the original video even more attention. The press revisits it because she spoke out," Cal said.

"Or maybe she just did it out of kindness. Cal, I hate to kick you out, but I need to go."

"Um, sure," he said. "We'll talk later. I'll check in with you, make sure you're all right."

"I'll be fine. That's not necessary."

"I saw a news report this morning. Two people attacked. On social media one of the local news stations says that one of the victims is Matteo Vasquez."

She said, "Is he OK?" She betrayed no emotion on her face.

"They just say they're in the hospital. A crowbar was left at the scene."

"I know you think I'm capable of violence…"

"You were here last night," he said. He softened his voice. "I'm sorry for what I said the other night, about everything, you attacking Jane, suggesting that you could be involved. I was upset. I don't want the divorce. And…I know you couldn't take a crowbar to two people."

"But you thought I could burn down a house with people in it."

"Perri…"

"We are in this together," she said. "We have been in it together since David died. I know I hurt you with the divorce. I'm sorry you're hurt. I never wanted that. But us not being married doesn't mean I don't care deeply about you or that we're not still a team when it comes to David's memory, or to getting through this nightmare." *So tell him about Shiloh.* She started to and then stopped. She had watched Shiloh leave after Vasquez, but that didn't mean he'd followed the man. It wasn't proof. Still, the police would have to be called. Shiloh could accuse her of being a coconspirator, even though she had known nothing of his plan. Guilt wrenched her. She would be at the station all day. And she would know nothing more about who had started this. If she knew…she could cut a deal with the police, and both Shiloh and whoever was Liv Danger would both be caught. But how long until the police knew Vasquez had talked to her and to Shiloh at her house? If

Matteo awoke and could talk, it would be soon. She was running out of time, so she had to act *now*.

The words started to form and then failed her.

"Are you all right?" Cal asked her.

"Yes," she managed. "I guess."

Cal watched her, concerned, as if he knew she was lying to him. "OK," he said. "We're in this together. I'll talk to you later."

He left. Ten minutes later, she headed for Highway 71 East, and drove to La Grange.

* * *

Randy Franklin wasn't happy to see her. He knew who she was the moment he answered the door. "What do you want?"

"To talk to you."

He looked past her. "Why, Mrs. Hall?"

"Who is it, Randall?" she heard an older woman's voice call.

"A former client with a question, Mom." He stepped out onto the porch.

"I'm sorry to bother you, but this is important, and now your voice mail message says you are shutting down your practice."

"The rent's paid for the next three months. I'll see then."

"Are you waiting out a bad situation?" she asked bluntly.

"My parents are both ill. I needed to come home to take care of them. Why is this any of your business?"

"Brent Norton."

His mouth thinned.

"His daughter, Jane, came to see you and the very next day you basically vanish."

"How did you know that?"

"Jane told me."

"That's not how it is."

"She told me quite a bit late last night on my porch. Like the fact that she came back after you left town. She stole two files from your office—one on my son, one on her father. Here's the weird thing. She says the file on her dad doesn't list a client."

"The client was anonymous. I was paid in cash."

"That would seem to violate some kind of licensing, I would think. An off-the-books job?"

He said nothing.

"There have been several people attacked and hurt who were connected to my son's crash. When you vanished, I thought you were one of them. But you're just here, hiding, and the attacks have changed. Gotten directly violent. Almost like someone else has done them." She wanted to see what Randy Franklin would say—he hadn't been hurt, or damaged, he had just withdrawn from Austin.

"Are you accusing me?"

"I don't know. Who was the client who hired you to follow Brent Norton?"

"If I told you, there wouldn't be a point to anonymity, would there?"

"Did someone come after you? Threaten you?"

"I'm not having this discussion."

"Matteo Vasquez is in the hospital. I assume as a journalist he won't be scared off by the attack on him; he'll redouble his efforts, and other journalists are going to close ranks around him and write about this now. I don't think you just came out here for an extended stay. I can either aim him at you or away from you. Who was the client?"

He didn't answer.

"Are you scared, Randy? Did someone threaten you? What Brenda Hobson wanted most was her house. What Shiloh wanted most was his fiancée. Both, lost to them. What matters most to you? Your parents, that they're safe?" She took a step forward. "If you're scared of being killed, me knowing the secret means you're safer. Don't you see that?"

Either he was tired of hearing her or she convinced him he couldn't stay silent. "My client was his wife. Laurel Norton."

She had to struggle to keep the smile of triumph off her face. "Why?"

"She wanted him shadowed. Who he met with, who he spoke to, where he went."

"And then he ended up dead."

"I had nothing to do with that."

"But...his file. Jane told me there were spreadsheets in it. Was he hiding cash?"

"How did she manage to steal my damn files?"

"She's clever. She always has been; it was easy to forget, considering how she was after the wreck," Perri said.

Randy Franklin gave a disgruntled sigh. "I took those spreadsheets as insurance."

"From his computer?"

"No, he had printed those spreadsheets out. I copied them and took them from his rented office. But I don't know where the spreadsheets came from."

"Was he cheating?"

"No, not a sign. But...in her reports about Brent, she did not want any mention of your husband."

Perri frowned. "What does that mean?"

"If I saw Cal and Brent meeting, or having lunch, I was not to report it. She did not want Cal's name in any reports."

How strange. "Why would Laurel ask that?"

He shrugged. "I don't know. I can suspect."

She made herself say the words. "That there was something going on between her and Cal?"

"Maybe. And if she filed for divorce against Brent, she didn't want Cal's name in the proceedings."

"How long did you follow Brent?"

Now the pause was long and she thought he wasn't going to answer her. "Until he died."

His meaning, so blandly said, took a moment to sink in. "Wait. You followed him to his uncle's house that day?"

"Yes. That was my assignment. After I arrived, I was called and told the assignment was canceled and to write my final report."

"Do you think he died by accident?"

His voice was soft. "No. I think I was not supposed to be there to witness anything."

Shock thrummed through Perri's chest. "Laurel killed him?"

"Or had him killed. But I had zero proof. Zero."

"Did you see any signs he was suicidal or depressed?"

"I would find it depressing if my wife paid a guy to follow me around. He was up to nothing. No other women, no drugs, nothing illegal. He went to his office—he was starting up a business for tax preparation, I think, a chain of those offices—and then he went home. He went to his daughter's events at school and sometimes he drove his daughter and her friends around. He went to his uncle's house because he'd inherited it and had some remodeling done and was getting it ready to put on the market."

"And after his accident you didn't go to the police?"

"No." He cleared his throat. "I hadn't even heard about

his death. The next day there was a box, like I'd ordered books online, at my office door. Inside was thirty thousand in cash." He looked away from her. "The cops didn't think it was murder. Suicide or accident. So I kept my mouth shut. My parents...they don't have much retirement savings. So. I stayed quiet." Shame colored his voice. "This is all going to come out, isn't it?"

"And then it was just coincidence my husband and I hired you to investigate the Nortons' daughter?"

"Your husband told me he knew I did good work and could be trusted. He didn't want to say who had recommended me to him." He bit his lip.

She kept very still, but her mind raced. "OK. I want you to think. You said you had to purge anything regarding Cal from the reports at the request of Laurel. Did you follow Brent Norton anywhere else? Any other place?"

"If you want to tell the cops about me, fine. Go ahead. My folks needed the money. They can come after me, not them. They didn't know. My brother and sister both died young and I'm all they've got." Now his whisper had grown into a growl of defiance.

"I don't care about that right now," Perri said. "Was there any other place Brent went?"

"He went to Houston once—I had an associate of mine follow him from the airport there, but it was a meeting with an investor. Then once he went alone, here, to a marriage counselor. Alone. You know, like maybe asking if he needed to get counseling, which I could have told him yes for free. That was it."

"All right..."

"Oh. Yes. Because I had to cut it. He went to your family's lake house."

"To see my husband?"

"No. Alone."

The kids. The kids had gone to the lake house, according to Jane's account of that night. "And he did what?"

"Walked around it. There was a satellite dish off the roof he looked at. He seemed to be waiting. Then a man came. I didn't know who he was, but anything connected to Cal wasn't to go into the file. The lake house was his, so I didn't take notes to put into the report. They talked, briefly, and then they both left."

"Who was this man?"

"I don't know."

"You didn't take a picture?"

"No. It wasn't to go into the file."

"Do you remember the license plate, the car?"

"No."

"You said you took those spreadsheets from Brent."

"I broke into his office once. The spreadsheets were there, on his desk, along with some notes in his wife's handwriting. I know it was hers because she wrote me checks. I made copies of both."

"What was in her handwriting?"

"A long web address, very random. Like the kind you wouldn't ever accidentally type. And some code. I think it must have been to access something on the web."

"Did you try?"

"Yes. I got a 'denied permission' page. Got no farther. And then after I got that money and gave it to my parents, I didn't ask questions about Brent Norton anymore. And you and I never had this conversation, Mrs. Hall. I need to go tend to my dad now. He gets confused." He got up to go inside. "I would leave this alone. Nothing points to any crime, except someone bribed me to stay quiet, and what's done is done. You might not like where an answer leads you."

He shut the door on her as she sat unmoving on his porch.

The lake house. Kamala had gone there; the kids had gone there; and Brent Norton had gone there. Something was there, the key to all this.

52

Kevin texted Jane: I am still to meet your mother at her charity office; closed today, so will be private. Please remember everything that has happened is for the best.

Jane had the photo of her mother and Cal. She had, in her pocket, the other scraps that came from her father's file: the paper with the long-coded numbers and letters that seemed to lead to a hidden website, the folded spreadsheets. She didn't know what they meant, but she was going to give them to Trevor to keep for her, in case this went wrong. Because they could not be explained, they had to be part of the explanation of the mystery that lay at the center of her life. Her mother had loved her, and taken care of her, and written about her in ways she wished she hadn't, but now Laurel had lied to Jane, and the truth had to be brought to light.

Trevor picked her up a bit before two. He was in jeans and a dark T-shirt that was tight on his strong frame, and the shirt said SECURITY in big yellow letters on the front; he wore dark glasses. He did look intimidating. But he greeted her with a smile. A big, slightly goofy smile. Like the world might be OK.

"You took being my badass sidekick seriously," she said.

"I worked as a bouncer on Sixth Street for about ten minutes, but I'm not really a night person," he said.

They parked across the street from her mother's office. Her mother's car and another car were already there. "Is that car Kevin's?" he asked.

"I guess."

"Do you want me to come with you?"

"Yes."

"This is kind of personal, Jane. If you decide you want me to leave, to have privacy with her..."

"I know. But she loves her audience. This time *I* pick the audience."

"This is going to be brutal if your mom tells him to write up commitment papers."

"I've had a lot of brutal in the past week. It's about to get brutal for her." *I don't know if I can do this. What am I suggesting to my mom? That she had an affair and then my dad died? In an accident or suicide or...?* She couldn't think that next, inevitable thought. She couldn't. She felt feverish, sick. But it would have to be done.

They walked toward the office. She didn't know why but she reached out for Trevor's hand. She squeezed his hand and he squeezed back.

She stepped into the office. Her mother stood in her private office's doorway, Kevin sitting in a chair, looking miserable... and two large men in suits and sunglasses, hands folded in front of them, waiting like sentinels.

Jane laughed in disbelief.

"My apologies, Jane," Kevin said. "I had to tell her."

Her mother gave her a pitying smile. "Sweetheart, I'm sorry about this."

"About what?" Jane said.

"Trevor, please excuse us. This is a family matter," Laurel said.

"He's staying," Jane said.

"Trevor," Laurel said. "Please go. I won't ask again."

"Jane wants me here," Trevor said. "I'm sorry, Mrs. Norton, but no."

Laurel looked at the two men, jerked her head toward Trevor. Both men quickly moved forward and grabbed Trevor by the arms. As big as he was and even with his Security shirt, these guys were bigger and professional, and Trevor was hustled out quickly into the parking lot.

"Mother," Jane said.

"This is for your own good."

"What? Bribing a psychologist to lie to me? Manhandling my friend?"

"Jane. You are not getting better. I can't let you lead your life this way. Adam can't keep you in his dorm room and you've said repeatedly you won't live at home, so I had no choice. Kevin and Adam are both willing to testify as to you being a danger to yourself."

Wait, what. "Adam?"

"Yes."

"No. He wouldn't."

"He will."

"Why?"

"I'm not sure he's thrilled about your renewed friendship with Trevor."

That felt like a fist in her stomach. Adam's former girlfriend, Bettina, was right; she had misread her relationship with Adam, and what he wanted from it. And now he was getting his revenge for her not feeling the same way. She looked at Kevin. "Do you hear her?"

"Jane. Listen. What you're doing is dangerous. It's very hard for people to accept responsibility. To accept the blame of others. What you're doing..."

"What I'm doing?"

"It's a very nice facility. You'll thrive there. You'll remember more." Kevin tried to smile.

"I am remembering," she said, to see what reaction she got. "I'm remembering more and more."

"Then the hospital will help you process it," Laurel said.

"Mom, this isn't the nineteen fifties, this won't work. I'm lucid."

"You're a homeless amnesiac tied to arson and burglary." She stated this as if it pained her. She would be convincing to anyone that asked. "You'll be safe there."

"Tied to arson? No. I was in Adam's room the night those houses burned."

"Adam now says you took his car. It's in the commitment papers Kevin has drafted." Her voice was steady with the lie. It would make a good impression on a judge or a doctor.

Kevin said, "We know about you making Internet threats, Jane. The Liv Danger persona."

"That's not me!" The world, closing in on her like a collapsing building. Wouldn't a judge have to sign those? Wouldn't someone else have to examine her? Or how much had her mom greased the right palms? "Why are you doing this?" Her voice rose.

"To save you."

"No. It's for your book you want to write. I'm just the supporting player. I thought I was your daughter. I'm just a damn prop in your life."

The jab about the book scored a hit—Jane saw her flinch—but Laurel kept her composure. "That's so unfair." She looked at Kevin as if he would agree.

"So what, you're going to prosecute me? Tell the police these lies?"

"No. If you cooperate, I won't say a word to the police, and neither will Kevin."

"How long am I supposed to stay there, Mom?" Her voice broke. Her life, slipping into a grayness, much darker than the limbo she'd let herself fall into. "What, until you and Cal get married?"

Her words were like a shove. Laurel actually stepped back.

"Excuse me," Kevin murmured, going out the front door.

"That's a lie," Laurel said.

"I have a picture."

"No, you don't."

"Yeah, I do. You and Cal, kissing. Dad was still alive."

"You're lying."

"I stole it from Randy Franklin's files."

Her mother's mouth trembled. "So I can add burglary to your list of misdeeds when we arrive at the hospital."

"Go ahead. Did Dad know?"

"Jane, I have never—"

"If you deny this one more time, Mom, I actually will go insane and turn on you. Stop. Lying."

Laurel took a deep breath. "All right."

"Did Dad know?"

"No."

"Are you sure? Did it make him depressed or suicidal, finding out that you were cheating on him with his business partner and next-door neighbor?" She said the words like they were hard punches.

"That wasn't my fault. His death was an accident."

"You're paying off Kevin, you're encouraging Adam, why stoop to this? Why do you need me tucked away?"

"Can you not trust me?" Her voice cut to a whisper. "It's for your own good."

"Mom." She could show her the papers from Franklin's file. And have them promptly taken away by these hired goons. Her plan fizzled into nothingness.

The door opened and one of the men came back in. "Are we ready, Mrs. Norton?"

"*What?*" Jane screamed. "I'm not going anywhere with you all."

Laurel said, "Jane. Don't resist. These men are here to protect you and to make sure you safely reach the hospital."

"Where am I going?"

"It's a very nice hospital in the Hill Country. Chic, even. Like a spa." The excitement she tried to add to this announcement was the most ghastly thing Jane had ever heard.

"And when do I get out of this spa?"

"When the doctors say you're well enough. Let's not prolong this. Let's not make it ugly. I need you to trust me. Give me your phone."

Jane did. Her fingers brushed the papers folded in her jeans pocket. She hadn't yet given them to Trevor.

But then the man reached for her and Jane raised a warning finger at him; he brought his hand back and just opened the door for her. He gestured, almost gallantly, for her to step outside. In the parking lot, Adam Kessler stood next to Kevin, arms crossed, upset and defiant, and Trevor sat on the asphalt, hands into fists, the other man standing over him.

"You need to agree, or it will get ugly. You don't want

these two men beating up Trevor." Her mother said this to her from behind Jane, her voice a harsh whisper.

"He'll go to the police."

"And we'll all say he interfered with your removal to the hospital. I'll file charges. This is happening, and it's for your own good, his own good. For everybody's good."

What did that even mean?

"Just get in the car, Ms. Norton," one of the men said.

"Jane, I did this for you," Adam called to her. She showed him her middle finger.

"Jane?" Trevor stood. "Jane?"

"It's OK, Trevor," Laurel called. "It will all be OK. We will take good care of her."

Four steps from the car she thought, *No. They are not going to lock me up, even if it's a spa, they are not. They are not.* Not when she'd come this far. She grabbed her mother and shoved her into the guard and sprinted the other way. One of the men tried to intercept her and Trevor tackled him, both of them landing in the oil stains of the parking lot, the man howling as the side of his face scraped the pavement.

Jane ran. She ran down the hillside that led to one of the winding creeks that threaded through Lakehaven. These always flooded during the spring rains, but now, in the autumn, it was shallow and cold and choked with leaves. She ran and then saw one of the men chasing her. She didn't know where the other one was.

Don't, Trevor, don't fight them.

She started scrambling up a hill between the office park and a nearby road, the incline thick with oaks and cedars, slowed by the steepness. The man was gaining on her, calling, "Don't do this, Jane, don't. We are here to help you."

What if she found someone to help her? All her mother

had to do was show the commitment papers Kevin had drafted and all her denials would be worthless.

She ran. And behind her, she heard the crack of a gun-shot.

No, no, no. She nearly stopped but she saw the man closing the distance. *No, keep going.* She went behind the storefronts; there was a Dumpster, another tree-studded hill leading to a park. She couldn't outrun this guy. She jumped in the Dumpster, closed the lid behind her, covered herself in the gross garbage bags, a couple of which had leaked. She buried herself in the pile. Her cage smelled of rotting food and soiled diapers—one of the storefronts was a tod-dler learning center—and she held her breath. She could hear footsteps going past the Dumpster. She stayed still, barely breathing, fighting the urge to cough and gag.

Footsteps coming back. The lid being raised. She felt the weight of a bag landing on top of the bags that covered her.

"Can I help you?" a man's voice asked. Different than that of her pursuer.

"I'd like to look in your Dumpster. There's a young woman who may be hiding in there."

"And why?"

"She's being committed to a mental health facility and she ran from us."

"You got some ID?"

"The family hired me."

"You don't have any ID from a hospital or nothing?"

A slow beat of silence. "No."

"Well, look, she ain't in here. I just threw in a ton of garbage. No one's in there."

She couldn't see, she did not dare move. The silence stretched and stretched. The lid fell.

"If you see her…" the pursuer began.

"If I see someone, I'll call the police. Thank you."

She waited. Waited. It felt like a grave. He could come back, wait for her, drag her to a car and now she'd really look ill, the woman who'd covered herself with garbage. She counted to a thousand, disciplined and measured, then finally she crawled out from the Dumpster. She shivered. She wanted to head back to the parking lot, to know that Trevor was safe, that her mother was all right, because as mad as she was at her mother, there had been a gun fired. Which might bring the police.

But she didn't hear a siren. She crept back through the woods toward the parking lot, thinking, *This is stupid, they'll catch you.* She splashed a trickle of cold water from the creek onto her soiled face. She climbed back toward the lot, ready to retreat again.

They were all gone. Except Adam, who was sitting on the hood of his car texting. He stared at her.

She walked up to him. "Thanks for selling me out."

"Your mother is worried about you. And you smell like crap."

"There was a gunshot…"

"Oh, did you come back to see if Trevor was all right?" he asked sarcastically.

"Adam, don't. I was worried about everyone."

"Trevor was the one with the gun, genius."

"What?"

"Trevor had a gun and it went off when the guy took it from him. He unloaded it and gave the gun back to Trevor but not the ammo and then told him to leave or they'd call the police on him."

"Where is my mom?"

"With the guards and your doctor, looking for you.

They're in three different cars. I expect one of them will roll back through here at any moment."

Now her gaze met his. "If you care about me so much, why didn't you tell me and why would you do this to me now?"

Ten seconds ticked by in silence. Finally he said, "Why didn't you let me be the one there for you? Trevor walks back in and wow, all of a sudden, he's the hero. Not me. You need me until you don't, then you throw me aside for a dumb jock."

She could hardly keep her voice steady, she was so rocked by his betrayal. "You have been my dear friend, and I never meant to make you think otherwise. Trevor and I were involved. Really, really involved. Before the accident."

Adam's face blanched.

"And I don't know if the memories of how I felt about him are coming back, or I just like him now as a friend, but he had things that only he could tell me about that night. Me turning to him for help wasn't a rejection of you. I can't reject you if I don't know how you feel about me."

Adam turned away. She turned his face back toward her. She wanted to slap him, but she couldn't. She needed his help, so she forced her anger down.

"If you want to help me, really help me, help me get out of here. I think I know how to find out what happened that night. Or you can continue to act like a complete jackass who only pretends to care about me."

He stood up a little straighter. "Get in the trunk of my car."

"I don't trust you that far."

"You're not going to stink up my car."

"I want you to take me to Trevor's."

He shook his head. "That's a bad idea. I heard one say they were going to follow him, because you might go to his house."

How can I trust you? she thought. *It's not like I have a ton of options.* "OK." Then she told him where to go.

"Why there?"

"I have a reason. And when this is done, you and I can have a talk about…us." There was no "us"; there never would be. But he didn't know that. Her coldness amazed her. But this was what had to be done.

He nodded.

It took all her will to get into the trunk. He closed the lid. He could drive her straight to her mother. Either he regretted his actions or he didn't. Why did a guy have to be this way?

She lay in the stinking quiet, and when he opened the trunk again, she wondered if she was back at her house. She climbed out. She wasn't. She was, as requested, at the Halls' lake house.

"What exactly are you going to do here, Jane?" Adam asked.

"Wash off in the lake and then get inside the house. And that's a crime, and you can't be here. And you need to get amnesia for the last twenty minutes."

"Jane." He took a step forward.

And she put up her hands. "Thank you for bringing me here. But I am not having this long-overdue talk with you right now."

"I'm sorry. I'm sorry." Adam's voice broke. "You have to understand. I've tried to make so many things up to you. I thought…I thought I had hurt your dad. Giving him that hacker drive. Maybe he found out something he wasn't supposed to and he killed himself, or...I didn't know. So I thought the only thing I could do was take care of you. I tried. It was hard, because we had been so close and you didn't remember me at all. You knew Kamala and David and Trevor when you were little, but I was your most recent friend, and I was gone from your brain." He steadied his breath. "I just care about you a lot, more than I ever did before, and I miss the Jane I knew. I see flashes of her now and then. Not all of her."

"No one has been better to me than you have. No one. That's why what you've just done has hurt me so badly." Those words were true and she felt a ragged edge in her voice.

"You hurt me, too," Adam said. "But I'm not going to stand here and cry. I just want a chance with you."

She said nothing.

"I feel weird about leaving you here. Don't do anything dumb, Jane."

"I won't if you won't," she said. "But know this. If you tell my mom where I'm at, I'll never speak to you again." He nodded. She said, "Can I have that blanket you have in the trunk?"

"Sure. I'll find a way to help you. You don't have to doubt me." He gave it to her, seemed ready to say something else, but then got in the car and drove off. She shivered, watching him leave.

Behind an oak, not far from the water of Lake Austin, she stripped down to bra and panties, jumped into the cold lake, and, shivering, scrubbed the scum and garbage from her skin. She wasn't clean now exactly, but it helped. She used Adam's blanket to dry off and she tried to rinse the worst from her clothes, careful not to damage the papers in her pockets. The clothes didn't smell a whole lot better, but she still shrugged into them.

She walked around the house. Hoping for another shard of memory to pierce her mind and tell her what had happened here.

But nothing.

53

<hr />

IT MADE SENSE now, even without what Trevor and Kamala had told her.

They had bought a crowbar. Why did you need such a tool? To break into a locked or boarded-up place. The Halls' lake house was isolated, empty, and no one would have immediately thought to look for them there.

It sat a few hundred feet off Lake Austin, the lawn flat and green, sloping down to the water. Lake Austin always looked more like a river than a lake to her, winding through the beginning rises of the Texas Hill Country. She could see the houses on the opposite side. There was one that was a plain-looking ranch house that looked like it dated to the 1970s and hadn't been updated. The one farther down the lakeside was a Tuscan giant, all new architecture, high-end and glamorous.

She had come out here a couple of times, for birthday parties when they were little. David's birthday was at the beginning of summer and he liked the lake. She remembered that he'd nearly drowned out here, and Perri hated

the house after that, but Cal refused to sell. When they were
in third grade: her, Kamala, Trevor, and David, and other
kids. She remembered that: ice cream and cake, jumping
off the pier, swimming, the parents all watching over their
cocktails, nervous, the cool pleasure of the grass against
her bare, wet feet as she ran. They'd played freeze tag, the
dumbest game ever, but oh they'd had fun. She remembered being frozen by Trevor—despite his bulk, he was
fast—and David tagged her again, saving her, but Trevor
caught him and froze him before he could reach the tree
that was the safe base. David had sacrificed himself in the
game to save her.

It should have been a sweet, funny memory, but it made
the back of her throat hot with emotion. Her face, her head
hurt. She walked around the house. The land, the house,
had to be worth a fortune. But it was quiet and private;
something could be hidden here.

If only she knew what it might be. It was infuriating
to think the information was a ghost in her brain, un-
touchable, unreachable.

Then an offhand comment Amari had made rose in
her mind: Cal Hall had come to Happy Taco. She hadn't
thought about it much, but he had been in touch with Kamala earlier in the evening; that was in the texting record;
if she found David and Jane here, and she was incensed
enough to text Trevor—and yes, Kamala had admitted, she
had texted Cal as well. It was a possibility, done in anger.
Look what your perfect son has done.

She peered in through a window. Maybe this was the
window where Kamala saw them kissing. Kamala had said,
*I watched you through the window. You were crying. He
took you in his arms. He kissed you, but like he'd never
kissed me. He picked you up in his arms. You kissed him*

back. You—you wrapped your legs around his waist...He leaned you back against the wall...kissing you like you were everything to him and I was nothing.

She heard a car driving and stopping on the other side of the house. She peered around the corner.

Perri Hall. She froze. She watched Perri park. Then she saw Perri open her trunk and pull out a crowbar. It was sleek and steel and had a deadly cleanness to it.

Jane stepped out from the building. "Mrs. Hall?"

Perri looked like she was ready to drop the crowbar in shock. "Jane. Why are you here?"

"My mother attempted to have me committed to a mental home. She had hired goons to chase me and she got my best friend to betray me. They roughed up Trevor Blinn. I hid here."

For a moment Perri said nothing to this catalog of tragedy. "Um, you smell bad." *Like a crazy person*, Jane thought she would say.

"I hid from them in a Dumpster. My clothes don't matter. My mother...my mother and your husband were having an affair before my dad died. I'm sorry."

Perri tapped the crowbar against her own leg, gently. "That is really not a shock to me. I just talked with Randy Franklin." They shared their information. Jane felt sick at the revelations.

"Why did you bring the crowbar?" Jane asked.

"Because you all were here that night. With a crowbar. Let's go inside. Maybe it will prompt your memories."

Perri unlocked the door.

Jane followed Perri through the house. It was a second home, but the furniture was not hand-me-downs from the main house; it was nice, high-end, a beautiful home but sterile, as if it wanted for people. Jane walked through the rooms. No doors were locked, nothing padlocked where you might need a crowbar to gain entry. She found a room with a touch of David about it—photos, posters of Lakehaven football, a wooden Lakehaven Roadrunners baseball bat mounted above the bed. A large window faced the driveway.

"Anything?" Perri asked. And Jane shook her head.

"I hate this house," Perri said.

"Because David nearly drowned here?"

"Well, that, but Cal wouldn't ever sell it. We bought it when we couldn't afford it and he'd never sell it even when we needed the money. Our finances turned out OK, but I couldn't figure out why he loved it so. Maybe he saw it as a place to get away from me. Or just a place to be with David and shut me out." That last part came out before she thought about it.

Jane said nothing. There was no comfort to be given.

They finished their downstairs search and went upstairs. More bedrooms, for when the Halls hosted large parties. Most looked untouched. There was a master bedroom, facing out onto the lake, with a spectacular view.

"I haven't slept here in years," Perri said. "Do you think this is where...your mother and...Cal?"

"Don't think about it. You're divorcing him."

"I still love him." She said it like it was something she hadn't known.

Jane wanted to reach out and touch her, but she didn't.

Jane went back down the hall. There was a door near the far end of the hall. Jane could see faint marks of damage along the door frame and the wall—perhaps where a crowbar had once been forcefully applied. It was locked.

Perri ran her fingers along the marks. "Painted over. You

two came here and then this was painted over." She said it like something inside her was breaking.

Jane took the crowbar from her. Without asking permission, she started levering the lock off. It was hard work, and Perri grabbed the bar with her and together they pulled. The door's lock splintered. Perri kept her grip on the crowbar; Jane let go and stepped into the room. It was a small room, of no real purpose except for a small chair, a TV, and a card table. And, she saw, looking up, an attic door.

"Did you know this was here?" Jane asked. Perri shook her head.

Jane pulled the attic door open. A small stepladder folded out. She crawled up into the attic; the AC unit was on her left. To her right, toward the front of the house, was a wall and a door, dividing this small room from the rest of the attic. Padlocked. And scarred again from an earlier crowbar, but not painted over. Because no one would ever see it.

"Oh," Jane said. She nearly dropped the crowbar.

"Are you remembering?"

Jane covered her face. "I don't want to be here." Fear, like a fire, had lit in her gut, her spine, her brain.

Perri turned from her, taking the crowbar from her hands, and went at the second door, her breath coming sharp. This door was tougher and by the time she splintered the lock, Perri's face was drenched in sweat.

"I feel sick," Jane said. It was a sudden punch to the gut; she went to one knee.

"Do you remember this?" Perri asked, kneeling beside her.

"I don't... we have to get out of here."

"No, Jane, not yet. Maybe you should go outside and get some fresh air."

"No." Jane pushed herself up. "No. I need to see."

Perri put a hand on her shoulder and helped her up.

The two women looked at each other, and then Jane pushed open the door.

The first surprise was that this part of the attic—a large one, which ran the entire length of the house—was air-conditioned. The room was cold. Inside was a desk, four computers, a server array. It looked like the network setup for a small business. Perri thought, *How can this be awful?*

Jane went to the keyboard of one of the systems. She slid the hacker drive that Perri had found into the port.

"It wants to know common elements you might use for your passwords," Jane said. Perri leaned down and typed: her birthdate, Cal's, their anniversary, the names of the pets they'd had.

"Any other dates?" she read on the prompt.

"The date of the accident," Jane said suddenly. Thinking of the combination on her mother's safe, where she'd found her gun, found her hidden medical files. "Try that."

She did. The computer password was cracked in less than three minutes. The screen opened. Perri sat down in front of the screen. The icons on the desktop appeared to be links to server management apps, and to a distant server elsewhere, marked as being in Iceland.

A browser window opened by default. She pulled the paper with the coded letters and numbers from her pocket and spread it smooth so she could read it. In the space for the web address she started typing in *R34D2FT97S*: the long, nonsensical code she'd found in her father's file, the odd web address she'd tried earlier on her mother's computer. Then at the end she added the *.com*.

She could see David's fingers typing the same, like a flash. She closed her eyes and the image was gone.

"Randy said he saw a paper with a long series of numbers and letters. That can't be a website," Perri said, watching her type. "No one would ever remember the address."

"No one would ever accidentally type it in as an address, that's the point. It didn't work from my mom's computer. It must only accept visits from a list of preapproved computer IP addresses. Hers wasn't, but this one..."

Jane hit Enter. The screen opened to a banner that read, Welcome to Babylon. There was a prompt for username and password.

The jumbled numbers and letters below the address on the piece of paper. One marked "U," one marked "P." She entered the "U" code from the paper into username, the "P" code into password.

Jane hit Return.

The site opened.

"Oh, no. No," Perri said. "This can't be."

The front part of the site was old-looking, like a relic from the early days of the web. Only when one clicked through to the various categories did the design get more sophisticated.

Because this was a marketplace.

Sex slaves. Illegal drugs. Illicit weapons. Hacker services. On the first tab the current offer was a thirteen-year-old girl, kidnapped from Cambodia, available to buyers. Jane moused to another tab, and there was a long list of human beings, mostly women and children, available for bidding. Perri made a noise and couldn't look at it anymore, while Jane started to cry and moved the mouse to the arrow for illicit drugs. Offers appeared on the page, organized by prescription or by illegal. Oxycontin to heroin, cocaine to painkillers.

On another page, requests for hacker attacks against various organizations, individuals, and companies, from the United States to Europe to Africa to China, with payment in digital currencies. It got even worse. A forum of death, of hired killers offering their services. Jane read, numb, as some restricted their services, announcing they would not kill minors or political figures.

"What is this?" Perri said. "This cannot be."

Jane minimized the browser. "Stop looking at it." She found a spreadsheet app on the desktop, opened it. She pulled the spreadsheet printout from her pocket, smoothed it flat. She entered in the names and abbreviations from the spreadsheet against a catalog of files. HFK. Alpha. On the same dates as the entries she found listings. Payments funneled from...her mother's charity. Helpful Hands Reaching Out was a front, one of many channels to clean the money sent to this online marketplace.

Her mother was part of this.

"My dad must have found this when he was looking for proof of their affair. Then *we* found it..." Jane's voice cracked.

"Are you saying Cal came here when Kamala told him you were here...and found that you two had discovered this?" Perri pressed her fist against her mouth.

"No," Cal Hall said, standing in the doorway. "That's not quite what happened."

54

"STEP AWAY FROM the computer," Cal said. There was a gun tucked in the front of his pants. He had a Taser in one hand; he gestured with it.

"Don't you point that at us," Perri said. "Explain yourself."

Cal pulled a cheap, orange phone from his pocket. Orange. Like the one missing from the crash, the one Brenda had knelt on when she went to help David. Cal pressed a button, listened, said, "It's OK. We have a situation, but it can be handled. But I need you to be ready." Then he hung up and put the orange phone in his jacket.

Jane stared at him, and it was as if shards and slices of memory cut into the here and now, pierced her brain. This room. This terrible room. David sliding the hacker drive into the computer, finding a password, discovering the distant server, entering the username and the passcode. And then the terrible truth of the dark market.

"David went through the logs, the data records on the little hacker flash drive. He found the traces that my dad found. My dad was just looking for proof of e-mails or texts or something on my mother's computer to prove you two were having an affair. What he found was the spread-sheets with far more money than anyone would expect moving through my mother's charity accounts. So, being an accountant, he went looking for the source..."

"He found Babylon. I had no idea how he had done it...I thought the leak was Laurel. I didn't realize he must have had a hacker drive until it was too late. She told me she'd tossed all his stuff. I didn't know she'd given some of it to David. She didn't realize the harm she'd done."

"Our son. You let our son see this? Why would you do this, Cal, why?" Perri demanded.

"I don't 'do' anything," he said. "I help move money. That's all. I don't...I don't touch anything illegal."

"No, you just make it possible..." Jane said. She staggered back from him and it was as if the walls holding the hell at bay fell in her mind. "You. Oh. You. It was a chain reaction. David found the hacker kit. Maybe there is something on there that points to your affair with my mom. Then he found the money trail on your computer, too? This is what had to do with my dad. Both our parents breaking the law. What do we do? Talk about running to Canada. So we wouldn't have to face you all. Then we think, where would this be? We've found the locked doors in the lake house, maybe already when we're there being together sometime before; maybe there's proof behind them. Something we can use to protect us. Protect me, David, and Perri from you. We buy the crowbar. We break in. We find this. It's so much worse than simple money laundering. Then..."

"Then what, Jane?"

Jane shook her head, staring at Cal. "You put us into my car. You made me drive. You had the gun on me. To my head. You...you were in the car with us. *You were there*." Her voice rose into a shriek.

Cal fired the Taser. The needles slammed into Jane Norton and she screamed and collapsed. For a few moments Perri stood frozen in shock as Jane writhed on the floor. She threw herself at Cal, who shoved her to the floor and yanked the crowbar from her grip. When she came at him again, he hit her.

It was unimaginable. The father of her son, the man who had said "I do" to her.

55

Shiloh drove, looping through Lakehaven, the burn of revenge hard in his heart. After the adrenaline had faded from the attack last night, he'd felt at odds, loose, restless. He had tried to call Mimi, to inch his foot onto that thin ice, but she had told him to drop dead and not to call her again. She had been the one good thing in a long time, his reason to get up in the morning, his reason to (usually) not chase after a woman he wanted. And she was gone.

The rage needed an outlet. He had taken out the pretty black girl he'd seen Jane Norton talking to, and the guy who was with her...that reporter. They were both on his list of people who had been quoted in the old series of articles about Jane's accident and amnesia. The follow-up story would be about Jane and the Halls. Even if Jane wasn't Liv Danger, well, if she hadn't driven so recklessly, there wouldn't have been a wreck, Shiloh wouldn't have responded, and then none of this misery would have happened. He tried to tell himself he was doing it for poor Brenda and her burned-up house, too.

But now Jane had vanished and Perri Hall was gone; he'd driven past the circle and seen a police car at the Norton house. They must be questioning Laurel, or looking for Jane, about the attack on Bowman and Vasquez. It hadn't gone how he planned it and perhaps he needed to stage another attack. He had the list from the article of people who Matteo Vasquez had interviewed in the aftermath of the crash. There was the lawyer, Kip Evander, but he had a wife and kids he was around a lot and he hadn't gone to his office. There was this Kamala Grayson, Jane's best friend. Yeah, maybe her. She was pretty but he hadn't yet figured out where she lived.

But he did have an address for one of them. One easy-to-find target was this friend of Jane's and David's, this blond boy, Trevor Blinn. He had been interviewed in one of the articles, his picture taken along with Kamala Grayson as mutual friends of David and Jane. According to the news reports, Amari Bowman had been at a party and he'd called a police officer friend and gotten the address of the party she'd been at—a detective had talked to the boy. Shiloh was restless and curious. When he drove by the house once the next day, he'd seen the boy from the old news article getting into a black truck, wearing a shirt that said Security. He was a big kid, bigger than Shiloh, but he was weak. You could tell he was weak, he wouldn't stand up in a fight. Shiloh prided himself on his ability to read people's capacity to really fight, which very few had. Shiloh had driven off then, before he got noticed parked on the residential street. Neighborhoods had Faceplace pages now and they loved to warn each other when a stranger or a door-to-door salesman was around.

Shiloh had the crowbar. A crowbar could take care of

the blond boy real quick. Blond boy could be the dot under the exclamation mark of Bowman and Vasquez. He was tied, loosely, to the crash. He would fit the pattern of Liv Danger's attacks.

He had then decided to pay blond boy a visit. If blond boy fought back, then fine. He'd had to restrain himself from not beating on Amari Bowman or Matteo Vasquez again once they were down; the sense of power that had coursed up from the steel bar into his brain had nearly been intoxicating.

He had a taste for this, more than for the feel of Mimi's kisses against his mouth.

Yeah. The blond boy. He headed toward his house.

* * *

He didn't quite understand what happened next. He parked down from blond boy's house and sat and waited, and not ten minutes later a dark-haired boy came to the blond boy's house. He didn't know the dark-haired boy. The blond boy met him in the yard of the house; they talked; they seemed to argue a bit.

The blond boy shook the smaller, dark-haired boy and with his window lowered, parked two houses away, pretending to text, Shiloh could hear him yell, "Where is she, Adam?"

And the other boy apparently told him.

The blond boy headed for his truck and the dark-haired boy started to yell at him, *Don't be an idiot. Jane doesn't even like you. She doesn't like you and she doesn't need you. I'm the one who has been there for her, not you. I'm the one she chose to live with, after all. I just need your help, that's all. But we're doing this my way.*

For a second, Shiloh could tell, the words scored home, and the big kid paused. *Oh, looky, looky, who has a crush on Jane.* The dark-haired boy came toward the truck, like he was going to get in, but then the big blond shoved him back, knocking him a good ways across the yard. Then the blond boy got into his truck and roared off, leaving his dark-haired rival standing on the lawn.

Shiloh followed the blond boy.

* * *

The blond boy drove to a big, two-story house on Lake Austin. Shiloh followed, hanging back, but the kid didn't seem to notice him. *Nothing dumber than a guy in love,* Shiloh thought, knowing that was well true. As the blond boy slammed the brakes on his truck in the driveway, there was another car there, a Lexus that Shiloh recognized as Perri Hall's. No other car.

Blond boy ran into the house. The back door was ajar, as if someone had left in haste.

Interesting, Shiloh thought. He got out the second crowbar he'd bought. And waited by the door, to be sure the big dumb blond was alone.

56

THE POLICE HAD left. Jane clearly wasn't there, and Laurel shivered at the thought of the cops actually inside her house. She texted Cal on the cheap orange phone he'd given her, which she kept locked in a drawer in her office; she was to use it only to contact him and he would give her a new phone every month. He got them in bulk somewhere, he'd told her. The phone was so ugly no one would steal it, he said.

The police were here! Looking for J. I have men looking for her. What do I do? She pressed Send and thought, *This isn't going to make for a good chapter in my book.*

The text came back: Come to where the car crashed.

She stared at the words. Why? She texted back.

That's where your daughter is.

She's with you?

Yes. She remembers.

Laurel's chest tightened. Don't hurt her, please. Laurel's hands were shaking. She needs help. No one will believe anything she says.

You know it's not up to me. Get here. Wait for me if I'm not here. Don't hurt her, she texted again. But there was no answer.

Laurel ran for her car. She was scared that there would be a police car waiting, watching for Jane to return, but there wasn't. She nearly dialed the two hired muscles who were now over at St. Michael's, looking for Jane along her old haunts at the school and along South Congress; she might try to blend in with her old crowd. They had already determined she hadn't headed to Trevor Blinn's or Adam Kessler's house. But if she called them to where Cal had Jane...she would have to explain why her daughter was with this man. It was too many questions for private security.

Laurel opened her safe and found the gun. It wasn't where she usually put it. She loaded it, put it in her purse, and headed out the door.

57

PERRI THOUGHT, *He's going to kill that girl.*

Cal had held out a pair of plastic flex cuffs to bind the unconscious Jane's wrists—*You know, like he was prepared for this*, she thought with shock—and ordered Perri to put them on Jane. She stood across from the man she'd taken vows with, loved every night in her bed, kissed on a Paris bridge after attaching a lock to the railing with their names etched on it, bore a son with.

"Do it," he said, gesturing with the Taser. "Now."

"Cal…"

"Do it, Perri. For so long you've said she killed our son. Why wouldn't you make her pay?"

"You're Liv Danger. You. You hacked my computer. You set the fires. You targeted that lunatic, Shiloh."

He shoved her. "I don't want to hurt you. Do as I tell you."

"What are you going to do to her?" *To us*, she amended in her thoughts.

"Nothing, sweetheart. Nothing to her. She's not going to rat on her own mother."

Perri knelt by Jane and put on the flex cuffs, but not too tight.

"Tighten them. Do it right." His voice was steel.

She did as he said. "I don't understand this. I just don't. You were in the car with our son...?"

"Come on." He unplugged the computers with a kick of his foot against the cords, put the unconscious Jane over his shoulder, and gestured at Perri with the gun. "My car. You're driving. Do as I tell you and this will all be OK."

"*Cal*." It was as if their whole shared history were in that one, pleading word.

"I did what I had to do."

"Were you *in* the car when David died?" Her voice rose. Because that meant he had abandoned their son. In his worst moment of need, Cal had left David dying. It couldn't be so.

Cal kept his voice steady. "It's not what it seems. I will explain everything to you when this crisis is over. I am not having this conversation now. If you don't do exactly what I tell you, I will hurt you. I don't want to, but I will."

"I'm your wife." She nearly spat the words.

"You're leaving me. You're divorcing me."

It could not have been a greater shock to her than if he had struck her. "Cal..."

"For two years I've heard you hate on this bitch, blame her for everything wrong in our lives, and now you take her side."

"Cal, this isn't you."

"Shut up. Walk ahead of me. Run and I'll shoot Jane, I swear I will."

She believed him. She believed, in a rush, that Brent Norton's death was no accident, that Cal had killed his best friend. He would kill Jane. Maybe he would even kill her. She was nothing to him, perhaps only the vessel that had given him his son. "Were you with David when he died?"

"I'm not talking about that."

He shut the house door awkwardly and she, glancing back, saw it didn't close right. She said nothing. He, flustered and angry, opened the trunk of his car and dumped the limp Jane in it and slammed it shut.

"Drive," he ordered Perri, tossing her the keys.

"Where are we going?"

"To the crash site. Sort of."

"Why? Who did you call?"

He didn't answer.

"You cannot do this, Cal!" she screamed.

He ordered her into the car, gesturing directly with the gun. She obeyed. They drove onto Old Travis and had gone a quarter mile when she saw a large black truck racing past them. And then another dark truck following at a distance, but this one with Shiloh at the wheel. She glanced in the rearview; she had memorized his license plate. It was him. *Shiloh*. No. She assumed Shiloh was heading to the lake house. This had all gone wrong.

"Listen to me," she said. "I made a mistake. That attack on Amari Bowman and Matteo Vasquez, I know that wasn't you. It was Shiloh. He's trying to make Jane and her mother look guilty. He's out there, Cal, and he's going to hurt someone."

"Drive."

She did, following, she realized, the same path her son and Jane had followed. At his direction, she turned onto High Oaks. But before she reached the crash site, he said, "Turn in here." It was one of the three large houses on the road, its gates open.

The one man who had heard the crash and called the police. What was his name? James Marcolin. She turned in and the gates swung shut behind her.

58

SHILOH COULD HEAR the blond boy running through the lake house, calling Jane's name again and again. Oh, yeah, some affection at work here. All Shiloh had to do was wait and the idiot would just barrel out the door and Shiloh could take him down with one solid home-run swing. He tested the weight of the crowbar in his hand. Mimi had been taken from him; if this boy was Jane's version of Mimi, the one she cared about, then he would take him from Jane.

In the back of his mind he kept thinking how Perri Hall was going to react to this, if she would be suspicious of his hand in it. Didn't matter. She hadn't called the cops on him for Bowman and Vasquez. She wasn't an idiot. She would shut up as soon as he made it clear she was part of this, as much a conspirator against the Nortons as he was. He wondered what she'd be like in bed.

He slapped the weight of the crowbar into his hand, thought of the blond boy's head caving like a melon.

The sound inside stopped. No more calls for Jane. It

gave Shiloh pause. Maybe something interesting was in the house? He resisted the urge to rush inside. Wait for it. Wait. There was a second-story window directly above him. Had the blond boy seen him or his truck? He cussed and waited.

He listened: the soft ripple of the water on the lake, a distant dog barking, the hum of a boat's engine far down a bend of the lake. But he heard the door open on the other side of the house. He turned and ran around the house, the crowbar cocked back to deliver a crushing blow, and there was the blond boy, holding a wooden baseball bat, swinging with equal force at him. Shiloh barely got the crowbar up in time as the bat slammed down into him and then into his face. He felt his lip split but he pushed past the pain, like he'd told the patients to do as he stitched and held them together, and shoved back against the kid. The blond boy was big but Shiloh was strong and low to the ground, and the big kid didn't really want to hurt him.

That was the mistake. That, Shiloh thought, was why he would win.

They tumbled back and the blond boy started to yell, "Where is she?" in an enraged voice. But he was down, and Shiloh was on top and he swung the crowbar, connecting with the boy's shoulder. The boy howled. Shiloh raised it again, grinning, and the kid kicked out and Shiloh went flying back into the dirt.

The blond boy, his right arm useless, staggered to his feet.

This was bad. He'd gotten a good look at Shiloh's face. That had not been part of the plan. Shiloh had thought it would go like Vasquez and Bowman, where neither had gotten a look at his handsomeness. OK. So be it. The decision to murder this boy was quick and not barbed with a lot of regret. Mimi was as good as dead to him, wasn't she?

Shiloh swung again with the crowbar. The kid had moved the bat to his left—clearly not his dominant hand—parried with the bat, and Shiloh laughed—this was like a redneck swordfight. It would make a great story except he really couldn't tell it to anyone. He swung and caught the boy's hip, heard the crack of glass and plastic taking the blunt of the blow. He swung again and the boy stopped the blow, but the bat splintered, leaving a long, sharp shard in the boy's hands.

"Where is she?" the blond boy demanded, like he still had a weapon, still was in the fight.

Shiloh decided to play a bit. Make it last. Make the blond boy's ruddy face go full crimson. "What's it like to bone an amnesiac? Does she remember it the next day? Five minutes later?"

The boy didn't say anything. Shiloh laughed at his own joke and swung again, but the kid, moving faster than a big guy should, stepped into the swing and pile-drove a fist into Shiloh's gut. It hurt. He thought of all the football players he'd hated in high school, and then the thought got knocked clear of his brain when the blond boy hit him again, sharp and hard, with an uppercut that lifted him off his feet and caught his tongue between his teeth. He collapsed, in shock that he had been beaten. Through the pain in his center and in his head he felt the tip of the crowbar press against the hollow of his throat.

"Where. Is. Jane?"

He spat blood. "I don't know."

"Why are you trying to hurt me? I looked out the window and saw you waiting for me."

Shiloh didn't answer.

"Where is she? The inside of the house, did you break into those rooms?"

"I don't know where she is."

"Is this what happened two years ago? When they left here? Is this the same?" the kid said, his voice rising.

Shiloh didn't know what the blond boy meant. Everything hurt. He didn't have Mimi, he didn't have anything. He lay back on the grass and waited for the boy to pummel him. It was what he would have done.

The blond boy took the crowbar away from Shiloh's throat. He hit Shiloh's right arm once, breaking it, and Shiloh howled. The blond boy got into his truck and drove off.

Shiloh lay on the cool grass, writhing in pain, furious. He had certainly misjudged the blond boy. He dug his cell phone out of his pocket and called her number. "Mimi? Please. Please, wait. I need to go to the hospital. Please. Yes, really, I'm hurt. Will you come get me?" He listened, staring at the sky. "No, don't call an ambulance. You come, please, please. I don't know the address." He started to cry. "I'm not kidding, help me, please." Then he heard her saying, "I'm not falling for this, don't call again," and then he listened to the quiet of the lake, the distant birdsong, and knew he was going to always be alone. Always.

59

JANE?"

Jane shivered to full wakefulness, drool spilling from her mouth. Her head lay in Perri's lap. "Where are we?"

"In a house on High Oaks. Up from the crash site," Perri whispered.

"Where is Cal?"

"He left."

"We have to get out of here." Jane raised her head slowly.

"We're locked in this room."

"Why did you let him lock us up?" Jane said, still sounding stunned.

"He had a gun," Perri said after a moment. "And a Taser."

"You think he would use it on you?"

"On you."

Jane trembled.

"I can reason with him," Perri said, trying to calm her. "I know him better than anyone. He won't hurt me. Or you. But we have to get out of here."

"You said we're in a house? On the street?"

"Yes. I think it belongs to the man who called nine-one-one after the crash."

"James Marcolin? I talked to him. Why is he in this?"

Perri bit at her lip. "I think...I think if Cal was in the car with you when you crashed, he was forcing you to drive here. After what you and David found. It's the simplest explanation."

"I wasn't just trying to get away from Trevor...I was being *brought* here." She sharpened her focus, pushed the haze away. "James Marcolin's involved in this mess with Cal. So...it must be...If Cal was in the car and Marcolin heard the crash, he must have come down, gotten Cal out, then called the police."

Perri shuddered. "If he left our son to die..." Her hands closed into fists.

Jane took a deep breath, rallying her thoughts. "If he was bringing me here, it was to get rid of me. Or threaten me. If my mother is in on this, she's receiving and sending money for him through her charity, then...my mother...They won't hurt me if my mother's involved..." Her voice drifted off, unsure.

Perri studied the room. A small utility room, washer and dryer and cabinets, a dog's food and water bowls in the corner of the tiled floor. Cal had opened the door and gestured them in, saying to her, "Just stay with her, please, for a minute," as if he didn't have a gun in his hand.

"Cal," she had said. "Let's talk this through. Calmly. Please." She had told Jane she was still in love with him. She felt sick at the thought.

"Keep her quiet and calm. We'll talk when I'm back. And don't try anything." Then he bolted them in. What kind of place had a utility room you could lock from outside? Someone had imagined needing to keep a prisoner in this house.

If he was going to kill us, Perri thought, *he could have done it at the lake house. But of course he wouldn't want DNA or blood left at the house. He wouldn't ever want the police coming to that house.*

Perri stood up. She looked in the cabinets. Powder detergent, softener sheets, a stick of stain remover. A spray bottle of cleaner to treat stains: a weapon. She started to read just how bad it would be to get it in your eyes.

"Jane, we may have to fight. Do you understand?"

Jane nodded. She took the spray bottle from Perri. "We're not negotiating with them," she said. "If they come back here, it's to kill us or to take us somewhere to kill us."

"Jane, this is Cal."

"He's not who you think he is. He killed my father, or he knew about it. He left David to die."

"He must have thought David was already dead."

Jane pushed her in the chest. "Stop with the excuses! He walked away from him to protect himself. No matter what you think."

"Maybe he was unconscious and Marcolin took him up to the house."

"And he never told you?" Jane said. "He was here when you arrived at the crash site, wasn't he?"

"Yes."

"Did you see his car?"

She blinked. "No. No. We took my car back that night. I was in no shape to drive, he drove us."

"He isn't the man you loved. That man doesn't exist anymore."

Perri's breath came in hard, sharp spurts. Jane turned to the door, the spray bottle in hand, waiting. She would go for the eyes.

60

THEY MET AT the site of the crash. Cal Hall arrived first, Laurel Norton second. She parked along the street and hurried down the hillside, found him standing where the decline became much steeper, watching, staring at where her daughter's car had crashed two years ago. The gun was in her purse, but the purse was open and the strap on her shoulder. She couldn't go up to him with a gun in her hand. But she could reach it fast, even fire through the leather if she had to. She steadied her breathing as she reached him. She didn't like standing so near the cliff's edge.

"Is there ever a day you don't think about it?" he asked her. His voice shook slightly, but he took a deep breath, like he was in a yoga class.

"No," she answered. "Where is Jane?"

"She's safe. But she knows about the money you've moved for me."

"No one will believe her about anything once she's in the hospital, Cal. Please. We just have to drive her there, check her in. It's a way I can keep her safe and keep her out of ... trouble. Until I make her understand."

"You haven't been able to manage the problem, Laurel."

"We agreed." The fear was plain on her face. "You would build up this Liv Danger threat, you would frame Perri and make her disappear and Jane would go into the hospital and then we could be together."

"We could stage it so that Jane gets blamed for Perri," he said.

"I am not doing that to my daughter. No. She has suffered enough. I have suffered—" But then he grabbed her blouse, dragged her farther down the hill, and then his shove sent her over the cliff's edge. She managed to get her hand on the gun, but he moved too fast and fear froze her. One moment she was on solid ground, the next there was only air and gravity. She smashed along the oak branches, tried to grab at one of them with her free hand, felt her fingers break with the force; then she fell from branch to branch and hit the unforgiving earth. She looked up at where she had stood a few seconds ago, whole and unbroken, and she saw his distant face peering down at her.

But he loved her. He loved her. They were in this together. She still watched, unable to scream now, just a harsh-breathing wheeze. His face vanished from the edge.

She tried to call for help. Move her hands. She flailed; nothing seemed to work. Something was very wrong. She wasn't even sure her mouth opened. But her eyes could close, she felt them, the darkness coming over her. Were her eyes closed? She thought of Brent, sweet, foolish Brent, and Jane, who was neither sweet nor foolish and now ... the fear. Not for herself and the beckoning dark. But for Jane.

61

TREVOR DROVE THE truck along the same route he'd followed that fateful night two years ago. He zoomed past one of the grand houses. He saw Laurel's red Volvo parked along the road and he slowed, then turned onto the hillside itself, looking for Jane, aiming the truck toward the cliff's edge. He set the parking brake. No sign of Laurel. No sign of Jane. No sign of the men Laurel had looking for Jane, to cart her off to the mental hospital. This was a waste of time.

But then, where was Jane's mother? Her car was here.

He got out of the truck and walked the rest of the way down the hillside. "Jane?" he called. "Mrs. Norton?" He hoped Laurel's hired muscle wasn't around; his shoulder ached, it wasn't right from that crowbar blow, and he couldn't fight anymore. His good arm and hand ached from the punches he'd landed on the crazy man at the lake house.

He heard a noise. A soft call.

He went to the edge of the cliff. Looked down into a

maze of branches and jutting stone. Saw nothing. Heard the noise again, moved farther to his right.

Then he saw Laurel Norton. She'd fallen forty feet, apparently hitting branches along the way, which had slowed her descent but beaten up her body. Her arm moved and she made a noise when she saw Trevor.

"Mrs. Norton!" he yelled. She reached toward him. She was hurt.

And by her lay a gun, next to her purse.

He dug into his front jeans pocket for his phone and pulled it out. It was smashed beyond repair from one of the blows of the crazy man's crowbar.

"I'll go to the house and get help," he called. She could be dying right now. Panic filled his chest.

Laurel shook her hand, shook her head.

"No?" he called. "Why? Where is Jane?" He couldn't leave her to go look for Jane. Horror struck him. "Is Jane down there with you?" He couldn't see what was around Laurel.

He had to find a phone. "Your purse?" he called. "Is your phone in your purse? Can you dial?"

She tried to speak again but couldn't. One-handed, she pulled it from her jacket pocket. In her hand it looked unbroken, but she didn't seem to be able to press the buttons.

He heard voices coming. A man's voice. And at its sound, Laurel Norton moaned and gave a weak, gasping scream, terror contorting her face. He decided it was best that whoever was coming didn't see him. With his shoulder aching and still one-handed, Trevor started to make his way farther down the cliffside, feet carefully finding purchase.

He needed that phone. He needed that gun.

62

THE DOOR OPENED and Jane sprayed the cleanser.

But the man through the door wasn't Cal—it was the man she'd talked to through the gate. The witness who had called the police after the crash. James Marcolin. He staggered back as the cleanser hit his eyes and he roared. She tried to shove past him, but Cal Hall was there and he punched her in the face. She fell back, Marcolin's cussing booming in her ears. Then Perri beside her, trying to wrest the Glock from Cal's hand, Cal overpowering his wife and shoving her hard to the floor.

"Get up," Cal said, grabbing Jane by the hair. Her whole face hurt. He shoved the gun under her jaw.

"Cal, don't do this. Don't." Marcolin had moved past Perri, clawing at his eyes, gasping, turning on the tap water to rinse his face.

"I'm just taking her to her mother," Cal said. "It's going to be OK, Perri. Just shut up and let me handle everything. Stay here. Help him." Marcolin was still rinsing his eyes, hissing in pain and annoyance.

Cal shoved a cloth from a shelf into Jane's mouth, wrapped duct tape around her head. "I'll take her to Laurel and then I'll be back. And I'll explain everything to you."

Jane shot a beseeching look at Perri as Cal hustled her away.

"The spray," Marcolin gasped, squinting, "how long does it say to wash the eyes?"

She picked up the spray container and read it so he would believe her. "Fifteen minutes," she said. They saw her as nothing. To Cal she was no risk, no threat, someone who would do whatever he said; to Marcolin what was she—the dense wife or just the dumb mother of the dead boy? She stepped back from him. "I told her not to do it. It would just make Cal mad." She listened; the house was big and she needed to hear a particular sound.

She heard it. The shutting of the front door. She stepped out of the utility room and slammed the door shut, fumbling for the bolt. She slid it home as Marcolin yelled and threw himself against the door.

Police. Now. Cal had taken her phone, but there had to be one here in the house, a landline. She checked the next room. A spare bedroom, no phone. Next door down was a library. No phone.

She heard the blasts of gunshots from the laundry room. Marcolin must have had a gun under his jacket; he was shooting away the door lock.

Perri ran.

63

JANE COULDN'T SPEAK with her mouth bound with the tape. Cal hurried her down the street. Toward the crash site. She could see her mother's Volvo parked along the side. *Is he just going to hand me over to her and hope no one believes me at the asylum?* But as they got closer, she saw her mother wasn't in the driver's seat.

Jane screamed under the gag and tried to spin out of his grip. Cal locked the gun on her head. "The memories are gone, right? It's all going to be gone soon. You killed my boy. He...he wanted to get you away from this. From me. He begged. You were both crying as you drove."

Cruel blows of memory, pressing upon her. His gun to her head, like then, like now. She fought back tears. *Don't let him hurt me, David, please don't let him hurt me. Let me go, Mr. Hall, please, I won't tell.*

David's voice, an echo in her brain: *Dad, let her go, let her go, she won't talk. Please, Dad. You can't be serious; you can't hurt Jane. Are you going to send her to those people? You can't. Please, Dad, please.*

"He unbuckled his seat belt and grabbed the wheel from you. You screamed 'I hate you' at me, he screamed he loved you. And the car crashed. Him trying to help you escape. My son, my wonderful son. You took him from me. I blame you." His hand in her hair yanking her along. She tore at the tape, scoring her cheek.

"Taking you to your mama," he said, and they rounded the line of cedars and oaks onto the stony decline. She saw Trevor's truck, parked, twenty feet from the edge. Her eyes went wide.

Oh, no, Trevor couldn't be here, he couldn't, Cal would kill him. Where was her mother?

Cal skirted the truck, saw it was empty, gun pointed into the cab. He cussed under his breath and started dragging her toward the edge, in a hurry now. "Down there with her," he said. "You and her dead, then Perri. Rid of you all that ruined my life and I go on, the crazy wife who's been targeting people connected to the crash gets blamed, boom. All will pay. Finally."

The blame for David's death had twisted something in him: the affair with Laurel, leading to her father's death, leading to the crash, leading to Perri leaving him. A seed of blame that had turned into a strangling vine. A man who could not see the blame was all on him.

She fought him. She tore at the tape and tried to scream.

"Go ahead, get the tape off," he said, and she realized he didn't want it to be on her once he threw her from the cliff. Mom. *Down there with her. Oh, no, no, no. What had he done?* He ripped the tape from her face and from her hair. He pulled her to the edge and looked down, as if aiming his throwing of her and said, "What the hell?" She saw what he saw as she fought to pull away.

Trevor. Trevor was halfway down the cliff, descending,

half-hidden by an outcrop of rock and a thick oak branch. She couldn't see her mother. Cal tried to aim his gun down at Trevor and fire. Jane knocked him back from the edge, her arm still clasped in his iron grip. If she shoved him over the edge, she would go over with him.

Fine. She couldn't let him hurt anyone else. She was never going to be whole again anyway. She realized he couldn't shoot her and still make it look like she'd killed herself and Perri and her mom. That gave her a momentary advantage. She was small and he was big—not as big as Trevor but solid—but he wasn't expecting her to move *toward* the drop.

She started shoving him toward the edge. He realized her intent and his face contorted in shock. He fired the gun down toward Trevor, and Jane heard a cry of pain.

Then he swung the gun around toward her, his eyes bright with hate.

No.

64

PERRI RAN. SHE was beyond looking for a phone or a gun, she just wanted out of the house. She burst from the mansion. No sign of Cal or Jane. Cal's car was there, but she didn't have the electronic key. She ran past the open gate and onto the empty road.

If she turned left, she could run downhill to Old Travis, wave down a car. She felt sure Cal had not turned in that direction.

He was taking Jane to the crash site. She knew it with certainty. This scheme of his was falling apart and Cal was cleaning house. He was going to kill Jane Norton, the girl she'd hated with a fiery heart for the past two years.

For one moment she wavered. Then she turned and ran right.

She could hear the injured Marcolin howling, chasing her. He had a gun and she had nothing. She ran down the street, the curve bringing Laurel's red Volvo, parked, into view.

She heard a muffled scream, the crack of a shot.

David. David, I'm coming.

She turned and saw her husband and Jane fighting near the edge of the cliff. In front of a large black truck that was parked there.

The truck. She opened the unlocked door; the keys were in the cup holder. She started the engine and laid on the horn. Jane stared at her for one second, then tried to shove Cal over the side. Instead he picked her up, pinning her arms, and moved toward the edge, yelling over his shoulder at Perri to get out of the truck, he'd explain everything.

He was going to throw Jane off the cliff. Laurel's car— he must have already killed her. He'd killed Brent Norton. He'd framed Perri as Liv Danger, using her computer. And she'd played right into his hands, let him use her hate against her.

Not anymore. She started the truck, put it into gear, and powered it toward him, starting to slide down the steepness of the rocky decline.

* * *

Cal hauled Jane to the edge. He could simply drop her; she fought. *Not like this, not like this, not where I was supposed to die before*, she thought. At the edge he looked down and saw Trevor kneeling on the ground and holding aloft a gun—Laurel's—to fire it. Cal retreated, stumbling back, and Jane broke free, running to the right, toward the clutch of gnarled, thirsty cedars closest to the edge.

He looked up at the roar of the truck. Perri hit Cal straight on as she slammed on the brakes.

Cal flew well over the cliff's edge, a look of soft surprise on his face, and fell into the maze of tree branches with a choked scream.

Trevor's truck slid on the slope, tires fighting for purchase as Perri stood on the brakes, and Jane, stumbling, clutching at a tree, saw Perri's face through the windshield. Calm, resigned, staring back at her as the truck spun and then dropped over the edge with a thundering crash.

Jane froze behind the stunted cedar she'd grabbed in her mad scramble, the tree closest to the edge.

No. Perri and Trevor and her mom. No.

She heard footsteps sliding down the stone. Marcolin, his eyes red, holding a gun, stumbling down to survey the carnage. She crouched behind the tree and picked up a rock. He was fixed on the truck he'd just seen plummet into the canopy of oaks and cedars below.

Jane hit him, hard from behind, and he dropped to his knees. She hit him again, and then again, the rock messy with blood. He groaned and she hit him in the face. Twice. Three times. He made a choking noise.

She took his gun from him and then peered over the side.

The truck, in its spin as Perri tried to stop, had gone over backside first, smashing through the branches, landing rear-first and then falling onto its side. In the cab she could see Perri, lying still, not moving. Beyond the wreck she saw, through a gap in the branches, Trevor and her mother. He must have pulled her mother clear as the truck roared over the precipice.

"Mom!" she screamed. "Trevor!"

"Your mom's hurt bad, we need an ambulance," Trevor called out.

Jane went back to Marcolin's moaning form and took an orange phone from his pocket. She dialed 9-1-1, and for the second time teams rushed to the isolated cliffside on High Oaks.

Jane crawled back to the cliff's edge. Trevor ran to the truck's cab, peering inside, trying to see if Perri was still alive. Jane watched, gasping, listening to the emergency operator tell her that help was on the way. *Please don't be dead. Please, Mom. Please, Perri. Please. Please.*

65

So you're going back to school?" the therapist said. "You shouldn't push yourself too hard after such an ordeal." The therapist was an older woman, wearing a smart suit and very fashionable eyewear. Jane thought she was secretly pleased to have a notorious client.

Jane nodded. "After the trials. I want to get back to life. Back to normalcy. Whatever that's going to be now."

"You said you're going to sell your house."

"Yes. A nice family made an offer. And my mother, she doesn't want to stay in Austin. San Antonio's not so far." They talked for several minutes about her living arrangements, then the therapist asked about the people she read about in the news. Like she had a list in her mind.

"Your mother..."

"The FBI is letting her cooperate so they can trace more of the money Cal Hall cleaned through her charity for Marcolin and the Babylon website. There are lots of overseas payments, lots of banks and other law enforcement involved."

"You must have complicated feelings about your mom."

"She says she didn't know for certain that Cal had killed my father." She made her next words measured. "She said that when Dad and Cal's business failed, Cal offered to help her expand her charity, at a salary where she could keep our house, and he just asked her to 'handle' money transactions and she didn't ask questions—she says she didn't realize she was cleaning money used in buying drugs and sex slaves and weapons. Not even when my father might have found out she was cleaning money and then died. She bought the idea that he was depressed and killed himself, and she convinced herself that Cal was saving us from losing everything." Jane looked away. "She's my mom. I love her. But I don't like her a lot right now, and I'm not a big enough person to forgive her yet. Her image matters too much to her: the perfect mom, the perfect blogger, the perfect fund-raiser...just no. That image is gone. She'll have to make herself a new one."

"Will she walk again?"

"Time will tell if she recovers enough. She seems to be adjusting to the wheelchair."

"And you take care of her."

"Yes. I do." She made her hands into fists. "I will. She will have to make some adjustments in her life, though. I might have to put her in a facility for a while." She kept the edge out of her voice; the doctor might not appreciate the irony.

"And Trevor Blinn?"

She took a few seconds to answer. "We're friends. I don't think I'm quite ready for a relationship. I'd like to stand on my own and not worry about who's propping me up." And maybe more than friends, later, once she felt stronger. She felt no need to rush, and he was giving her space and time for the ordeal of the trials that lay ahead as a key witness against Marcolin's dark-market website, which had made millions in illicit profits, and against Shiloh Rooke for his attacks on three people.

"Let's talk about your dad. And David."

And they did. But she could talk more easily about them, and her mother now. She was on firmer ground. She knew it wasn't her fault. The blame and the guilt—didn't feel like it coated her flesh, burned her bones.

"You know, you should forgive," the therapist said.

"My mom?"

"Well, eventually, but I was..."

"Cal?" That was beyond her. And he was dead.

"No. Perri Hall. All that anger you carried for so long toward each other."

Jane said nothing.

"May I ask, did she really save you? She really ran her husband down in that truck, knowing it would likely veer over the edge? A woman who had hated you and attacked you at David's grave?"

"Yes. She did."

* * *

It wasn't like they were suddenly going to be best friends. Not at all. But Perri was glad Jane would soon meet her here. In this sacred place.

Perri stood in the bright sunlight above David's grave, leaning on her cane. The truck's cab had protected her, but she'd had a broken leg and arm, and back injuries, a collapsed lung. The recovery had taken time. The news stories had been exploding about a respectable pair of Lakehaven entrepreneurs operating an international illicit marketplace, to the tune of millions. Laurel had told all: hiring Kevin Ngota to fake commitment papers, helping Cal frame Perri as Liv Danger. Cal had found the characters notebook the kids had made and thought it would frame Perri effectively. He had set the fires in San Antonio, he had researched Shiloh Rooke and found his weakness and stolen the sex tapes, he had framed Perri by sending the Liv Danger postings from her computer, he had used another sophisticated hacking scheme to access her computer that Maggie hadn't spotted. All to set up a scheme where he could get rid of Perri and Jane, one blamed for torturing the other, the other blamed for a murder-suicide. He had clearly not disclosed all his plans to Laurel; and whether he had planned to let Laurel survive this process as well was unknown. Laurel had said she wanted Jane in a psychiatric facility so she would be safe. Her mother's instinct, no matter how stunted, had tried to shield Jane from Cal's machinations against his soon-to-be ex-wife.

Perri had confessed her role in withholding information from the police regarding Shiloh Rooke's activities; she had paid a hefty fine and was sentenced to a thousand hours of community service. The Bowman and Vasquez families had sued, and she had paid for their medical bills and suffering out of her own money. Cal's money was all frozen. Shiloh was charged with three counts of attempted murder and was in jail awaiting trial, and awaiting a visit from Mimi that would never come.

The world Perri had known had been swept away, except for the quiet of her home, and the comfort she got from sitting in David's room.

"Hello, baby," she said to the grave, sitting down on the cool grass. *His death was not at all what I thought it was.*

She could never let her grief go, but she had to find a way to move on, to try for joy again and to not be caught in the prison Cal's lies had made for her. "I miss you. I can't imagine what you carried, knowing about your dad and what he'd done... and oh, I wish you could have told me. It might have been so different. But I don't blame you. I love you."

A truck pulled up. New. She'd paid for that too, even though that nice boy hadn't asked. Trevor Blinn was at the wheel, and then on the passenger side Jane got out. Jane said something to him and shut the door. Trevor stayed in the truck, but nodded and waved at Perri, and she nodded back.

Jane was holding two bunches of flowers. She didn't walk toward David's grave; first she walked toward her father's, several rows away, and laid down the first batch of flowers. She touched Brent Norton's headstone. She turned and headed back toward the truck, and there was a tentative moment when Perri thought she might not approach. The last time they'd both been here they'd fought over David's grave. A low, bitter moment. But Jane walked past the truck and toward Perri.

Perri opened her arms. They embraced. Jane knelt on the grass beside her.

"Those are lovely," Perri said.

Jane put the bouquet on the grave. "Thanks." They were silent for several seconds, then Jane said, "I saw the For Sale sign in your yard."

"Oh, I can't stay in that house."

"But David's room..."

"That house is an anchor to me. Cal did everything to give it to us and then give us more, more, and more, and I don't need it. He paid it off with money earned on the pain

of others. No. David's with me always. Room or no room."
Perri cleared her throat. "I wish David had told me about
the two of you."

"I wish I remembered why we hadn't. I guess he was
ashamed we'd cheated on Kamala. He probably didn't
want you to think less of him. And maybe I didn't let him,
because I was cheating on Trevor, and I was ashamed of
that."

"Trevor is a great kid, Jane."

"Well, he's been sweet on me since first grade. You have
to admire his loyalty."

"And how do you feel about him?" It was, Perri realized,
the kind of conversation she and Jane might have had if
the families had never fallen into their tragedy. The second
mom, the trusted friend, giving life advice.

"He's everything I could want. I am just such a lot to
take on. It's hard to let someone try. Because he might give
up."

"That boy doesn't have any idea of how to give up
in that brain of his. And neither do you. Not a bit." She
touched her shoulder. "If you want to be with him, be with
him. Build the life you want, Jane, free of all this mess,"
Perri said, nodding toward the truck and Trevor. "You de-
serve whatever makes you happy, after all this."

"So do you, Perri."

She tried to nod. Happiness, maybe, one day. Right now
she'd just take being grateful for her memories of David,
for being alive. For being free of the blame, of the hate
she'd felt.

"Here," Perri said. "David would have wanted you to
have this." And she handed her a notebook. "It's where
Liv Danger—the good version, the wonderful idea you and
David had—lived." Jane paged through the stories and the

drawing. She looked at the back of the notebook. Tayami, the Japanese brand. Where her suicide note, written in fury, had been torn free from. The paper was luxurious and David's drawings were wonderful.

"Finish it," Perri said. "Find an artist who can share David's vision. Write Liv Danger's story. I think you know about being a hero now."

Jane closed the notebook. Maybe work could be good, and she could reclaim her and David's creation from how it had been badly used.

"Perri?"

"Yes?"

"I remember something. A lot more. Not all of it. But...when we found out about all this awfulness that night, it was so much to carry, but...David didn't know how to tell you. Neither did I. We wanted to get you away from it. From Cal. We wanted to protect you. I remember that."

The tears welled up in Perri's eyes. "Oh."

"David loved you so much. So much."

Perri wiped the damp from her eyes and took a deep breath, and she took Jane's hand. Jane glanced up in surprise. "It's going to be all right. It really will be better. That's life. It does go on. We have to go on with it. Forward."

She would never remember the parts of her life she had lost, but she knew who she was now. Who she had been, who she might become. And that would be enough.

"I'll remember that," Jane said. "I will."

ACKNOWLEDGMENTS

For their support in writing this book I'd like to thank: Jamie Raab, David Shelley, Lindsey Rose, Ed Wood, Peter Ginsberg, Shirley Stewart, Holly Frederick, Jonathan Lyons, Sarah Perillo, Eliane Benisti, John Q. Smith, Kelly Coulter, Chip Evans, Melissa Greenwell, Matthew Praisner, Todd Praisner, and Steve Basile. As always, deepest thanks to Leslie, Charles, and William for their love and support.

You will not find Lakehaven on a map; nor will you find St. Michael's University in Austin. You also won't find "Faceplace" as a widely used social networking site.

Any errors or manipulations of fact for dramatic purposes are all on me.

TURN THE PAGE FOR A PREVIEW OF *THE THREE BETHS*, JEFF ABBOTT'S EXCITING NEW PSYCHOLOGICAL SUSPENSE NOVEL COMING THIS FALL.

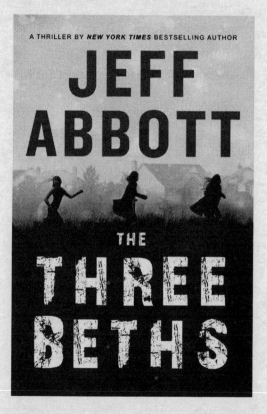

A THRILLER BY *NEW YORK TIMES* BESTSELLING AUTHOR

JEFF ABBOTT

THE THREE BETHS

1

MARIAH DUNNING SAW her missing mother standing on the other side of the crowd.

The food court at the mall—ugh—had been one of their mother-daughter hangouts. Mom genially loathed the food court. Mom was particular about what she ate, while Mariah was not—chicken biscuits, Mongolian barbecue, pepperoni pizza, none of which Mom would touch and all of which Mariah would work off playing basketball. And when Mariah got the summer job during her high school years selling tickets at the movie theater, a back corner booth at the food court was a place where they could meet and share a sacred hour between Mom's business trips, Mom saying, "Well it's better than airplane food—I think."

Mariah had not been to the food court since Mom disappeared. She had been careful to avoid it on the few outings she made to the mall. But she and her father had gone to the Apple Store to buy Mariah a new computer and a new iPhone; it made Dad happy to give her gifts even though she was an adult who could buy her own gear. His gifts were like a hug, sideways, when you didn't know the depth of the other person's feelings. The food court wasn't a place she wanted to be; it made the back of her brain itch, made her feel like she couldn't sit still. Dad had said, "Let's get a snack," and he was trying so hard to make today fun that Mariah didn't have the heart to say no. But in the middle of the music and the loud conversations Mariah glanced up from her pad thai and she saw her mother. Mariah froze, the chopsticks in her hand, the tangled noodles hanging like a noose.

Her mother had vanished nearly a year ago, and then there she stood, peeking out from behind a sunglasses display at the edge of the food court. Dark glasses, red lipstick, pale skin, even the distinctive twist of scar at the corner of her mouth that could only be Mom's. For five seconds Mariah couldn't move, couldn't make a noise; she felt like she might never speak again. She gazed at her as if she were in a staring contest with a ghost. She stood, dropping the chopsticks into the bowl.

Her mother retreated behind the display. Gone.

"Mariah?" Dad asked, glancing up at her. "What?"

"Mom is standing right over there." She pointed, her hand shaking.

Dad stared for a moment and then turned. "That can't be."

Mariah started to walk fast, then to run, threading her way through the maze of tables and diners.

"Mariah?" Dad stood, craning her neck. "Where are you going?"

"I saw her." Mariah ran, heedless, toward the sunglasses display. She couldn't see Mom any more. She shoved past two women, nearly knocking one's tray of Chinese food over and the other's milk shake to the floor. "Mom! Mom!"

"Mariah!" Dad called, low and urgent, as if he didn't want people to notice, hurrying in her wake, apologizing to the people Mariah collided with, apologizing to those she dodged. "Mariah, wait." He made his voice steel, trying to stop her.

"Mom!" she screamed, loud and long, as if she could leash her mother with the sound of her voice. As if Mariah were still a child instead of twenty-two years old. She moved fast, but blindly, hardly seeing the people she pushed aside. She circled the sunglasses vendor. Mom was gone. She spoke to the clerk: "There was a woman just here—dark hair, dark coat, scarred mouth. Forties. Where did she go?"

The clerk shrugged. "I'm sorry. I didn't see her."

"She was just here!" Mariah's voice shook as she glanced around.

"I'm sorry," the clerk repeated. "I didn't see her." People were staring, watching. Mariah saw a girl aim a smartphone at her.

Mariah hurried beyond the display, past four other mall carts, out into the wide hub where two wings of the mall came together. Ahead of her was a two-story department store, to her left a wing of the mall with a bunch of apparel specialty shops, to her right the ever-busy Apple Store and several smaller stores.

"You didn't see her," Dad said, touching her arm, and she flinched away. "Sweetie, if it was her she wouldn't have run. You imagined it."

I didn't, Mariah thought. *She was here. I saw her.*

"You didn't," Dad said, as if Mariah's thoughts were displayed on her forehead. "Mariah. Let's go." A tinge of embarrassment touched his voice. "We don't need this."

"What's your damn problem?" a woman demanded, a

spilled chocolate milk shake running down the front of her white blouse. Her eyes were bright with anger.

"She's so sorry," Dad said, watching a mall security guard approach. "Please, let me take care of your cleaning bill for that." He opened his wallet, began to count out twenties. His voice desperate for them not to be noticed.

"Hey. Haven't I seen you on TV?" the woman said.

"No," Dad said. "No."

Mariah ignored them both. *She wanted to see you. She came and looked right at you. No sign of her, either, to the left or right.* So Mariah ran full tilt for the department store ahead of her, Dad calling her name in a pitiful bleat.

Mariah tore through the department store, dodging a woman spraying perfume samples then turning and grabbing her arm. The sample bottle fell and shattered and the lavender aroma of the French perfume rose hard in the air.

"A woman, black hair, black coat, did you see her go past?"

"Um. I think so. She went out that exit." The woman pulled away, fright in her eyes.

Mariah ran to the nearby exit, jostling around a woman with a baby stroller, fury and impatience driving her out into a small side parking lot. She scanned the cars.

"*Mom!*" she screamed. But Mom was gone. She saw a blue car, the only one pulling out of the lot. Dark blue. Honda. The car sped away, and was gone.

It must be her. It had to be her.

Mariah ran to her car, thankful she'd driven, and not Dad because she already had the keys. She got into the car, jabbing at the ignition, wheeling it backward before she could even get the door shut all the way. In the mirror she saw Dad running toward her, his expression frantic. She powered down the lane, racing out into traffic, narrowly missing an oncoming minivan loaded with a mother and kids. The mother honked and screamed at her, and Mariah screamed back "Sorry!" and pulled the car out of its swerve. The Honda turned, headed down the steep hill that led to the mall's exit onto a cross street.

She followed, blasting through a four-way stop and turning at the same hill. The blue Honda took a hard right, away from the highway, back toward the center of Lakehaven. Mariah accelerated; her old Ford sedan straining at the boost. She started to close the gap.

Get up next to her, she thought, *confirm that it's Mom. You're not crazy. It's Mom.*

She accelerated, drawing closer to the Honda, and then the Honda veered into a sharp turn. Mariah overcompensated, control drifting from the wheel, and she spun into the oncoming lanes. She saw the markings of a police sedan, the sirens atop the roof as she spun toward it and then the car hit her Ford's rear, spinning her again, and she came to a jarring halt. Shaking. Looking at the Lakehaven Police car in her mirror. The Honda was gone.

"Get out of the car, now!" the officer's voice yelling at her sternly, and she trembled because now people would have something else to say about her family, a bright new flame of shame. She bit her lip.

Mariah Dunning got out of the car, hands up. "Hello, officer. I have a bunch of guns and gear in the trunk. And I've got a telescoping baton in my boot. Just so you know."

2

AN HOUR LATER, Mariah and her dad were dropped off by a rideshare service at the driveway of their modest house not far from Lakehaven High School. Home was a 1960s ranch house, the type that had often been torn down repeatedly in this Lakehaven neighborhood and replaced with a much larger, grander McMansion squeezed onto the lot. Sometimes when Mariah came home she'd see her father standing at the window, peering out if there was a For Sale sign in a neighbor's yard on Bobtail Drive. There had been several in the past year. People fleeing the Dunnings and cashing in on the renovation craze. She wondered if her father was worrying about a teardown happening and hiking his property taxes or just hoping for new neighbors, ones who didn't know about his wife's disappearance. Neighbors who didn't look at him with thin smiles that seemed to whisper, *How'd you do it, Craig? How'd you get rid of the body?* The gossip always seemed to convey with the sale. The new neighbors never said hello when Mariah or her father were in the front yard or shooting baskets in the driveway.

She'd gotten him to venture out of the house today, for the first time in weeks, and it had all gone wrong.

Mariah had moved home right after her mother vanished. She knew she should get her own apartment again, but she couldn't. She didn't feel ready to leave Dad quite yet...to leave him alone. She'd finished her degree in computer science at the University of Texas as fast as she could; she didn't like to leave Dad on his own, even for classes and labs. She got permission from her professors to do group assignments on her own, even though it was harder, so she wouldn't have to leave him to dwell in his own darkness.

It was the two of them against the police, and against the world. And parties and service projects and all the other résumé padding and fun having of college had ceased to matter to her, gone on the wind of her mother's vanishing. It was too hard to explain to people with unsullied pasts and bright futures: *Well you see my mom disappeared without a trace and no we don't know if she was murdered or kidnapped or if she just walked away from her life and my dad was the prime suspect in her disappearance but nothing could be proven so we live in limbo. What's your major?*

Now Mariah felt a hot embarrassment rise from the small of her back, spread through her chest, redden her face. She'd lost control. The control she kept in place for the world's eyes. And now Dad *knew*. The gear in the trunk, the file box with clippings about her mother, the guns and the police baton and the Taser, the laptop loaded with software designed to trace and find people. She'd had to explain it all to the police, in front of her father, when he'd been brought to the station. She could have argued that she didn't have to explain anything. But telling them this had made them sympathetic, and they'd let her go without a formal charge. One of the officers had stared at her father the whole time; oh, they all knew Craig Dunning.

He was, in their eyes, guilty. The guy who got away with murder.

Her dad got a pitcher of iced tea from the refrigerator, shuffling, walking like a man carrying too heavy a burden. Craig Dunning had been a football player at Lakehaven High and then at Rhodes College up in Memphis on scholarship. He was a broad-shouldered blond with blue eyes and a strong jaw. In college he had done some modeling for a couple of southern clothing catalog companies. Mom had kept a portfolio of his work, to his total embarrassment and Mariah's vast amusement. She liked to pretend to be horrified at him posing in modest swimwear and suits and cable-knit sweaters. Whenever she saw one of his modeling shots, she'd make sure to say, "Ewww I thought the point was to sell the clothes," because he knew she was teasing him. Her handsome dad. There was no interest from the pro football scouts, so he'd put his trophies and disappointments on a shelf and he'd gotten a master's in accounting and worked his way up to partner in one of the national firms in downtown Austin. Now he "consulted," which meant he didn't go downtown or wear a suit and the firm sent him work he did mostly from home. Sometimes he rallied enough to go in for a meeting or a call, but he no longer went to the firm's holiday party or the Fourth of July picnic. Now he was rail thin, sunken cheeked, ash gray streaking his hair. He had loved just one woman in his life and the loss of her was like a physical mark on him. He was still a handsome man, but the joy that once animated his best feature, his smile, was gone. To Mariah, he was like a painting you could look at and say, "Yes, the lines are all in proportion, the colors are right, but something is missing."

"You're lucky Broussard is not pressing charges," Craig said. Lakehaven's police chief, Dennis Broussard, had listened to Craig's account of Mariah's...confusion with a stony silence. *Yes, we're going to get her back into therapy. No, she has not imagined seeing her mother before. Just stress.* Ignoring the officers' stares at him because they thought he might be a murderer. And here was his daughter, with a car trunk full of weapons and gear, like she was planning a robbery or a heist.

"Do we have your consent to search the car?" the police had asked.

She had said yes. What else was she going to say? A towing service had already taken her car and the police cruiser.

"You shouldn't have given your consent for them to search your car," Craig said, as if he knew her thoughts. "Why would they need to? They could plant drugs or something."

"Dad. They're not going to do that. Get real."

"They hate us. Or me, rather."

"I didn't have much choice. I was at fault, Dad."

"You don't...you don't need those weapons and gear. And saying it's to hunt down Mom's kidnappers. You can't say stuff like that to the police. They don't like people trying to do their job. It's dangerous, Mariah. I'm amazed they didn't arrest you."

"The police don't like us anyway."

"They don't like me," Craig said. "They feel sorry for you. Especially Broussard."

Sometimes Mariah had seen Broussard, in his own car, driving slowly past their home. Like he wanted to stop. Or simply put eyes on her father. It had been Broussard, who, summoned to the scene by an officer because the Dunnings were involved and Mariah had claimed to be chasing her missing mother, had stopped to get the stranded Craig at the nearby mall and brought him back to the scene. Mariah imagined it had been an awkward few minutes together in the car for the two men. Her father had not shared any details.

Craig poured iced tea for them both, and Mariah took hers with a shaking hand. She had to ask. "Did you see her?" She hoped he'd say, *Yes, she did look like Mom, I see how you thought what you thought.*

"No, honey, I did not." Craig sounded tired. Not angry. Not annoyed. Just exhausted.

"Did you see the blue Honda?"

"Well, the police saw it but they didn't see the driver." Craig's voice went soft. "It was probably just an innocent woman who panicked when you chased after her."

It was Mom, Mariah wanted to say, but she didn't. He didn't believe her. No one did. They sat in silence for a minute.

"I wonder if the mall has parking lot security tapes." Mariah's tone had calmed, become thoughtful. "I could ask."

Craig took a deep breath. "Mariah, stop right now. You are not calling the mall and asking them to review security tapes. They will ban you from going back there. You drove recklessly, you damaged a police car, and the only reason the cops didn't arrest you and haul you off to jail is that they felt bad for you."

Mariah didn't like those words, so she ignored them. "I really thought it was Mom. I did."

"I know you think you did, sweetheart. I know. What I wouldn't give to see her…" His deep voice cracked, and he took a deep breath. "Can we please talk about what all you had in your car? Wrist ties and guns and a Taser? Who are you planning to kidnap?" His gaunt face was pale with worry.

Mariah set her tea down. "I told you. I legally bought the guns and the gear."

"Why would you have an armory in your car, sweetheart?"

"I have to be prepared for when I find Mom, in case bad people have her. Dad, it's OK. I took classes on how to use this stuff."

He sat across from her, took her hands in his. "Classes?"

"And online videos."

"Honey, you are not some sort of bounty hunter or movie detective. Mariah, this stops now. You can't do this to yourself. Or to me." His voice cracked.

"The police quit looking," she said. "Someone has to find Mom. Find out what happened to her."

"I love you so much. But you didn't see your mom today," he said. "Do you understand that, Mariah? That woman wasn't your mom. This is...this is your grief playing tricks on your mind."

Her voice shook. "Even if...I still have to know what happened to her. I have to know who took her from us." She fought to keep her voice steady. "I have to know."

"No, you don't! I mean...not like this. We just have to keep the faith the police will find her someday. But you, you stay out of it."

Mariah took a deep breath. "Dad, I never got the chance to fix things with her, I..."

"I don't know how to make this right for you. I wish I did. I wish I could make people understand how hard this is for us. More than anything."

Because of Lakehaven, Mariah thought. Because of so

many people who had been sure her father had killed her mother, somehow made her body vanish. Although there was no evidence. No proof. And no other suspects in their circle of friends and acquaintances. Only the low, ceaseless whisper of innuendo and hearsay. But that constant drip was poison enough to nearly kill a man, leave him a shell. Beth Dunning had never reappeared—not on a credit history, not with a phone call, not on a security camera. She had snapped out of the world.

"Let me fix us a late lunch?" Mariah asked. They'd abandoned their meals at the food court. Craig usually cooked; he was much better at it than Mariah. But she wanted to do something nice for him.

"No, I'll fix it. You want a grilled cheese?"

She nodded and hugged him, and to Mariah he felt like skin and bones underneath the jeans and the Lakehaven basketball booster club shirt faded in the years since she had played on the team. *I'm sorry, Dad*, she thought to herself.

Craig turned away and padded over to the refrigerator. He got out butter and sliced cheese, set a pan on the stove, and began to assemble a cheese sandwich, melting butter in the skillet. "This feels like a point of no return. We can't do this again. You could have hurt yourself badly. You could have hurt a police officer. Or an innocent person. Do you think this town would ever forgive us for anything more? I'm not going back to people throwing rocks at the house or spray-painting threats in the middle of the night. I'm not putting you through that again."

The phrases "KILLER LIVES HERE" and "WHERE IS BETH," in bright red on their garage door. She would never forget. Some of the neighbors had helped them clean it up—but she could see the doubt in their faces. "Dad..."

"I think we need to have a service for your mom," he said. "We have to wait for her to be missing seven years to have her declared legally dead." Craig bit his lip. "But...maybe we go ahead and have a memorial of some sort. We let her go."

"No." She shook her head.

He met her gaze and there was a steadiness there she hadn't seen from him in a long time. "This grief...fine—it can ruin me. But it cannot ruin you. You have to move forward with your life. What if your clients hear about today?"

"How would anyone hear?" Mariah was a freelance web designer. She had only three steady clients, the largest one a hip clothing boutique called Lucy-Lou, which did a high volume of online sales.

"People talk on social media. They're a damn lynch mob. Maybe someone recorded your scene at the mall on their phone. Or took a picture of you being put in the police cruiser. Maybe someone posts it. You think there wasn't someone from Lakehaven in that food court? And the police blotter, they post that in the town paper. It'll be on the Lakehaven news website." His voice cracked. "This can't happen. Not everyone looking at you this way..."

She had no answer to this. She thought of the teenager with a raised smartphone aimed at her. People were so ready to record the awful moments for someone else. She could imagine the status posting: Girl hallucinates seeing missing mother in food court, ends up in car crash with cops. Surely no one would be that cruel. Then surely, she knew, they would.

"I could go see a therapist," she said quietly. "If you want me to. You said so to the cops."

"I don't think that's necessary." Dad eased the hot sandwich out of the pan, put it on a plate, cut it into three equal strips, just how Mariah liked it. He handed her the plate and started making a sandwich for himself. Not looking at her. Wanting, she thought, for the conversation to be over. Any time she'd mentioned talking to someone professional—a grief counselor, a psychiatrist—he'd resisted. She could go herself. She was an adult. But if he didn't like it, it felt like a betrayal. She thought he must worry about what she would say about him: *Everyone thinks my dad is guilty, and I don't, but... what if...*

She sat down with the sandwich, but it had no taste; the butter and cheese and soft bread just felt like grease in her mouth. "I mean, I'm surprised you don't want me to talk to a therapist."

"All it does is make people miserable. We have to learn how to deal with grief on our own," Craig said. "And I want you to stop this idea of finding whoever took your mom. The police—it's their job. Leave it alone. Promise me you'll stop."

He waited. She wanted to say, *The idea of finding Mom is my therapy, it's the only thing that makes me feel better.* Instead she said, "I promise."

And then a vicious little voice borne of hurt and pain and sadness said in the back corner of her brain, *Why doesn't Dad want you to see a therapist or find out the truth? Why?*

And she strangled that little voice in her mind, quickly, before it could speak its poison again.

3

CRAIG CURLED UP into his leather recliner in front of a huge flat-screen television. He fired up one of the streaming services. He would binge through hours of shows, often mesmerized most of the night. He slept very little, cocooned in the soft glow of the stories. Many nights he just slept in the recliner, which worried Mariah; it seemed unhealthy, but her attempts to get him to sleep normal hours all failed.

Mariah told him she was going to her room to read. She had stopped watching much TV; crime dramas made her edgy and reality shows were full of people with invented problems. Books had been her refuge. She shut the bedroom door and leaned her head against the wood.

She hadn't come up here to read.

She locked the door, quietly. Dad always seemed to hear the lock clicking into place, and in those dark days after Mom disappeared, he had been afraid Mariah would hurt herself. She had been afraid of the same with him. She dimmed the lights. She lit a candle her mother had given her on her fifteenth birthday. She thought candles made for crappy gifts, but this one she had liked; it smelled of vanilla and cinnamon, and she lit it only when it was time for her quiet secret ritual. It made her think of Mom, the warmth of her hugs, the smell of her skin, the strength of her.

They could laugh, even during the fights, the disagreements, the screaming matches of her teenage years. She loved her mother so much and sometimes she'd acted like she hated her. She'd never told Mom how much she loved her. This failure seemed to widen the hole in her heart.

She stepped inside her small closet and reached behind her hanging clothes. She slowly eased out a large corkboard. Papers and photos were pinned to it. Pictures of Mom, printouts of news accounts of when she'd vanished, sketches of men from around the country who were suspected in the disappearances of women. There were printouts of postings by a crime blogger and podcaster who wrote under the name Reveal and had taken a brief interest in her mother's case. A schedule of the day she'd last been seen: March 4. The bits and pieces of her mother's case—and she'd mounted them like she was a detective on a TV show, or Claire Danes on *Homeland* hunting a terrorist, trying to see the data and the connections all at once, spot the unseen ties that would lead her to the truth. She used to sleep with the corkboard over her bed, as if the data would sift down into her mind and reveal the answers in her dreams. But she never remembered her dreams since Mom vanished, even if she awoke sweating and confused and near to tears. Her father had told her, in a quavering voice, to stop this foolishness and take the corkboard down. He told her this wasn't healthy. She thought it was all that was keeping her balanced. She told him she'd thrown it all away, but instead she'd just slid it into the closet behind her clothes.

She hadn't added anything to the board in a long while. There was nothing new to say.

She sat at her laptop and started to type in what she always did for the ritual: Beth Dunning disappearance Austin

The results appeared. The news stories from the time, from both the Austin and Lakehaven papers and from the local news stations. Her mother's story hadn't gotten much national coverage, a bit on CNN and some of the others, and then the world moved on. She knew most of them by heart. And the entries from Reveal's crime blog—but there was a new entry under Reveal's blog entries.

She clicked on it.

WHAT'S IN A NAME?

There are certain cases that I've written about numerous times. One of those is of Bethany "Beth" Blevins Curtis, who vanished from Austin eighteen months ago in an apparent desertion of her husband. She has made no subsequent contact with friends or family and has not left any kind of digital trail. Six months later, Beth Dunning of Lakehaven, a suburb of Austin, also vanished, her car found in an empty lot in the hills above Lakehaven, where she and her husband were planning on building a home and where she often went for quiet time.

Two Beths, vanishing without a trace from the same city in less than a year.

A six-month interlude is consistent with certain serial killer cycles...but have you ever heard of a serial killer who chooses victims with a particular name? I haven't. And I haven't found a notice of another Beth disappearing this past year, though, for which we should be grateful there is not a name-obsessed serial killer lurking in our fair city (for a history of Austin and serial killers, see my earlier series of podcasts on America's first serial killer, who terrorized Austin in the 1880s, known as the Midnight Assassin, also known as the Servant Girl Annihilator). But wouldn't the psychology of someone who so hated a name that he had to kill victims bearing it be fascinating? Of course, neither woman's body has turned up to suggest a serial killer, so this is likely a coincidence, but an interesting one.

I noticed this unhappy coincidence when I was writing up my exciting new Calendar of Unsolved Cases, a new feature on the website that will link to my previous blogs and podcasts, tied to the major date of each case. These are two very different disappearances, but the names and the time frame struck me. I think it's always interesting to look for coincidences and see if they are something more.

Is it not the most human endeavor to seek the pattern of order in chaos?

If you agree, then hit up my PaySupport, so I can keep doing this podcast for you . . .

To seek the pattern of order in chaos. Yes. Mariah almost nodded at the screen. Patterns must be found. That was what she needed: a pattern, an explanation that made sense in a world that didn't.

She clicked on all the links to the Beth Curtis case.

The first was to an article from a tech news website on the disappearance. Bethany Blevins Curtis. Dark shoulder-length hair, wide mouth, cheekbones that Mariah envied, nice smile, age twenty-seven. She worked as an office manager for a transportation company in south Austin. She was married to a man who was a rising star in technology, CEO and founder of a small software company preparing for a public offering of its stock, valued at millions. Mariah tried to remember if she'd heard about this case, but she didn't watch the local news much before Mom vanished. And, as she read, she agreed with Reveal: this might not even have been a disappearance as much as an abandonment.

Eighteen months ago on September 4, Bethany Blevins Curtis had apparently left her home in north Austin, cleaned out half her joint banking account shared with her husband, Jake, boarded a Southwest Airlines flight, and flown the short jaunt to Houston. A security camera caught her walking alone through the Hobby Airport terminal. The video was posted on a Faceplace page dedicated to her, apparently run by a friend: Bethany Curtis in a crowd, dark hair, floppy brown hat pulled low, a muted scarf tied around her throat, dark glasses. Glancing over her shoulder. Somehow she had eluded the cameras in the airport, they'd lost her after she deplaned. Had someone picked her up? Had she already arranged for a car to be there waiting? Did she shed her coat and scarf and hat and walk undetected? She was simply gone.

Mariah sighed. This case wasn't like her mother's. Mom had not emptied a bank account or flown on a plane and been spotted in the airport security videos. Mom had gone to work at the software company where she was a sales rep, left for lunch, and had never been seen again. Beth Dunning's car had been found parked in Lakehaven near some property she and Dad owned and had been planning to build a house on. Mom had always liked being out on the property, a large empty lot with a stunning view; it was peaceful, and she liked to talk about the house they would build. It was a place she went for quiet, to escape the pressure and busyness of her job, imagining the house that would stand there one day, with its lovely views of the hills of Lakehaven.

Reveal was right: the only similarities were the name Beth, the women's residences being separated by a matter of a few miles, and the short time frame between the cases.

She went back to the links on the Curtis case. The other Beth left behind a husband, Jake, a software entrepreneur who steadfastly claimed he had nothing to do with her disappearance. He had a company that went public a few months after Bethany disappeared—apparently his investors stuck with him. He'd made millions. That got some press from both local media and the tech industry media, as if perhaps he'd gotten rid of his wife so as not to share his new wealth. But Bethany Curtis had very clearly walked away of her own accord. No new evidence, so no forward motion. Mariah read a follow-up article on the one-year anniversary: Bethany Curtis had still not left any kind of digital trail. No use of credit cards, no withdrawals from her bank, no pinging of her cell phone by towers. She had left her life, then left…everything else. Even with taking enough cash to live on for a while, it was a bad sign.

Mariah printed out the articles on Bethany Curtis and pinned them in an empty corner of Mom's corkboard. She pinned the photo of Bethany Curtis next to Mom's.

And then she made up her mind. She had to know. The time span, the similarity of the names, no trail for either of them—this was suddenly a hunger, a need to know that gnawed at her. She would find the pattern, if one was there.

And if there was any way to make the connection back to her mother.

She emailed Reveal: Hi, Mariah Dunning, Beth Dunning's daughter here. Read your post about my mom and Beth Curtis. Want to meet me for a drink tonight? I wonder if you're right about patterns.

Reveal's answer came faster than she thought it would: I sure would.

Meeting him was defying Dad. She'd come up with a good reason.

ABOUT THE AUTHOR

Jeff Abbott is the *New York Times* bestselling, award-winning author of seventeen novels. His books include the Sam Capra thrillers *Adrenaline, The Last Minute, Downfall, Inside Man,* and *The First Order* as well as the standalone novels *Panic, Fear, Collision,* and *Trust Me. The Last Minute* won an International Thriller Writers Award, and Jeff is also a three-time nominee for the Edgar Award. He lives in Austin, Texas, with his family. You can visit his website at JeffAbbott.com.